HOW TO
Rescue A Rake

JAYNE FRESINA

sourcebooks
casablanca

Copyright © 2016 by Jayne Fresina
Cover and internal design © 2016 by Sourcebooks, Inc.
Cover art by Judy York

Sourcebooks and the colophon are registered trademarks of Sourcebooks, Inc.

All rights reserved. No part of this book may be reproduced in any form or by any electronic or mechanical means including information storage and retrieval systems—except in the case of brief quotations embodied in critical articles or reviews—without permission in writing from its publisher, Sourcebooks, Inc.

The characters and events portrayed in this book are fictitious or are used fictitiously. Any similarity to real persons, living or dead, is purely coincidental and not intended by the author.

Published by Sourcebooks Casablanca, an imprint of Sourcebooks, Inc.
P.O. Box 4410, Naperville, Illinois 60567-4410
(630) 961-3900
Fax: (630) 961-2168
www.sourcebooks.com

Printed and bound in Canada.
MBP 10 9 8 7 6 5 4 3 2 1

"We certainly do not forget you, so soon as you forget us. It is, perhaps, our fate rather than our merit. We cannot help ourselves. We live at home, quiet, confined, and our feelings prey upon us… All the privilege I claim for my own sex (it is not a very enviable one, you need not covet it) is that of loving longest when existence or when hope is gone."

—Anne Elliot, *Persuasion*

Prologue

1815

HALFWAY UP A TREE…

Sometimes a man had to go out on a limb.

Captain Nathaniel Sherringham, a gambler who had dangled at the end of a great many theoretical limbs, and frequently lost his shirt there, was nothing if not persistent. But for once he found himself quite literally up a tree and potentially about to lose more than a linen shirt.

Still, if he ripped his breeches and got stuck while climbing this tree, it couldn't be for a better cause. Hopefully, the note he carried in his coat pocket was about to impress Diana Makepiece enough that she'd give him another chance to plead his case, this time while he was sober. Whatever his means of getting that note into her hand, she ought to be moved by it. And should he amuse her by getting trapped in the branches or savaged by blackbirds in the process of delivery, all the better.

Despite her haughty manner, Diana had struggled

to hide her chuckles if he walked into a wall, or got poked in the eye by a lady's ostrich-feather headdress. With her dark sense of humor, she'd take delight in seeing him stranded up there, and if he fell a few feet and broke something, she would be even more amused. Mayhap he could arrange a black eye too. The hilarity would surely bend her double, but only when no one might witness her elegant shoulders relaxing.

"Captain Sherringham," she would say in her somber voice, and with her querulous eyebrows on alert, "I would have sewn you some wings, had I known you were trying to fly."

Oh yes, Nathaniel's misfortunes were frequently her source of private glee. Yet, perverse as it may seem, this was the woman he wanted and he was not giving up yet. Diana had recently suggested that his optimism in the face of impossible odds was part of his "wretched" charm. That was enough to give him hope.

Now here he was, inching along creaking tree limbs, making one last attempt to win Diana over before he left Hawcombe Prior, risking his new buckskins in the process.

It was fortunate that although the early morning air pinched his skin with cold fingertips, frost had not yet set in. There was certainly little else in his favor as he scaled the oak tree behind the cottage where Diana and her stern mother lived. Nothing more than reckless bravado.

He looked down to the gnarled roots where he'd set young Jamie Bridges on guard. When he whistled sharply, the boy turned his sleepy face up. Nathaniel jabbed two fingers toward his own eyes and then pointed at the cottage. Jamie nodded, frowning a little, and leaned back against the tree trunk, waiting for the penny he'd been promised and the safe return of his sling. He was possibly the world's most disinterested lookout.

Nathaniel couldn't get much higher in the tree, so it was time to take his chance. He knew her window; it was open. Diana had told him once—in a rare, unguarded moment—that she liked to sleep with fresh air blowing in, even when it was winter.

He took the folded note out of his pocket. The small square of paper was tied with string to a crab apple, which he estimated would give it just enough weight. Carefully, he aimed the borrowed sling and fired. His message flew gracefully across the short distance and through her window, bypassing any other barriers. Such as her mother.

All that remained was to wait and see if Diana came to the old bridge to meet him. If she didn't, he would set off on his journey and never think of her again.

The branch across which he stretched gave an ominous creak, and he suddenly had no need to worry about his descent because the law of gravity saw to it for him.

"Never seen a grown man climb a tree before," young Jamie grumbled, scratching his head and looking down at Nathaniel's sprawling form.

"And you haven't now. Remember?" He groaned. "Not a word to anyone."

"Don't get all aerated, Sherry. I ain't stupid." The

boy yawned. "I ain't the one climbing a tree for a woman already engaged to marry another."

Indeed, Nathaniel thought with an inner groan of despair while brushing dead leaves from his uniform jacket, when *would* he learn to give up on a lost cause? But he was a gambler, wasn't he? It was what "Sherry" did best.

Which, much to his chagrin, wasn't saying an awful lot for his other abilities.

One

Just when Diana thought she was safe, hidden successfully from the biggest nuisance in Buckinghamshire, that shrill voice rang out. "Ah, here I find you, Miss Makepiece, perched in the corner, quiet as a church mouse."

For a petite woman, the parson's wife created a surprisingly large cloud of dust and a considerable rumpus as she plowed through the dancing crowd to collapse on a chair beside Diana.

"Gracious, you ought to make some noise and move about once in a while, or you might fade entirely into the wall plaster." The lady chuckled at her own wit. "That won't improve your sad lot in life, will it, poor dear?"

"Oh, I don't know, Mrs. Kenton," Diana muttered. "Sometimes the idea of invisibility is not without appeal."

"What's that? Such a timid little voice you have, when you use it at all. Your presence is so easily overlooked that I am surprised you have not been sat upon."

Apparently Mrs. Kenton paid no heed to her husband's sermons about the meek inheriting the earth.

Digging a fork into her slice of cake, she dramatically regaled Diana, and everyone seated nearby, with the story of her struggle at the refreshment table. In that place of greed, violence, and malice, she'd been elbowed in the eye, thumped about the head by a fiercely wielded reticule, had her slippers stamped upon until she was certain every bone in her foot was broken, and bravely thwarted the near theft of her best lace handkerchief. Any listener unaware that her quest had merely been for cheesecake might think she'd survived a riot at the Bastille.

Some people underestimated the advantage of being quiet and unnoticed, Diana mused, gazing up at the rafters. Woodworm larvae, for instance, were possibly burrowing away up there, munching tunnels capable of bringing the entire structure down upon the dancers' heads. Yet the stealthy little creatures went about their business without making a sound heard by the human ear.

If only certain people did the same.

The parson's wife choked on her cake and, in a wheezing breath, exclaimed, "I am underwhelmed by the selection of refreshments. Had they invited me to join their committee, I would have set them straight, but they must have been too afraid to ask me. I am always so busy with all the other duties I take on, I daresay they did not want to impose."

"Naturally. There could be no other reason for excluding you."

"Two shillings to get in and another *sixpence* just for

tea and cake. Exorbitant prices for a small town hall! It's not the Upper Rooms at Bath, for pity's sake." Having set the empty plate in her lap, the parson's wife briskly fanned the underside of her chin. "You have eaten nothing and you are so very thin. It borders on unsightly. A lack of padding on one's bones is terribly aging, you know. Will you not have some cake?"

Yearning only for solitude and for her bones to be left in peace, Diana shook her head.

"Sarah Wainwright looks very well this evening," Mrs. Kenton continued in Diana's ear after only the briefest of pauses. "Such an amiable creature, now that *I* have pried her out of her shell. As I warned her—and as I tell you—a young lady who is painfully reserved and too often mute in company risks ending her days friendless and unloved."

There was a difference between being mute and choosing not to say aloud every stream of thought that came to mind, thought Diana.

The parson's wife continued. "But Sarah really ought to be told that shade of yellow does her no favors. With a sallow complexion one must be so careful, and if only she would take my advice for the dressing of her hair."

Oh, why did people feel the need for conversation, even above the music? Unless someone needed to warn of a fire breaking out in that crowded place or to inform her of a rampaging madman with an ax, Diana could think of nothing so urgent that it needed to be howled into her ear by Mrs. Kenton, who leaned close enough to disturb Diana's ringlets with the blast of every annoying word.

"She was such a gaunt little thing when she first arrived. Thanks to my intervention, she has grown into a handsome gel these past few years."

Handsome. Diana's jaw tightened. That particular tribute always felt begrudging to her, as if the givers couldn't bring themselves to say the object of their discourse was truly pretty. When used as praise for a younger woman, it was a consolation prize, one of which she had, on several occasions in her youth, been the recipient. Only once had a man called her "beautiful." And then look what had happened. Unaccustomed to such bold declarations, she hadn't known what to do with herself or how to respond.

And where was he now, for all his grand talk? Gone more than three years without a word to anyone he once professed to care about. Typical.

Some would say Diana only had herself to blame. *Ha!* As if it mattered to *her* where the most irritating, unreliable man went or why. It was no surprise at all that he'd taken himself off in such dramatic fashion. One could only stir up a modicum of astonishment that he'd left the place fully clothed, apparently with both boots still on his feet, and without bloodshed.

In an effort to relieve her headache, Diana relaxed her previously clenched jaw, tipped her head back very slightly, and let her gaze seek airy space above. This resulted in her sighting a trapped sparrow that fluttered about the rafters of the old hall. With every swoop of the confused bird, her own inner distress grew swiftly.

"Perhaps Miss Sarah Wainwright will have better luck than you, dear," Mrs. Kenton continued loudly, every unencouraged syllable clanging through Diana's sore head and causing several folk standing nearby to glance at her over their shoulders in pity and bemusement. "'Tis a great shame you never had the benefit of my friendship and advice when we were that age."

Diana thought that if Mrs. Kenton's "friendship" had been used upon Napoleon ten years ago, the war would have ended much sooner than it did. The lady's talents were wasted in Buckinghamshire.

"I would have found you a husband, Miss Makepiece, before it was too late and you'd lost your bloom. Now here you sit, twenty-seven and all hope gone." The lady began to hum loudly along to the music, causing several folk nearby to turn as if they thought a bee had invaded the room. Mrs. Kenton paused again and exclaimed, "That young fellow dancing now with Sarah Wainwright seems very keen and attentive."

Suddenly Diana could not sit silently any longer. "But young men can often appear to be something they are not. When the next prettier thing crosses his line of sight, probably with a larger dowry and a significant bosom, he will promptly forget Miss Wainwright and her amiable handsomeness. All men are duplicitous and fickle."

The parson's wife looked at her in surprise, pausing the rapid motion of her fan.

Diana sighed. "The perils of pushing a quiet person to speak, Mrs. Kenton. Unfortunately, you might not always want to hear what they're thinking."

After that, the lady kept her vociferous commentary mostly directed at the ears of the luckless soul on her other side.

Oh dear, thought Diana, *I let my temper get the better of me in a public place.* That was not proper and very unlike her. She decided it must be due to old age and the fault of this hall, where noise and memories persisted.

Compounding her weariness, Diana was recovering from a spring cold, which had left her not only in low spirits and with a pimple on her chin, but also with weakened patience for too much clamor and vitality. A most unfortunate circumstance since she was now surrounded by an abundance of both.

"You *can* take Sarah to the Manderson assembly on Tuesday, Diana, can you not?" Rebecca Wainwright, Sarah's stepmother and one of Diana's dearest friends, had exclaimed in a hurry as they'd left church on the previous Sunday. "It is to be the last dance held there until September, but I have too much to do. With the baby so fractious and teething, I do not like to leave him…and Luke does not return from London until Wednesday, so he cannot escort his daughter. Justina has her hands full with her little tribe and cannot get out."

It was, of course, a well-known fact that unlike her friends, Diana had nothing else to do, having no husband, children, or house to manage. Unwed and past her youth—halfway to death, if one listened to the parson's wife—she was a woman in want of purpose, always reliable and available.

"Mrs. Kenton insists she can chaperone and she won't take no for an answer, as usual," her friend had added with an urgent whisper, "so you must go too, for balance, or I fear Sarah will not forgive me."

So there Diana was, trying to keep the peace and

make everybody happy—a state for which any decorous, well-raised lady should always strive.

Diana raised her fan again to hide that stubborn, vexatious pimple. Still hoping to relieve her pounding headache, she was about to close her eyes when she heard a woman's voice above the music and stamping. A voice other than Mrs. Kenton's.

"Oh, Sherry! You are so very bad! What can one do with such a naughty fellow?"

Diana felt time stop. The music faded. Trying to hear more from the people standing somewhere behind her, she had tipped so precariously to one side that she almost fell out of her chair when Sarah Wainwright abruptly shot out of the crowd like an arrow from a longbow. "I broke my fan!"

Diana stood quickly, feeling as if she'd been caught doing something she should not. With a quick smile, she exchanged the broken fan for her own. "I'm sure you need the cooling benefit more than I do, since you are dancing."

Sarah thanked her profusely and then exclaimed, "You look very pale, Diana."

"Do I?" Raising an unsteady hand to her cheek, she pressed it there, hoping to encourage some color back again. "Perhaps I was not as recovered from my cold as I thought."

"You poor dear," Sarah exclaimed, grasping her hand. "I shall fetch you some cake."

"No. Thank you. Although cake is the cure for a great many ills, I have no appetite for it at present."

"How tired you must be. Your hand is so cold, even through your glove! We should go home at once. I will ask for our carriage to be brought around to the steps."

Cold? How could she be cold in this stuffy hall? Diana assured the girl that she was perfectly content to wait for the last dance. She didn't want to spoil the evening; these events were far too important for eighteen-year-old girls.

Having urged Sarah's return to her eager partner, Diana casually moved back toward the wall until she felt a sturdy beam at her shoulder.

Her mama was right, as she so often proved to be. Diana should not have come out to Manderson before she was fully recovered. She should have—

"Good God, it's been so long since I was here," a male voice exclaimed on the other side of the beam. "The old place hasn't changed though. Not a bit."

Diana froze, clutching Sarah's broken fan so tightly that the horn cut into her palm through her glove and would leave a red dent in her skin. For one startled intake of breath she thought he had addressed his comment to her, but he had not, of course. He was not even aware of her presence. Thankfully. She wished for the wall to absorb her completely, as Mrs. Kenton had warned her it would. The pimple on her chin throbbed, and she was sure it grew larger by the second.

"And are your memories of the place sweet, my dear Sherry?" his companion inquired. "I daresay you charmed many young ladies in this room, you sly devil."

"A great many."

"But never one in particular?" the woman demanded, her tone coy.

Diana stared at the nearest candle flame as it stretched tall, undisturbed by the slightest draft while she held her breath.

"No one in particular," he said. "You know me, the more the merrier."

Their voices moved away, merging with the general commotion, and Diana finally exhaled with such a hard sigh that the bold candle flame nearby was nearly extinguished. Still partially wedged behind her beam, she slowly turned, scanning the crowd for a sight of his sun-kissed head and that ridiculously well-carved physique.

A stout gentleman moved aside, taking a cluster of women with him, and Diana found the owner of the name—and the laugh—that had plucked her attention out of the weary void. For the first time in more than three years, there he was, his fine, foolishly arrogant profile smudged by candlelight.

He was back. Of course he was, she thought scornfully. He'd returned after all that time, just when she looked her very worst and had a pimple the size of a holly berry on her chin. When else might he possibly return but at that very moment? She would have laughed out loud at her own misfortune, if she'd had no fear of being heard and looked at.

Yes, there he stood. It was him, and no denying it. Captain Nathaniel Sherringham, "Sherry" to his closest friends.

The most frustrating, infuriating man she'd ever known. A man who dared accuse her of having vinegar in her veins and a heart like an icehouse.

The irreverent, imprudent gambler who once in

utter madness—and very probably in his cups—had proposed marriage to her.

The man who had once called her beautiful, but to whom she was now apparently "no one in particular."

Two

HE SIPPED HIS PUNCH, HIS GAZE TRAVELING SWIFTLY over the dancers. No faces he recognized tonight. Had they all moved on in his absence? Three and a half years was a long time to be gone, he supposed, but he had not expected this hollow sense of sadness and loss in his gut. As he'd said to his companion, the town hall assembly room hadn't changed at all. Only the people had.

Nathaniel knew he should have written to his sister, Rebecca, and let her know he was traveling into the county. Had she come there to meet him, at least there would have been one face he recognized, even if she did immediately start nagging him about being gone so long and never sending a letter to let her know where he was. Letters were not his forte, and she ought to know that.

He watched a young girl in a yellow dress as she skipped beside her partner in a country jig, laughing and pink-cheeked, glowing with the spirit of youth. Made him smile.

"Don't you want to dance?" the woman at his side demanded.

"No. It's too late, Caroline. This is the last dance of the evening."

His companion looked around in disappointment because they'd arrived when the ball was almost over.

"Oh, I suppose it's just as well," she exclaimed with a weary droop of her shoulders. "I am feeling sick and my head is spinning. This dreadful crowd has a very peculiar, unpleasant odor…" She covered her nose with her small fingers, wincing.

"That is the scent of the country, Caroline."

"But indoors too?"

"Inevitably someone brings the outdoors indoors. On their shoe."

She shuddered and clutched his arm.

Darkly amused by her performance, which seemed to suggest she'd been raised in a palace rather than three small rooms above a shop in Cheapside where her father was a glove maker, he reminded his companion, "Well, you wanted to experience a dance among the *rustics*, as you call them."

Nathaniel's fingers drummed slowly against his punch cup, recalling this tune and a time, long ago, when he'd danced to it. Turning his attention back to the dancers, he gazed beyond the faces of the people there and saw those that used to be present. Ghosts of his past.

❦

A graceful hand in a white silk glove, its touch so light, like a fledgling bird uncertain about its perch.

A coolly knowing glance from shining green eyes beneath black, curling lashes.

Ebony hair, so startling against translucent, ivory skin.

"My mama says you're a good-for-naught scapegrace, so you needn't try to flirt with me. I'm only dancing with you because your sister is my friend and she asked me to. Please don't try to impress me. It will only embarrass us both."

Well, that told him where he stood from the start.

"Oh, I do love to be danced with as a favor to Rebecca," he had replied with teasing hauteur as he rose from his bow. "Nothing fluffs my vanity and pride more than to know my little sister must bribe and cajole her new friends into standing up with me, Miss Makepiece."

She'd eyed him warily, but with just a touch of curiosity and bemusement. "Your vanity requires fluffing? It seems every bit as plumped up already as a proud songbird's chest feathers."

Immediately he had noticed two very alluring things about her. No, not her bubbies—although they would come to his notice too, in time. Nathaniel had been drawn first to the young lady's very dark and shapely eyebrows. Like the stalks of two restless exclamation marks that had fallen over onto their sides, they emphasized everything she said, made every word seem important and challenging, even when it came in such a calm voice. Not just calm, he reconsidered, but emotionless. The eyebrows gave away what her voice would not.

Her steady, poised hand laid over his own forced Nathaniel to slow down, to look where he was going for once. Diana Makepiece moved with elegant, ladylike steps and didn't erupt into giggles like many girls her age with whom he danced. She even danced this rather wild country jig with grace. She made everyone around them look like concussed drunkards with two left feet. Especially him.

Other people had watched her with quiet admiration, for her looks were very refined and unusual, exotic for the Buckinghamshire countryside. He'd heard it speculated—in hushed tones—that her father was possibly of foreign blood, although whether that blood was Greek, Italian, Spanish, Cornish, or Irish no one could confirm.

Much to Nathaniel's frustration, his practiced, teasing wit was not enough to win a smile from her lips. But when he stubbed his toe, she smirked and her brows twitched. His infamous charm couldn't raise the slightest blush, yet her slender shoulders shook with the effort of remaining somber when he was prodded in the eye by the tall feather in another lady's hair. Thus he discovered a strange way to amuse the ice maiden. Good thing he was naturally clumsy. And hardheaded.

❧

"What are you smiling at, Sherry?" His companion nudged his arm again in a habit that was becoming as annoying as the presence of a persistent fly buzzing around the dregs of his punch.

"Was I?" Nathaniel didn't want to share those memories with Caroline, so he put his smile away and shuttered the little scene that had played through his mind's window.

His green-eyed girl must be Mrs. Shaw by now. *Don't think of her.* He had promised himself he would not, yet barely a quarter of an hour in that room had brought her back to him.

How different she was from the woman on his arm tonight, he thought, glancing down at Caroline. How *had* he become burdened with this spoiled, loud creature? She liked to say they were two wounded souls together, and they did rather limp along. "We're two of a kind," she often remarked.

He hoped not. It had given him a jolt to hear that she considered her personality and habits to be the same as his.

Caroline was a divorcée, cast off by her husband, Admiral Sayles, after a scandalous affair with an exiled French aristocrat. She scrabbled along from one reluctant host to the next, getting money where she could. Now she'd turned to Nathaniel for assistance, and having known her in his younger years, he felt he should come to her aid. He had never been able to deny a woman in distress. Unfortunately, his gallant spirit had a habit of earning him more trouble than praise. In this case that was certainly true, for since he'd offered her a helping hand, she had not shown any desire to release it, instead holding on with a fierce grip.

"Since my dear cousin Eleanor was lost to typhus only weeks before her wedding, I'm quite certain her mother will welcome my company to cheer her spirits," Caroline had said. "My aunt is always inviting me to visit her in Bath."

"Yes, but does she *expect* you to accept the invite? A surprise visit is often more imposition than anything else."

Caroline's only concern, however, was for herself. "A change of scenery and air will certainly be of benefit to me. My health suffers. I have been betrayed and abandoned, left to manage as best I can. Why would my own aunt turn me away?"

Since no one else would help her, Nathaniel had assumed the task of delivering Caroline safely to the one remaining relative who might take her in, but on the way he had business to tend. They were obliged to stop here overnight, and Caroline, hearing by chance about the assembly room dance, would not cease her moaning until he agreed to take her. In truth, he had felt some curiosity to see the place again. One of his old hunting grounds.

"At least let's get some more punch, Sherry," she exclaimed. "I'm parched. It's too hot in here. I fear I might faint. I am very dizzy."

He offered to find her a chair, but she preferred her place standing at the edge of the dance floor. "Goodness no, why would I sit with those old ladies and chaperones? No one can see my dress if I sit down."

"But I thought you were not feeling well."

"I do suffer a steadily increasing weakness and the most awful pains through all my joints," she insisted, suddenly remembering that fact. "Not that anyone ever cares." With this said, however, she declared herself capable of remaining upright at least until he returned with her replenished cup. As long as he was not gone too long.

Nathaniel left her tapping her feet at the side of the room while he returned to the table of refreshments by the door.

As he waited to refill Caroline's punch cup, he felt a sudden stroke of air that seemed, somehow, in that stifling ballroom, to have found its way under his tall collar. He glanced up.

A woman had just walked over to a nearby window and opened it. With her back to Nathaniel, she shooed a small bird out into the fresh, spring night air, and then she stood there a moment, probably taking a few cooling breaths herself. She had dark hair, a slender neck devoid of jewelry, and a plain gown with a high collar. He thought for one dreadful moment that she might be Diana's mother, that old termagant Mrs. Rosalind Makepiece. The memories were certainly haunting him tonight.

The woman in the dull-colored, unflattering dress still had her back to him as she walked away into the mob, struggling against the flow. Now he knew it couldn't be Mrs. Makepiece, or that cluster of young girls would have parted as quickly as the sea for Moses. Nobody ever got in that woman's way.

Except Nathaniel, of course. He had never stood aside for her.

"I do not like you, sir," Mrs. Makepiece had said to him once. "My daughter is destined for greater things."

Well, at least she was direct, but since he didn't particularly care whether she liked him or not, her comment didn't prevent his appreciation of Diana. When Nathaniel found a woman he fancied, he pursued her energetically and without disguising his intentions, regardless of anyone else's opinion. He seized life by the seed bags, to put it bluntly, and saw no cause to limit his own happiness to please others.

Ah, he thought suddenly, perhaps Caroline Sayles was more right than he cared for her to be when she pointed out their similarities.

His sister used to laugh at him. "I've never seen you work so hard, Nate! You put more determination and dedication into chasing Diana than you put into anything."

He knew his sister thought it was merely a teasing game of sorts, a challenge to his vanity. Nathaniel had thought the same. In the beginning.

The first sign of something different being afoot came when old habits and the familiar parade of petticoats and pretty faces no longer made him content. But Nathaniel could not reconcile himself to the idea of giving up all other women for the sake of one. He believed in "gather ye rosebuds while ye may," his favorite poem—the only one he'd ever memorized—being "To the Virgins, to Make Much of Time."

And Diana certainly never encouraged his attentions.

But when he heard news of her engagement to another man, Nathaniel was cast utterly adrift. Sinking deeper and deeper into a violent depression, he'd come up with a list of three possible plans over several jugs of ale at the local tavern.

> One. Kill W. Shaw.
> Two. Kidnap D. Makepiece (until she concedes her mistake).
> Three. Kill W. Shaw.

He was never a very great schemer.

In the end, having sobered up only slightly, he

proposed marriage to her instead. It was ill-planned, badly timed, and desperate. He had no experience with humility.

Not that she considered any of this to be a mitigating circumstance.

In his mind now, he heard Diana's voice as clearly as it had been when she berated him on the last day he saw her. Even then she had spoken coldly, condescendingly, using emphasis without raising her voice.

"Nathaniel Sherringham, you're a *boy*! You don't know what you want from life. You greet every day as if it's your first and yet your last. You have no direction, no discipline, and no appreciation for the consequences of your actions. As my mama says, everything for you is about the pleasure of the moment, and your fancies are too fleeting.

"How can you look after a wife when you cannot look after yourself? This ridiculous proposal is nothing more than another impulsive, addlebrained idea upon which you would merrily wager—like betting on an outside chance in a horse race just because you feel sorry for the beast or like the color of his tail. Well, I, sir, do not gamble."

A sharp pain stabbed deeply through his chest as he thought again of those green eyes shimmering with light and shade. The gently arched brows seeming bemused, pitying him for that maladroit proposal.

Then had come the severing cut to his pride when she left him waiting on that old stone bridge until he could no longer imagine she might come. Apparently even laying open his heart to her in that foolish note, fired by sling through her window, had not thawed her feelings for him.

Still watching the slow, awkward progress of the bird rescuer across the hall, he saw her stumble. Whether she was pushed accidentally by the surging crowd, or whether it was the fault of her own unsteady footing, he couldn't be sure. Seeing that she was quite unnoticed by anyone else, Nathaniel put down his empty cups and moved swiftly toward her.

A large gentleman had unknowingly caught the hem of her gown under his chair leg, and as he talked and laughed loudly with his drunken companions, the woman's distress was ignored by all. Nathaniel thought he must be the only one who could hear her agitated, *"Excuse me."*

He moved forward quickly, demanding that folk stand aside. The woman swiveled around, her hands tugging on her skirt. Apparently she'd decided to sacrifice the gown rather than try further polite methods to get her captor's attention.

Nathaniel arrived behind the loud group, ready to help. "Madam, can I—?"

She looked up, startled and annoyed.

And he gazed down into a pair of simmering spring-green eyes. The light in them was livid, tart, frustrated. But upon seeing him, it changed immediately to astonishment and alarm, then something akin to fear, before it flickered and died away, like a candle flame caught in a draft.

Now those eyes were dull, empty.

He could not speak. He could barely take a breath.

Was it only three years and six months since he last saw her?

"Diana." The name burst out of him, just when he thought his tongue was frozen by her icy regard. "*Diana?*"

She was so changed, frail and faded.

"Captain Sherringham," she replied, her voice tired, her head bowed as she looked down at her trapped skirt again. "You're back."

The weary resignation in her voice irritated him. He might as well be a returning infestation of greenfly, he thought angrily. Now she would not even look up, intent on hiding her face.

He recovered enough to reply with his customary jocular teasing. "Yes, I am returned, but don't worry. I shan't blot the horizon long with my presence."

"That will be a pity for some ladies, I'm sure. You'll still find some addled enough and at liberty to seek a rake's company."

"Good. I do love a woman with a taste for merry thrills."

"And thrillingly merry bad taste."

She wrestled with her skirt, but since she didn't have the physical strength to secure her escape, her actions became more frantic and even less effective. The large fellow now noticed her struggle and tried to move his chair, but only succeeded in dragging the leg further along her skirt and rending a larger hole in the hem.

Where was her husband? Nathaniel wondered. Why did William Shaw leave his wife unattended?

Nathaniel folded his arms. "I came over to make this gentleman move off your gown, yet I hear not a word of thanks."

"Fortunately, Captain, I haven't been waiting around for you to save me," she muttered.

"I didn't imagine you had. It would have been foolish to do so, since you gave me my marching orders once before."

"For a man with itchy feet, marching orders are a gift."

"Itchy feet?"

"A man who is never still, never content, must always be going somewhere. Running away."

"*Running away?*" He was incensed by that comment. She dared to accuse him of that after what *she'd* done to him—left him standing on that bridge like a simpleton? She might at least have come to say good-bye. He didn't expect miracles, but would a few words have been too much? They might have parted under better terms, and he could have apologized for his undignified proposal.

Her face in shadow, she said, "As my mother says, some men won't stop running until they trip and fall face-first into a grave."

Ah yes, the delightful Mrs. Makepiece. She and her opinions were always mentioned sooner or later. "Speaking of which"—he spat out the words—"I almost mistook you for your mama tonight."

He heard one inhaled gasp, and then Diana gave another furious tug to her skirt. Apparently a pricked temper gave her the needed burst of strength at last. Her skirt ripped free of the gentleman's chair and she walked away without another word, torn hem trailing after her.

Somehow moving his feet in the other direction,

Nathaniel returned to the refreshment table. But he decided against refilling Caroline's beverage or his own. His hands trembled with so much anger that he might be tempted to smash the punch bowl to the ground.

"I say, aren't you that Captain Sherringham?" A woman standing by the cake was squinting hard at him.

He didn't recognize her. She was short, plain but well-maintained, about his age. Her lips gathered in a tight pout as she awaited his answer—almost as if admitting his name would be the same as confessing guilt of a crime.

"Captain who?" he murmured.

She stared hard, a deep line forming between her brows.

"Ah, wait!" He held up a finger. "Sherringham. That dreadful, brazen fellow from whom no innocent young woman was ever safe. Gambling debts up his backside. No responsibility. No discipline or willpower. Terrible habit of drinking too much and swearing in polite society. Never out of bed on the right side of noon, countless women left ruined in his wake when he *runs off*."

She blinked rapidly. "Well, I—"

"Never met him before in my life."

"But you—"

"And frankly, madam, I am shocked and offended that you would mistake me for that reprobate."

Turning swiftly on his heel, he walked away. Whoever she was, let her swallow that with her cheesecake.

He knew what they all thought of him, but they were about to be surprised.

Captain Nathaniel Sherringham was no longer the rudderless, jolly rake everybody loved to mock. He was a man of determination, purpose, and considerable means.

He was also a man who had learned not to lead his life as if it were an open book.

Yes, he was back. And in control.

Things were going to be different this time.

Three

THE AIR IN HER MOTHER'S PARLOR SEEMED EXCESSIVELY warm and stale the next morning. Diana thought perhaps she was still suffering the effects of last night's debacle, but glancing around at her friends and fellow book society members, she saw them all in some state of similar discomfort.

Lucy Bridges had requisitioned an old copy of *La Belle Assemblée* to fan herself so violently that she'd wafted half the dried petals out of a dish of potpourri beside her. Meanwhile Justina Wainwright dabbed her perspiring forehead with a jam-stained napkin, subsequently leaving a few sticky crimson blobs above her eyebrow. And her sister-in-law, Rebecca, resorted to loudly puffing out unladylike breaths, while popping open the buttons of her lace chemisette. Since there were no men present, Diana supposed it was safe to allow some exposure of skin, but really she ought to do something to cool the air before the unveiling went too far. Where Rebecca was concerned, one could never be sure what she might do next, and a petticoat lifted to the knee may soon occur if this heat was not alleviated.

It was good cause to open the window, she decided hastily. Her mother did not care much for an open window this early in the year, but she cared even less for too much bosom and ankle on display.

Having opened the parlor window, Diana returned to her chair and reached over to pour the tea, just as Sarah Wainwright—the society's youngest and newest member—bounced with sudden excitement and exclaimed, "You will never guess who I saw at the Manderson Assembly Rooms yesterday."

Diana temporarily lost control of the teapot's spout, splashing tea into her saucer and across her mother's second-best tablecloth.

"A notorious"—Sarah lowered her voice and glanced nervously at the parlor door—"*adulteress!*"

Rebecca Wainwright passed Diana a napkin to help mop up the spilled tea. "An adulteress? Good Lord, and in Manderson of all places."

"It is quite true," Sarah insisted. "She was pointed out to me. A Mrs. Caroline Sayles."

Diana dabbed at the tea stain and gave a small sigh of relief, for she had expected another name to fly out of Sarah's mouth. Until she remembered that Sarah Wainwright would not know Captain Sherringham by sight. He had left the village shortly before she came to live there.

"They say Mrs. Sayles has run off from her husband *five* times," added Sarah, eyes popping.

"Goodness," Rebecca exclaimed wryly. "If I were her husband, I would have changed the locks."

"Well, it seems he has now done so. It was a most scandalous divorce and all over the London papers."

"You shouldn't listen to gossip," said Justina Wainwright primly, but then she leaned forward. "What did the adulteress look like?" Always eager for lurid details, she was probably looking to use them in whatever story she was currently writing.

"Nothing very special, I must say. For an adulteress, I expected something quite different. But I can report that she wears an excess of rouge." Pausing, Sarah glanced sideways at Lucy Bridges, who was halfway through a jam tart and had bulging cheeks that were suspiciously robin's breast in hue. "But apart from that, I saw nothing extraordinary about her. She looked like any other woman of middle age, just slightly sillier."

"Middle age?"

"About thirty," Sarah replied. "Although all the powder and rouge might make her look that old."

Diana bit her lip and stirred her tea violently.

"I do wish I could have gone to the dance and seen the adulteress," exclaimed Lucy, scowling fiercely at the crumbs left on her plate. "It is most unfair that I cannot go anywhere more interesting than these book society meetings for another fortnight at least. Papa has forbidden me to leave the village or attend any functions in mixed company."

"You are in mourning for your grandmother," Diana reminded her.

"Yes, and thanks to her, I have missed the last assembly dance of the season."

Rebecca gave a scornful snort. "How inconvenient for you that your poor grandmother chose this month to shuffle off her mortal coil."

"Well, she didn't even like me and made no bones

about it, so why should I feel sorry?" Lucy glanced over at Diana. "Oh, and by the by, before I forget, Mama asked me to thank you for the scones you brought over. Although they were not very well risen and rather hard, she said since you have naught else to do, perhaps you might make us some more. Little Timothy devoured four and he's such a troublesome eater usually."

Before Diana could explain that they were not scones but Welsh cakes, Lucy turned back to the others and snapped, "Grandmama said I was a terrible, flighty girl and that I should be shut away in an attic with nothing but bread and milk until I was beyond my *most trying age*."

Rebecca laughed, and Justina, seated beside her on the sofa, said, "I fear that would have been a long wait."

Lucy stuck out her small chin. "Oh, you are all so clever and smug now. But I remember, Jussy, when you were always in trouble, and it was not so long ago when you were getting me into it too! Before Mr. Wainwright came here and married you."

"You make it sound as if he tamed me."

"Everybody says he did."

"I can assure you he did not!" Justina straightened her shoulders in protest. "I tamed *him*, if you must know."

Rebecca intervened with her shilling's worth. "But Luke says you've made his brother much naughtier than he used to be."

"I made him smile more. Is that a crime?"

"It depends, dear Jussy, upon the methods you employed to achieve that smile." At that they both chuckled until Lucy dropped her cup into her saucer with a clatter.

"Oh, don't start cooing again about your dratted husbands," she cried. "I am rendered nauseous by hearing about them and their latest gallant deeds every time we come to this stuffy parlor. We're supposed to be discussing the book."

Lucy was usually the last person present to show any interest in the book they read, but little pleased her these days. She had been foundering in a permanently sour mood ever since her mother birthed yet another baby boy that winter, giving Lucy the pleasure of *six* younger brothers. This was bad enough, but when her curmudgeonly grandmother's demise severely curtailed what remained of her social life, that was the last straw.

Diana looked on as her friends bickered. It seemed as if there was too often tension in their book society meetings, and they no longer had sweet, even-tempered Catherine Penny to bring peace in her gentle manner. Since she had moved away from the village to become Mrs. Forester, the loss of her steadying influence was greatly felt. Diana might have taken over the role of adjudicator, being the eldest remaining in their group, but as an unmarried lady past her prime, her consequence was naturally diminished and she slipped further down the order of precedence with each passing year. No one would listen to her advice.

It was young Sarah who made a valiant effort to steer the conversation back into pleasanter territory. Glancing at Lucy's even redder face and tightly pursed lips, she said, "But I must tell you more about the dance. Oh, and Samuel Hardacre was there, Lucy, in a very smart new coat and asking about you."

"I am also heartily sick of *that* subject," Lucy snapped. "Since I wasn't there, but forced instead to sit home in black ribbons and eat flat, burnt scones, what does it matter to me that you danced so many times that you wore out your slippers? Or that a man who smells of damp wood chippings, has rough hands, and wears his hair too long asked after me? I am quite sure I wouldn't give a sixpence for that dreary, oafish carpenter, and you may have him for all I care."

"But I don't want—"

"Oh no! Of course the village carpenter is not good enough for a Wainwright, is he? I, however, the daughter of a lowly tavern keeper, can expect to get nothing better."

"Lucy, I'm sure Sarah didn't mean to—"

"Go on then, rub salt in my wound! Remind me again that I was not there while you danced with every eligible man in the county! That I am almost *one-and-twenty*"—she emphasized the number by pressing a fist to her heart, as if it cost her blood to say it—"and should be out finding a husband. Yet I am stuck at home every night in mourning for a woman who despised me. I have no prospect of any good company or handsome bachelors in sight. I have no escape! I suppose you will finally feel sorry for me when I too am twenty-seven, have lost all my opportunities, all my looks, and am destined to die an old maid."

As her tirade drew to a shuddering, impassioned halt, every other eye in the room turned sheepishly toward Diana. Three teacups were hastily raised in unison. A fourth—Lucy's—was merely banged about in its saucer, for she was too caught up in her own problems to realize that mentioning the specific age of twenty-seven was sufficient for everyone present to know whom she meant.

Diana felt a headache coming on again. Or perhaps it was the same one from last night and it had not yet left. "Shall we turn our attention to the book then?" she asked.

They all hurriedly agreed and Diana gave another small sigh of relief when Sarah opened their borrowed copy of *Persuasion* and began to read aloud.

> *He was at that time a remarkably fine young man, with a great deal of intelligence, spirit, and brilliancy; and Anne an extremely pretty girl, with gentleness, modesty, taste, and feeling. Half the sum of attraction, on either side, might have been enough, for he had nothing to do, and she had hardly anybody to love; but the encounter of such lavish recommendations could not fail. They were gradually acquainted, and when acquainted, rapidly and deeply in love.*

Diana, once previously resolved to avoid memories of Nathaniel today, now found thoughts of that reckless man thrown into her path again.

Should she mention seeing him at the dance in Manderson? If his sister later discovered he was there, would it not look strange that she kept the information to herself? But raising the subject seemed a challenging prospect. Until she had actually laid eyes on him yesterday evening, she had not known how his return would affect her.

Her pulse, she had found, still changed its rhythm in his presence and threatened to embarrass her.

He annoyed her so, made her nervous, made her forget her composure. There was also, so she'd discovered, a twinge of…regret.

It made no sense.

She'd turned down his marriage proposal for very sound, practical reasons, and even if she had suffered some vexing, nervous emotion the next morning, his swift abandonment of the village immediately after suggested that he'd come to his sober senses, seen the truth in her words, and realized the futility of pursuing her further.

Her mother—always right about so many things—had pointed out that Nathaniel was neither reliable nor sensible. He relished a deliberate ignorance when it came to bills and responsibilities. His manners, while open and charming, were never restrained but shared equally between all the women he knew.

"He probably flirts with you, Diana," her mother used to say, "merely because he knows how it torments me to see you being made an object of ridicule."

One could never tell with Nathaniel where the jokes ended and the real feelings began. Part of her didn't want to know. Facts were easier to deal with than emotions. Her mother, the greatest influence in her life, dealt in facts and therefore so did Diana.

Sarah read on in her clear voice.

> *Captain Wentworth had no fortune. He had been lucky in his profession; but spending freely what had come freely, had realized nothing…*

The man, as her mother had said, was rootless, a gambler. He spent money as fast as he made it, had no appreciation for the polite ways of society, and seemed to make his own rules. All true, and he would gleefully admit it to be so. It was part of his awful charm that he knew his own faults and never tried to deceive anyone about them.

> *Such confidence, powerful in its own warmth, and bewitching in the wit which often expressed it, must have been enough for Anne; but Lady Russell, saw it very differently. His sanguine temper, and fearlessness of mind, operated very differently on her. She saw in it but an aggravation of the evil... Lady Russell had little taste for wit; and of anything approaching to imprudence a horror. She deprecated the connection in every light.*

There was also an underlying worry for Diana's mother, another reason for her disapproval of Nathaniel. Mrs. Makepiece had eloped with a man of whom her proud family did not approve. The mésalliance was brief, for he died early, but as with most missteps in life, the consequences of it stretched on. He had left his young wife with a baby daughter in her arms and a sack full of debts on her back.

Since most of her haughty family had snubbed her, Diana's mother was forced to rely upon the charity of an unwed brother who was then the parson of Hawcombe Prior. She became his housekeeper, and when he died, he had left them a small annuity and a few bits of china. The new parson did not require a servant, so she and Diana had been forced to find new accommodations.

Then the Sherringhams came along and Mrs. Makepiece found herself paying rent to the eccentric, salty-humored major, her new landlord—a man she considered socially inferior. Oh yes, her fall from grace might have obliged the lady to take in private pupils for French and music lessons, but her pride remained undented. She still thought her blood finer than that of anyone in the village.

Shortly after the Sherringhams arrived in Hawcombe Prior, Diana's mother wrote to her very grand relatives, seeking forgiveness for past sins. These fine cousins, the Clarendons, had finally begun to acknowledge her again, and the sinking lady grasped desperately at this slender branch.

"You must know, Daughter," she exclaimed once to Diana, "that any close association with Nathaniel Sherringham—a young man of no breeding, no manners, and no fortune—will finish us completely with the Clarendons. And certainly do him no favors either."

Again, her mother's advice was perfectly sound. It was evident that with his looks and charm Nathaniel could find a richer prospect, a wife with many more advantages. Diana was not lively like him and did not bring smiles to a room simply by being in it, the way he did. She preferred shade and quiet corners from which to observe the action. Nathaniel needed the sun. He thrived in it.

He needed a woman who would never be bothered by his flirtatious streak. Perhaps a woman just as capricious as Nathaniel, a jolly girl who liked a good time and didn't worry about his notoriety.

His proposal to Diana, all those years ago, had been rash, sudden—a gamble, like most things he did. He'd delivered it with his usual lighthearted humor, and the idea of marriage had likely come to him the same way, as a jolly good joke of which he would soon tire. By the following morning he must have come to his sober senses and seen the error in binding himself to one woman.

> *The belief of being prudent and self-denying, principally for his advantage, was her chief consolation...*

But this morning she pondered his laughter again. So confident, hearty, and warm. That sound had not changed. Oh, she hoped life had treated him well. For all his faults and despite his utter unsuitability for *her*, she wanted him to find happiness.

> *Her attachment and regrets had for a long time clouded every enjoyment of youth; and an early loss of bloom and spirits had been their lasting effect.*

He had kissed her once, on the day before he left Hawcombe Prior for the last time.

Appalled that the memory should sneak its way in so determinedly, Diana stared down at her overfilled teacup and watched the liquid surface tremble. She closed her eyes.

It was a kiss taken without her permission, and she could not forget how it felt—the rush of unwanted emotion coursing through her body. She had never known the like of it before or since. That night she had been unable to sleep. Wretched man. What had he done to her?

"Diana?" said Sarah suddenly. "You're shivering. Are you cold?"

Diana set her cup and saucer on the table and hastily grabbed her knitted shawl from the arm of the chair. Jussy got up to throw more coal on the fire.

Outside the window, Mrs. Kenton was herding a troop of little boys along the lane, chattering at them the entire time as she corrected a skewed hat or a misbuttoned coat. Her husband had begun taking in student boarders to help pay his bills, which gave the lady more to do with her time and her organizing skills, much to the relief of Diana and her friends, who had all fallen foul of her attempts to manage their lives from time to time.

These days Mrs. Kenton was too busy for much more than the occasional remark about fabric choices, the "right way" to dress a bonnet, or how a woman past blossoming ought to stop wearing her hair in a fashionable style and don a lace cap when indoors.

Thinking of that last comment, which was thrown in her direction quite recently, Diana raised a hand to her own tumble of neat curls. She went to such trouble every evening to attain those ringlets by twisting and tying her locks in rags before bed. It was a practice she'd continued nightly without fail ever since she had hair long enough.

But perhaps Mrs. Kenton was right and she *was* too old for those uncovered ringlets.

❧

Later, when her friends had gone, Diana went into the kitchen and found her mother seated by the fire, applying ox gall to remove a small stain from her favorite old shawl.

"Mrs. Bridges was very grateful for the Welsh cakes, Mama. I said I would make some more."

"Hmph. I've never known a woman to put her hand out so often and so shamelessly, yet she never returns the deed."

Pulling an apron over her dress, Diana replied that she would happily forgo something to make up for the added expense of baking ingredients.

Her mother frowned over her shoulder. "'Tis they who should be bringing cakes to us for all the times you entertain those rambunctious little boys. Why that daughter of hers can't look after the little brats I don't know. Too busy finding new ways to plump up her bosom, no doubt, and making eyes at the carpenter when she should be home helping her mama with that brood."

Diana could tell her mother was in a high state of dudgeon, for otherwise she would never let a word like "bosom" slip out.

"Of course, in respectable families very young children are sent out to a wet nurse, not kept underfoot at home," she added crisply.

"You did not send me away, Mama."

"No, but I had only you to tend." Her mother sniffed. "No one else to manage or keep content. I did not birth a child a year and then let it roam about disturbing the neighbors as if I had naught to do with it. People who make too many children should accept responsibility for them. It's not for you to be looking after those little boys all the time, Diana."

"I don't mind it. What else do I have to do, Mama?"

"Plenty about this house! *I* can hardly ever find you when I need you these days. Always off in your own world, idly daydreaming." Her mother added scornfully, "And what worthy literature are you and your friends reading now?"

When Diana told her the name of their new book, Mrs. Makepiece shook her head and dabbed at her stained shawl with greater fervor.

"I hear the lady who wrote those books died a spinster, so you can see where it got her. I would have thought you too old for those silly novels."

Diana was tempted to warn her mother that in her virulent determination to remove a slight blemish from her precious shawl, she would take all the color out of it too. Instead she stepped down into the pantry and stared at the shelves. There, pushed to the back and gathering dust, her mother kept a few ingredients deemed too luxurious and expensive for everyday use. Exotic spices reserved in case they had a special visitor—a Clarendon, for instance. Years ago Diana had chirped to her mother, "You do know King George isn't coming to visit Hawcombe Prior, don't you, Mama?" and received a clip 'round the ear for her trouble.

Those precious ingredients sat there in readiness, waiting for a chance that may never come.

She wondered what would happen if she brought some of those jars out into the light. But it was a passing idea, a spark of rebellion soon stamped out. Diana reached for the familiar bottles.

Perhaps she ought to be beyond her enjoyment of romantic novels, she mused, but Anne Elliot's story had touched her heart. She understood how persuasion, like a constant drip of water over many years, can eventually make a mark, even in solid rock.

Four

NATHANIEL WAS SURPRISED TO SEE THE PIG IN A POKE tavern with shutters closed over its crooked, ivy-fringed windows and the front door bolted. Yet another change to the place he had visited so many times in the past. There was no sign of life within, no smoke billowing from the chimney, no children shrieking or dogs barking. It was as if he had unknowingly died and now walked in an unsettled dream where everything was the same on the surface, but not quite as it should be when one looked closer.

Then, as he turned his mount to head across the common, he spied a familiar face at last.

Three ladies walked down the High Street, deep in conversation. They had not yet seen him, but the bright auburn hair of his sister, Rebecca, was unmistakable, even with most of it hidden under a straw bonnet.

Nathaniel grinned and urged his horse into a canter.

"Well, if it isn't my rotten little sister, Rebecca! I thought your husband would keep you under lock and key for his own peace of mind, as well as the general safety of the village."

His sister's astonishment turned quickly to laughter and joy, much to his relief. "Nate! For the love of—why did you not write?"

He dismounted to greet her. "I didn't want to give you any warning," he teased. "But it seems as if someone already knew I was coming, for they boarded up the tavern as a precaution!"

Rebecca's hazel eyes shone warmly up at him, springing with tears that were quickly swiped away. "Mrs. Bridges's mama died and so they are closed for the mourning period." She reached up, tapping his cheek lightly with her fingers. "How typical that your first visit should be to the local tavern and not your loving family."

"It was not a visit of pleasure," he replied, "but one of business with Mr. Bridges."

Clearly, she didn't believe that. As he knew she would not. "Oh, it is very good to see you looking so well, Nate. Is it not, Jussy?" She stepped back to take in his full height. "So finely dressed too." Squinting, she added, "Your luck must have improved."

"You might say that."

Now her friend Justina joined in the welcome. The two girls had grown up in his absence, he noted—no surprise, since they were now wives and mothers. But whenever any amount of time passed between sightings, he was always struck by the considerable changes as if his mind expected them to remain forever little girls with muddy petticoats.

"You have several new acquaintances to meet," said his sister. "You have a little nephew, to begin with."

"Aha! I must set about corrupting him at the

earliest opportunity. I've been remiss in my duty as his mad uncle."

"And I have two seedlings," Justina told him, "who, along with Becky's son, have been left this morning to the care of my poor husband, so I cannot leave them long or I might return home to find him trussed up in the pantry with a flowerpot on his head, while the new litter of piglets runs riot through the house."

Nathaniel smiled. "Your boys take after you then, Jussy."

"They are both *girls*," she replied smugly, as if she'd had a say in the matter, "and yes, they do take after me."

Rebecca added, "To the great despair of her husband."

They all laughed.

He remembered Darius Wainwright as a dour fellow who couldn't crack a smile if his life depended on it. Nathaniel could not envision how Darius and lively Justina Penny had ever found common ground. Opposites attracting, perhaps?

"Oh, but you have not yet met Sarah Wainwright," his sister exclaimed, drawing the other girl forward from where she hovered in the background. "Sarah is my stepdaughter."

"Miss Wainwright." He bowed. "I am delighted to make the acquaintance of an instant niece." Her small face looked familiar but he could not immediately place it.

Her eyes were round, thoughtful, and rather intense. The sort of eyes that might come in useful if she had a spy to interrogate. "Captain Sherringham. I have heard much about you."

He laughed. "You may as well believe every bleak

word, for the truth is probably a great deal worse than the gossips of Hawcombe Prior can conceive." Glancing down the street in the direction from which they'd traveled, he asked if they'd been plundering the village's one and only shop. "I see no packages, so it seems you left Mr. Porter's shelves stocked for once."

"We've been to a meeting of the book society," his sister replied. "Don't you remember? You used to call us the Book Club Belles."

As if he could forget. "Still under the influence of dangerously subversive novels, eh?" he teased. "I never did think young ladies should read novels. It gives them entirely false expectations of men and of life."

His sister used to claim she was no romantic—a fact Nathaniel disproved easily by pointing out her love for books in which the hero always gets his woman, justice prevails, and they all live happily ever after.

An event that happened in real life as often as the Prince Regent passed up a new pair of breeches.

"Have you seen Papa yet?" his sister demanded.

"Hmm? No." He tore his eyes away from the small cottage in the midst of a row that crossed the end of the High Street. The Book Club Belles used to congregate in the parlor of Mrs. Makepiece's cottage. Obviously today they'd been to some other cottage in the lane, for he couldn't imagine starchy Mrs. Makepiece still putting up with his sister and her friends now that Diana was married and gone to Manderson.

"It might be best if you let me come with you, Nate."

Nathaniel was still looking down the main street to where it met a grassy path known as "the Bolt" for its narrowing shape and its convenience as a shortcut. At the far end of the Bolt, not visible to anyone unless they passed through it, the trees had reached across and tangled their branches overhead, making a cozy arch. A favorite haunt for secret lovers. That was where he once proposed marriage to Diana Makepiece. Where she tore his heart out and trampled it. There were probably still pieces of his flesh in the ground. Perhaps they had grown into sad, thorny weeds.

"Nate, did you hear? I said it might be best if I come with you and prepare Papa, or the shock could do him in."

Since no one mentioned Diana, he was determined to say nothing about her either. It was not as if he yearned to hear details of her wedding or anything else about the woman. She was nothing to him now.

"How long will you stay?" Justina asked.

"We'll see. I am undecided."

"But what have you been up to all this time?" They could tell from his clothes, of course, that he was no longer in the army.

"Oh, this and that." He gave them what he hoped was a mysterious, narrow-eyed look.

"I believe I saw you at the Manderson assembly dance yesterday evening, Captain Sherringham," said Sarah suddenly.

So that was where he'd seen her pert face. She was the merry young miss in the yellow dress, enjoying a rowdy country jig.

"Your companion is not with you today?" she added, casting a meaningful glance at his sister and her friend.

"No, she remains in Manderson, recovering from a sore head." He had left Caroline reclining on a chaise, being tended to diligently by the landlady at the Royal Oak in Manderson.

"A lady friend?" his sister demanded. "You must introduce us at once."

"Oh, I don't think that's necessary. I am merely escorting her to relatives as she could find no one else with whom to travel."

His sister gave him one of her skeptical looks. "Well, we had better go and see Papa." She linked her arm with his. "I was going to have luncheon at the manor with Jussy, but now Sarah will have to go alone. I will join her there later."

Still no mention of Diana. Why would there be? It was doubtful the friends saw much of her these days. He may not even catch another glimpse of her himself while he was there. Not that he wanted one anyway. At breakfast he'd casually asked the landlady of the Royal Oak about the prominent town resident, Mr. William Shaw, and learned that he had married at the end of last summer and had recently returned from a long trip abroad with his wife. The extended travel did not seem to have done Diana much good, he thought grimly. Perhaps that was why she'd looked so tired when he saw her yesterday.

"Goodness, your face just went very dour," exclaimed his sister.

"Indigestion," he snapped. "It bothers me from time to time."

Suddenly Sarah Wainwright cried out in alarm and pointed, "Sir Mortimer Grubbins! What is he doing now?" Across the common, a large Oxford Sandy and Black pig was rooting aimlessly through a cottage garden, the gate hanging wide as if he had opened it with his own trotters. "Mrs. Dockley's peonies do tend to be his favorite! He must have got out again. Oh sakes! He will not stay put lately. I do not know what has got into him."

The pig lifted its snout and grunted loudly over the wall, munching the luckless blooms belonging to the oldest resident in the village.

"We had better go and get him quickly," exclaimed Justina, "before he does any further damage to the poor lady's garden."

Sarah took hasty leave of the little group and dashed across the common, shouting to the errant beast who calmly grunted in response. Justina followed close behind, waving over her shoulder as she left brother and sister to walk down the road together.

"So...the Book Club Belles still meet." Nathaniel led his horse by the reins. "I am glad to see not everything has changed. Your friendships are as strong as ever."

"Yes, although marriage has taken one of our number from the village, of course. We miss her terribly. Her husband does not bring her to visit nearly enough."

He swallowed as best he could with a tight throat and looked away at the low clouds.

"I was sorry you did not come home for *my* wedding, Nate," his sister added.

"I knew nothing about it," he snapped, still thinking of the other nuptials he had not attended. Then, recovering, he cleared his throat and continued in a gentler tone, "Until I heard from some of my old army friends, quite by chance, that the lovely, flame-haired

Miss Rebecca Sherringham had taken herself off the market by marrying infamous Lucky Luke Wainwright of the Nineteenth Light Dragoons and various dens of iniquity from Bombay to Brighton. A man fifteen years her senior and with a harem of lovers in his past. They took great enjoyment in teasing me about that."

She chuckled. "I suppose it was a shock to you, brother dear."

"Not overmuch. You always were terribly impulsive and attracted to trouble."

She slapped his arm with her reticule and they walked on together.

"I heard it was something to do with a gambling debt?" he added.

His sister protested, "Luke needed me. Someone has to take care of him."

"Oh, yes, the poor invalid! How is that notorious limp of his these days? You do know he always used that for sympathy from the ladies. The severity of his lurch depended largely on the desperation he felt for getting a woman into his bed."

"I see you still like to expound at length upon subjects of which you know little to naught."

"I also know that he shot himself in the thigh quite by accident while cocking his pistol, yet he tells all manner of heroic tales about the acquisition of his wound. Poor, simpleminded woman, I daresay you were taken in. Like all the others."

"Indeed I was not."

"You were always so very particular about men and especially about the ideal husband. Now look at what you married. Still, I suppose even a stubborn, scolding woman like you needs a man eventually, just to control your hysterical humors—"

"My *what*?"

"—and the Wainwrights *are* stinking rich. No doubt you could overlook all his sins for a comfortable, well-feathered nest. Women are mercenary creatures."

"Stop it at once! I will not have you tease me about falling helplessly in love. Unless you would like me to torment you in the same way."

He looked down at her. "Tease all you like, Sister. I have nothing to hide."

Rebecca's eyes gleamed. "Don't you?"

"Certainly not."

"Never fallen in love?"

"Good God, no."

"But what about—"

"There are far too many lovely and obliging girls in the world requiring my attention. It would be selfish of me, don't you agree, to reserve all this manly beauty for one woman?"

"Nate, you are the very limit."

"Although I am thirty now. I suppose, sooner or later, I must marry if I want a son." He gazed off into the distance, feigning deep thought. "Perhaps, before I'm too old and set in my ways, I *ought* to find a suitable young woman who doesn't try my patience too much."

His sister chuckled again, the breeze fluttering through her bonnet ribbons. "And what will be the qualities she must possess, apart from an ability to tolerate your antics?"

"I'm not so difficult to please." He grinned down at her, "Any pretty, fair-haired girl between fifteen and—oh—twenty-five. Not so old that she can't be trained to behave and not so clever that she thinks too much. Someone exceedingly grateful for all that I give her, who knows her place and never questions me."

"Nathaniel Sherringham, I pity any woman you set your sights upon."

Thus, joking together, they walked onward to their father's house.

Five

REMOVING THE LAST BATCH OF WELSH CAKES FROM the iron skillet, Diana laid them out to cool and then took up some mending. She sat beside her mother who was shelling peas, dropping empty pods into a basket by her feet and letting the little green gems cascade through her quick fingers into a china bowl in her lap.

"The first crop of the season," said Diana, smiling. Shelling peas had been one of her favorite chores as a child, despite her mother's complaints that she was too slow at the task. Diana, of course, had to count the peas in each pod she opened, for if she found nine, it meant she would have to marry the next man she saw. How she loved the sight of those bright green pearls nestled in their velvety purse, knowing that no human had ever laid eyes on them until she did. Her impatient mother had usually snatched the bowl away to finish the job herself.

"I suppose you saw no one of any interest at the assembly dance yesterday, Diana?"

"No, Mama. Just the usual faces. It was horribly

crowded despite the entrance fee." Diana squinted as she threaded her needle by the flickering light. The afternoon shadows stretched into the kitchen, bringing the day to a premature close with the threat of a spring storm. Her mother had already lit an oil lamp since the firelight was inadequate.

"Sarah Wainwright was much admired, no doubt." The last two words were snapped off as another peapod was ruthlessly split open.

"Yes. She danced every dance."

Her mother's lips turned up at one end. "Although I cannot see much cause for her popularity. She has a sly look about her and a certain gaucheness in her manners."

"I always thought that was shyness, Mama. I could hardly call Sarah gauche."

"A naturally quiet, reserved girl has dignity. But *she* is either silent and sulking or bursting out with inappropriate questions and remarks. The appearance of shyness is merely her *lying in wait*, gleaning information to be used later. She's a scheming creature, you mark my words." Her mother glowered at the peas in her bowl.

"But her family is rich, of course, and that makes all the difference these days. Money is too often prized above breeding. We must say nothing of her illegitimacy or of her mother who once danced across a stage. That must be overlooked because she will have a fine dowry and the Wainwright name. Not that they are anything more than pirates and rum smugglers."

"Mama, the Wainwright brothers manage a respectable shipping and import business."

"Respectable, indeed! Men seldom come from nothing to make a fortune by legitimate means."

With a quiet sigh, Diana continued to mend the torn trim of her best frock. She had stepped on it yesterday when she got up out of her chair in haste to give Sarah her fan and that had loosened the hem—leading to disastrous consequences later that evening. But she had better not think of *him*, not in her mother's presence. Rosalind Makepiece had an uncanny ability to winkle out secrets just by reading a person's expression.

"No sign of William Shaw and his bride at the assembly rooms now they are back from their travels abroad?" Her mother dropped another disemboweled pod to the basket by her feet.

"No." Diana drew her needle through the material and paused a moment before adding quietly, "Mr. Shaw made his fortune through trade, Mama, and I never heard you disparage his means as you do those of the Wainwrights."

"William Shaw is a perfect gentleman," her mother grumbled, ripping open another pod. "He was raised with proper discipline by his grandmother, who came from a noble, ancient family. His shop holds a royal warrant and sells only the very best and most respectable English goods. William Shaw always behaves with impeccable manners. He knows where deference is due. By comparison the Wainwright men are wild brutes."

"Wild brutes?" Diana almost laughed.

"There are many professed 'gentlemen' who could learn a thing or two from dear William Shaw," her mother continued. "It is unfortunate that you could not see the value of his affections while you still had them."

"Do you not wonder, Mama, how long I would have kept those affections, even if I had married him? He was, after all, affianced to another woman less than a fortnight after I ended our engagement."

"He only did what a proud man must do to save face after being humiliated."

"But I think—"

"A man as well settled as William needed a wife, Diana. It is the natural instinct in the male creature to seek out a worthy mate as quickly and efficiently as possible. If he is sensible and capable of affording a wife, he knows it is his duty."

With her mother's voice slowly fading, Diana's mind returned to Nathaniel's dangerous, forbidden kiss. Most unwise. Not in the least sensible. Certainly not dutiful.

Her gaze fixed on the kitchen window above her mother's head, Diana observed the first tickle of rain against glass. The thick heat was at last breaking and the storm that had hovered for most of the afternoon was finally set free from the threatening clouds.

She set her sewing on the table. "I'll close the parlor window, Mama. I had it open to air out the room." On a spring day, one of Diana's greatest pleasures was opening windows to let in the sweet scent of blossoms. If she had her way, the windows would always be open. Her mother, however, preferred the chalky fragrance of potpourri and protested that an open window let in more flies and odors than it did fresh air. Especially when the dairy farmer, Mr. Gates, had just driven his herd to the meadow by taking a shortcut past their cottage and down the Bolt.

"I should send you to our cousin Elizabeth, now she is settled near Bath, and see what she can make of you," said Diana's mother sharply. "A change of society—and one that is vastly improved—would do you good. Besides," she said, sighing heavily, "there is nothing here for you now. Just those ridiculous novels. They do naught but inspire a head full of dreams."

Thank goodness for those books, thought Diana.

She left the kitchen, entered the silent parlor, and walked to the open window. She hovered there for a while, reluctant to close it just yet, breathing in the outside air. Even speckled with damp it had a good fragrance, full of life and rejuvenation.

Her thoughts wandered back again to the summer afternoon when William Shaw had stood in that parlor with her for the last time.

〰️

"Miss Makepiece…Diana?" After an engagement of two years William had still hesitated to call her by her first name. "I'm not certain I heard you correctly."

Tearing her gaze from the music sheets on the pianoforte, Diana had looked at him and repeated, "I'm sorry. I cannot marry you." She'd been struggling desperately for a way to put it kindly, and in the end, simple felt best.

The man standing before the cold, empty hearth straightened his shoulders, snapped the case of his fob watch shut, and looked at her with a slightly furrowed brow. "But…you are four-and-twenty, Miss Makepiece," he had said with the ponderous solemnity she might expect from a doctor announcing she'd acquired a terminal disease. It was rather uncharitable—not to mention impolite—of him to point out her age, she thought. "Your looks will not last forever."

Diana wondered what her mother would have made of that lapse in his much-lauded manners.

"What other prospects can *you* have?" he'd muttered, shaking his head. "You will be quite sunk without me."

Diana had replied civilly, "I know you will soon recover from this disappointment." After all, it wasn't as if she would bring any fortune to the marriage, and if he was only marrying her to gain some benefit from a connection to grand relatives in Oxfordshire—as she suspected, having witnessed some of his humiliating attempts at social climbing—he must be better off without her. "And you will find a wife to make you far happier than I ever would."

When William left the house for that last time, Diana had taken a moment to prepare herself before she went out to give her mama the news. She must not be smiling with relief. *Think of something tragic instead*, she had chided herself crossly.

Not that the effort saved her from chastisement.

"I blame this entirely on those silly novels you read and the rash marriages your friends have lately made!" her mother cried. "That has influenced you to make a terrible misjudgment. Well, I don't know who you think I can get for you now. We've wasted years on this engagement. Your prime is gone. I don't know why you're putting that bread crust out for the birds. We can't afford to feed them now too!"

Breaking through these memories, a breeze kicked up and rustled the music sheets atop the old pianoforte. She picked up the papers and tidied them.

Her fingers hovered over a tattered edition of *Campbell's Country Dances and Jigs*. Usually kept hidden behind the other music, it contained a tune to which she and that reckless, flirtatious, entirely unsuitable gambler Captain Nathaniel Sherringham had once danced. She never played it now, but Diana could run her gaze across the notes on the paper and hear it in her mind, where it could not be spoiled by one of her mother's scornful comments about how clumsily that young man had danced.

Listening to the music in her head was one of Diana's naughty little secrets. She didn't have many. But for her, the sweet notes of music were a treasured escape from chores. Rain now dampened the music sheets, so she closed the parlor window and twisted the latch shut.

If Nathaniel returned to Hawcombe Prior, she would undoubtedly see him again, even be thrust into the same society on occasion. But she would be calm, ladylike. She'd greet him as an old acquaintance, as she should have done yesterday evening if she had not been flustered and embarrassed about her pimple and so many other indescribable, inexplicable things.

So determined, she hastily drew the curtains closed.

※

Nathaniel flung open his bedchamber curtains and opened the window. Restless and hot, he couldn't sleep. Pacing in only his buckskins, he welcomed the cooling, gentle raindrops as they blew in. With his father's merry encouragement he'd imbibed a little too much brandy after dinner, and that wouldn't do at all. He refused to fall into old habits. Coming back to Hawcombe Prior was bound to reopen some wounds, but really he should be strong enough to bear it without needing alcohol to dull the pain. He would not make childish excuses for his bad behavior. He was an adult, a man—no longer a boy shirking his responsibilities.

He smiled wryly. Took him long enough to get there, didn't it?

Caroline Sayles must wonder what had happened to him, for he'd expected to be back in Manderson by nightfall, instead of spending the night at his father's house. He would send her a message in the morning and warn her that their journey to Bath must be delayed a few days. He couldn't very well approach the tavern keeper about business while the man was in deep mourning. Keeping Caroline away a few more days might also do her aunt a favor, he mused grimly. That unfortunate lady had so recently lost a daughter and probably had no idea she was about to be descended upon by a niece with more imaginary illnesses than a child hoping to escape an algebra lesson.

Besides, necessary delay gave him an excuse to linger a few days more in Hawcombe Prior.

It was quiet there, peaceful, comfortable. He'd lived in many places in his thirty years and never stayed anywhere long, but somehow that village felt like home. His father had retired there almost ten years ago, purchasing some land and property and then settling in to enjoy his last years in comfort. Sadly, it had

not turned out quite as the major hoped. Thanks to
an overgenerous temperament and a kind heart easily
tapped by the unscrupulous, he could never bring
himself to charge his tenants full rent and had soon run
through his savings.

As Nathaniel had recently learned, Rebecca's husband
had gotten the major out of a sticky spot a few years ago
by buying up some of his fields and assuming landlord
duties. Now the major was happier, with less stress hanging over his head and his accounts managed ably by his
son-in-law at Willow Tree Farm. No one dared try to
cheat "Lucky" Luke Wainwright out of the rent due.

Apparently, only the residents of that short row of
cottages at the end of the High Street still paid rent
directly to the major. Nathaniel thought his father
probably insisted on that because he enjoyed making
haughty Mrs. Makepiece pay him. Her superior atti-
tude had always grated on the major's nerves, as it did
on his son's.

At dinner last night his father had had news to share
on any and everything except Diana, and Nathaniel
had not felt able to raise the subject in a casual way.
The conversation never seemed to come close enough
to be diverted in that direction.

He should simply have asked after her and been
done with it. One quick, nonchalant remark could
have ended this pain, but instead he was drawing
it out, like a slow blade scraped over his skin. Self-
punishment, he supposed, for his sins.

She was another man's wife. What else could they
possibly tell him about her now? And why should he
care to hear it?

He had kissed her under the trees of the Bolt. How sweet her lips had tasted, even directly after rejecting his proposal. Their taste did not match the bitter words that came out of them, probably because those words were her mother's, not her own.

Nathaniel laughed contemptuously and shook his head. What asinine fellow would kiss a woman *after* she rejected him? A fool who didn't know when to give up, when to quit the battlefield.

But despite his intention to hate her, other feelings, raw and primal, dominated his thoughts.

She should be with him now. She should be *his* wife. He'd wanted her from the first moment her hand was placed upon his. That first dance in Manderson when they were so young. Nathaniel couldn't account for it, couldn't understand it, but back then he had not been the sort of man who studied reasons. He'd acted on impulse, driven entirely by his bodily instincts. He'd known immediately that she was special, the one woman who made him feel calm, who made that busy, reckless young man want to stop, sit down, and put his boots up. Perhaps even get fat and surround himself with children.

Diana and her mother had had other plans. He was not good enough for them.

The injustice bit cruelly into his flesh and clung there. He could not shake it off. His desire for her had been too great.

Often at night, in need of comfort and release, Nathaniel lay in bed with his eyes closed and pictured Diana beside him. That's where she belonged—naked, with open eyes, her lips damp from his kisses, her cheeks flushed, her hair spilled loose over her shoulders. Given the chance, he would have made love to her in such a manner that she knew her place was with him, that she felt as he did and understood they were made for each other.

Really it was ridiculous that he'd ever proposed marriage to her. He wished he could forget it. Undoubtedly she had. If he saw her again, he would treat her with as much chilly disinterest as she had shown him.

In the years since he'd left Hawcombe Prior, Nathaniel had learned to be less transparent about his thoughts and feelings. He kept his instincts and his hot blood reined in. Usually.

Alas, his mind and his limbs were too restless tonight.

Storming back across the room to the washstand, he poured water into the bowl and splashed his face. Unfortunately the water was frigid cold, so it woke him further, rather than soothing him into drowsiness.

Nathaniel dropped heavily onto his back across the narrow bed and gazed up at the low ceiling, memories of the green-eyed girl plaguing his thoughts.

❧

"I certainly would never marry you, Captain. It is quite out of the question. What can you be thinking?"

"I know I'm a rogue with a repertoire of wicked jokes, absolutely no sense of propriety, and the grace of a plow horse on the dance floor"—he grinned—"but I do not believe you can say you have no feelings for me whatsoever. Say that you do not, Diana. Say it and I'll believe you."

"Don't be so ridiculous. Of course I have feelings for you."

In that second his heart had lifted. Only to be trampled and shattered in the next instant when she added, "I find you annoying, provoking, petulant, spoiled, and slightly unhinged. My feelings are that and only that."

Recovering as best he could, he replied on a short exhale, "I suppose some feelings are better than none."

She'd looked at him then in surprise, those expressive brows arched high. "If you can be content with that, it is no wonder you're always pleased with yourself. I daresay if I didn't care what people thought of me I could be eternally smug too and congratulate myself at every opportunity on my faults."

❧

Proving herself a mercenary, Diana had sacrificed herself to another instead. A man of "stability" and wealth, handpicked by her mother; a man for whom she felt even less than she had for Nathaniel.

"William Shaw rouses no emotion in me at all," she'd admitted, "and I am thankful for it."

To her, emotions were an abomination.

Nathaniel supposed that was why he had kissed her—to try and make her feel something real, something her mother had not taught her about.

Now she was just another girl he'd once kissed. There were many.

He sat up again and groaned. No good. Couldn't sleep. Needed to be doing something.

So he left his room and went downstairs to the

quiet kitchen where he spent a good hour polishing his boots. By the time he was done they gleamed like glass, his arm ached, and he was quite certain he'd erased all thoughts of Diana—now Mrs. William Shaw—from his mind.

Six

He had not forgiven Anne Elliot. She had used him ill; deserted and disappointed him; and worse, she had shown a feebleness of character in doing so, which his own decided, confident temper could not endure. She had given him up to oblige others.

—*Persuasion*

It was with a much clearer head and happier temperament that he rode to Willow Tree Farm the next morning after breakfast. He was delighted to meet his little nephew for he'd always been fond of children. They were artless, curious, and had not yet formed a single judgment on anything more serious than whether or not they liked strawberry jam.

As for his sister's stepdaughter, Miss Sarah Wainwright, he reserved his opinion for now. Her eyes were just a little too knowing, and she was the quiet sort. He'd had his fill of those. The girl became more animated, however, when prompted by his sister to bring out her portfolio of sketches.

One of the first sheets that fell out onto the table portrayed a too-familiar image and made Nathaniel start so suddenly that he bit his inner cheek.

"This is Diana Makepiece," said Sarah. "It was very difficult to get her to sit for me, and when it was done, she said I could keep it. I thought she might want it framed, but she did not."

Across the room, playing with the little boy on her lap, his sister had turned to look at him. He felt the cautious regard in her worried gaze, so he forced a smile and said, "Ah, but who is this?" He focused Sarah's attention on another sketch, a drawing of one of the harvest workers apparently. His hand remained a moment on the picture of Diana and, when he thought he could do so unobserved, he glanced at it again.

Couldn't help it. Ah yes, why not torture himself anew?

Sarah had called her Diana *Makepiece*, so this must have been drawn before her marriage.

In the sketch her face was calm, just as he remembered it from before—not as it was two nights ago when she seemed extremely agitated. She was staring away from the artist. Diana was not the vain sort and must have hated sitting for a portrait. No doubt she did so just to please Sarah, for she always complied with the wishes of her friends. She did not include him in that group, of course, despite his efforts.

Nate remembered walking across the meadow with Diana in one of their stolen moments alone together. He had chased after her, tumbling over a stile to tell the ingrate that she was beautiful.

He'd never seen her blush before then. "Don't be silly," she'd said, looking flustered and covering her cheeks with her hands. "For goodness' sake."

But she must have known how she looked. She surely had a mirror to see for herself and could have heard compliments aplenty whenever there was a dance to attend. Her beauty, however, was of a different variety than the usual rosy-cheeked, buxom country girl. Perhaps that was why she failed to recognize its full worth. He saw that possibility now, although at the time he'd been nonplussed by her lack of confidence. Three years of absence from a situation could cause a man to look at it from another angle. Through new eyes.

Nathaniel studied the portrait as long as he dared, sneakily following the charcoal lines and curves with a sideways glance, the direction of his gaze hidden by lowered eyelids.

Until her likeness was covered by another sketch and then another, for Sarah Wainwright was a prolific artist.

There were sketches of plow horses, dogs, and that very large pig called Sir Mortimer Grubbins. Soon, as the pile mounted, there was nothing of Diana left visible.

"Should I call you Captain or Uncle Sherringham? Or Uncle Nathaniel?" Sarah asked suddenly, her eyes very wide and earnest, as if this was a most pressing matter.

"Hmmm." He pretended to consider her question with equal solemnity. "Uncle Sherringham sounds awfully old and dry. Indeed, I do not like the *Uncle* much at all. It brings to mind a stodgy old man with rancid breath and bulging waistcoat buttons. Would a simple *Sherry* be appropriate, do you suppose? It is what all my friends call me. Those that are still speaking to me, that is," he added with an arch grin.

She nodded. "Very well, I shall call you Sherry."

"Perhaps you can sketch my brother," said Rebecca, "if he will sit still long enough while he is here."

Nathaniel replied teasingly that he thought the real thing much more endearing, unless, of course, his future bride might want to keep his image in charcoal for the times when they were not together. "I would not want her to go into a decline if she does not have my handsome face before her every day."

"Are you going to marry that lady you were with at the assembly dance?" asked Sarah, sounding slightly scandalized by the idea. "The one with all the rouge?"

"Good Lord, no." She'd almost taken his breath away with that question. "Mrs. Sayles is just an acquaintance."

A strange look passed between his sister and her stepdaughter.

"An *acquaintance*," he repeated. "A traveling companion. I am charged with delivering her to relatives in Bath."

"Well, I must say that's a relief," Rebecca muttered.

While Sarah took her drawings back to her room, Nathaniel whispered, "I told you, sister dearest, my bride must be between fifteen and twenty-five, sweet-natured and adoring, full of maidenly innocence. That hardly describes Mrs. Sayles, I fear."

"Maidenly innocence?" his sister scoffed as she fought to regain one of her bronze locks from her son's tightly determined fist. "How typical that you would expect virtue and considerable naiveté from your bride, while you, for years, have been free to gain experience of that nature wherever and whenever you desire it."

With an amiable shrug, he replied, "A man should always seek knowledge and gain a familiarity with certain practices in order to guide his new bride." He winked. "Such an education is invaluable, and no woman has ever had cause to complain that I lack skill."

Rebecca snorted. "I'm quite sure you've never *heard* any complaints because you make yourself scarce the next day to escape fathers, husbands, brothers, and other consequences of that nature."

"What a thing to say to your own brother."

"I can say it to you *because* you are my brother. And someone has to show you the error of your flirtatious, unguarded ways."

He laughed. "I never seduced any fragile maidens, I assure you."

She looked skeptical. "I knew plenty of naive little misses who took your flirting seriously and suffered when you forgot them entirely the next day, once you were sober."

"I never forgot a single one! I remember them all fondly and always made certain to send them a gift."

Sarah dashed back into the room as if she feared missing any part of their conversation, and now he endured two sets of eyes studying him with a great deal of worrisome consideration. He suspected they were already running through a list of potential brides who might take him in hand.

When his sister once again pried for details about his business, Nathaniel was deliberately vague.

"I don't know why you cannot say," she exclaimed. "Clearly you wish people to know you've done well, or you would not be dressed that way."

"Of course. But they don't have to know exactly how well or how I managed it. Let them wonder."

"They will assume the worst. That you came by your new wealth by some illicit means."

He laughed. "Perhaps I did. But the woman I choose to marry will have to be brave and take me on"—he patted the side of his nose with one finger— "dark secrets and all."

"What woman do you think will possibly be induced to take you knowing nothing about your life?"

"It's a test, Sister. This way I can be sure she loves *me*, not merely the accessories that might come along with marriage to me."

"An addled woman blinded by love, you mean."

He widened his eyes innocently. "Are not all women addled to some extent?"

While she was still shouting at him for that comment, Luke Wainwright came in, walking with a cane. A short, stout, ugly dog—one that had featured in several of Sarah's sketches—trundled solidly, with a certain degree of self-importance, at his heels. "Captain Sherringham! We are glad to see you returned after so long. I have you to thank for the acquisition of a wife, you know."

"Ah, I did hear something of that matter." He glanced at his sister, who blushed under her freckles. "A gambling debt, was it not? One of mine probably."

Luke grinned broadly. "If not for that debt you once owed me, Sherringham, your sister would never have given an unsightly old sinner like me a kiss on the lips. And if not for that kiss, she'd never have been forced to marry me." He limped to the window seat where his wife sat and placed a kiss on her forehead, then one on the baby's soft hair too. "Now that's a pleasant sight to come home to after a morning in the fields." With a look back at Nathaniel he added, "You ought to get yourself one, Sherringham. A wife, that is."

"Oh, I intend to. I am fully open to the idea of acquiring a wife now and babes at once, many of them."

Luke took the child from his wife and carried him under one arm to wash his face in the scullery. The dog, having sniffed Nathaniel's gleaming boots, flopped down by the fire and rolled leisurely onto his back, presenting a belly for Sarah to scratch in a motion that seemed quite routine.

"Well, don't run hastily into marriage," said Rebecca. "I know how impulsive you can be, Nate. You must make sure she is the right woman for you before you marry. I would hate for you to make a mistake and be unhappy, trapped."

"I promise you, Sister"—Nathaniel put on a somber face—"I am far from the fool I once was."

She looked doubtful, so he returned to his usual flippant tone.

"However, a man of thirty cannot afford to let more time slip by while he dillies and dallies. He must seize his chance with the first merry and agreeable young thing in his path. Something lively. Yes indeed!

The less thought I put into it, the better. Expectations can too easily be shattered and disappointment leave a man's heart in ruins if he wants too much and cares too deeply."

He stopped abruptly, realizing his tone had turned serious just when he had not meant for it to be. So he clapped his hands together and exclaimed merrily, "I can hardly wait to see who you shall pick for me. Let her have a good bosom, a pretty face, and a quiet voice. Apart from that I'm not particular."

"What about teeth, Brother?" his sister remarked wryly.

He pretended to consider. "A few would be handy, of course, but one hesitates to ask for too much."

❧

Diana took her Welsh cakes to the Pig in a Poke, and while there she heard the news she'd dreaded from an excited Lucy.

"Captain Sherringham has returned to the village!"

Diana managed to look surprised, or so she hoped. Lucy seldom bothered to assess anyone else's feelings and was so full of this news that she scarcely glanced at Diana's face as she told it.

"He sent a message to my papa." Lucy leaned close and lowered her voice dramatically. "He has some business to tend while he's here, but Papa will not tell us what it is. What do you suppose it might be? What could the captain wish to speak to my papa about in private?"

Diana politely declined to speculate.

But Lucy did plenty for the both of them. "Well,

I don't flatter myself too much, I think, if I suspect it might have something to do with me. He has shown me many kindnesses in the past and seems to find me amusing company. As my mama says, he is of an age now when he must be thinking to settle down and I am unattached."

"Yes."

"I can imagine no other reason for Captain Sherringham to desire a private discussion with my papa. Although I do not know how I feel about it. To be sure, he is exceedingly handsome and witty, but it is so unexpected."

Diana began inching toward the door. A few moments later, after Lucy had observed, "You look rather crumpled today, and your hair is lank and listless…" she took her leave, explaining that her mother needed her at home to help kill some ants.

In no haste to return to the cottage, Diana chose the long way home. Instead of circling the common and going back down the High Street, she took the path along the stream toward the old mill. The ducks were out with their little ones— fluffy gold-and-brown smudges sailing along in a line behind them. The happy, peaceful scene should have kept her thoughts from wandering.

Should have.

Hands tucked into her muff, she marched along the bank, disturbing dandelion seeds and trampling long grass with a speed and violence that hardly lent itself to quiet reverie.

It made perfect sense for Nathaniel to return here to see his family. Of course it did. It was possible that he had also come back for a bride, and Lucy Bridges was the right age, certainly. She had a colorful personality, a lively temperament, and was undeniably pretty. She had spirit and boldness. She also knew how to speak up for herself.

Unlike Diana.

Nathaniel had once said to her, "Have you no will of your own? No gumption? Do not be a passive bystander in your own life, Diana."

She sniffed, shaking her head as she stomped along.

He might think she took the easier path rather than struggle against her mama's wishes, but then "Sherry" never thought of other people's needs, did he? Nathaniel regarded life as sport, coming and going as he pleased, never worrying about consequences. He called it confidence. He was proud of it.

Foolish, imprudent man!

Now, as she imagined Nathaniel's wedding to Lucy—oh Lord, would it take place right there in Hawcombe Prior?—a wretched pain in the region of her preciously guarded heart brought Diana to a halt on the path. There was also a shocking pinch of jealousy, when she had no right to feel it.

She'd always known he would have to marry someone. Someone other than her.

If only it didn't have to happen here, on her doorstep so to speak.

Alarmed by the intensity of her objections to the idea, Diana shook her head. What did it matter?

Resuming her brisk pace, she came to the stone bridge, where her thoughts turned to the long-ago days when she and Catherine Penny had played together, tossing sticks into the stream below, waiting to see whose drifted by first on the other side. Always together in those youthful days, Cathy and Diana were close in age and of similar temperament.

When Cathy went off to be married, leaving the village and Diana behind, it was a hard desertion to manage. At least Diana knew her friend was genuinely happy and that must be her comfort, but Mrs. Makepiece had disdainfully dismissed Cathy and her husband as "too giddy." She predicted their marriage would end in tragedy "as such reckless and sudden matches often do."

Well, thought Diana, *you should know, Mama.*

As for herself, she would never marry. Why should she? At her age the last thing she wanted was to suddenly be forced to adjust her life, to share it with a man. There were plenty of times when she liked to be alone to read a book, and the likelihood of that once a woman married was slim. Her mother, of course, would remind her that it was a woman's duty to marry and bear children. It was her only purpose in life. But then her mother had no appreciation for novels.

When Diana was a little girl, she had shocked her mother one day by declaring, "If I were rich I would never marry at all, but I'd take a lover and he would be obliged to please *me* for *my* money."

That declaration was also blamed on her choice of reading material.

Funny that she should remember it now—how she'd been hot-faced and defiant, standing in her mother's kitchen. As far as she recalled, she might even have stamped her foot. Why the subject ever came up, or what inspired her to such a wild thought, she had no idea.

It was a moment of revolution, a spark her mother quickly extinguished by assuring Diana that there would be no more books for her if she continued in that vein.

Pausing now at the peak of the bridge, Diana leaned against the mossy stone and gazed down into the sun-dappled water. A strange tear of sadness threatened, and a hollow ache started in her breast where that harsh pain had been a moment before. It must simply be a yearning for the sunny days of youth and for Cathy at her side again.

Nothing made a well-guarded heart hurt more, Diana had discovered, than the absence of something it once took for granted. Or something of which it never knew the full measure until it was gone forever and could not be won back. Perhaps it was not always good to have a heart so protected, for when it did feel pain, it was almost unbearable and she did not have practice healing it.

But if Diana mentioned such a thought to her mother, there would be a scornful huff and a reminder of the undone chores from which those "unnecessary ponderings" had distracted her.

She set her muff on the parapet to free her hands and then reached into her coat pocket for bread crumbs to feed the ducks.

Suddenly hearing hooves clattering over the bridge toward her, Diana flattened herself to the wall so the rider could pass. Expecting to see someone from the village, she prepared to greet them with a friendly smile as usual.

But the person she encountered was not the black-smith or the carpenter, or any other jolly, local face.

It was Nathaniel Sherringham.

Startled by the sudden sight of him coming rapidly toward her on his horse, she spun around so sharply that she nudged her muff from the edge of the parapet and it tumbled into the water with a splash.

Seven

Nathaniel had slightly longer than Diana to prepare, for he had seen her before she was aware of his presence. She was leaning over so far to watch the ducks sail by below that his heart had leaped in panic. He was ready to jump out of his saddle and dive to the rescue—he supposed even a woman who had insulted him the last time he tried to help her ought to be rescued—but the only thing that fell was the fleece muff.

When she saw him, her face paled. Her lips parted and she reached behind to clutch the stone ledge.

He had slowed his horse and now came to a halt on the hump of the bridge where she stood. Determined to keep his face empty of any expression, he stared down at her, waiting for something—a smile perhaps, some sign of gladness to see him. This time, let her be the first to speak. Could it be so hard for the damn woman to greet him? Others had welcomed his return with warmth. Why couldn't she? It wasn't as if she was in any danger of him renewing his attentions.

But there was no sound from her. Only parted

lips, and cheeks sunk in as if she were stuck on an inhaled breath.

Finally he grew too impatient. "Madam," he snapped out in terse greeting. Why was she there alone? Again she was unattended, Shaw nowhere in sight. "Are you on your way to visit my sister?"

She tipped her head back slightly, and gentle sunlight reached under her bonnet to touch her face. His pulse had almost ceased to beat. For so long he had held her face in his memory, and now she was before him again. Yet changed.

One small word squeaked out of her. "No." She looked as if she was not sure where she was going.

No smile warmed her expression. If anything, her countenance drained the sun of its heat, and when that word emerged from her lips, she looked perplexed. He stared down at those lips he'd once kissed. Their color was faded and they turned down at the corners, wobbling slightly.

He thought of riding on and saying nothing more, but found that to be quite impossible. "Pleasant weather," he said. Damn her. He would make her be polite to him even though she thought him so unworthy.

She merely nodded.

Nathaniel rested one hand on his thigh. "You look"—He decided not to lie. After all, flattery had never got him anywhere with her—"very ill. Is something amiss, madam?"

"Amiss?" A sharp, humorless laugh escaped her as she looked away from him. "I'm afraid it's simply the passage of time, Captain."

"Ah. I suppose so. And time is seldom kind to women."

Once, she'd accused him of being a boy, aimless, immature, and selfish. He'd waited more than three years to return the wounding thrust.

It did not feel quite as satisfying as he'd imagined. And he realized that rather than assuring her of his new maturity, he had just done the opposite.

Her gaze swept back to him but briefly, vexed. Then she looked down over the parapet again. Nathaniel waited, staring down at her, the horse restless under him.

"Shall I fetch it for you, madam?"

Her hands still grasped the stone behind her. "Fetch what?"

She'd forgotten it already. Clearly the muff meant nothing to her.

"The item you dropped, madam." He paused and then added, "Unless, of course, you tossed it away deliberately."

She was breathing rapidly now, a little color returning to her cheeks. "Why would I toss it away—?" Her brows lowered in a deep frown, and then he knew she understood his meaning.

Yes, he had recognized the muff he'd bought for her. He'd given it to her the last autumn he was there, while they stood under the sheltering golden leaves of the Bolt and he tried to dissuade her from marrying Shaw.

Warm your hands in this, Diana, until I can return again to warm them for you.

Nathaniel was quite sure she would never have

dared tell her mother who'd bought her that muff. Indeed, he was shocked to see it was still in her possession for several years before being resigned to the murky, weed-laden depths of the stream.

"It is floating away, madam," he pointed out.

"I–I can…" But her words floated away in the same manner as her muff and she did not move.

Nathaniel dismounted swiftly and looked over the other side of the bridge, where he spied the object caught in some reeds beside the supporting pillar. He would leave it there to rot. Serve her right.

When he turned back to look at Diana she was walking away hurriedly, apparently having made her decision to abandon it.

Fury ripped long talons through his attempt to remain detached.

❦

The stones slipped under her feet as she took the downward slope of the bridge at a reckless pace. It was not like her at all to risk a twisted ankle, but this was an emergency.

Madam, he had called her in that deep voice. As if they were barely acquainted.

Madam. How cold it had sounded, and how stern his face had been when he looked down at her from his snorting horse.

Nathaniel had always had an easy smile and a mischievous gleam in his eye. That had changed, along with so many things. His blue eyes were cheerless today as they bore down upon her.

He looked older too, she thought, but more

handsome than ever. How was such a thing possible? The injustice made her even more annoyed and lent speed to her pace until she turned to the right onto the grassy bank of the stream. Then she had to slow down to keep from tripping over the tussocks on that steep slope.

Now, where was her muff? Her darling, precious muff. Diana's blood cooled in the shadows beneath the bridge, but her heart still thumped hard and fast. With one hand resting on the stone abutment to steady herself, she studied the water and the reeds, searching desperately. The ground was wet and soft because the sun had not yet reached there to dry it. Her walking boots sank in a few inches, the mud sucking her down and making the most hideous squelching noises as she pulled her feet out again.

As if she needed his help to retrieve anything for her! As if she were a weak, defeated female. An old lady unable to help herself—just like two nights ago at the dance. Why did he think she needed him to rescue her constantly? How did he suppose she managed when no man was around?

Hopefully he would not stay long. Would just take his bride and go away. Diana would certainly do nothing to encourage his stay. Even if he didn't want Lucy, there would be others. Men were prideful, vain creatures and he was never lost for admirers.

She spied a flattened stone boulder and thought that would be a good place to stand while she sought her fallen muff. It was a little mossy, but if she was cautious...

❧

Nathaniel had rushed back down the other side of the bridge, removed his hat and coat, and looked around for a long stick—something with which to capture the muff. Having discovered the location of the fallen item before he ran down to the stream, he was soon wading into the weeds, makeshift fishing hook in hand. He didn't care about his fine, costly new boots and breeches. What did they matter now?

Much to his surprise, as he rounded the first pillar of the bridge he saw not only the trapped muff bobbing among the reeds at its base, but also Diana, thrashing about in the water.

The stream was no deeper than three feet in that spot, but weedy, thick tendrils wrapped around her as she tried to stand.

He had never heard Diana curse until that moment.

When she saw him, the woman shut her mouth and glared as if he were responsible for pushing her in. She was standing upright finally but soaked from head to toe, her bonnet flattened to her head and strands of dark hair hanging down the sides of her face.

It took every shred of his willpower not to laugh out loud. Oh, how far the haughty had fallen.

"What, pray tell, are you looking at?" she demanded, her shoulders back, spine straight, as dignified as any lady could be in those extraordinary circumstances.

Nathaniel pondered her prim face and weed-laden figure for a moment, his head cocked to one side. "I'm not entirely sure. I thought I knew it once. But I've never seen it quite so moist."

He had not meant to joke, but his heart was gladdened to see her looking for the muff—to know that she thought it worth saving, after all. He'd never expected such stupid happiness over so small a thing, and the humor bubbled out of him before he could maintain a stern face.

"You'll catch more fish if you bring a rod, madam."

Did she just curse again under her breath?

"I am in no mood for frivolity," she gasped, pulling a long weed from her sleeve.

"Quite. At our advanced age I don't suppose we can afford it too often."

In the shadows and dancing ripples of light that moved under the bridge, the color of her eyes had regained a startling brightness. Earlier he had thought them dull and darker than he remembered. But now her eyes were back to sparking and shimmering again. How he had missed that look! It stopped his pulse for a moment.

But she was right about the frivolity. His days of joking with her, flirting with her, were in the past. They must be. She was married now, and he had struggled to patch his heart up before because of her. He would not endanger it again.

Nathaniel reached with his stick and hooked the muff, lifting it slowly and carefully from the reeds. It hung limply, dripping water. "Yours, I believe, madam."

He had to take a few steps closer until she could grasp the recovered object and when she did so, it was with a quick motion, impatient, almost snapping his stick in two.

Reluctantly her lips moved. "I must thank you, Captain."

"Must? Don't do it because you *must*. Do it because you want to. Unless, of course, you don't want to."

She looked down, the shimmering green of her eyes hidden from his view. Drops of water fell from her crumpled bonnet brim to her cheek and looked like tears.

Nathaniel straightened up, tossing the stick into the water. "I would rather have a sincere thank-you from your heart." He had said too much, no doubt, but he couldn't help himself. Better than saying too little. Or nothing at all.

When she turned away, her skirt and coat swishing in the water, he added breathlessly, "God forbid, madam, that I add gratitude to the burden of your duties."

She halted and he thought she might turn and berate him. Good. He welcomed it. He was ready to get a lot off his chest. He wanted to quarrel with her. Perhaps he would finally draw out her emotions.

Instead, she waded to the bank and did not look back at him.

"We'll call it water under the bridge then, shall we?" he yelled. Ah, old habits. Still trying to make her smile, despite everything.

As she came out from the shadows, Diana was illuminated in bright sun for two beats of his heart, and then she was gone again.

Eight

"I HAVE ABSOLUTELY NO INTEREST IN MEETING THAT man again," her mother declared. "Why should we be hauled out on a rainy evening to fawn over *his* return? Trust him to come back again like a bad penny."

The note from Rebecca had arrived on Friday, inviting them to a small gathering at Willow Tree Farm. There was no mention of Nathaniel's return, but Diana had felt it best to warn her mother. Mrs. Makepiece did not care for surprises of any kind.

"If we don't go, Mama, it will look rude, considering our long association with the Sherringham family."

"As if I care what it looks like!"

But of course she did. Appearances were very important to Diana's mother.

"No one else is aware that he ever proposed to me, Mama." Occasionally she'd had cause to suspect that his sister might know, but Rebecca never raised the subject so Diana didn't either.

After expelling a few more energetic grumbles into the air, Mrs. Makepiece was forced to agree it might be best to get it over with. As Diana pointed out, no one could guess how long Captain Sherringham would remain in the village, and avoiding him forever would be impossible.

Diana said carefully, "We should be natural and polite with the captain, Mama."

"What can you mean by that? Don't you think *I* know how to behave?" came the scathing reply. "I have nothing to say to the man and neither do you, I'm sure."

"But the past is behind us now. There is no cause for you to hold it against him after all these years." For her friend Rebecca's sake she didn't want to seem aloof. She certainly didn't want anyone thinking her upset by the notion of Nathaniel marrying Lucy Bridges. "It is not as if he is likely to repeat his mistake with me, Mama."

"Indeed not. Even he couldn't be so very stupid as to bother *you* again. He'll have his eye on someone younger. Some naive petticoat with money to fund his reckless wagering."

So the two women walked out to Willow Tree Farm that evening through a fine drizzle of rain.

Rebecca met Diana at the door and was immediately cross with her. "I would have arranged the carriage for you, had I known you were coming," she exclaimed. "How could you think to walk all the way here in this weather when you are still recovering from a cold? Poor Diana!"

"Why did you think we would not come? You did invite us."

"Well, I assumed—" Catching Mrs. Makepiece's stern eye, her friend quickly shook her head and ushered the newcomers through the vestibule. "Of course you must come in and get dry and warm." Drawing Diana aside she whispered, "You look so pale and tired. Sarah said you were quite unwell at the dance, and it was my fault that you were there! Now you've come out in the rain! My fault again. Poor Diana. You look dreadful."

Diana stared at her friend and didn't know what to say. She had glanced briefly in her mirror before she left the house and thought her appearance acceptable, if nothing remarkable. She wore her hair in a knot at the nape of her neck, a more severe style than usual, but she didn't think it anything worth commenting on. She certainly couldn't fuss over her appearance before seeing Nathaniel again. If she did, her mother would be suspicious and *he* must not think she ever regretted turning him away.

"Thank you, I must say," she said finally. "I can always rely on you for the brutal truth. Now all I need is Mrs. Kenton's opinion and advice, and then my evening will be complete."

"My daughter took it upon herself to go swimming after fallen coins yesterday," Mrs. Makepiece snapped, having followed closely to overhear their conversation. "She has no one to blame but herself if her cold lingers. She does not take due precautions or a word of my advice. Soaked through, she was."

In response to Rebecca's puzzled expression, Diana explained, "I dropped my reticule in the stream. The string broke from my wrist, and then I slipped trying to retrieve it."

This was the best excuse she'd been able to think

up. While her mother would never have thought it necessary to chase after a muff that fell into the water, she would definitely be angry if Diana lost her purse of coins.

"For goodness' sake, come to the hearth and get warm," Rebecca exclaimed.

The Wainwrights' farmhouse was a spacious building with large, timbered rooms. Luke Wainwright had undertaken many repairs and improvements since he purchased the place from his father-in-law, and it was much grander than it had been before, although in a comfortable way. Even Diana's mother was surprised, but she hid it well of course. When Rebecca urged her guests to take chairs by the fire and dry their feet, Mrs. Makepiece replied that she preferred to stand, as if accepting the luxury of a padded, brocade seat in that company was the first step toward sin and debauchery.

Then the dreaded moment was upon them. "You will remember my brother, no doubt," said Rebecca, bringing Nathaniel over to where they stood.

"Yes. No doubt." Mrs. Makepiece could barely bring herself to look at him, let alone move her mouth, but when she did raise her eyelids, shock flashed through her gaze like sparks from a blacksmith's hammer. Diana felt it too.

Although she had seen him twice already since his return, she had not, on either occasion, been calm enough to take much note of his appearance or attire, other than to allow herself the galling acknowledgment that he remained as handsome as ever. Now she realized he was very well dressed indeed, the cut of his jacket in the latest style, the material costly. He looked every bit a gentleman of means and consequence.

"Madam." He bowed to her mother and then to Diana. As he straightened up again there was hesitation. Did he not know what to call her? Or was the tersely uttered "Madam" meant for both women, she wondered. Whatever the cause of his quizzical expression, it apparently prevented him from addressing Diana directly.

Justina and Darius Wainwright arrived in the next moment, and his sister swept him away to greet them.

Diana caught the faint trace of a sneer on her mother's face and then heard her remark, "I daresay he had a lucky win at the tables, but he will waste it all on his appearance. As one might expect of such a vain fellow. All surface and no substance. Always be wary, Daughter, of property dressed up beyond the means of its owner. There will be cracks hidden by furnishings, mold on the wall covered by sly paintwork, and leaks patched up with temporary fixes." Her mother looked around the room and added, "Go and sit down, Diana. You look very obvious and desperate standing in the middle of the room. Don't draw attention to yourself. It's not ladylike."

Not waiting for any response from her daughter, she walked away to converse with Mrs. Kenton who, with her usual need to be the center of Hawcombe Prior society, had arrived early for the party. Diana's mother had a curious relationship with the parson's wife. She did not like the lady much—thought her brash and vulgar—but although she would never admit it, she *did* like the endless seeds of gossip she could "inadvertently" collect by brushing against the woman occasionally.

All the principals of the village were there, including the Porters from the shop, and Dr. and Mrs. Penny. Only the Bridges were absent, still in mourning. Diana was surprised to see so many braving the rain that evening, particularly since news must have circulated by now of Nathaniel's return. He had never been very popular among the mothers of the village. She would have expected many of the more haughty residents to stay away rather than mingle with the notorious rogue.

Luke Wainwright's mutt ambled over to greet Diana and she stooped, giving the creature a quick scratch behind the ears, but even he soon left her standing alone as if her company was too dull to be tolerated for long, her attention inadequate. She looked around the room, but everyone seemed busy with their conversations and no one encouraged her with eye contact and a smile. It was the worst thing in the world to walk up to folk already involved in a discussion and try to foist oneself upon them.

If only Catherine Penny were there, Diana thought sadly. She was always at ease with Cathy because they were two quiet girls together. But one never knew what Rebecca and Justina might say or do next, or what one might hear by joining one of their conversations already in progress. Diana was not much fonder of surprises than her mama was.

She had begun to feel awkward and superfluous when, thankfully, she was saved by Sarah Wainwright, who wanted her opinion on a design for a new gown.

As they pored over sketches at the table, it was not long before the conversation turned to the unofficial guest of honor.

"I am to call him *Sherry*, he says," Sarah told Diana as they stood by a small table at the window. "He has come home to find a wife, you know."

Diana swallowed, catching a breath. "Oh." She checked in her peripheral vision that everyone else was engaged in their own conversations. Her mother was completely attentive at that moment, listening to Mrs. Kenton. The two women liked to complain together almost as much as they liked to complain *about* each other.

"We're going to find him one. Perhaps you can help."

Diana focused on Sarah's drawings. "One what? For whom?"

"A wife. For Sherry! My stepmama says he has always danced away from matrimony and has feared binding himself to one woman." Sarah lowered her voice even further, making Diana lean in to hear. "Apparently he has had a few near misses in life but sobered up the next day to hurriedly escape the consequences." Sarah studied her face. "I hope you are not sick because I dragged you out to the Manderson assembly dance on Tuesday!"

"Goodness no," Diana managed tightly. "I am much improved."

"But your eyes are watery and your nose is very pink. In fact, you look positively wretched."

"It is merely the end of this cold. I am much better than I was." Even as she said it she felt a sneeze coming on, but managed to subdue it to a very small squeak into her handkerchief.

"Poor Diana." Sarah laid a commiserating hand on her arm. "You *are* under the weather. Your hair has lost all its curl."

She smiled as widely as she could, her face hurting from the strain. "I have given that up, Sarah."

"Really?"

"Time for a change, I thought. I am no longer a young girl. Next step will be donning the lace cap of an old maid, as Mrs. Kenton has advised."

Sarah looked confused for a moment but then nodded, apparently agreeing this would be a sensible idea. In her tender young eyes, twenty-seven was indeed ancient and she didn't yet understand Diana's dry humor. Not that Diana was even sure she'd meant the comment as a jest.

"I did so admire that little embroidered book cover you made Jussy for her birthday. I wondered if you would show me how to make one," Sarah was saying. "My stitches are not nearly as neat as yours, though. My lack of skill will, sadly, dictate a simpler pattern."

Knowing she would likely end up sewing the book cover herself, Diana agreed that she would "help" Sarah. What else did she have to do?

Apparently he has had a few near misses in life but sobered up the next day to hurriedly escape the consequences.

No doubt she, Diana, was one of his "near misses." That was why he had left the village immediately without another word to her after his failed proposal.

A moment later, young Sarah's mind had already moved on to other subjects. "Do say you will play for us tonight, Diana! No one plays so well as you, and I want to dance with Sherry. He promised he would dance."

"Of course I will play for you." Even with a hot, foggy head and a scratchy throat, what else could she say when asked so sweetly? Better she make herself useful rather than stand about getting in the way and being "obvious."

❧

Despite everything he had imagined saying to Mrs. Rosalind Makepiece when he saw her again, Nathaniel no longer felt the need to fire his arrows. In fact he did not wish to speak to her at all. The anger was still there, but tamed for now, caged. He blamed this calmer temperament on his new clothes. One had to be on one's best behavior in such a fine suit of clothes. His tailor may not be Schweitzer and Davidson, but he was almost as costly. It was rather like donning a suit of armor, he mused.

In the past, except for the Book Club Belles, who were always more daring than they should be, the ladies of Hawcombe Prior had given Nathaniel a wide berth. But tonight, when he presented a tidier figure in expensive garments, they gathered about him eagerly. It also helped, he suspected, that they knew nothing about his business, and he avoided the subject. An air of mystery drew the gossips in like bees to clover. That amused him, and he may as well get some entertainment from the evening.

He certainly would not reveal to any of these women how he'd come by his wealth. Not yet, in any case. Let them wonder for a while. A few of them—Mrs. Makepiece, for instance—would never approve. It would give her a fresh reason to look down on him. Not that she needed any more.

But he was pleased to see a few of the residents of Hawcombe Prior again. Dr. Penny had been a good friend, inviting Nathaniel into his study to share his troubles and a glass of wine on several occasions. The doctor was an excellent listener and he worked his remedies in such a quiet, unassuming way that one seldom realized how clever he was.

That evening, the doctor's bright eyes twinkled merrily as he inspected Nathaniel's new attire. "You have come to set the young ladies' hearts aflutter again, Sherry," he exclaimed with a low chuckle. "I can see I had better stock up on smelling salts and indigestion pills."

"I am on my way to Bath, sir, and will not stay here long."

"To Bath?" The doctor looked distressed. "I was there once. Didn't take to it."

"I am escorting a lady there to visit her relatives. *Not* that sort of a lady. I barely remember how I became commissioned with the task of escorting her there, but it seemed no one else was willing to travel with her and I have since discovered why." He grimaced. "Still, I promised I would deliver her safely. And then I shall be free to enjoy the sights and perhaps even find a bride while I am there. I hear there are plenty of eligible wenches on parade in Bath."

The doctor snorted. "Oh yes, there are plenty on parade indeed. The streets are full of 'em." He shuddered. "Like cowpats in a field."

Nathaniel laughed. "I shall have to pick my way through them with care."

"I must say it is a pity you cannot stay longer,

Sherry. This place gets very dull without a resident rake about to thrill the girls into fainting fits and nervous rashes, their mamas into hysteria, and their fathers into apoplexy."

Nathaniel replied that he would try his best to liven things up for the doctor while he was there.

When Sarah Wainwright begged for dancing and space was cleared in the room, she quickly requisitioned Nathaniel as her partner. He had not expected to dance that evening, but she was insistent and it gave him a reprieve from painfully polite conversation at least. Although there were only four couples willing to dance, that was adequate for the size of the room and just enough for a cotillion.

As he and Sarah joined hands, he glanced over at the pianoforte where Diana played, her skilled fingers flying over the keys, her eyes upon the music.

"You remember Diana, surely," said his partner, following the path of his gaze.

"Yes." He was puzzled to see her there without her husband. Yet again. "She married William Shaw, I hear." There, the words were out.

"Married? Oh, no. Diana had a terrible disappointment. Did you not hear of it? Her fiancé married another woman. It was very tragic. Now she is left brokenhearted and resigned to the future of an old maid."

His pulse slowed, almost came to a dead stop. He looked over at Diana again. Her eyes were fixed upon the music, although he doubted that she needed to follow the notes. This was a tune she must have played many times.

"But I was told…"

Nathaniel had to wait until he was reunited with his partner in the dance before he could learn any more.

"Then who is the Book Club Belle who moved away and whose husband seldom brings her to visit?"

"That would be Catherine Penny—now Mrs. Forester! She is very much missed since she moved away, although I did not have the chance to know her well before she married."

Catherine Penny, of course. What a fool he had been to forget Cathy's marriage! She was always so quiet and well behaved that he had often overlooked her, especially in the company of her noisier sister, Justina. Catherine Penny—that dear, sweet, darling girl. He suddenly thought of her with far more fondness than ever before.

"Diana always plays for us," Sarah continued. "I go to her for lessons twice a week, but I'm afraid I'm still not very good. She is much more accomplished at the pianoforte than anyone else and does not mind sitting at the instrument all evening."

"She does not care to dance?"

"Never. She prefers to play the music. Diana has given up all activities of the young."

He remembered again the first time he took Diana's white-gloved hand, when she said she only danced with him to please his sister. It must have been almost ten years ago or thereabouts, the year his father first moved to Hawcombe Prior. The first time he'd laid eyes on her and thought about how there was a light within the girl. It shone through her skin, making her look almost angelic.

But the light was gone now. She stared at the music before her, and the eyebrows that had once captured his attention were drawn fiercely together as if she might need spectacles. He knew how much Diana loved music—had heard her many times, humming quietly to herself and tapping her toes, when she thought she was alone and would neither be heard nor observed. Tonight, however, there was no sign of pleasure on her face as she played for the dancers.

"I would not have known her," he said to himself as much as anyone. "She is so changed."

Suddenly Diana looked up and her gaze collided with his. Had she heard his comment above the music? There was a spark between them, as if two swords—his and hers—clashed in the night, and then her gaze returned to the music book open before her. She played on without missing a note.

The dancing continued for some time and, as Sarah had assured him she would, Diana stayed at her post.

While his feet followed the steps—occasionally moving in the wrong direction and causing Sarah equal shares of frustration and amusement—Nathaniel struggled to get his thoughts in order. All his preparations of self-defense had been made in the expectation of Diana's marriage. Knowing that she remained unwed broke the wall he'd carefully built and sent questions tumbling through his mind. But he kept quiet.

"Lucy Bridges will be furious to have missed this party, especially when she learns there was dancing," Sarah exclaimed. "Her father hardly lets her out of the house. He says it is improper while she's in mourning for her grandmama."

"I am sorry to hear that."

"She is only allowed out for book society meetings. Being shut in has made her quite short-tempered. Just like our dear old boar Sir Morty, who doesn't care much for fences either. I pointed out the resemblance to her recently, and she went into quite a rage."

He smiled. "We'll have to think of some way to cheer her spirits. I remember Miss Lucy Bridges as a lively and amusing young lady."

Sarah looked at him with wide, thoughtful eyes. "Yes, I do not think you will find *her* so much changed."

While the dancers rested, he watched Diana stand and move over to the sideboard for some wine. No one had offered to bring her any, despite the fact that she'd sat there playing for them half the evening. Looking around the room, he realized all the guests were too preoccupied with themselves and their conversations. Diana was very much alone as she stood with her head bowed, pouring the wine.

She had not married. He didn't know what to make of it. Her mama had always been so set on William Shaw that it must have been a shock to both women when he married elsewhere.

How small Diana seemed now. Had she lost inches in all directions? There was a time when his gaze would immediately go to her when he entered a room. Now he was not sure he would have noticed her at all, if not for their history.

While Nathaniel observed her slyly, Diana covered a yawn with her fingers and leaned her hip against the sideboard. Then she gave a tiny, hesitant sneeze.

Rebecca suddenly dropped to the sofa beside him. "You have certainly caused a stir with your refusal to tell anyone what you've been up to these past three years. I suppose you're enjoying yourself."

"Very much."

"Well, I shall ask you nothing more about it. I suspect it might be something I wouldn't want to know, in any case."

"Quite so, Sister."

She gave an exasperated gasp. "Since when have you become circumspect, Nate? There was a time when you kept no secrets and your life was an open book. Every sinful chapter was exposed without hesitancy. And if you tap one finger to the side of your nose again in that despicably annoying fashion, I shall be tempted to take those fancy new boots of yours and hold them to the fire."

"I warned you, Sister. I'm a changed man. Older and wiser."

"I hope that is the case, Nate," she said, softening her tone. "I know I had never seen you in such low spirits as when you left here the last time."

"A long time ago." He rubbed his thigh with one hand. "And I soon shook that depression off. Nothing ever troubles me for long." After a pause, he added casually, "I hear your friend Diana's engagement was called off."

"It was. Some months after you left."

"And you did not think it necessary for me to know when I returned?"

"Why should I?"

He glared at his sister.

"You didn't ask, Nate. I did not think it wise to raise the subject until you did. Considering…"

Nathaniel waited and when nothing more was forthcoming, he snapped, "It means naught to me. I merely asked to be polite." He huffed, leaning back in the chair, resting one ankle across his knee, his pose relaxed. "I would not want to make a faux pas. That is all."

"Of course."

"If I should mention anything to Miss Makepiece that causes her distress—"

"It might be best if you do not talk to her of anything but the weather and her health, don't you think? You managed to cause her enough distress in the past."

He took further umbrage at that. "What did I ever do to cause *her* any suffering?"

"Oh, you know very well."

"Indeed I do not! You had better tell me, for I wouldn't want to be accused of doing it again."

His sister gave an extravagant sigh. "Perhaps flirting is so deeply ingrained in your behavior that you don't even know when you're doing it."

Nathaniel looked at her, puzzled.

"Any pretty woman who passes your line of sight becomes a target for your charm, brother dear. It is a habit that would keep any sensible woman from letting you into her heart. But it might be that one very dear, extremely sensible, reserved young woman can't help feeling fondness for you. And that can only end in tragedy because she feels everything deeply and dares not show it, while you take nothing seriously, and as you just said, nothing troubles you for long."

He frowned. "Then this…woman, whoever she is, ought to speak up. How am I supposed to read her mind?"

"Perhaps such a woman suffers from shyness. Not everyone is like you, Nate, or has your confidence."

"Shyness?" he scoffed. "That is simply vanity in disguise. A bashful person assumes everyone is looking at them and waiting for pearls of wisdom to fall from their lips. I have no time for shyness."

Rebecca shook her head. "Vanity takes many forms, and thinking you know everything is one of them. So is never bothering to put yourself in someone else's position to view life through their eyes. Demanding the attention of every woman in the room just because you can is another."

"I don't understand what you're trying to tell me."

"Of course not." She patted his knee. "You're a man. The male brain's capacity for absorbing new information is limited."

Annoyed, he grumbled, "Am I not supposed to be polite and gracious to ladies? If I stood in a corner and refused to converse with anyone, I suppose that would make me a villain too. Claiming dainty shyness would not save *me* from scorn."

"Well, my dear brother, you must continue as you think best. Consider how your carefree, indiscriminate flirting has worked for you up until now."

Nathaniel deepened his frown. *Indiscriminate flirting*? He'd always been polite to ladies, had grown up under his father's tutelage when it came to dealing with women. The major, admittedly, often got himself into trouble by being a little too bawdy, but he had taught his son the importance of flattering the ladies and making them laugh.

"No woman can be cross with you for long, if you know how to handle 'em," he would say. "Just like a child can't keep weeping and whining with a mouthful of sweet, sticky toffee."

So Nathaniel's first instinct was always to befriend a lady, to listen and nod, and then—when the moment was right—to sweeten her up, tease her, and make her blush. The ladies might not always approve of him, but they never forgot "Sherry," and they couldn't ignore him.

Major Sherringham loved to hear stories of Nathaniel's conquests. They would sit together after dinner, sharing a laugh and deepening their bond over brandy and a mutual appreciation of the fairer sex. Once the major's health forced him to retire and kept him mostly confined to his house, he lived vicariously through his son's lusty adventures.

Nathaniel didn't have the heart to tell the old man that a few of those adventures were pure fiction. Or at least exaggerated for effect. His seductions and conquests, true or embellished, were things for which he'd earned his father's admiration and as such were well worth the effort.

All this considered, Nathaniel couldn't see what was wrong with his methods when it came to the "handling" of females.

Rebecca leaned closer, lowering her voice to a scant whisper. "It may be amusing to surround oneself with bunches of pretty flowers—the more the merrier when they are easily tended and inexpensively acquired. But every gardener knows that the most beautiful bloom is often the rarest, the most difficult to nurture, and yet the most gratifying to possess."

"Now you have truly lost me, Sister," he murmured. "I know nothing about gardening."

"You are being deliberately obtuse. I shall converse with you on this subject no longer."

Thus he learned nothing about the whys and wherefores of Diana's broken engagement. Sarah Wainwright had described the event as "tragic," but with the usual dramatic tone any girl of eighteen might use. Something, however, had definitely taken its toll on Diana. She was wilted, her colors washed out, her flame extinguished.

But it could be nothing to do with him. For once no one could lay the blame for a lady's problems at his feet.

His sister got up and moved away, giving up for now. It always made him smile that she—his little sister—tried to advise him. Since their mother died when they were young, Rebecca had taken charge of things and tried to manage both Nathaniel and their father. She had set herself an uphill task, but was never daunted by it. He had to admire that gumption, however annoying it was to suffer her lectures from time to time.

He noticed Sarah stirring people up again to dance, but one look at Diana on the other side of the room suggested she was in no fit state to play all night long. Dark shadows were visible under her eyes, and her hand shook as she sipped her wine.

She had steadily played her way through one book

of dances already and was clearly not in the best of health. The woman should probably be home in bed, wrapped up warmly and fed soup. Even if she protested. He knew how stubborn she was.

Not that it was any concern of his. Because she was nothing to him now, of course.

❧

She had not seen him drink a single glass of wine all evening, but he was still talkative and charming with the ladies in the room. That much had not changed.

From the corner of her eye, Diana watched him entertaining the others, quite at his ease despite the long absence. Nathaniel was the sort who could immediately find interesting conversation with anyone, even a complete stranger. She begrudgingly envied the fool that skill and the freedom to use it, for she had been raised to hold her tongue and speak only when spoken to. And when she did speak, she was taught that she must say the right thing in the proper way. As a consequence it was often easier for her to say nothing at all rather than to risk chastisement.

Nathaniel, however, said whatever he wished to say. In the past, his ebullient nature had forced her to speak even when she should have remained silent. She knew that was part of what made him dangerous, as far as her mother was concerned. He made Diana want to say things she ought not to. His spirit was infectious.

The balance of the world was unfairly tipped to the benefit of men, she thought with a burst of sharp anger. They could come and go when they pleased, say and do much as they wanted without reproach.

She, for instance, had broken off an engagement in the most polite and kindest way possible with a man who clearly did not care much for her anyway and who became engaged to another much younger and richer woman within a fortnight. Yet *Diana* had been the target of gossip; she was the one who was punished. Her behavior was tut-tutted over, not his. Apparently William Shaw was merely doing what came naturally to the male animal.

Speaking of which…oh Lord…Nathaniel was advancing toward her. "Prowling toward her" might be a more accurate description for this particular animal.

Her heart thumped, obscuring all other sound in the room.

Once again, escaping from the corked bottle in which she kept it, the memory of his forbidden kiss seized her in its heated grip. As her lips touched the rim of her wineglass, she felt his flesh instead of cut crystal. The savage desire in his kiss haunted her. Why had she not prevented it? He'd kissed her *after* she rejected his proposal, when she could not possibly have expected it. His audacity had left her frozen in astonishment. So much so that she was unable to sleep that night after it happened. Instead she'd lain awake, reliving his proposal and fighting strange sensations of which her mama would never approve.

The next morning her friends came to tell her that Nathaniel was gone without even saying good-bye. That kiss was all he left behind, and Diana had resigned herself to never having another like it.

Nor did she want one, thank you very much.

Now he came here again to torment her and

reopen that dangerous memory. Did he remember the stolen kiss, or was it just another mistake regretted the next morning?

On his course across the room Nathaniel was halted a few times by ladies eager to converse with him. As always he charmed and joked. The ladies ate it up. It was thoroughly ridiculous, really. An embarrassment to womanhood.

His progress had begun again and he was looking at her. Diana looked around for somewhere to go, away from his trajectory. She should have found an escape by now since it was taking him long enough to arrive before her, but her legs refused to take her away.

He stopped again to whisper something to his brother-in-law, and then Lucius Wainwright nodded and left the room.

The troublesome rogue male had not taken his eyes off her and continued to advance toward her.

Perhaps he intended to pour himself some wine. She finally moved away from the decanter of Madeira, but he did not reach for a glass. He stopped and it was plain that he meant to speak to her.

The scoundrel seemed taller than she remembered. Was it the new clothes that gave him such a powerful aura this evening? The high collar of his dark burgundy evening jacket, the ruffled, cream silk cravat, the waistcoat patterned with lines of vertical gold thread, the perfectly fitted breeches that showed off the fine musculature of his thighs? He'd always been handsome in his uniform, but this was new and different. It didn't shout for attention, but instead gave him an air of quiet confidence and authority.

Superficial change, of course, as her mother said.

"Miss Makepiece," he murmured, "I have taken the liberty of asking my brother-in-law if the carriage might be brought around for you and your mother."

She squinted, not really wanting to take all of him in. This close. "Oh. Yes?"

"You've been here quite long enough, I think."

He was getting rid of her, pushing her out the door, the sight of her heinous to him now. All the blood seemed to have drained out of her. All the life.

"How nice of you to see me off, Captain." Unlike three years ago, she thought angrily, when he didn't even say good-bye. Just because she had told him a few unvarnished truths he didn't care to hear.

"My sister tells me you walked here in the rain and that you are only recently recovered from a bad cold."

"That must have been a very dull conversation for you."

"I was told I should stick to your health and the weather." He gave her an odd, brief smile. "So I thought I did rather well by combining the two subjects."

"I appreciate the thought, Captain." She hoped he had not seen her hand trembling, but as she tried to set the glass down, he reached to take it. The tips of his fingers touched hers and wine spilled on the sideboard.

"Sarah was about to ask you to play again, and I saw you were not up to it," he said.

Diana stared at his long fingers touching hers, the skin several rich shades darker than her own. She couldn't breathe. Once when she was very young, a lightning bolt had struck the ground not far from where she stood. It had made her entire body sing and the little downy hairs on her arm lift. Nathaniel's touch had an identical effect.

"But I knew you could not say no," he added. "Not to her, in any case."

Looking up, she was caught in the blue flames of his regard as they tore into her briefly and then his eyelids lowered. Just in time, because Diana's mother was upon them in the next moment.

Nathaniel bowed sharply and walked away.

"What did *he* want?" her mother demanded.

Diana took a breath at last, life returning to fill her lungs. "He has asked for Mr. Lucius Wainwright's carriage to take us home. He must have seen that I was tired, I suppose." She still felt that purring hum vibrating through her bones. It made everything in the room seem brighter and louder. Herself included.

"You have not had anything to eat. Your health will not improve if you don't eat, Diana. There is plenty of—"

"Mama, I have no appetite. Please don't fuss! For pity's sake, I don't want anything to eat."

Her mother's eyes sharpened. "There is no need to raise your voice, Diana."

Contrite, she closed her lips tightly.

"It is just as well we are leaving," her mother remarked with a sniff. "You must be overtired. I knew we shouldn't have come, and against my better judgment, I let you persuade me."

Diana wanted to laugh. As if *she* had ever wielded the force of persuasion. She wouldn't know how to begin.

On the journey home, she stared through the carriage window, her head spinning, her heart beating like an overwound clock that would soon burst a spring and send cogwheels flying all over.

He had touched her fingers and looked at her with those stormy eyes full of…what? Anger? Scorn? Nathaniel seemed altered in some ways. Older, calmer, sterner. She almost caught herself wishing he had not changed so much, for the changes confused her. She knew how to manage the merry, carefree Nathaniel of years past, but this one presented challenges.

Exhausted by the many different pains he'd caused simply by saying a few words to her, Diana was relieved to be leaving his irritating presence. She pressed her aching head back against the swaying wall of the carriage, hoping this dizziness would soon pass.

"So this is the Wainwrights' new carriage," her mother muttered, running a gloved hand over the well-padded leather seat. "Astonishing what some folk will waste their money on. But then the Wainwrights have no need to budget."

Diana sighed. "Doesn't it make you wonder, Mama, why God lets some folk become so rich while the majority of us are poor?"

Her mother's answer was a pert: "It's not the money one has that is important, Diana, but what one does with it. How one acts when in possession of wealth."

Diana let her head roll from side to side with the motion of the carriage. "And what would you do with it, Mama? If we were rich?"

There was a lengthy pause. Just when she thought her mother would dismiss the question as frivolous and accuse Diana of drinking too much wine, she was surprised to receive the sudden, loud, and adamant response, "I would not shell another pea. I know that much!"

While Diana choked on a chuckle, her mother added, "And I would get a peacock."

"To cat?"

"No, foolish girl! To walk about the lawn with its pretty tail on display." Her mother's voice had turned positively dreamy as she looked out the window at the dusk-shaded view. "I always rather fancied having a peacock when I was a girl."

Diana stayed silent, too amused by this odd confession to risk spoiling the moment.

Nine

…He was not altered, or not for the worse. She had already acknowledged it to herself, and she could not think differently, let him think of her as he would. No; the years which had destroyed her youth and bloom had only given him a more glowing, manly, open look, in no respect lessening his personal advantages…

"So altered that he should not have known her again!" These were words which could not but dwell with her. Yet she soon began to rejoice that she had heard them. They were of sobering tendency; they allayed agitation; they composed, and consequently must make her happier.

—Persuasion

"IT'S BEEN DECIDED! WE ARE HOLDING OUR BOOK society meeting out of doors today," Sarah exclaimed, dashing through the door. "We're having a picnic! Isn't it a wonderful idea?"

Diana frowned. "What if it rains?"

"Oh, it won't," replied Sarah with the blissful naiveté of the very young. "Look, the sun is out."

As if that ever meant much at all. Sometimes Diana thought she was the only Book Club Belle with caution in her soul these days. Again she missed Cathy. "Yes, but—"

"Come on, Diana, make haste! Put on your bonnet. We are all going to Raven's Hill in the cart. What fun we shall have. This will surely put some color back in your cheeks, poor Diana!"

Poor Diana.

How often had she heard that lately? It may as well be marked on her forehead.

There was barely time to slip into her coat, grab *Persuasion* from the parlor table, and let her mother—who was working in the vegetable garden that morning—know she was going out.

Mrs. Makepiece looked up from pulling weeds, shaded her eyes from the sun with one hand, and advised Diana not to sit on any damp grass. In a tolerant mood for once, perhaps enjoying the improved weather, she raised no objection to the idea of a picnic or of her daughter going out without her. She didn't even feel it necessary to warn about suspicious gypsies or unscrupulous strangers they might meet on the road.

Since last night and the party at Willow Tree Farm, Diana's mother had been full of gossip about Nathaniel, harvested mostly from the parson's chatty wife.

"Mrs. Kenton saw him at the Manderson assembly dance with an infamous adulteress," she'd told Diana at breakfast. "Naturally he had the gall to deny his own name when she confronted him there, but she knew who he was. He couldn't fool her. He's up to no good, of course. Why else would he pretend to be someone else? He keeps his common mistress shut away in Manderson, out of sight, while he parades about here in those fancy clothes waiting for fish to bite. I knew he had not changed."

Thus Diana learned of the existence of his tawdry companion ensconced at the Royal Oak. It was no more or less than she should have expected from the rake, and it barely caused her an intake of breath. She was able to ask her mama which jam she wanted from the pantry without even a blink or a long pause to betray her reaction to this news.

"What would Mr. Bridges have to say if he knew about the adulteress, I wonder," her mother had added.

"Mr. Bridges? What could it signify to him?"

"Captain Sherringham came back here in fancy clothes to court an unsuspecting bride. And we may all guess who he has his eye on now. That flirtatious, idle creature at the tavern. He ran off with her once before, if memory serves."

"Mama, that is a slight exaggeration. Lucy rode to Manderson one morning without telling anyone, just because she was feeling ignored and unappreciated. Captain Sherringham happened to travel the same road that day when he left Hawcombe Prior. He found her and sent her home again quite safe."

"That's the formal story her family came up with. You mark my words, there can be only one reason for the captain to call on Mr. Bridges while the tavern is closed for business. I daresay the family would welcome anybody taking that girl off their hands. They cannot afford to be too particular."

She had buttered her toast with firm swipes of the

knife. "At least we know the captain will not bother you again. He told Sarah Wainwright that he found you so altered he would never have recognized you."

Diana caught her breath and spooned a large helping of jam onto her toast. "I neither expected nor wanted to be noticed again by Captain Sherringham. The thought never crossed my mind."

"I would hope not. Don't use too much jam, Diana. We're almost out of the raspberry, and there won't be any more until it's made this summer."

As her mother's thoughts turned to making jam, she was almost cheerful for once—an unnatural state that hovered precariously like a china cup on an ill-balanced saucer. Diana felt it necessary to be as quiet as possible and do nothing to upset the tilt of that delicate saucer. Perhaps leaving the house for a few hours would be a good thing.

As she followed Sarah out the front gate, she saw her friends gathered in "the cart"—a sturdy but not very comfortable vehicle generally used to transport Luke Wainwright's pigs and sheep to and from the market. Today it was filled with fresh straw bales and loaded with a different, more fragrant cargo. Apparently the fine new carriage could not be spared for their jaunt—or else Rebecca and Jussy had decided this would be more fun. The latter was the more likely scenario.

The group gathered in the back of the cart was rather noisy and excited that morning, because all the children had been brought out too. Justina explained, "My Wainwright simply refused to have the girls at home with him again today, and it's the nursemaid's half day."

Rebecca sat in the front to drive the horses, and Justina leaned out from the back to help Diana up. She was immediately clambered upon by the children, of whom she was very fond. The little ones did not care what clothes a person wore or how much of a fortune they had, or whether they had a great number of clever things to say. As long as there was a warm, welcoming lap and the possibility of a game or two, they were happy.

Lucy was already seated on a straw bale, eagerness adding natural color to her cheeks today. As she said, at least this meeting was taking place in a new location and therefore had a sense of novelty about it. "Your mama's parlor can get awfully stuffy, Diana. And goodness knows, you could benefit from some spring air too! Poor thing. How wilted you are from the lack of sun."

The cart pulled forward with a sudden jerk that almost knocked her off her straw bale seat. Everyone else squealed with excitement, Rebecca yelled a hasty apology, and then they were off at a slow, rather bumpy pace.

The air was warm that morning, the birds singing merrily. Diana glanced up at the sky and saw only a few fleecy clouds rolling by, nothing to threaten rain. Yet. She tried to be as carefree as the others, for they would not want her dour warnings casting a shadow on their day out.

"I know," shouted Sarah, "let's sing a song!"

Inwardly Diana cringed. She loved her friends dearly but few of them could hold a note. The more excited they were, the noisier they were, and they liked their music the same way. Diana had been told that she had a very musical ear, but since she was rarely given the chance to hear music played flawlessly, or without someone yelling or stamping over it, this advantage seemed destined to be wasted.

She had seen a sketch once in the newspaper of a concert performance, during which the audience was seated and apparently attentive while the orchestra played and a luxuriously curved Italian lady sang. *That would be nice*, she thought wistfully. Just to listen to the music for once and not be correcting someone's playing.

Her friends, meanwhile, made their own music fearlessly, not caring who heard or how offended a sensitively tuned ear might be.

At least her mama needn't worry about highwaymen and bandits on the turnpike road, Diana mused. Anyone who thought of apprehending them would hear this noise and surely run for cover.

⁓

Nathaniel called at the tavern that morning to leave his condolences for the family. Mr. Bridges, he soon discovered, was out—called to a meeting with the solicitor in Manderson—but his wife was more than happy to welcome a visitor. She was very like her daughter: she loved company and her spirits had suffered from the loss of it during this mourning period.

"You must come to dine with us, Captain," she exclaimed, eyeing his fine suit of clothes and the silver pin in his cravat. "I know Lucy will be overjoyed to see you. She has talked about little else since you left. It's Captain this and Captain that. Never stops!"

"Really?" He smiled at that, doubting it very much. Lucy was the sort to forget about anything once it was not immediately before her, and it had been more than three years since he was last in her presence.

"Although she will be disappointed that you are no longer in your red coat. My daughter has always had a great fondness for soldiers."

Now that he *could* believe. He'd met a lot of young girls like Lucy hanging around army camps. But he suspected it would not be considered gentlemanly to make such an observation, so he said, "Are you sure your husband wouldn't object if I join you for dinner? You are, after all, still grieving for your mother's passing."

She flapped her hand at him. "I think we've all suffered enough for it, and he cannot begrudge us ladies a little good company." Again she eyed his silver pin. "The best sort of company. For our dear Lucy."

After agreeing to join them for dinner the following evening—thinking he might afterward have an opportunity to discuss business with the tavern keeper—Nathaniel took his leave of Mrs. Bridges and steered his horse across the common to find the carpenter, Sam Hardacre, standing outside his workshop with a very peevish expression on his face.

"Cap'n Sherringham," he muttered in sullen greeting as Nathaniel's horse drew near. "So it's true and you *are* back." It didn't sound as if this caused the fellow much pleasure.

"Mr. Hardacre, I see you've expanded your shop

premises. I heard about your father's passing. I'm sorry. He was a good man."

"Aye, he was." Sam's brow darkened in a heavy frown. "Not enough of *them* about."

"Very true."

Sam wiped his hands on a rag and glowered up at Nathaniel. "Planning to stay long, Cap'n?"

"Just until I conclude some business with Mr. Bridges." He was accustomed to people thinking they had some grievance against him. Apparently he had the sort of face that caused people to distrust his motives even when he was perfectly innocent, but he had no idea what he could have done to Sam Hardacre. In fact, as far as he recalled, he'd lost quite a bit of coin to the young man in the past over card games at the tavern. In all likelihood he'd paid for part of the carpenter's expanded premises, he mused. "I'll soon leave you all in peace again, never fear."

"Good. And hopefully as you found us."

When Nathaniel asked if he'd seen a cartload of young ladies driving by recently, Sam replied snappishly, "I have." He pointed with the business end of a hammer. "Went up Raven's Hill." Then he turned away, shoulders rounded. "I daresay there's naught I can do about it."

"Mr. Hardacre, do you have something you wish to say? I believe in a man speaking aloud if there is something preying on his mind. Nothing can be done for those who do not help themselves."

Sam growled, "I've naught to say to you."

"Excellent. Well, I shall bid you good day." Frustrated, Nathaniel tipped his hat to the back of the other man's head and rode off to follow the Book Club Belles on their jaunt.

Gentlemen were usually strictly banned from their little society, but Nathaniel wasn't one to let rules get in his way. Besides, it had been his idea that they take their meeting outside for a picnic today. He had suggested it to Sarah when they were thinking of ways to get Lucy Bridges out for an airing to improve her spirits.

"What you all need, young lady, is a picnic in the sun," he'd said. "If Mr. Bridges only lets your friend out for book society meetings, then that must be your chance to cheer her up."

"Yes," Sarah had exclaimed, "and how much nicer than sitting in Mrs. Makepiece's stuffy parlor with her listening through the walls."

He couldn't agree more.

Urging his horse into a gallop, he headed for Raven's Hill.

～

It was Diana's turn to read aloud, although she was constantly interrupted by one or another of her friends' children, who could not sit still but had to be chasing birds, collecting worms, or drooling on somebody's muslin every few minutes.

She plowed onward with the bright sun beaming down upon the page. Earlier she'd felt a little improved and had thought the warmth of the day could only help. But nothing worsened a stuffy head more, she now found, than sitting outside surrounded by noisy children and pollen.

Sarah very sweetly offered to hold her parasol over Diana's head to keep the glare off her page, but the girl was every bit as distracted and inattentive as the little children. Since she kept letting the beaded fringe of her parasol descend over the words being read, it was, all things considered, more time consuming and interruptive than it was useful.

And it was during one of those moments—just as the wobbling, ill-managed parasol tipped once again over Diana's head, bumped her in the eye, and obscured the words of her book—when a horse could be heard thudding through the grass toward them. Hidden behind this fringed obstruction and waiting for her eye to recover, Diana was prevented from recognizing the new arrival immediately. Therefore, she was also the last to offer any sort of greeting.

Not that the unexpected guest waited for a welcome or apologized for interrupting.

Under the fringe of the parasol, with her smarting eye closed, she watched Nathaniel's boots dismount, leave his horse in the shade of a tree, and bring his arrogant carcass to sit on the blanket among her friends. His presence stole their attention from the characters in the book, so Diana paused a moment until they were all settled again. Then she read on.

> *The evening ended with dancing. On its being proposed, Anne offered her services, as usual; and though her eyes would sometimes fill with tears as she sat at the instrument, she was extremely glad to*

be employed, and desired nothing in return but to
be unobserved.

It was typical of Nathaniel to follow them to
their picnic, of course. The cad might not be a great
reader, but no gathering was more attractive to him
than one of ladies who professed not to want a man
among them. He used to appear at the parlor window
during their book society meetings and startle them
all by suddenly knocking on the glass, pretending to
be "spying on what wicked hussies get up to when
gentlemen aren't around."

Mrs. Makepiece would later be infuriated by the
smudge marks his knuckles left on her glass panes. All
part of his amusement, naturally.

Once, too, he spoke to her. She had left the instru-
ment on the dancing being over, and he had sat down
to try to make out an air which he wished to give
the Miss Musgroves an idea of. Unintentionally she
returned to that part of the room; he saw her, and,
instantly rising, said, with studied politeness,—
"I beg your pardon, madam, this is your seat";
and though she immediately drew back with a decided
negative, he was not to be induced to sit down again.

Under the swaying shadow of Sarah's parasol,
Diana felt her pulse grow uneven and too fast, making
her feel as if she might jump out of her own skin.
Her injured eye kept tearing up, so she covered it
with one hand and read on with only half sight and a
mounting headache.

Anne did not wish for more of such looks and speeches. His cold politeness, his ceremonious grace, were worse than anything.

Success! She had read to the end of the chapter without rousing anyone's suspicion of her scattered nerves. If only she might find some way to soothe her head.

"So this is the story that holds the Book Club Belles enthralled now," Nathaniel exclaimed, setting his hat on the blanket and sweeping quick fingers through his gilded hair. "Another foolish heroine. And who is the love of *her* life?"

"There is none," chirped Lucy. "She was once engaged to Captain Wentworth, but called it off when she heartlessly changed her mind. Now she's just an old maid and he has come back handsome and rich. I really do not like Anne for she is very immature and always feeling hard done by."

This was a hilarious comment considering the nature of the person who made it, but while the others fell about laughing, Diana and Nathaniel remained solemn.

"She sounds like a cowardly young woman who has no one to blame for her trials but herself," he said. "There is nothing worse than a woman who wavers easily when she faces a little obstacle, who cannot stand up for her own passions and would rather pretend she has none."

Diana felt such a hard pinch in her heart that it took her breath away. She moved Sarah's swaying parasol aside to get a better look at his face, but immediately regretted it as they all exclaimed over her sore, squinting eye. She covered it again with one hand.

"But please, don't let me spoil your enjoyment, ladies," Nathaniel exclaimed as he saw her placing an embroidered marker in the page, ready to close the book.

"It is the end of the chapter," she murmured, not wishing to share more of Anne Elliot's sad story with him when he was so ready to dislike the character.

"But you must read on. I am anxious to know what happens next to this poor Anna girl and whether she will ever learn to speak up for herself."

"Her name is Anne, and she can speak up for herself. She waits until she is certain of what she has to say. Unlike some people who speak the first thing that comes to mind and regret it later."

Nathaniel shrugged, his eyes narrowed against the sun. "Some folk think too much. They become inert, unable to act out of fear. If we all worried about the dreadful things that might happen, nothing would ever be done, nothing good achieved, nothing new discovered."

"But fewer mistakes made. Less pain caused."

"I would rather risk some pain than close my heart away from contact and chance to keep it *safe* and therefore have no joy at all."

"Anne Elliot has feelings. Many of them," Diana exclaimed in defense of her favorite character. "She just does not care to expose them to the ridicule and derision of others. Especially when those feelings can do no good for anybody she cares about and it would be selfish of her to express them."

"Then she is a fool, and as I suspected, her problems are her own fault," he scoffed, chewing on a blade of grass. "I'm sure no one around her labors under such indecision and hesitation. There is selflessness and then there is martyrdom."

With her unwounded eye, she looked up at his smug countenance and felt her temper rising. Carefully and with as much dignity as she could manage while somewhat resembling a pirate, she replied, "And to imagine, Captain, that I did not think you joined us to discuss books. I felt sure you were merely here to distract us and cause mischief."

A gleam of surprise lit his gaze with an extra spark of clear, piercing blue. "No indeed, you mistake me. I am always reading!" He glanced at his sister. "Next to gardening, it is one of my favorite pastimes. I absorbed every word. Please, do continue."

Diana had no inkling what he meant by the remark about gardening, but clearly it was a joke between him and Rebecca. He sat casually on the blanket, one knee up, his arm resting across it, his fingers loosely linked. The scene might have been an oil painting, she thought. A moment captured for posterity of a privileged, golden young buck with no cares in the world.

With a taut sigh, Diana declared that she would concede defeat to the sunny day and the pleas of the children who wanted the picnic basket opened.

Since Nathaniel's gleaming presence was a novelty that made Anne Elliot and Captain Wentworth's problems dull in comparison, no one else made a convincing protest against pausing the story for now.

As Lucy declared, "On such a sunny day, who wants to read a book?"

"If it were not for books," Sarah sharply reminded her, "you would not even be allowed out of the house. It is only because of the book society that your papa let you out."

Nathaniel swiftly turned to Lucy and offered his sympathies for the demise of her grandmother.

"Well, she was ancient and terribly mean to everybody," Lucy replied. "She always thought my mama could have done so much better when she married my papa, and she took it out on all of us. Oh, what sort of cake did you bring, Jussy?"

"How dreadful," Nathaniel muttered. "I have never understood why people shouldn't marry as they please. A great deal of unhappiness would be avoided in the world if people married for love."

"I agree," said Lucy firmly. "But some folk don't like others to be happy because they are miserable themselves."

"Precisely." Nathaniel smiled dashingly at the young woman. "Miss Bridges, hold very still."

She froze, eyes wide. "What is it, Captain?"

He raised a hand to her shoulder and captured a ladybird that was about to crawl onto her fair ringlet. As Lucy gushed with gratitude, he examined the creature on his finger, then blew gently until it took flight.

No one seemed to notice that the ladybird next landed on the crease of Diana's open pages. She moved it carefully to the safety of a blade of grass before she closed the book. She had just done so, when one of Justina's daughters launched herself at

Diana's back, clung around her neck in a stranglehold, and refused to let go.

Diana cajoled the little girl to let her breathe again, but she was not heeded. Across the picnic blanket, Justina was preoccupied with arguing with her other daughter about whether or not the child could have more than one biscuit. The other ladies paid no attention to Diana's struggle, too busy examining the contents of the picnic hamper. Packed by the Wainwrights' excellent French chef, it was a veritable feast of delights.

Diana's head throbbed and her desperation mounted. The child, assuming this was merely a game, was heavy on her back, her arms tight. To throw the giggling bundle off her could result in injury, and to discipline a child who was not one's own was always a difficult business.

Then suddenly she was rescued. The naughty girl was plucked from her back by strong hands and tossed playfully into the air. Squinting, Diana looked up and found Nathaniel behind her, his tall form outlined by the sun's bright glare. She had not even known he was on his feet or standing nearby until that moment.

No word passed between them, but a glance of hesitant thanks and one of mildly surprised acceptance were exchanged following this simple act of kindness.

He had come to her rescue yet again, and from his expression, he didn't know why he had done it. She could not imagine why he had either.

The spiteful sun stung her eyes as she watched Nathaniel's tall silhouette spinning around, letting the naughty child "fly" through the air. How strong he was.

Of course the children loved him because he was fearless and knew how to tease them. Unlike some men, he did not mind how silly he looked while doing it.

Diana fought to compose herself, hoping none of the others had seen her hot face. She needn't have worried, for there was soon a much larger disturbance.

Convinced a wasp had invaded her petticoats, Lucy Bridges began a squealing pantomime that provided more entertainment than anything else that day. Having turned in a rapid series of flapping spins, Lucy suddenly tripped over a tuft of grass and appeared to faint. Which, of course, required Captain Sherringham to put down the child and tend to her immediately.

The "wasp" was found to be an almond sliver from the top of a bakewell tart. Lucy suffered nothing more than a bump to her forehead, and the moment of madness was over. But the young lady was so shaken that she could only be consoled by requisitioning Sarah's parasol to keep the sun off her face and having Captain Sherringham sit beside her to valiantly fight off the advance of menacing insects.

Not wishing to be thought peevish about the parasol or antisocial by leaving the picnic blanket, Diana suffered quietly for a few minutes and then stood.

"I think I will enjoy a little walk," she said. "Do excuse me."

Hastily she walked away to find shade.

Nathaniel was never very good at sitting still and was almost as restless as the children. Consequently, as she moved away from the picnic blanket, Diana heard him suggest a game of hide-and-seek.

"You will not play, Diana?" Jussy called out.

"No, no." She waved. "I am on the hunt for bluebells."

Soon she had put a fair distance between herself and the joyful shrieks of the others. Her headache began to ease a little as she moved through the cooler, quieter shade, and her pulse settled into a more familiar rhythm. Her eye had ceased to smart, although her lashes felt damp.

For some reason the lashes of both eyes were moist, not just the one that had been wounded by Sarah's parasol.

Ten

THE GAME OF HIDE-AND-SEEK WOULD HAVE BEEN OVER very quickly if Nathaniel had not pretended to miss the excited squealing of the children. Rather than spoil the fun, he good-naturedly remarked upon the curious calls of so many rare birds among the trees as he walked along with Sarah—the two of them nominated to hunt.

"There must be a great many exotic birds nesting here this spring," he said with a wink.

She laughed and grabbed his arm. "Come on, Sherry. I think Lucy went this way. You must seek her out and I will find the others."

He realized that Lucy Bridges was the potential bride that Sarah had picked out for him. His step-niece was not subtle and clearly had little experience with matchmaking, although she fancied herself skilled in the art. Unfortunately he had exposed himself to this by taking an active interest in getting Lucy out of the house and telling Sarah that he remembered the young lady favorably. It was not, of course, the first time one of his spontaneous good deeds had caused him trouble.

Aware of this error, he quickly let Sarah know that her intentions for Lucy were misaimed. "I am fond of Miss Bridges. She is amusing company, but she is not the girl for me."

Sarah put her nose in the air and replied, "Aunt Jussy says that men never know what's good for them."

"I can assure you that your aunt is wrong about me."

"But we women," she said haughtily, "spend a great deal more of our time in deep thought and we see things that you do not."

"Do you indeed?"

"My stepmama said that you were once very keen on Diana Makepiece." She bent over to pick some daisies and seemed thoroughly unaware of the cannonball she'd just shot into his chest.

There! He should have known his sister would never be able to hold her tongue. Good thing she didn't know about his marriage proposal. Diana would never have told her; he knew that.

Nathaniel cleared his throat. "It was a passing fancy. Many years ago." He was beyond it now. Quite beyond.

"Yes, I did think it must have been a hundred years in the past. Diana is resigned to spinsterhood. She has even stopped curling her hair. William Shaw broke her heart when he ended their engagement. Horrid man."

He said nothing. He still had doubts about Diana's guarded heart ever being in danger from anyone. From that dry crust Shaw? Not likely.

"Mrs. Kenton, the parson's wife, says nobody will notice Diana now because she's too restrained and meek. Men don't see her. She says it's a great shame that poor Diana lost her one chance because she won't have another." Sarah studied the daisy she'd picked. "In truth, I don't think Diana really wants another. If she did, she'd make more effort. She could still be quite pretty if she tried, but she's given up and it does take greater effort the older one gets."

Nathaniel nodded. "And why did William Shaw abandon her?"

"He found someone else." She looked over her shoulder and then lowered her voice to a whisper. "Lucy says it's because Diana wouldn't let him kiss her, even after they'd been engaged two whole years."

"And how would Miss Bridges know this?"

"She saw them once, walking in the Bolt. William Shaw tried to kiss Diana, and she pushed him away so hard that he almost fell over. Lucy heard Diana say something about memories and how she didn't want them spoiled. William was very red-faced. A short while after that, the engagement was called off."

"I see." Nathaniel's heart was tentatively warmed by this news. It didn't mean that the memories Diana cherished were of him, of course, but he wanted to believe they were. She wasn't the sort of girl to make a habit of kissing gentlemen under the arches of the Bolt.

"But unlike Diana, Lucy is eager to find a husband and she believes it's miserly to withhold one's affections. She would kiss anyone who asked."

"How altruistic of the lady," he murmured, amused.

"Lucy may seem somewhat shrill at times and silly, but she is a sweet girl underneath it all."

"I'm sure she is." They had walked up the slope and now came to the old stone ruins of a shepherd's hut on the brow of the hill. "Amazing that this place still stands," he remarked. "It takes a battering from the weather up here and has no one to maintain it, yet here it has stood for so many years."

"My papa says that if something has a strong foundation and is well-built in stone, it will stand forever."

"Unless it is deliberately destroyed, of course."

"Deliberately?"

"By someone wielding a very powerful hammer. Someone who knows where the vulnerable spots are."

"Even if the walls are knocked down, the foundation will still be there to show where it once was. Papa says that land holds memories much longer than people do. Think of all the people who have lived up here. They must all have left their mark in some way."

"Possibly." Nathaniel ran his hand over the mossy stone wall of the old hut. "But this place is lonely now and sad with no one to live in it, no one to put light in the windows at night. It has lost its last inhabitant and will never have another. Not now. It has been left to the elements and ghosts too long with no one taking care of it. There is no heart alive within it anymore."

Suddenly he felt a deep and heavy grief, as if he were mourning for the shepherd who had last lived there. He shook his head. "Enough of this grim talk. We should be hunting." But the weather had turned to match his mood. Clouds had gathered seemingly out of nowhere, and the first prickles of rain touched his cheek when he looked up. "But I fear rain will bring a premature end to our game."

Sarah agreed and they turned back down the hill toward the cart.

She heard their voices growing fainter and exhaled with relief that they had not seen her inside the hut, standing just on the other side of the wall. Diana had been resting there in the cool shade when she first caught the sound of people approaching. Not wanting to be found, she'd stayed where she was and prayed they would not destroy her solitude. Then she overheard their discussion about memories, followed by Nathaniel's somber speech regarding the shepherd's hut no longer having lights in its windows at night, and people taking a hammer to cause deliberate destruction. The symbolism was not lost on her.

Raindrops, fat and slow, began to spit on her through holes in the old rafters. Thankfully, Sarah and Nathaniel had already begun to move back down the hill when Diana sneezed. It exploded so suddenly that she had no time to cover it with her handkerchief, but she thought they must be far enough away not to hear.

The rain quickened, pitter-pattering against her bonnet brim and soaking through the shoulders of her muslin, for she'd left her coat on the picnic blanket. The ground at her feet was soft, and a puddle soon formed around her toes. Typically, the rain had waited until people ventured bravely outside before pelting them with spiteful glee.

Diana left the shepherd's hut and started picking her careful course down the soggy slope, but when she looked up, squinting against the rain, she saw a small blob in the distance, rushing away down the turnpike road toward the village. The Wainwrights' cart.

They were leaving her behind in their haste to get home and dry.

Was she so easily forgotten, just as Mrs. Kenton had told her?

Your presence is so easily overlooked that I am surprised you have not been sat upon.

Another sneeze bubbled out of her. If she were Justina, she would laugh at her misfortune and run home, jumping in all the puddles on her route. If she were Rebecca, she would shake her fist at the rain clouds and curse. But Diana felt no such strength today. She had no one waiting at home except her mother, who would probably shout at her as if the rain were her fault. She considered—for just a moment—sinking down onto the grass and letting the flood sweep her away.

Until she heard hooves pounding uphill toward her.

He had not gone with the others. He shouted her name, bellowed it through the rain in an uncouth manner as if he would bring her to heel. The rake who called her a fool, thought her weak, and had the audacity to set his cap at one of her friends while keeping an adulteress mistress had ridden back to find her.

Why? So he could tell her again how ill she looked? To advise her to eat cake?

Her pulse renewed with determination, she set her face against the rain and walked on.

∽

"Miss Makepiece," he called out to her as he slowed his horse. "I told the others I would find you. They were anxious to get back because one of the children had indigestion and Miss Bridges worried for her new bonnet. She did not want her father to know she'd been out so far in the rain, and flattened ribbons with running black dye would most certainly give her away."

Her small, pale face winced up at him. "I can find my way home, Captain. I was not lost. It was not necessary for you to stay."

Just as he expected. Damnable, stubborn, predictable woman. He reached down, offering his hand. "Come up behind me, Miss Makepiece. I won't bite."

Her eyes widened, the flare of emerald quite spectacular while raindrops hovered in her long, thick lashes and reflected the color like tiny prisms. "I certainly cannot ride with you." Walking hurriedly around his horse, she stumbled onward down the hill.

Nathaniel rode after her. "I can get you home in less than half the time it will take you to walk, yet you would rather drown yourself than take my hand and sit on my horse for ten minutes."

"It would not be proper," she sputtered, her gaze fixed on the wet grass, her heels slipping as she quickened her pace to escape him. "What would my... What would people think?"

"I've heard of cutting off one's nose to spite one's face, but I've never seen it demonstrated quite so vividly."

"Please go away." She tripped but stayed upright. Only her bonnet was dislodged, slipping back off her head and hanging around her neck by its wet ribbons.

"Don't be so damn foolish, Diana!" He lost his temper. Drawing alongside the anxious woman, he reached down again. This time he scooped her up with one arm, hoisted her over his lap, and set his horse for the road. Even sopping wet she weighed little more than a bundle of kindling wood. She was desperately in need of a few good meals, which angered him even more.

"How dare you," she gasped.

"Be still or you'll scare the horse."

He had given her the option of riding behind him and she had rejected it. Now she would have to suffer riding in front of him on the horse, with both her legs laid over his right thigh and his arms closed around her. Served her right for being stubborn and putting herself in danger. She could have tumbled down the slope, fallen under his horse, and broken a limb or worse.

At least his body gave her some shelter from the rain, he thought, trying to calm his pulse and remember that he shouldn't care about this woman. So what if she ran around getting soaked and endangering her health? It was not his concern.

Yet he could not stop caring.

"This is just like one of those novels you like so much, is it not?" he shouted wryly above the clattering hooves as they finally hit the stone road.

"No, it is not," she replied, her voice as stern as possible through chattering teeth. "The gentlemen in Miss Austen's novels would never capture a lady against her will."

"Then it's no wonder her books are so long—if everyone tiptoes around, quibbling and fussing before they reach a conclusion. A good, sound kidnapping, and possibly a spanking, would bring smart resolution to the heroine's fate."

From what he could see of her face it was pinched and tense, any sign of humor hidden. "You will kindly put me down as soon as we get to the bridge, Captain. The rain is easing already."

"Indeed I shall not. Kindness would mean delivering you to your gate, madam. I cannot leave you to walk that distance in this weather. As a gentleman, it is my duty to—"

"As a gentleman, you would put me down."

"Stop squirming or you might fall."

"Look, it is little more than a drizzle now."

That was true. The heaviest rain had passed quickly and remained now as nothing more than a damp mist with hazy, diffident sunlight slipping through the clouds.

Nathaniel warned her, "Those clouds could darken and split open again at any moment. Such are the joys of an English spring and summer. Have some caution, madam."

"Caution?" she sputtered. "*You* talk to *me* of caution? I did not think you knew the word."

When he urged the horse into a gallop, the sudden thrusting, forward motion pushed her light, slender form back into his arms, her shoulder against his chest. She seemed determined to keep her face turned away from him, but with her crumpled bonnet hanging at her back, her pale, vexed brow was not far from his lips. He could smell the soft violets of her perfume, could taste it on his tongue. Unleashed by the rainwater, the fragrance was even stronger than usual.

Struggling to keep her balance, she had placed one hand on his buckskin-clad thigh. Almost at once she took it off again, curling her fingers into a fist in her own lap. But the touch had ignited a spark of flame inside him, and despite the wet weather, that bright, hot, quivering light grew and stretched.

Before he even knew the thought was in him, he said, "If you give me a kiss, Miss Makepiece, I will do as you ask and set you down before we are in sight of your mama's house. There, see? I am being reasonable."

He felt her stiffen against his body as if she held her breath. But then the words came out of her in a rush. "My mama was right. You have not changed at all, Captain." She shook her head. A lock of black hair had fallen loose from her pins and it tickled his cheek, catching on his stubble.

"Some things about me *have* changed. Some never will. No matter how I might wish they would." He stared at the road ahead, trying to remember his determination to despise this woman. But it was hard. *Very hard indeed*, he thought, grinding his jaw. Especially while she was a captive in his lap and he had her at his mercy. "It seems I am destined to be the villain in your story, Miss Makepiece."

As he had observed last night at his sister's farm, Diana seemed smaller than he remembered, more fragile. It brought out his protective instincts, he supposed. When he saw her stumbling along in the rain without her coat, he had thought only of her safety, of the need to rescue her. He was almost overwhelmed by it. How quickly that gallant desire had transformed into the need to bribe a kiss from her reluctant lips. And now to demand more, for his forearm rested across her lap and every stride of the horse caused his sleeve to brush her muslin and the legs beneath.

That little bit of contact had an extraordinary effect

on Nathaniel and sent a procession of wildly passionate images through his mind. He thought about riding off with her, never taking her home at all.

Now why on earth would his mind wander that way when he was determined not to forgive her, not to let himself fall into old traps?

"You bring out the wicked in me," he muttered, bewildered and not knowing why he still felt this way for a woman who had rejected him so heartlessly.

"I do not suppose your *wicked* ever goes very far away, Captain. Men often have a much more difficult time abandoning the follies of youth, so my mother says."

She had to keep mentioning her mother, didn't she? That was enough to cool any man's ardor. "And what do you think? If you have a separate thought in your head that was not put there by your dear mama."

"On the outside you are a chameleon and can alter to suit your surroundings. But within, you are what you always were."

"Which is?"

"A cheeky, flirtatious scoundrel who lives to be the center of attention and would take any opportunity to steal a kiss. From any woman. Even one he cannot have any serious thought about. He likes games. He likes to see how much he can get away with. Just like a boy. And he will never grow out of it, because he does not want to and he does not have to. Let other people bear his responsibilities. Let them stay behind to pick up the pieces."

"I see."

"You asked for my opinion."

He groaned. "I think I prefer it when you are mute with supposed shyness after all."

"You had better put me down at the bridge or I shall know for sure you have not changed your"—she sneezed so violently she lifted out of his lap for a moment—"ways!"

He closed his arms tighter and more securely around her because she was so wet that he feared she might slip out of his grasp. "You're ill, Miss Makepiece. It would be careless and ungallant of me to make you walk home from the bridge." As she opened her mouth to argue, he added, "By all means, lecture me again about propriety and Miss Austen's gentlemen heroes. I'm sure not one of them would leave a lady in the rain to find her own way home. But I cannot win. Damned if I do, damned if I don't." He laughed without much mirth.

"At least while you rail against me, your lips are safe from being kissed, because the very second they are still, you know a rogue like me will steal from them. I would rather not have the temptation, so do keep chattering and abusing me with your insults, even as I rescue you from the weather and your own stubborn will."

Apparently she didn't know what to say to that. By encouraging her to talk he had, ironically, confused her into silence.

Shy? No, she was not shy. But she was wary, so accustomed to living by her mother's rules that she couldn't imagine any other way. The opinions she expressed were her mother's—he was sure—not hers. Perhaps she did not know the difference.

"It surprised me to find you still here, Diana," he said. "I had expected you to be married by now to William Shaw." His sister would glare at him or kick him under the table for raising the subject, but it had to be said. "Did your dear mother find something amiss with the fellow eventually?"

She shot him a quick frown. "He married another."

"So I heard. And left you brokenhearted." Her gaze went to his lips, and almost at once she looked away again. He thought of what he'd just heard, about her refusing to kiss William Shaw and not wanting to spoil memories. He wanted those memories to be of him, but it was difficult to believe she had fond thoughts of their past encounters. The damn woman hid her feelings so well. Perhaps Lucy had misheard or misinterpreted what she had witnessed in the Bolt.

"I know what it is to be rejected, Diana. To have one's heart thrown aside and trampled. I know it all too well, but I never imagined *you* would be affected."

She struggled again, intent on leaping free of him and his horse. "Your heart has never been in any real danger."

"Why do you say this?" he exclaimed. "Aha! Of course, you think me still a boy for whom life is a jest."

"That proposal was reckless, thoughtless, and immediately regretted. As you proved by leaving the next day, once you realized your mistake."

"Mistake?"

"When you woke to a new day, you had already changed your mind and seen the foolishness. Is that not why you left?"

He could not believe his ears. "You did not read my letter, Diana?"

"Letter?" A short, hard laugh gusted out of her. "Now you pretend you wrote to me? There is no need for lies, Captain. It is all in the past. Let us not revisit that error, I beg you." She seemed to wilt in his arms, as if all the air had gone out of her.

"I wrote to you that morning, Diana. Before I left the village."

"How very amusing, I'm sure. You should go back to your mistress who waits for you in Manderson. She might believe your lies."

"My mistress? Do you by chance refer to Mrs. Sayles?" He chuckled, the idea of Caroline being his mistress too patently ridiculous. "Is that what the rumor is now?"

"Not that it matters to me. It is no business of mine."

"It certainly is not, since you didn't want me. Even after I opened my heart to you."

She was not listening. Too busy fretting about being seen on his horse now that they neared the village. "You understand nothing about me if you think I am naive and easily led," she gasped. "Taken in by your practiced art of seduction. Like all your other *near misses*."

"Seduction? I only asked for a kiss. How quickly your mind leaps ahead, Miss Makepiece. Tsk-tsk. Must be all those horrid novels you read."

"You are impossible. You take nothing seriously."

She had almost elbowed him in the groin. "Diana, sit still before you knock us both off this horse!"

"Now you see me again like this—*poor Diana*—and

for vengeance you think it jolly good fun to tease and torment me, bribing me for a kiss." Ah, her temper was mounting. He knew it because she was listening less and less to what he said, building a conversation with herself.

"Alas, you guessed my dastardly motives. I want to kiss you simply for revenge. And since you can pretend that you were forced into it, you won't need to feel any guilt. But if you're going to swoon, please do it after the kiss. I like my victims to be conscious when I use my villainous arts on them."

Diana muttered scornfully, "In and out of our lives you flit. The moment you grow weary of this village you can be off again with no strings to bind you."

"I understand Lucy Bridges is not as stingy with her kisses as you are, Miss Makepiece."

Oh, that she heard. The fussing woman caught her breath. "Yes, Lucy would suit you very well. I'm sure she could overlook your faults. She could be content with a pretty surface. If anyone can put up with you, she can!"

Nathaniel momentarily lost his grip and she slipped out of his arms. It was fortunate that he'd slowed his horse, but she still stumbled. A lady was never supposed to run anywhere and Diana was usually so well composed, yet now she took flight as if he might physically harm her. Perhaps she truly thought he would put her over his knee and spank her as he had teased.

He recovered, leaped down, and caught up with her at the foot of the bridge. "Diana! There is no need to run from me like this. What has got into you?"

She was breathing hard, leaning against the stone wall, and trying to keep a nonchalant face. "I am going home, Captain. There is no cause to chase after me in this dramatic fashion. Kindly go…"—Diana looked around anxiously and then pointed farther along the turnpike road—"go that way, so that we are not observed together."

"I will go whichever way I choose." Nathaniel folded his arms.

He could see her trying to hold in her temper, squeezing her lips together. Showing a hot temper would be improper, of course.

"It doesn't mean I'm following you," he added. "Why would I?"

One of those dark eyebrows arched and lifted.

Annoyed by the smug, cool doubt and still wanting to lure her emotions out, he exclaimed, "You made your feelings plain three years ago, madam. You need have no fear that I came back for you. I am not that same reckless fool. If that's why you run from me, you waste your energy."

She pointed over his shoulder. "Oh, look! A rainbow."

He turned.

The woman seized her moment and ran off again. But she only got four or five steps across the bridge before he caught her again, lifting her off her kicking feet.

Eleven

HE CARRIED HER TO THE ARCHED DOOR OF THE OLD mill at the foot of the bridge and finally set her down. The doors were padlocked, but there was a broad entrance under which they could take shelter.

Diana, who had never imagined being so manhandled in her life, was appalled. But she was also exhausted and could not fight any further.

"You burned my note, I suppose," he accused, breathing hard, probably from the exertion of chasing after her and carrying her like a sack over his shoulder. "Did you even bother to read it?"

"There was no note from you." She'd seldom heard of him writing a letter to anyone. To his sister perhaps, but only once or twice in all the years she'd known them. He was notoriously lazy with his correspondence and everyone knew it. How could she believe him now? Why should she?

Nathaniel clearly assumed that William Shaw had called off their engagement. Like everyone else, he couldn't believe Diana ever made a choice of her own or had any sort of will that was not directed by her mother. But she would not enlighten him to the truth. If she told him it was her own decision, he would only assume in his usual bigheaded way that she'd rejected William because of *him*.

And it was too late for all that. Their moment—such as it was—had passed.

Then there was Lucy. The girl was so eager to marry and she was the merry, sociable sort. Suited to Nathaniel.

In the shifting shadows of the mill doorway he looked like a carved statue of a pagan god come to life. Like a fallen angel with that fair, sandy hair kissed by the memory of summer and those cerulean eyes, so intense and searching. Every woman he met fell under his spell, and Diana—always the quietest girl in the room, always observing—had seen how he basked in the adoration. She didn't believe he would ever give that up to focus his attention on one woman. One woman could not possibly keep his lively, lusty attention forever. There would be heartbreak, especially if the woman he chose made the error of falling in love with her husband.

Whenever they had danced, Diana had felt people staring at her, as if they couldn't understand why he chose her as his partner when he could have had any pretty girl in the room. She wondered herself. Mischief, she supposed. Her mama was always right.

"I sent you a message the morning I left, Diana," he said. "I fired it myself through your bedchamber window with a sling."

"You did *what*?"

He ran a hand over his face, flattening rain-drenched spears of hair to his brow. "I climbed that damnable oak behind your mother's cottage. I didn't want to leave without giving us another chance."

She tried to think, but her mind wouldn't cooperate. *Don't believe him, Diana. He's a rogue and a charlatan. This is another of his practical jokes, no doubt. Any moment now he will burst his seams with laughter.*

Diana sniffed. "What did this supposed note say?"

He frowned.

"And don't bother making something up, Captain, for I will know you're fibbing. It comes naturally to you and always did. But I never fell for it, did I?"

The frown broke with exasperation and then reformed with scorn. "Oh, you know me. It was childish nonsense. Just what you would expect. Good thing you never read it."

"Don't tell me then," she grumbled into her handkerchief. "It hardly matters now anyway. The years have passed, and we are both too old for climbing trees."

"Quite," he snapped. "Three years is an eternity."

For me it has been, she longed to say.

What had his foolish note contained, she wondered, suddenly morbidly curious. He seemed embarrassed now to tell her. Had it been a hastily scrawled line, *Will you marry me, yea or nay?* That was how life was for him—easy and straightforward. He never saw potential problems.

Suddenly Nathaniel seized her hand. "We should start again, Miss Diana Makepiece, and put the past behind us."

"And why, pray, would we do that?"

He lifted her gloved fingers and pressed his lips against her knuckles.

"Captain?" she demanded.

He met her frown with a narrow-eyed, somewhat menacing appraisal. "Your opinion of me might improve."

"Well, it could hardly get any worse."

Nathaniel's hand tightened around hers and tugged her closer. "I am not all bad. We may become friends."

Skeptical, Diana tried to retrieve her hand, but his grip was too strong. "I wouldn't hope too hard, Captain." She admired his spirit; she envied his lively manner and his fearlessness. But to feel more for such a capricious man would be a mistake. "I think you should—" A dark, devious twinkle sizzled in his blue eyes and made her draw an anxious breath. "Do not think of it!"

He blinked, but the wicked sparkle remained. "Do not think of what?"

"*That.* It is not proper!"

"I'm afraid not. It is, however, necessary."

"Captain Sherringham, if you dare—"

The words were stolen away as his mouth lowered to hers, claimed her lips. She'd said the wrong thing, of course. In his case, saying "if you dare" was like waving a red rag at a bull.

Diana was almost lifted off her feet, left to hover on her toes as he took his kiss. His tongue touched hers and stroked it gently. A raindrop that fell from his eyelashes to her cheek was warm and soft, tickling her skin as it trickled down the curve like a tear and finally gathered on the ridge of her jaw. Until the tip of his tongue followed it and then licked it away.

She was stunned speechless.

"If you don't believe me about the note," he whispered, his lips warm against her ear, "ask Jamie Bridges. It was his sling I used."

Every inch of his hard body was pressed against her, and in her wet clothes she had little defense. He must feel her heartbeat. She might as well be naked. The wicked thought flashed through her mind as if he had put it there with his kiss.

"Ask him," he repeated. "Unless you're afraid." A flash of white teeth showed as he smiled. Oh, that lethal charm. He would never lose it. "The world might tip upside down if I was proven honest for once."

Nathaniel's eyes shone down at her and she was caught up in their brilliance, like a fly trapped in a spider's web.

"I once fell out of a tree for you," he whispered, sounding bewildered.

"That would explain these bouts of madness," she reasoned.

"You don't want to believe me, do you?"

"It's not something you should be proud of, Captain. It was a remarkably foolish thing to do. If it's true."

He raised his other hand to her brow and stroked a stray curl away. "I can show you an interesting scar if you'd care to see evidence."

Fortunately a rumbling sound warned of wheels approaching and broke through the threads of gossamer that held them both enthralled. He released her hand and she tumbled dizzily back to earth.

"I do not want us to part under a cloud," Diana said as she stepped into the shadows to avoid being seen by whoever passed. "Let us say good-bye this time as *friends*, not in anger."

"You can be friends with a—what was it—a cheeky, flirtatious scoundrel? A moment ago you made me sound like the worst of men."

"This cold has shortened my temper. As I said, your behavior is none of my business." She simply couldn't give him more than friendship; he must understand. Anything more was out of the question. They were completely ill suited in every way.

His horse had followed them over the bridge, cropped at the wet grass for a moment, and then come to find him. Now it nudged Nathaniel's shoulder with its long nose and whinnied.

"The rain has eased, so perhaps you can walk me home, Captain," she said. *What harm could that do?* she thought. Perhaps they *could* part civilly, as friends.

He looked away from her, his jaw set hard, his lips pressed angrily together.

"It is for the best, Captain," she added. "You have many other prospects and—"

"Prospects?" he snapped, turning back to glare at her. "Oh yes, tons of women who want me to kiss them and would never run away as if they thought I wanted to chop them up with an ax."

"Well, then." Diana forced a smile.

For a long moment he stared at her, then finally he bowed his head. A drop of rain fell from the tip of his nose. He took the horse's bridle and walked out the doorway. She hesitated, not certain what he meant to do, but then he gestured that he would help her mount. Apparently words were beyond him.

It was not a sidesaddle, but she could manage if she sat carefully, and they didn't have far to go.

Nathaniel walked, leading the horse and letting her ride.

⤫

That kiss had been a mistake. It only served to remind him of what he couldn't have. He suspected she was lying to him about not reading his note. But how quickly he had forgotten that he despised her, he mused.

It was troubling, infuriating.

When they reached her mother's gate and he helped her down, she kept her eyes averted.

"Good-bye then, Captain. I wish you well," she said stiffly. "May all the harsh words be forgotten and do say we shall part as friends."

It was as if she was performing for an audience, giving a demonstration of how adults should behave. He knew she taught music lessons now to supplement her mother's income. Did she also teach etiquette to bored young people? He could imagine her rapping knuckles with a hard stick.

Her mother must be watching. That was the audience for whom she was acting out this display of nonchalant politesse.

Nathaniel found it impossible to speak, so he bowed, opened the gate for her, and watched Diana walk into the house. She did not look back.

Twelve

"DIANA!" HER MOTHER WAS IN THE SHADOWS OF THE hall, waiting with her hands clasped before her as Diana came through the front door. "Where have you been?"

"I was at the book society meeting, Mama. I told you before I left." Her fingertips felt odd, as if pricked by hundreds of tiny pins at once, making the removal of her gloves suddenly a difficult enterprise.

The door to the parlor was open and she knew her mother must have been in there, watching through the window as she and Nathaniel came down the High Street. "You know very well what I mean, Diana. Where have you been with *him*?"

Struggling now with the wet knot in her bonnet ribbons, Diana replied, "Mama, Captain Sherringham offered his horse and escorted me home. It is nothing to fuss about."

"Nothing to fuss about?" Her mother advanced, eyes wide and dark with fury. "A lady's reputation can only be lost once, Diana! The entire village will have seen you on that man's horse in such a state of dishabille. How could you?"

When her mother reached to help her with the knotted ribbons, Diana murmured weakly, breathlessly, "Mama, I can manage."

"I want better for you, Diana. Better than I had. Can you not see what he is?"

"It was only a ride on a horse. Hardly an elopement."

"Do not use that tone with me!"

"Mama, I think you've let your imagination run away with *you* for a change. Not me."

Her mother drew back, her face white. "You know very well how rumors can spread in this village. I have not worked my fingers to the bone and earned all these gray hairs raising you so that you can throw everything away on a rake who will—"

"I know all this. Don't you think I know? You instilled it in me from the day I was born."

"Yes, and he wasn't there then, was he? Oh no, didn't want to be troubled with a baby. Left me alone to manage. Couldn't even turn up at the church...on time. Left *us* to the shame."

Diana could see the veins popping in her mother's hands as they smoothed over her gown. And then it all began to blur, colors melting into one another.

She tried to set her bonnet on the hook and missed. The edges of her vision fizzed and bubbled. Falling backward, she hit her shoulder on the spinning wall. She turned her eyes up to the ceiling, and a damp patch in the plaster between the old, low beams was the last thing she saw before it all went dark.

❧

When she opened her eyes, she was in bed and Dr. Penny's kind face leaned over her as he listened to her heartbeat.

Her limbs felt very soft, and she was grateful that she didn't need to do anything but lie still. She hurriedly sent her thoughts back in time to see if she had done anything humiliating. If one had to faint, she supposed doing so in one's own front hall and out of public sight was the best way.

Beside the bed, her mother waited to hear the verdict, her face tight and angry. As if this was something else Diana had done to disappoint or shame her.

Shame. Yes, she remembered that word being yelled at her in the hall. "I'm sorry, Mama," Diana whispered. "I don't know what happened." Nathaniel's kiss had happened, she thought grimly, and just as he'd predicted in his sarcastic way, it had indeed caused her to swoon.

Her mother's mouth opened in surprise and she unclasped her hands, letting them hang at her sides. "For goodness' sake, Diana, it is not your fault."

It wasn't? Then it was the first time the blame was not hers, she thought bleakly. For twenty-seven years it had all been her fault—from her mother's thickening waist to her worn nails and the threads of silver multiplying in her hair. Diana knew that if she had not been born, her mother might have remarried, would certainly have had more time for herself, would not have had her merry youth curtailed so soon.

"You looked angry at me, Mama."

"For pity's sake, I am not angry at *you*."

Dr. Penny patted Diana's fingers where they lay

above the coverlet and smiled. "You had a dizzy turn, m'dear. Frightened your mama, but you just need some solid rest and a warm bed. Soon you will be right as rain. This cold has brought you low."

She saw her mother's shoulders sag slightly in relief. "Diana has not had much appetite lately, Doctor. She will not eat." Then she shook her head crossly and added, "So stubborn!"

The doctor smiled again and with his soothing, serene tone said, "Then you must find things that *do* entice her to eat. All young people can be tempted by something. Let her have whatever she desires."

When he called her "young," Diana felt a tear in her eye but blinked it back.

"This cold has worsened her condition, but I believe the underlying problem could very well be a lack of iron in her blood. Anemia. From what you tell me of her irregularities, Mrs. Makepiece, your daughter could benefit from my special tonic. Jussy can bring it 'round later when she visits the patient. In the meantime, keep Diana warm, rested, and comfortable. Nothing to cause anxiety or upset."

"She reads an awful lot of novels, Doctor. And they do excite her passions, I fear. In my day novels were never encouraged reading material for young ladies."

"Oh dear, yes." The doctor looked down at Diana and she thought she almost caught a wink, but perhaps he simply had dust in his eye. "These modern girls get up to some terrible habits, but if they did not have those books on which to spend some of their time and unleash their horrifying curiosity, goodness only knows what they would get up to, eh?"

Mrs. Makepiece persisted. "You do not think her reading material might be to blame?"

"Perusing the newspaper these days, my dear lady, is likely to cause a person far more discomfort than reading a work of fiction."

As they moved toward the door, she heard her mother say, "I had thought to send her to Bath, Doctor. To stay with my cousin. She might take benefit there from the waters. And I hear it is not such a crowded place these days."

"Bath?" Dr. Penny paused and glanced back at Diana. "Yes, I think once she is feeling stronger and the remnants of this cold are fought off, a visit to Bath might do her a great deal of good. My son-in-law plans a trip there very soon, I understand. He can travel with her and save the trouble on your nerves, madam."

"To let her go without me?"

Dr. Penny was already removing his white wig as he reached the door. He only wore it on official business and complained it made him itch. "I think, madam, the change will do you both some good, and she will have your cousin to watch over her in Bath."

Diana lay in the quiet room and closed her eyes. She thought of what Nathaniel had said, of how he'd climbed the tree outside her window to deliver a note. What a thing to do, and yet quite like him, of course. What was *not* as believable was the idea that he might put pen to paper for her.

When her mother came back to the room, Diana asked if she might have the window open for some fresh air. Seeing her mother ready to disapprove, she added coyly, "Dr. Penny said I should have anything I wanted, Mama."

"That was food, Diana."

"Yes, but he also said I am not to be upset."

Her mother stared, her lips puckered.

"If you open the window a little for me, Mama, I will eat a good supper. There, is that not fair? Fresh air will help my appetite." Oh, what had gotten into her? Nathaniel's forbidden kiss, of course. He was a terrible influence.

Finally her mother agreed and opened the window slightly. The air was warm, the rain gone for now. Light birdsong swept in, along with the distant sound of a dog barking and the rustling of budding tree branches. She could smell the blooming honeysuckle that grew on the trellis arbor in the back garden.

Diana smiled. It was pleasant to have her mother concerned about her health. Genuinely concerned, not just enough to shout at her for not eating her potatoes or not sitting with a straight spine.

Doctor Penny claimed she'd frightened her mother when she fainted. Diana had never seen her mother frightened by anything. Appalled or disgusted by something, but never afraid.

Her mother opened the bottom dresser drawer and took out a quilt that hadn't seen the light of day for years. Diana remembered it from her childhood. On rainy evenings long past, her mother would get that quilt out and wrap them both snugly in it while they read *The History of Little Goody Two-Shoes* by the glow of candles and firelight.

But once Diana was old enough to try her mother's

patience, the quilt was folded and tucked away, keeping it safe from damage and sunlight. Possibly from the effects of moral decline too.

Today, however, it was laid reverently over her bed for an extra layer of warmth.

"Mama, you said something earlier about my father not making it to the church on time. What did you mean? He was late for the wedding when you married? But he did get there eventually, at least."

Her mother turned, bent, and made much of closing the stiff drawer. "He was never on time for anything."

Over the years Diana had saved little nuggets of information about her father as they came her way, but those scraps were few and far between. She didn't like to ask questions, because they made her mother cross and short-tempered. Today she decided to take a chance while she had the advantage of being sick in bed.

"Papa was an officer, wasn't he?"

"Yes. I told you that. He was also a scapegrace and I should have known better."

Her mother had once shown her a silhouette she'd made herself and placed in a small oval frame. She'd kept that picture of the "scapegrace" all these years. "And he was killed in battle, was he not?"

"Yes."

"But he left you no widow's pension."

Her mother finally heaved the stuck drawer shut and then straightened. "There was something amiss with the papers." She gave a small, disdainful huff. "He was never careful with such things."

"You had no recourse? Surely a solicitor—"

"Would cost me more coin than I could have collected, as I have told you many times."

But Diana did not think she'd raised the matter more than twice in the past. She wouldn't have dared. "You must have worried when he was late for the wedding."

To that her mother made no reply. She had found a mark on the dresser mirror and was rubbing at it furiously with her sleeve.

"Where did you marry?" Diana persisted. "In Oxford, I think you told me."

"Oh, I don't remember the exact place. Some little church."

"Do you have the license?"

"What on earth—"

"I would like to see his handwriting. Just to know what it was like, Mama. I have so little that was his."

Her mother frowned, her brows drawn together. "I will look for it. Now do get some rest, Diana. Try to sleep. I'll bring you some soup when it's ready."

Then her mother swept out, leaving the door ajar in case Diana needed anything. Having her mother tend to her was like being sick as a child, Diana thought wistfully. Oh, if only people didn't have to get old, grow up, and face responsibilities.

Some never did, of course. Like Nathaniel.

Her mother was right again. He dressed up nicely and put on a good act, but he was the same underneath, the same bad little boy trying to get away with improper behavior, trying to lead her astray for his own amusement.

Turning her head on the pillow, she looked at

the curtains as they billowed gently in the warm spring breeze.

Couldn't even turn up at the church…on time. Left us to the shame.

The pause was significant because Diana's mother never stumbled over words, never made a mistake with her tongue.

❧

Nathaniel arrived for dinner with the Bridges that evening and immediately saw that Sarah Wainwright was not the only soul trying to make a match between himself and Lucy. He had treated it lightly before, but with his sister's lecture still fresh in his mind, he realized how his friendly nature— his desire to help a lady in distress—might have been misunderstood.

He was placed at the table beside the chattering young lady, and she and her mother paid him great attention throughout the meal, to the exclusion of anything or anyone else. Not that the other diners cared. Mr. Bridges sat at his end of the table and seemed distracted, contributing little to the conversation.

"How glad we were to see you back again, Captain," said Mrs. Bridges with a hopeful gleam in her eye. "We had quite begun to despair of your ever returning to our little village."

"I daresay you have been to many more exciting places," Lucy added.

"A few," he replied. "But I must say, Hawcombe Prior continues to be my favorite. No matter where I go, I think of this village with deep fondness. In some way, the air here has got into my blood and makes me think of it as home."

Lucy and her mama exchanged broad smiles. "Well, we are gratified that you think of us so highly," the elder lady said.

It was painfully obvious that he needed to say something to deflate their expectations before the situation worsened. "I wish I could stay longer. Alas, business takes me away again very soon."

"But you just got here," sputtered Lucy.

"I am merely passing through, Miss Bridges. Perhaps I will return in the future, but I cannot say when." He shrugged and smiled. "That is why I always warn people never to wait for me. I am the most unreliable of men when it comes to planning. I can suddenly get a thought in my head and be off in a moment."

Mr. Bridges finally paid heed to the conversation. "It is good you are a bachelor then, Captain." He glowered down the table. "A man with a wife and children cannot come and go as he pleases. He has to settle and take measure of his responsibilities."

"Indeed, sir." Miss Diana Makepiece had assured him of his failings yet again that day. In case he might have forgotten what she thought of him. How quickly she had retreated into her mother's house and shut the door, as if she could not get away from him quickly enough.

"But we heard you had come to find a bride, Captain," muttered Lucy.

He laughed gently. "That was just a jest, Miss Bridges. I fear young Sarah Wainwright took me seriously. She does not know me as well as the rest of you.

Surely you know that the things I say should be tasted with a pinch of salt."

After that, both females at the table showed their annoyance and disappointment by banging tureens and lids about. He thought again of what his sister had said about his flirting and the trouble it could cause. But he didn't always know when he was doing it, or what might be construed as "flirting."

Was his annoying little sister right after all?

After dinner he retired with Mr. Bridges to the tavern storeroom, which apparently also served as the fellow's sanctuary—a place where he consulted his ledgers, calculated his accounts, and mostly just escaped his wife and children.

"So, Captain, this business you wished to discuss with me had naught to do with my daughter after all." Mr. Bridges pulled up two chairs around a barrel and bade his guest to sit. "You've caused quite a stir in this house, I'll have you know."

"Yes, so I see. I'm sorry. It was not my intention."

"Aye. Fellows like you always say that." Mr. Bridges poured some port for them both. "But I know my girl gets airy ideas in that head of hers that bear little resemblance to reality, so I'm sure it ain't all your fault."

Nathaniel took the glass he was offered. "The Book Club Belles do tend to get romantic notions after they read those novels." He hesitated. "I must put a word in for Samuel Hardacre, however."

"Yon carpenter?"

"He's a solid young man, hardworking, ambitious, reliable, and honest. And I believe he has a keen eye on Lucy. Although he hesitates to say it."

But the tavern keeper puffed his chest, stretched his legs out, and crossed his ankles. "Well, my girl will have bigger fish on her hook now. Soon enough she and her mother will have something else to put a spring in their curls." As he exhaled a gusty sigh of contentment, his ruddy face cracked in a broad smile. "We're about to be rich, Captain."

"Indeed?"

"That crotchety old baggage, my wife's mother, went and left us a nice bit o' property in Hampshire and some coin too. I ain't said a word yet, but I just signed the papers and we shall be off to Basingstoke by summer's end. Can you imagine the surprise on the lasses' faces when I tell 'em?"

"Then you'll be leaving the village?"

"Once I find someone to buy this old place."

It couldn't have worked out better for Nathaniel. This was exactly the business that had brought him to Hawcombe Prior.

◈

Rebecca, Justina, and Sarah came to return her coat that evening, all three very anxious to see their friend. They were distraught about leaving her behind in the rain, but the race to get a sick child home had momentarily panicked the group.

"My brother insisted he would find you," said Rebecca. "Poor Diana! To be caught in the downpour."

She assured them they were forgiven for leaving her behind. "After all, I wandered away from the party. It was not your responsibility to look after me."

Her friends exchanged strange, secretive glances.

"Sherry did find you, did he not?" Jussy asked with an airy sort of unconcern that was almost believable.

"Yes. Not that it was necessary. I was capable of finding my own way home."

Again the odd looks. Evidently the news of her riding his horse down the High Street had traveled with the speed of fire through dry kindling.

Diana sighed and blew her nose loudly. They had better not get any ideas about her and the reckless captain, just because he was wearing a new suit of clothes and they thought she was an unhappy, unfortunate spinster with no other prospects.

But their company soon lightened her spirits, and even when Sarah let it slip that Captain Sherringham was dining with the Bridges and the other two women glared at her, Diana carefully showed no reaction beyond a polite smile.

She had other things to think about and look forward to. Fortunately.

"I am being sent to Bath," she told her friends solemnly as they sat around the bed. "Mama has written to our cousin Elizabeth." It made Diana feel special that she was being "sent" anywhere, for she'd rarely been farther than Manderson. It was too expensive to travel far, and her mother would never condone the wastefulness. Until now. She was eager to get her daughter away from Captain Sherringham, of course.

"Oh no!" cried Rebecca. "Why would you want to stay with that dreadful snob, Elizabeth Clarendon? I cannot see her companionship making you feel any better, only worse!"

"She is not a Clarendon now," Diana reminded her.

"She is Lady Plumtre. And she has invited me several times now to visit. She will not be put off forever."

Her mother's cousin had married a baronet the previous year and now resided just outside Bath in what her letters described as "merely an adequately sized manor." The main reason for her discontent appeared to be the fact that she had to share a pretty piece of parkland with a larger house in which her husband's mother and his unmarried siblings lived.

Sir Jonathan Plumtre was a newly knighted baronet, a wealthy merchant banker who had inherited considerable property, but he did not think it fair to turn his mother and siblings out of the big house when his father died, so he and his bride lived in a smaller house on the estate. To think of proud, haughty Elizabeth reduced to living in "an old stone cottage with only tiny, damp rooms and more drafts than windows" had given the Book Club Belles many a laugh.

"*Poor Diana.*" Rebecca reached for her hand with both of her own, as if to save Diana from tumbling over a cliff. "To spend your spring away from us and in her wretched company. It cannot be borne!"

Jussy, on the other hand, exclaimed that she thought Bath might be a very good idea. "I would invite you to stay at our townhouse in the Crescent, but unfortunately my husband's stepmama and her family are in residence, and I would not wish *that* society on anybody."

"Oh, can I go?" Sarah almost leaped out of her chair. "I have so wanted to dance at the Upper Rooms. I know Bath is not as fashionable as it once was, but I should love to see it."

Rebecca intervened swiftly. "Diana is going there to rest and recuperate, not to chaperone noisy young girls about in society." She squeezed the patient's hand. "I fear we have already asked her to look after you too many times lately when she should have been nursing this cold. We've all been caught up in our own lives and should have been looking after *her*!"

"There will be time enough for you to go next year, Sarah," Jussy added, comforting the girl with the promise that they would all go and have a vast amount of fun. "I once said I would never go there again, not even for a lifetime supply of hot chocolate, but since Bath is where I met my beloved Wainwright, I can have nothing against the place now. This time, however, it is Diana's turn to spread her wings and have adventures without us. She will return and tell us all about it."

"But what of *Persuasion*?" cried Sarah. "We cannot finish it without Diana."

"No," Jussy agreed. "We will wait until she returns to find out how it ends. She is going to live her own story in Bath, and when she comes home, she'll give me plenty of material for my next novel."

Diana smiled warmly at her friends and their optimism. It would be strange to go so far with none of them at her side, but Jussy was right. It was time for her to experience more of the world. She was a little fearful, yet excited too. A change of scenery would surely do her good.

As for Captain Sherringham, she had wished him well and put the past behind them. She hoped. Going to Bath would get her out of his way. She need not be witness to his courtship of Lucy Bridges. Or any other woman.

Her mother came up later to see how she fared and to show her a new beaded trim she was sewing on Diana's best gown.

"You must put on a good face in Bath," she told her daughter. "I won't have Cousin Elizabeth sneering at your clothes."

"Mama, I believe that a sneer is Cousin Elizabeth's usual expression. As such, I assure you I can never take offense at it."

"But I must pack your trunk with care, for there will be some important social engagements while you are there. The Plumtres are very well connected."

She guessed her mother was thinking that eligible bachelors must fall from the clouds over Bath. "They are new wealth though, Mama, just like the Wainwrights," she pointed out wryly. "They are not old nobility. Cousin Elizabeth claims they lack fashionable manners, that Mrs. Fanny Plumtre wears a worsted pinafore all day and was born the daughter of a shoemaker, and that her daughters know nothing of the rules of precedence when going in to dinner. Are you sure we should approve of the Plumtres? I might come away with shockingly bad habits."

"It would be very nice if you came away with a suitable husband."

"I thought I was going there to convalesce."

"And so you are, Diana, but if an eligible bachelor should take an interest—"

"I will think him unhinged." She chuckled dourly. "I admire your frugality, Mama, in killing two birds with one stone."

Her mother frowned. "I see you're feeling better

already. Dr. Penny's iron tonic must work wonders. You sound inebriated, for goodness' sake. What is in that bottle, gin?"

"Don't fret, Mama. I will be on my very best behavior in Bath."

"I know you will." Her mother hesitated and then leaned over to kiss her forehead gently. "You have always been a good daughter."

Diana felt her heart warm with surprise and joy.

"We have had only each other for twenty-seven years. It will be strange indeed not to have you here, Diana."

"But you will be busy teaching my students as well as your own while I am gone. You will have no time to feel alone. And I will return before you know it."

"I meant when you are married, Diana."

"Oh." Her mother's enthusiasm, it seemed, was renewed by the prospect of this trip.

"There is nothing I have ever wanted more for you than a respectable, suitable marriage."

Diana replied quietly, "One that eluded you, Mama?"

"What can you mean?"

The breeze buffeted the curtains, and outside the window a sparrow chirped. Shadows and sunlight shifted and flickered, making ghostly shapes that danced around Diana's room. She took a breath and valiantly proceeded. "He didn't marry you, did he? My father didn't turn up at the church. He deserted you." In that moment of panic and desperation when Diana had come in from riding on Nathaniel's horse, her mother had made a rare slip.

She stood very still at the foot of the bed, lips pressed tight, eyes weary. Lowering her lashes for a moment, she swallowed visibly. "Where do you get your ideas? Those novels, I suppose." But her voice was faint, pushed out under pressure.

"Why did you not tell me, Mama?" Diana persisted gently.

Fingers clasping the lace at her throat, her mother managed finally to say, "There are things in this world that one must try to protect one's children from. Especially daughters."

"The truth? What good would protecting me from the truth do?"

Her mother sighed heavily. "I wanted to protect you from the shame."

"Mama, I don't care what people think of me. My friends would love me no matter what I was."

"An innocent's view of the world, indeed," her mother muttered. "I had neither the money nor the family support to shield you. And I meant *my* shame, Diana. Do you think I wanted you to be ashamed of me, knowing what I had done?"

"But you were in love with him. The fault is not yours."

On a halting breath, her mother continued. "Yes, I made a fool of myself falling in love. And in sinful lust."

"What was he like, Mama?" Diana asked softly. "What was he really like? You never told me much."

After a pause, the reply escaped on a frail whisper. "He was handsome. Beautiful, really. All the ladies pined for him. When he gave me his attention, I was flattered, swept up in it, would do anything to keep it, for I knew how it wandered. He was generous when he could not afford to be, lavish with his presents and his love. He knew how to make a naive girl feel special, wanted. But when his attention passed, I felt nothing but pain and humiliation that I had ever succumbed to it." She gazed forlornly through her daughter's bedchamber window.

"Perhaps you are still in love with him, Mama?"

"Nonsense," came the sharp response as her mother recovered briskly. "I learned my bitter lesson. I do not want you to suffer the same."

Before Diana could answer, her mother left the chamber, one hand shielding her face.

The sparrow outside ceased its song and the breeze died down. Diana looked around now with newly opened eyes. She felt sadness for her mother. All these years of struggle were even more poignant. No wonder she was so scathing about Sarah Wainwright. Watching that girl taken in and loved by her family must have stung, reminding her mother of all she'd not been able to give her daughter in the same circumstances. Her own family had not been so forgiving.

Hard as it was to imagine her mother losing to the wicked temptation of the flesh, it must have happened. That mysterious army officer had encouraged her to run off with him and then left her with child, escaping his responsibilities and abandoning them both to the censure of the world. The deceit she was forced to play must have mortified her proud mother.

And when she looked at Nathaniel, she saw a man who was just the same.

Thirteen

THE BELL CORD THAT HUNG BY MRS. MAKEPIECE'S front door had the springiness of one that was seldom pulled. It wasn't frayed from use, as many were in that village. In fact, it was rather grand for the small cottage and might have been at home on a larger house where a servant came to answer the bell when it rang.

But the wooden door beside it was chipped and had weathered badly. It did not match the grand bellpull or the superior haughtiness of the women who lived behind it.

Nathaniel tugged hard, and there was a lengthy pause until he heard steps in the hall. The door swung open.

Mrs. Makepiece almost stumbled when she saw him there on her step, a bunch of pale pink tulips in his hand.

"I heard that Miss Makepiece is unwell. I'm quite sure you won't allow me to see her, but please give her these. If she cannot get out at present, I thought I would bring the spring to her."

Diana's mother took the flowers, her face empty of expression.

"I hope she is feeling better," he added.

Just as he thought she would not speak, the dour woman surprised him by exclaiming, "Diana is stronger than she appears. Her health will soon improve. She will not be brought down by a cold."

"I am glad to hear it, madam."

He tipped his hat and was about to leave, when she muttered, "Just as she will not be brought down by the antics of a man who thinks to use her, to take advantage of her."

Nathaniel paused, then turned back. "I cannot imagine who would try to take advantage of your daughter, Mrs. Makepiece."

"A man perhaps who thinks he catches her at a low point, when she feels left out because her friends' lives have moved on. A man who enjoys a challenge and cannot be content until he has made a conquest of every woman to whom he takes a fancy. A man who has been out in the world and has experience of the sort that my innocent daughter does not."

The tulips were already drooping from her fist, as she choked the life out of their stems.

Nathaniel pointed to them now and said, "That's what you are doing to your daughter, madam. But you always preferred your flowers dead and dried in a bowl, did you not?"

She glowered fiercely, the flowers trembling.

"Your daughter is devoted to you, madam. I daresay you will have her at your side for the rest of her life. I hope you treat her well, as she deserves."

He could have said so much more, but her ears

would not hear. She would surely never pass his concerns on to Diana. So he walked away.

What, he mused, would Mrs. Makepiece do when she found out that he'd purchased the Pig in a Poke tavern as another house for his brewery, when she saw the new sign with "Sherringham and Mawbry" painted beneath it in gold and red. She would still turn her nose up.

Ever since Nathaniel had enjoyed a substantial win at the Newmarket races and used it to pay off his debts and invest in a brewery, he'd imagined coming back to Hawcombe Prior one day and putting his sign over the tavern.

However wealthy he became, he wanted to leave his mark—his name—there in Hawcombe Prior, as he had done all over Somerset, Gloucestershire, and Oxford. The Sherringham and Mawbry brewery was flourishing with a tied estate of fifty public houses across the countryside, and Nathaniel's tireless enthusiasm had pumped new lifeblood into the business. He liked ale, he liked taverns, and he liked people. He'd been told he had a charmingly persuasive manner. It was, therefore, the perfect business for him. He thrived in it and had found something he could make a success of at last.

Nathaniel had returned to Hawcombe Prior thinking Diana married to another, yet purchasing the Pig in a Poke was still something he had to do to get her out of his veins for good. Like putting an official ink stamp on a document or a wax seal on an order of execution.

He stopped and looked back at the Makepieces'

cottage. If she'd heard him at the door, he would have expected Diana to peer out of the parlor window at least. To give him a wave. They'd known each other ten years—since she was seventeen. All that time she'd kept him under her spell, but she didn't even mean to do it. She had no idea of the power she held over him. Sometimes he didn't think she felt anything for him but scorn or pity. It seemed she wavered between the two. She was not the sort of woman who would ever indulge in bold displays of affection or talk about her emotions. It wouldn't be proper.

But, as he had said to Diana, he simply could not behave himself around her. He said too much and she said too little.

It was, therefore, for the best that he was leaving.

"Who was at the door, Mama?" Out of bed today, Diana paced in the kitchen by the fire.

Her mother walked in carrying the wilted tulips. For a moment it looked as if she might toss them into the fire, but suddenly she thrust them toward Diana. "That restless rogue Sherringham. He left you these, but he had no time to come in."

Diana stared at the flowers. "Oh." Slowly she took them from her mother's fist. "They look… sad."

"I daresay he stole them from someone's garden."

She wondered why her mother had even told her they were from him, why she hadn't consigned them to the fire. Rebecca would say that a man only sent flowers when he was guilty of something. Diana got the feeling that guilt was certainly involved when these flowers were delivered into her hands, but she wasn't sure it was Nathaniel's.

A few petals had already dropped to the flagged floor and she saw her mother itching to sweep them up, so Diana walked out through the back door, worried the flowers might lose more petals simply from that withering regard.

"Don't wander out there in the cold," her mother exclaimed, back to her usual stern manner today.

"I have my shawl, Mama, and besides, the sun is out again." She sniffed her flowers, hiding her smile within the petals.

For a while she stood watching an industrious sparrow as it flew back and forth, collecting sticks for a nest up in the branches of the old oak. She liked to imagine this was the same bird she had set free from the Manderson assembly room last week. How nice that would be if the bird had followed her home to raise its babies in the tree under her bedchamber window. A fanciful idea her mother would sniff at.

Sheltering her eyes from the sun's glare with one hand, Diana looked up into the oak and caught a gleam of something trapped in a notch of the rough bark where a thick branch met the trunk. It was too high for her to reach, but it looked like…a button. A tarnished, weathered brass button of the sort that might be lost from an army uniform.

She clutched her flowers tighter.

He had come back to Hawcombe Prior, but not for her. Surely not for her.

❧

"Well, I must say, one moment you abandon me here in this muddy, unfashionable ditch of a town for days on end, and then you come back and announce that we are leaving immediately!" Caroline could barely get her words out. Feebly sprawled upon a chaise under the window, she made no move to pack her things, despite his urgings of haste.

"Caroline, we must be on our way. If you don't pack your trunk and pull yourself together, I'm afraid I'll have to leave you here in this *unfashionable* place, because I am not coming back."

That got her up at last. "What happened? What have you done that has you in such haste to go? Have you seduced some local maiden and need to take flight to escape her father's blunderbuss?" She tittered, still reclined with one hand pressed to her brow like a bad actress.

"Not this time," he replied dryly. "My mission here is concluded. I can now deliver you to your aunt as I promised. And get on with my life."

The sooner he got away from here and back to business, the better. He was irritable, restless. When such a fever had come upon him in the past, he would have found a nearby tavern in which to blur his worries and forget his disappointments. These days he found that travel helped. Speedy movement and finding something to keep him busy and his thoughts occupied until the mood passed.

"But what about me?" she whined.

"I just told you. I shall deliver you to your aunt in Bath, as you begged of me when you came to my lodgings."

She lifted her head enough to peer at him sulkily. "You mean to be rid of me. It seems your interest in me has waned since we came into the country."

He sighed. "Caroline, I told you when we took to the road together that there would be nothing of that sort between us."

"But why not? We could do well together. Neither of us takes life too seriously. You charm the ladies and I charm the gentlemen."

She finally slithered from the chaise and wandered over. "We shared some good times once."

"Long ago," he said sharply, moving away from her and stepping around the open trunk. "My definition of 'good times' has changed since then."

Pouting, she set her hands on her waist. "You don't mean to take me under your protection then?" she demanded, forgetting the headache that had supposedly weakened her until she could barely speak. "Be careful of my silk shawl!"

"Caroline, I offered to escort you to Bath. That is all. I do not desire a mistress." How tired he was of women like her—pushy, loud creatures demanding his notice and forcing their way into his life. "I am off women!" he exclaimed. "Tired of them hanging on me!"

There was much to be said for the company of a quiet woman who didn't want to be noticed. He was beginning to appreciate that fact more than ever.

❧

The day before she left for Bath, Diana learned of the Bridges family's windfall.

"We are to spell our name with a *y* now," Lucy told her as they met outside the village shop. "And I shall have far better prospects than some silly village carpenter."

Diana congratulated her, although she felt extremely sorry for Sam Hardacre. Did those new prospects include Nathaniel? She could not bring herself to ask.

As Lucy and her troop of brothers moved away, Diana held Jamie Bridges back by his collar and asked if he had ever lent his slingshot to Captain Sherringham.

The boy's face was the picture of innocence as he replied that he knew nothing about it.

"I ain't seen nothin'," he exclaimed proudly.

"That's a double negative, Master Bridges."

"I hope you're spelling that name with a *y*," he replied cockily. "And giving me the respect I deserve now I'm rich."

"Respect is earned, young sir, not purchased."

He promptly stuck out his tongue and ran off to join his siblings. Like a clucking, weaving line of ducklings they followed their sister across the common. Diana was left to wonder about the tarnished brass button she'd found.

How else could it have become lodged in the oak tree if not from Nathaniel's uniform? A magpie perhaps?

Unless soldiers made a habit of climbing that tree to look in her window.

An amusing thought indeed. She had better check every night just to be sure.

Fourteen

DIANA WAS ACCOMPANIED ON HER JOURNEY TO BATH by Justina's husband, who offered the use of his own carriage, since he was visiting his stepmother to make certain her recent ideas for renovations to a house there would not result in the roof caving in or his bank account being severely strained. The lady seemed to have questionable taste and absolutely no financial sense. The renovations had been under discussion for some time, but Darius Wainwright had avoided the visit as long as he could. Diana suspected it would not have been made even now, if not for her need of a gentleman escort and Justina's insistence.

Since the companion travelers were both of a reserved nature, their journey by carriage was mostly quiet and completely uneventful. Diana was glad of it. As they traveled, her senses were filled with all the new sights, sounds, and smells of life beyond her experience, and she wanted to let them all soak in without the interruption of polite conversation. Darius Wainwright obliged by having his head in a newspaper quite often.

On their route they made several stops at various coaching inns, and on more than one occasion Diana saw dray carts with the name "Sherringham and Mawbry" painted on the side. What a strange coincidence, she mused. Nathaniel would laugh at the irony of a distant relative, or someone simply with the same name, owning a brewery. He had always been fond of good ale. Too fond.

As the carriage rattled along, Diana caught her reflection in the window, smiling sadly. Oh no! Was that a tear gleaming in her eye? She hastily wiped it away.

Each mile they traveled took her farther from Nathaniel, but only physically, she realized. If anything, her mind was fixed upon him more than ever. Ironically it was worse even than the sadness of leaving her mother and the Book Club Belles behind. At least she knew she would see *them* again.

Oddly enough, Nathaniel had accused Diana of having no feelings, when in fact the opposite was true. She knew now that she had too many. The only way she could manage their number was to keep them quiet and subdued, as was proper. As her mother had taught her.

For comfort on her journey Diana had brought along the copy of *Persuasion*. It was sneaky, she supposed, to finish reading it behind her friends' backs, but none of them had been enjoying Anne Elliot's story as much as she had. Diana was sure of that. Now she would have the opportunity to read it alone, without hearing anyone else criticize Anne at every pause. She wanted the freedom to sigh over Captain Wentworth and pity sweet Anne without needing to justify her feelings or stop reading when the others were distracted by their far more exciting lives.

Soon she would be in Bath and surrounded by new faces. It would be pleasant to have *Persuasion* at her side, the familiar characters keeping her company at night.

But thoughts of Nathaniel continued worming their way into Diana's thoughts through Anne Elliot's eyes as she studied the character and motivations of her Captain Frederick Wentworth.

> *She understood him. He could not forgive her; but he could not be unfeeling. Though condemning her for the past, and considering it with high and unjust resentment, though perfectly careless of her, and though becoming attached to another, still he could not see her suffer, without the desire of giving her relief. It was a remainder of former sentiment; it was an impulse of pure, though unacknowledged friendship; it was a proof of his own warm and amiable heart, which she could not contemplate without emotions so compounded of pleasure and pain that she knew not which prevailed.*

Diana closed her book and stared out the carriage window again.

It would do her no good to dwell on that man. She was meant to find renewal and refreshment on this visit. Her strange, confused fancy for Nathaniel—that charismatic troublemaker—had to be squashed. He would marry Lucy and be far away again by the time she returned to Hawcombe Prior.

Then perhaps she could find peace, no longer torn between duty and desire.

Even if he had once climbed the oak tree to throw a message through her window, that was just a moment in his reckless past.

If only she knew what that note had contained. He would not tell her now, of course. His pride was wounded. The contents of that mysterious letter would remain his secret and she could only cause herself pain by imagining the things it might have said. If it ever truly existed.

What did it matter now?

Life had moved on for him.

She looked down at her ringless left hand where it was spread on the cover of her book. Miss Jane Austen had never married, as her mother pointed out, yet look what she had managed to achieve!

Diana cheered her spirits by reminding herself that she had survived perfectly well without a husband. She would continue to do so.

As the carriage trundled along toward Bath, Diana became resolved to experience as much of life as she could while she was there. To not let herself mope or tire even for a moment. She would prove that she was her own person. She had all her limbs and considerable intelligence, and thanks to Dr. Penny's tonic, she was recovering her health.

After all, Diana, along with Minerva and Vesta, was one of three virgin goddesses in Roman mythology. They didn't need men either.

❧

"How good of you, Captain Sherringham, to bring my dear niece to Bath," exclaimed the small lady who greeted Nathaniel and Caroline in a dreary parlor several days later.

With her slow gestures and drooping demeanor, Mrs. Ashby reminded Nathaniel of a weary old cat—the sort that seldom moved from its warm spot by the fire except to follow a treat. There was a distinct odor of mustiness about the woman's person as she moved forward with slumberous grace. A dingy lace cap trimmed with a wilted black ribbon hung listlessly around a delicate, powder-pale face from which two downward-slanting gray eyes peered out at him.

"I did not think she would ever come again. But here she is. I shall have to put out the best china, shan't I?" She glanced fearfully at Caroline. "So seldom these days do I have visitors to my humble little abode."

Her niece said nothing, but yawned widely. Nathaniel expressed his condolences for the passing of the lady's daughter.

Mrs. Ashby nodded with her eyes closed, as if her head was too heavy for the motion. "It is a great hardship to lose one's only daughter, one's only child." She dabbed her moist eyes with a handkerchief. "But I must press on. I daresay it won't be too long before I am reunited with my Eleanor."

Not knowing what to say to that, Nathaniel made a few harmless comments about the building and its convenient spot in the center of town.

"There is much to be said for convenience," Mrs. Ashby agreed, drooping further, "but it is not a fashionable part of town, you know. My daughter was rather aggrieved that we were reduced to living here. Not that she ever complained. Even when she fell ill, not a bad or impatient word crossed my Eleanor's lips. She suffered greatly, Captain, but with bravery."

Caroline interrupted to apprise her aunt of the many ailments *she* suffered. The journey had apparently exacerbated many of her imaginary conditions, from the way she now described them. Her cousin's demise had taken attention from her, of course, and that would not be borne.

Her aunt listened with great forbearance and then rang for tea—the ubiquitous restorative. Nathaniel would have made his escape as soon as it was polite, but Mrs. Ashby sat beside him, trapping him on the small, worn sofa, and talked further about her deceased daughter, clearly preferring his company to that of her niece.

Years of flirting and charming the ladies had left Nathaniel with an inability to overlook tears or to turn away when he sensed he might be of some use. One of the few things he'd been good at as a young man was cheering a lady out of a sad mood. He'd always thought it was bad form to walk away from someone in distress. Therefore he remained in Mrs. Ashby's damp, grim parlor long after he had meant to take his leave. Whenever he began to rise from the sofa, her face fell half an inch, and thus he stayed and drank yet another tepid cup of overly sweetened tea.

At one point the lady took an oval portrait from the drawer of a small Pembroke table beside the sofa and showed it to him. As she unwrapped the black velvet cloth and placed the small portrait in his palm, she explained in a soft, wavering voice that her daughter had sat for the miniature painting as a wedding gift for her fiancé.

"It was just sent to me from the framer. See how pretty she was, Captain. I have the duty of passing this into her fiancé's hands this very evening. I wish I did not need to part with it, but my Eleanor would want Mr. Plumtre to have it. The portrait was meant for him. If only the task of delivery had not been set upon my shoulders. I shall not know what to say to the sad fellow."

Nathaniel studied the portrait and dutifully proclaimed the pale, very gaunt Miss Eleanor Ashby to be a "rose indeed." But his mind was filled with another face, eyes shining up at him, lashes wet with rain. He could not escape Diana's power. She might be out of sight, but never out of mind.

"She was the sweetest of daughters, Captain." Mrs. Ashby wiped her eyes again and while he still held the portrait, waiting to pass it back to her, she suddenly had an idea that raised her spirits. "Why, Captain, you must dine with us at the Plumtres' this evening at Wollaford Park. Perhaps you can give Eleanor's portrait to her fiancé and save me the discomfort. Oh yes, surely you could! It would be the very thing!"

He was astonished. "But, madam, I do not—"

"You have a kind face, Captain, and a smile with much warmth." She was set upon the idea even after so short an acquaintance. "It will be easier for a man, I think, to fulfill the duty. Especially a gentleman such as yourself with no attachment to the matter."

"Surely, you—"

"At Wollaford you will meet my oldest friend, Fanny. She is Mr. Plumtre's mother and a sprightly widow. She and I have known one another many years. Goodness, the merry times we once had together." She paused, sighing, screwing her handkerchief tight in her hands, and tugging on his sympathy. "Her family is such a support to me, for without them now I would be"—she glanced over at Caroline— "quite alone."

Preoccupied with assessing the view from the window, Caroline remarked that her tea was cold, as well as slightly bitter.

There was a pause and then Mrs. Ashby attempted a more cheerful tone. At least for half a sentence. "It is lucky indeed that you come at this time, for the Plumtres have just taken up residence at Wollaford for the summer. I doubt I could have amused you by myself, had you come earlier in the spring while they were all still in London. Dear me, no. I am not very interesting company at the best of times, but of late… with Eleanor gone…" She ruffled the surface of her tea with a lilting sigh, her voice fading.

Nathaniel assured her that he was in Bath on business and only for a short stay, so she need not worry about his entertainment. "I merely delivered your niece safely to you for company in this time of grief. And I'm sure she has come only to comfort you, not to seek society."

"Company? Yes…of course." Again she cast her niece a dubious glance.

"I haven't been here for ages." Caroline surveyed the small parlor with utter disinterest. "How odd it is not to see Eleanor sitting there on the sofa sewing away with her little fingers, so meek and mouse-like. Is it not strange how the presence of one nondescript creature can be missed when it is not there?"

Nathaniel winced at this thoughtless comment and Mrs. Ashby was silent, gazing at her lap.

"Dear, dear Eleanor," Caroline added with a yawn, toes nonchalantly tapping on the carpet. She must have caught Nathaniel's stern glare, for then she sat up and went on. "I was so grieved when I heard that I struggled to finish my lemon ice and had to go directly to my chamber. I didn't get up again for a week and had to be served all my meals in bed. Even now I am not my full self. I shouldn't be surprised if there is some horrid tumor lurking in me. Or a fever waiting to strike me down."

Nathaniel cleared his throat. "Fortunately you remain capable of speech." If only her tenderness for her cousin and aunt was as deeply felt as her own imagined pains.

"The Plumtres will be pleased to see you, Caroline," said Mrs. Ashby, soldiering bravely on. "Jonty was married last year to a very fine and fashionable young lady from Oxford. A little too fine for me, I fear. But his sisters are still unattached and lively young things. And then there is his brother, George"—she turned to Nathaniel—"my Eleanor's fiancé. We do not know what to do for George. He buries his sorrow, as he buries his nose, in volumes of intense poetry."

Caroline sighed heavily and said under her breath but still audibly, "Sakes! It's been six months at least."

Mrs. Ashby pretended not to hear. "But the girls

will brighten up the evening for you no doubt, Captain, if you are so good as to join us at Wollaford. Susanna is just turned eighteen and her sister, Daisy, a year younger, I think. Delightful girls, always pleasant company."

"Those Plumtre girls are terribly wild," Caroline murmured, pausing to yawn again. "They have no regard for any other person's nerves. To them, everything is a great lark. It's no wonder their brother wanted to marry Eleanor, if only for some peace from his noisy sisters. They always give me a horrendous sore head."

Again Mrs. Ashby's eyes watered at the careless, passing mention of her daughter's name.

"In any case"—Caroline rolled onward—"Sherry isn't here to amuse silly girls. He's apparently off the company of women." She sneered. "Doesn't want them hanging all over him."

Nathaniel cast her a stern look, but she was yawning again, her eyes closed.

What he had said was that he wasn't in the market for a mistress, but he could not say that in front of Mrs. Ashby. So he turned to the lady beside him and smiled. "Your friends sound delightful. I very much look forward to meeting them."

He could see he would have to stay tonight and appease Mrs. Ashby by fulfilling the task she dreaded. Additionally, the thought of leaving this poor woman to her niece's selfish company seemed callous. It might be said that he had added to the woman's burden by delivering her niece to Bath, where she was clearly not wanted and would only cause distress and inconvenience. The least he could do was complete this uncomfortable errand for the mourning aunt.

❧

Diana was relieved to find the Plumtres not at all the way her mother's cousin had described them in her letters. She had some warning of that likelihood prior to her arrival—knowing Elizabeth's disdain for most things and people—but it was still a relief to discover that they were pleasant, kind, generous folk without the slightest pretension.

She met Sir Jonathan first upon her arrival at Wollaford Lodge. "You must call me Jonty," he assured her in his booming voice. "Everybody does, you know. Have done so since…well, ever since I can remember, what ho?" He was a smartly dressed, ruddy-cheeked, affable fellow who laughed a great deal, even at himself.

There was a marked contrast between his manners and those of his wife. While Elizabeth looked down her fine nose at most things, her husband found everything and everyone remarkable and worthy of his attention. Diana took to him at once, for he was the sort of person who entertained with his chatter, had much to say on the smallest of subjects, and never demanded much reply.

As soon as her trunk was unpacked, he insisted on taking her across the park to meet his mother and sisters, despite his wife's attempt to stall the introduction.

"I really do not think I care to dine there tonight," Elizabeth said. "That mournful woman Mrs. Ashby will be there again, I suppose, sniveling into the consommé. I hope you know she lives in Westgate Buildings, of all places."

"Well, if you prefer to stay at home, Lizzie, you must do so. I can accompany your cousin. My sisters are very eager to meet her. I cannot let them down."

Elizabeth sneered. "Of course you cannot let *them* down. God forbid. My wishes, on the other hand, can be ignored. As for my cousin, she must be weary. She is of frail health and the last thing she needs is your sisters leaping all over her like a pair of overexcited hound pups. And how many times must I tell you not to call me Lizzie? It is so dreadfully pedestrian."

The fellow laughed jovially. "I am a scatterbrain, my dear. Whatever shall you do with me, eh?" He turned to Diana. "You must not mind my boisterous ways, Miss Makepiece. I am an annoying flibbertigibbet. If you are tired after your journey, perhaps you would rather stay in. My sisters can wait to meet you another day."

But far from tired, Diana felt rejuvenated in her new surroundings, and she suspected an evening spent solely in Elizabeth's company would bring her down again. The last thing she wanted anyone to think was that she stumbled feebly around, swooning at every opportunity, too weak to put one foot before the other. *Frail health*, indeed!

So she assured Sir Jonty that she was looking forward to meeting his family. "I am not at all tired, and I would very much enjoy dinner at Wollaford Park. In fact, I believe it might be considered rude of me not to go, if they've been looking forward to it." She smiled.

Elizabeth stared. She was never happy about losing an argument, and it must have been a shock to hear her usually quiet cousin not only expressing an opinion but doing so with determination and without her mother's prompting. "I was *sure* you would prefer to stay *in*," Elizabeth said, her voice tight, her eyes unblinking.

"Oh, but you are quite mistaken." Diana smiled again, wider. "I would prefer to go out."

When it became evident that she would otherwise have to spend her evening in lonely splendor and miss a good dinner, Elizabeth eventually—and with extreme reluctance—agreed to attend with them.

Bolstered by this small victory, Diana spent extra time that evening on her dress and her appearance, anxious that no one should mistake her for a sickly, pitiful creature. Apparently that was how her cousin Elizabeth had described her to the Plumtres, and Diana wanted to let them know at once that this was false.

She took out one of her brighter, most springlike dresses—a light green, floral-print muslin with puff sleeves. She often wore a lace chemisette beneath for additional modesty, but not tonight. The air was warm and she did not want to feel overdressed. The Miss Diana Makepiece in Bath and Somersetshire would be unfussy and unrestricted. Unburdened.

For once, she could go out without fearing what her mother might catch her doing or saying. It was an awful sort of freedom, and she was not certain that this adventure would not go to her head. With a few minutes to spare, she returned to *Persuasion*.

*...entering Bath on a wet afternoon, and driving
through the long course of streets from the Old Bridge
to Camden Place, amidst the dash of other carriages,
the heavy rumble of carts and drays, the bawling of
newsmen, muffin-men and milkmen, and the ceaseless
clink of pattens, she made no complaint...*

*...after being long in the country, nothing could
be so good for her as a little quiet cheerfulness.*

As she closed the book and set it on the bedside
table beside the bottle of Dr. Penny's tonic, Diana
heard her host calling up the stairs to inquire if she
was ready. Her mother, she mused, would never
approve of a gentleman bellowing up the stairs in such
a fashion. But she did not mind it. Sir Jonty's hearty
voice was like an encouraging clap on the shoulder.
Sad thoughts could not be completed or allowed to
fall into moroseness when they were forever interrupted by the sound of raucous, unbridled laughter
and her pompous cousin being called "Lizzie" five
minutes after she'd once again protested the use of
the nickname.

A calmness had come over Diana. For once she was
not nervous about meeting new people. She was new
to them too, an unknown quantity. She could reinvent
herself and be bold like Rebecca or mischievous like
Jussy. Even flirtatious like Lucy. Well...perhaps not.

Perhaps she would simply be herself. Whatever
that was.

She descended the stairs to find Sir Jonty in the
hall, merrily refusing his peevish wife's demand for the
carriage, while pointing out that the weather was fine

and the daylight lingered so there was no reason not to walk across the park.

Diana agreed at once that she would rather go on foot. After all, she'd spent several days in a coach and was anxious for a chance to stretch her legs. Her cousin glared at her with far more anger than seemed necessary, but her host declared, "There, it is settled! Miss Makepiece desires to walk and so the vote is passed. Never mind, Lizzie. A leisurely stroll will give you appetite for a good pudding, what ho?"

However, their pace was neither "leisurely" nor could it be called a "stroll." Sir Jonty proved to be a brisk, energetic walker. He swiped at the grass with his cane as they went along and bellowed congenially to the three leaping springer spaniels that accompanied their small party.

By the time they arrived at the large Jacobean manor house known as Wollaford Park, Diana felt very warm from the exercise and quite windblown, but there was no time to collect a breath or tidy her hair because Sir Jonty's sisters were suddenly upon them. Elizabeth's description of the girls was, on this occasion, not an exaggeration. They did indeed leap around like frisky, boisterous young hounds, and no one seemed capable of bringing them to heel.

On the other hand, Sir Jonty's brother, George, was withdrawn and sullen. He surveyed Diana with heavy-lidded, lugubrious eyes and, in a cheerless monotone suggesting there could be no hope of such a thing, expressed a wish that she might enjoy her stay. During their march across the park she'd been informed of George's bereavement to prepare her for his demeanor, but it was still such a contrast to the rest of his family that she found it startling.

The widowed matriarch of this brood, Mrs. Fanny Plumtre, was no taller than Diana's shoulder but sturdily built. She had a round, sweet face and her voice was laden with a rich Somerset burr as she referred to the dusk as "dimpsey" and the bees on the lavender outside the drawing room window as "dumbledores."

Whenever the lady slipped one of these colloquialisms into a sentence, Diana watched her cousin Elizabeth's lips pinch tighter in disgust, her shoulders become even more rigidly squared. Not that the amiable Mrs. Plumtre paid heed to her daughter-in-law's haughty expression. Like her son, she retained an easy smile and took eager, sanguine interest in everything around her.

"We are so excited to have you here at Wollaford," she exclaimed to Diana, clasping her hands firmly. "I cannot think the last time we were all this excited."

Diana suspected it was only a few moments earlier, because she already saw how every little thing that happened was greeted with excessive delight by the ladies of the house. From the arrival of the sherry tray to admiration of an apricot sunset that slipped through the leaded windows and made a diamond pattern on the rug at their feet.

The Plumtre daughters were pretty, vivacious creatures, sharing many rolling-eyed glances with each other and failing to smother giggles at every arrogant remark their sister-in-law made. As a new arrival and a relative of Elizabeth's, Diana was inspected with wary curiosity, but once the sisters found her to be quite different from her cousin, they wasted no time extending friendship.

"You must come dancing with us in town, Miss Makepiece," the younger sister, Daisy, cried when they learned that Diana had never been to Bath before. "What fun we shall have showing you all the sights!"

"Public balls in the Upper Rooms are not what they were," Elizabeth commented coldly. "Nobody of importance goes there anymore."

"*We* go there," Daisy replied.

Elizabeth merely arched an eyebrow.

"Jonty has promised to hold a ball here at Wollaford this year," said Susanna. "Surely you will look forward to that, Elizabeth, for private dances and parties are considered quite the thing these days."

Elizabeth scoffed. "To have people trampling about the lawns, scratching the floor, and not knowing when they have stayed too long? Oh yes, I can hardly wait."

Daisy chirped up again. "And we must take you to the Pump Room, Miss Makepiece. And shopping... Oh, there is so much for her to see, is there not, Mama?"

Mrs. Plumtre agreed that there was, but added gently, "We must not wear poor Miss Makepiece out. She is here to convalesce, you know, not to charge about hither and thither."

"Quite," muttered Elizabeth. "My cousin will not be dashing all over the place with the two of you. Might I remind you she has come to visit me? *I* invited her. Am I to sit home without my guest while you take her charging off about town?"

The sisters looked at one another and sighed meaningfully.

"Of course you must come too," Susanna managed in a taut breath. "We didn't mean to exclude you, Elizabeth."

Daisy bit her lip and slumped in her chair—no one bothering to correct her posture or her impolite comment. Sir Jonty played with his dogs, not following the conversation at all, and his brother had picked up a book as if no one else were present. Mrs. Plumtre fidgeted in her chair, seemingly keen to find another subject but not progressing any further than opening her mouth, closing it, and exhaling a humming sound.

"Well, it all sounds wonderful," said Diana suddenly, her voice firm. "I mean to take everything in while I am here, and I am sure I shan't get tired." They all looked at her and she continued confidently, "After all, who knows when I might have another opportunity to visit Bath? I promised my friends at home in Hawcombe Prior that I would have many adventures to relate upon my return. And if they are not wild adventures or very many in number, my friends will all be exceedingly disappointed."

It was not like her to be talkative among strangers, but she pushed herself, not wanting her hosts to dismiss her as another Elizabeth—a Clarendon relative—too haughty and superior for her surroundings.

The young ladies of the house seemed extremely pleased with this reply. Plainly, their sister-in-law's failure to appreciate Bath and its entertainments would never improve their opinion of her, but in Diana they had found a willing tourist.

Hearing her clear, determined voice, George Plumtre even put his book away, as if finally noticing there were other people in the room.

Fifteen

THEY WERE ABOUT TO GO IN TO DINNER WHEN MORE guests arrived and were shown in by the footman.

The group of three entered the drawing room—first a small elderly lady in mourning ribbons, and a younger woman displaying abundant cleavage, too much jewelry, and hair a suspiciously bright shade of copper.

But behind them, tall, lean, and magnificent in a dark green evening coat with an ivory silk cravat, was none other than…a man the very image of Nathaniel Sherringham.

How could it be?

Diana felt stuck to her chair.

His gaze swiftly traversed the room and stumbled to a halt when it found her.

There was a moment of confusion, which assured Diana that he had not come there on purpose to follow her, and then he blinked and looked away.

What was he doing at Wollaford? Oh Lord. Had ever a woman been so abused by fate?

Diana wound her fingers together in her lap and finally

remembered to breathe. She was a new woman today, a brave woman. Not sitting in a corner, hiding in shadow.

The lady in mourning—Mrs. Ashby—explained in a faint, sad voice, "This gentleman was good enough to escort my niece to Bath. I persuaded the two of them to join me this evening. I do hope you don't mind." She directed this last sentence at Mrs. Plumtre, who hastened to assure her that it was no trouble at all to accommodate two more at her table.

"We always have room at Wollaford Park, do we not, Jonty?"

"Of course, Mama. Plenty of room at the trough, what ho?"

Diana saw her cousin Elizabeth wincing as if someone had stood on her foot and belched in her face.

While Nathaniel bowed to each lady in the room, Diana's pulse skipped and danced. She almost didn't dare look up at him, but she had to. How could she not? How could her eyes ignore his male beauty?

Each time she saw him, it was as if his looks had improved yet again—or perhaps it was simply because she dared look longer. His manners certainly had changed for the better since their first meeting ten years ago. He did not fidget restlessly the way he once had when he entered a room. He now exuded a quiet confidence that commanded attention.

"This is my wife's cousin," Sir Jonty boomed pleasantly. "Miss Diana Makepiece came to us all the way from the wilds of Buckinghamshire."

Her eyes met Nathaniel's. A slight smile turned up one end of his lips. "Miss Makepiece, I am delighted to make your acquaintance."

So he meant to pretend they'd never met.

She was relieved. They could act as if they were strangers. It would be a clean page for both of them.

Her cousin Elizabeth would not know of their connection. Although she'd met Rebecca Sherringham during brief visits to Hawcombe Prior, she would be unlikely to link the captain to his sister. Elizabeth was not the sort to remember names unless they were attached to nobility or great wealth, and she had considered Rebecca too uncouth and far below her notice.

In fact, Diana was amused now to watch Elizabeth inspect Nathaniel with transparent appreciation and flap her fan hard enough to be in danger of taking flight. Her cousin was not the only one instantly rendered breathless, of course. The young Miss Plumtres gazed up at him with enormous calf eyes and completely forgot to say anything for ten minutes, which was the longest they'd been silent since Diana arrived.

When Nathaniel introduced his companion as Mrs. Caroline Sayles, Diana realized this was the infamous adulteress. She tried not to care. After all, it was, as she'd said to him, none of her business.

The moment Mrs. Sayles's name was spoken aloud it had an echo effect, speedily circling the room on a fraught whisper. The woman's infamy must have spread far and wide because even the Miss Plumtres seemed to know of it. They glanced at each other and then at the colorful guest with unconcealed and lurid inquisitiveness. Diana hoped her own expression had not betrayed her too. It would be far more ladylike to pretend she did not know the things that were said about Mrs. Sayles. A proper lady never listened to gossip or let down her guard to stare in complete horror—the way cousin Elizabeth was currently doing.

Keeping her own composure as best she could, Diana felt Nathaniel's wondering gaze touch her frequently. This coincidence of them being thrust together again must be just as bewildering to him as it was to her. However calm she kept her expression, Diana was bursting inside with startling and intense pleasure at seeing him. His company and his warm smile were unexpected gifts that caught her with her drawbridge and her defenses down.

Although he spoke with his usual self-assurance during the introductions, Nathaniel seemed subdued, as if he was making an effort to be less effusive. She couldn't imagine why, because he should have been in his element, surrounded by heaving bosoms and pretty, adoring faces.

But a curious thing happened. He looked most often at Diana and saved his smile for her alone. It was tempting to imagine she was the only woman he saw tonight, but that would be foolish vanity.

That did not mean that Diana, the virgin goddess, shouldn't smile back at him.

Hadn't she made up her mind to be more sociable here, to venture out of her shell and be brave?

When he caught her responding smile, he looked askance, touching his cuffs with fingers that suddenly seemed endearingly nervous. She couldn't think why he would be. It was only a smile, for pity's sake, and he must be accustomed to many of those from women.

Testing her power, she smiled at him again, and he almost tripped backward over the edge of a rug.

Clearly he wasn't prepared for the newly improved Bath and Somersetshire version of Miss Diana Makepiece.

❧

In the warm marmalade tint of candlelight, Diana's face shone with more vibrancy than he had seen it of late. The surprise of finding her there was slow to pass and still skidded and bumped through his body as they sat down to dine. Just when he had despaired, there she was before him again.

Although there were many conversations at the table—for the Plumtres were a loud family, and they did not wait for each other to stop talking before they began—his ears were tuned to Diana's voice and his eyes led to hers most often.

Tonight she engaged in the discussion more than usual. Perhaps she was making an effort while she was out in company without her mother at her side. She was bolder, letting her light shine again. The freedom could only be good for her.

Nathaniel's gaze followed the elegant arch of her slender neck and traveled to the little dip below her ear where he longed to place his lips and dampen her skin with his tongue. It would be all the sweet dessert he needed.

Instantly he closed the door on that thought. She was a lady, not a strumpet. Diana had offered him friendship as they stood together by the old mill door, hiding from the rain. He didn't know what her feelings were beyond that, and he shouldn't let his own desires run away with him again. Remembering his sister's advice about safe topics of conversation, he said, "Miss Makepiece, I hope the weather was pleasant for your journey. Few things are less convenient or more uncomfortable than travel in bad weather. Spring can be unpredictable."

"Yes. It was quite favorable, Captain." Usually she would volunteer no more information, but tonight she swallowed, took a breath, and added, "A husband of a very dear friend traveled with me. He was a good companion so I did not mind the length of the journey." With no mother to deliver a cutting glare when she spoke, Diana's voice gained volume as well as spirit. "He enjoyed his newspaper and I enjoyed my book. I do not think two people have ever traveled so far together in proximity without the need to quarrel or say anything much at all."

"And how do you find Bath?"

"I have not seen much of it yet, except through a carriage window, but I look forward to exploring the town." She smiled, and he thought of a tightly budded rose slowly unfurling its petals.

The young Plumtre sisters began advising her about all the places she should visit while she was there. Nathaniel would have joined in, but Caroline, seated beside him, fought for his attention by plucking at his sleeve again. He saw Diana glance at the woman in mild bemusement. Did she still think this was his mistress?

No doubt Diana had not believed his protests to the contrary, and now here he was with Caroline still at his side. This would probably be proof enough for Diana. Yes, her lips were smug, a little twitch dimpling her cheek. And her eyebrows were back to their old mischief, expressing the things she would not or could not say aloud. He imagined her thinking, *Oh, Sherry, you haven't changed at all.*

How glad he was to see those eyebrows alive again.

"Will you stay long in Bath, Captain Sherringham?" Sir Jonathan shouted down the table at him.

"I…may stay longer than I intended." Glancing at Diana through the tall candles, he saw her look down at her plate. He followed the graceful movement of her fingers as she picked up her knife.

Sir Jonathan went on to question him about whether he liked hunting, shooting, cards—all the usual pursuits of a gentleman. When cards were mentioned, Diana's eyes briefly found his again.

"I do enjoy a game, Sir Jonathan," he answered, "but not to the extent I once did. I've wagered too much in the past and finally learned to curb that impulse. And others. Mostly."

"Ah, all young men have a rite of passage at the gaming tables. 'Tis naught amiss as long as it is all in good fun, what? I like a little wager myself. But you'll find plenty here to keep you busy. I always say there is something for everybody in Bath. I never went in for this sea bathing that is so popular now and lures folk off to Brighton and Weymouth. As my sisters were telling Miss Makepiece, there is a great deal of good entertainment here."

"Yes," Nathaniel replied. "I see that there is."

Diana kept her gaze lowered, refusing to meet his.

So then Nathaniel said, "Actually, Sir Jonathan, I came to find myself a wife."

He heard Caroline's knife clatter against her plate. All other noises ceased. The ladies present appeared to breathe as one, exhaling a mighty sigh in unison. Except for Diana, who ate on as if he had not spoken. Candlelight sizzled under her black lashes and specks of gold leaf danced among the emerald of her eyes.

"You never did!" Caroline exclaimed crossly. "You're not fit for a permanent relationship, and you said that many times!"

For a moment, everybody paused what they were doing. Diana looked mortified for the woman. Not that Caroline Sayles appeared to note the effect of her impolite remark. Nathaniel, racing to the rescue as usual, gallantly tried to smooth it over for her with a little teasing jest.

"My dear Mrs. Sayles, a man is entitled to change his mind. Or is it only women who claim that prerogative?"

"Claim what?" she snapped, spraying his sleeve with little flakes of salmon.

"I hope to find a lady going spare in Bath," he continued, calmly wiping a napkin over his arm, "anything between fifteen and thirty, robust and merry, likes to dance… I'm not terribly fastidious."

The elderly Mrs. Plumtre laughed. "I like a man who's honest and direct about his purpose, do I not, Jonty?"

"Indeed you do, Mama." Sir Jonathan joined her in a hearty chuckle. "You had better watch out, Captain Sherringham, about making such bold statements in the presence of young ladies, or you might find yourself ambushed! Susy and Daisy will be after you now, and I don't envy you trying to escape my little sisters."

He and his mother continued to laugh, and the two young girls blushed. Diana's eyes finally looked up again and sought his, bemused.

Sir Jonathan's mother found some breath between her chuckles and exclaimed, "Surely a gentleman such as yourself has had many opportunities to find a bride."

"I was in the army and traveled extensively. There was no time to consider a wife and family until I was in a position to settle down. I daresay that was what Mrs. Sayles meant. There was a time in my life when I enjoyed the freedom to come and go. I made the most of it."

Again he felt Diana watching him.

"Now I am thirty, financially prepared, and my business thrives. I recently—very recently"—he threw her a quick glance—"decided this is as good a time as any."

"Very sound," his genial host agreed. "I waited a good while before I chose to marry. One gets one's gun aimed at the hog before one pulls the trigger, what ho?"

His wife, Lady Plumtre, glowered at the fellow, her nostrils flaring.

He went on, oblivious, beaming at his wife. "Now we wait for the first litter, of course, to hear the clatter of merry little trotters, eh, my dear?"

She set her glass down with a bang that almost cracked the crystal.

Nathaniel caught Diana swallowing the urge to laugh, just as he did the same. In that moment, he lost the last remnants of anger he'd nursed against her for rejecting his proposal. It was impossible to remain bitter when sharing a joke with her.

Yes, she was looking much improved, flourishing in new surroundings like a plant moved to a bigger pot. Thinking of his sister's gardening analogy, he chuckled softly.

A quizzical look passed over Diana's face and he straightened his lips, staring at her for a moment and wishing he could see inside her mind.

"And what is your business, Captain?" Lady Plumtre inquired stiffly.

He forced his attention back to the conversation. "Hospitality, madam."

"Inns?"

"Some, yes, but more specifically the ale and cider served within them."

Diana's eyes flared with a sudden understanding. "I believe I saw your name several times on my journey to Bath," she said softly, as if speaking only for his ears.

"I daresay you did."

"But I did not know it was the same Sherringham. I had no idea, for you never said." Her lashes flickered. "I mean to say…when we were introduced tonight, I did not realize you were the same Sherringham." A light flush swept her face, but no one else seemed to notice her slip.

There was something entirely too naughty about her expression. Something new. He'd never felt such heated desire surge through his blood. But he had misread her before, let his fanciful imagination run away with him, and then suffered great hurt.

It could not happen again. He was not the same reckless boy.

"You have never come close to being engaged, sir?" jolly Mrs. Plumtre persisted. "A handsome fellow like yourself, I wager you have broken many hearts!"

"I did think myself in love once, but the lady did not return my affections. I proposed and was summarily rejected." Nathaniel stretched one leg under the table, found her toe with his, and pressed it lightly. Alas, the impulse to misbehave was still there. He hadn't quite outgrown it, he realized, chagrined.

Diana raised her napkin to her lips. When he slid his foot under her hem and touched her ankle, she almost leaped out of her chair.

"How terrible!" exclaimed one of the Plumtre girls—he didn't know which she was, but the expression on her rosy face exuded compassion through the candles. Her sister agreed with a kittenish mewl of sympathy.

"It cured me of the thought of marriage for some time," he added somberly. "But perhaps it was for the best. I was young and aimless then. I had made no plans for the future, and the young lady was wise to point that out to me. Although at the time I found her brutal honesty hard to bear, I have come to understand her reasons, even if I cannot fully forgive her for the words she used."

"You've never mentioned this before, Sherry," cried Caroline. "You said there was never anyone special."

He laughed uneasily.

"You didn't want a wife, you said, because then you might have to spend every night with her," she added.

Gazes raced up and down the table, some confused, some amused, at least one lady appalled. Even George blushed. As for Diana, he couldn't tell. Her brows were still, her gaze lowered.

Nathaniel explained in a light tone, "I meant only that regularly closing one's eyes for an extended time in the company of a woman does seem a risk, does it not? After all, familiarity breeds contempt, as they say, and a woman in a vengeful rage—as a wife sometimes will be—can be a terrible creature."

His host agreed wholeheartedly. "One keeps separate bedchambers. And even a bolt on the door to keep a spouse at bay. My wife finds that quite necessary from time to time, what ho, Lizzie?"

This conversation had gone altogether too far for Lady Plumtre. She looked as if she longed for the release of sudden, swift death.

But Nathaniel stole a hasty glance at Diana and caught the slightest twitch that betrayed her lips to be on the verge of uncontrolled laughter again. Her breathing was labored, her delectable bosom rising and falling rapidly in the kiss of candlelight. Like two peaches in a pretty muslin handkerchief, ripe for tasting, he mused.

He cleared his throat with a short cough. "I suppose separate sleeping arrangements are wise. I should not want to give a wife access to my defenseless form while I sleep. Who knows what she might get up to?"

The candle flames fluttered wildly as the ladies around the table reacted with gasps and giggles. Diana threw him a warning look, trying to be stern.

"She could put mustard on my tongue while I snore," he added, "and shave all the hair off my…head."

Mrs. Plumtre covered her mouth with both hands. Her eyes were wide one moment, but screwed up with good humor the next, and her shoulders shook with stifled laughter. Her daughter-in-law's mouth tightened, creases settling around it in a well-established pattern.

"But I suppose I can be brave and submit to the dangers of marriage as other men before me have done." He chuckled, wiping his mouth on the napkin. "Invest in a few sturdy bolts. For both our sakes."

"Well, it is good for us that other young lady turned you down before," Mrs. Plumtre cheerily assured him. "Now my girls will have the pleasure of buying new gowns and bonnets in which to chase you around the Pump Room. The gentlemen's hunting might be over for the season, but the ladies' sport has just begun." She winked, breaking into more laughter that shook her curves and was contagious, sweeping up the rest of her family. Except for her daughter-in-law and grim-faced George, the bereaved fiancé who seldom contributed to the conversation.

The sound of Mrs. Ashby blowing her nose into her napkin like a ship's foghorn reminded them all of her presence, her lost daughter, and that engagement recently undone by tragedy. Mrs. Plumtre guiltily bottled her laughter and patted George's hand where it rested beside hers on the tablecloth.

Abruptly one of the Plumtre sisters exclaimed, "Perhaps you are still in love with that lady who refused you, Captain. What if you saw her again? You might feel the same now as you did then."

"Nonsense," her sister-in-law said bitterly. "Men do not retain that first flush of desire for long. Their attention spans are not equal to those of women." She glared in her husband's direction, but Sir Jonathan was enjoying his salmon and not listening to a word she said.

"But look at Georgy," the younger girl insisted. "He is still in love with Eleanor, and she's de... I mean"—she blushed—"she's not coming back."

"That's probably *why* he's so fond of her," Lady Plumtre drawled as she picked at her food. "No one is ever quite so well thought of as they are when they're dead."

This cold remark, dropped heavily and callously, left another deep hole in the conversation, until Nathaniel, anxious to save Mrs. Ashby's feelings from further hurt, said quickly, "Well, I can promise you all that since my disastrous marriage proposal to the lady who once spurned me, I have learned my lesson. I have grown up since then. Which, ironically, is what she advised me to do." He paused for a sip of wine. "I often wonder what she would think of me now. If we ever met again...if I might have improved in her eyes."

Look at me, Diana. But she would not look up now. Those green eyes refused to see how he had changed.

Sir Jonathan's hearty laughter stirred the candle flames again, and then he boomed down the table, "As my mama says, hunting is over, but no doubt you like to ride, Captain. I'd happily show you around the estate while you're here. I'm planting a good number of new trees and have just begun to build a Grecian folly by the lake. You must come with me tomorrow, Sherringham, and allow me to show off, what ho? Another fellow's opinion is always welcome, and you shall have luncheon with us at the lodge if the ladies have no objection."

"I would like that very much, Sir Jonathan." Nathaniel's smile was directed at Diana across the table, but she still avoided eye contact.

"You trip along tomorrow and we'll have a cold luncheon with pork pie and cucumber, eh? Just the thing for a spring day." Ignoring his wife's furious scowl, he waved his wineglass at Nathaniel. "And you must call me Jonty. Everyone does, you know."

"Then I insist that you call me Sherry. It is the name I am most often called by my friends." The young Miss Plumtres burst into frothy giggles, as if he'd said something remarkably funny. After a moment he realized this jollity was caused merely by his smile. Hastily, he checked the reflection of his teeth in the blade of a knife and, finding nothing unsightly stuck there between them, continued to smile. Why not? He liked to make ladies laugh, of course. Surely there was nothing wrong with it. When he experimented, widening his smile, this produced yet more breathless chuckles and considerable heaving of the young ladies' bosoms.

Suddenly he looked over at Diana and caught her rolling her eyes. She now turned to George Plumtre, asking him gently about his fondness for poetry.

Nathaniel's smile faded.

He didn't think he had behaved too badly. But he couldn't help his mood being jocular, his spirits light and merry. She was there before him again, so how could he not be happy? He might have said things a gentleman shouldn't in the company of ladies, but that was her fault. She made his heart beat too fast, and he wasn't made of stone like her. He'd tried to be when he came back.

God *and* the devil knew he'd tried.

❧

So that was how he made his money. A brewery. Diana heard him talking more about it after dinner as he and Jonty sat together by the fire, the dogs sprawled at their feet. Her mother would probably not approve of a fortune earned through ale, she mused, so it was just as well he kept the source of his new wealth close to his chest and under his beautifully embroidered waistcoat.

He was not engaged to Lucy Bridges, then. Or Lucy Brydges, she mentally corrected herself, remembering the family's rise up the rungs of society. The realization that Nathaniel was still unattached swept over her in a cool wave of relief, although it shouldn't matter so much. Poor Lucy must be disappointed. Hopefully the sadness would soon pass for her. If only the young woman would open her eyes and see how much she meant to Sam Hardacre—but he was a quiet soul who kept his feelings hidden to preserve his pride.

Diana knew all about that and felt great empathy for the man.

Nathaniel would say it was the carpenter's fault for not speaking up. "Sherry" had no understanding of the difficulties faced by those who were not blessed with an excess of self-confidence.

A smile teased her lips as she thought of his brazen announcement at dinner. *I came to find myself a wife.* Only Sherry would have the gall to say that in the company of several unmarried ladies.

But despite that comment and his lapse at dinner, he definitely was trying to dim the light now. Although he answered the Plumtre sisters' many impertinent questions, he did so in the manner of a benevolent, patient older brother. The naughtiness he'd exhibited earlier in the dining room was now carefully packed away and he was on better behavior.

He did not sit near Caroline Sayles and seemed cool toward her. There was no sign of affection or even friendship between them. Left alone, Caroline sat with a plate of marzipan on her lap and slowly tasted her way through it, nibbling little pieces of the colored sweets and putting each one back to try another. Although she had complained of an upset stomach earlier that evening, her appetite seemed unaffected. From across the room Elizabeth watched this with ever-increasing horror and kept trying—in vain—to get her husband's attention so he would take the plate away.

But Diana, who knew what it was to be the target of disapproving gazes and to feel awkward and out of place, felt some compassion for Caroline Sayles. She saw all that discontent and ill-mannered squirming and twitching as nerves. Caroline picked at her teeth, drank too much wine, and frequently adjusted her gown, but since no one engaged her in conversation what else was she to do? She could not leave until the man who had brought her was ready to go. In the meantime, it could not be very pleasant to know that one was being gossiped about, one's dirty laundry aired by strangers. At some point, Diana supposed, it must chafe upon even the most audacious spirit and cause a callused, toughened skin.

In Diana's left ear, George Plumtre was reciting some dull, woebegone poetry, reading from the book in which he'd been absorbed earlier that evening. Diana had lost interest several tedious verses ago, unable to concentrate while her gaze traveled across the room and her ears followed, listening for Nathaniel's voice. But George's rumbling recital rolled onward with a great deal of emphasis on all the wrong words, jerking her attention back and forth.

"Mr. Plumtre," she said when at last he finished, "I do think perhaps you might find something more cheerful to read. Once in a while."

He looked at her. "But I am grieving. I mourn the loss of my darling Eleanor."

"Of course. Your grief is understandable," she replied gently, "but you must allow yourself to heal eventually, and wallowing in the constant company of such poetry will not help that process." Now that she'd begun expressing her opinions out loud, Diana found the process very freeing. And much easier the more she did it. *Best not get carried away*, she thought. *Wouldn't want to turn into another Mrs. Kenton!* "That is merely my supposition, however. If you feel it is helping you, then by all means continue. You would know what is best for yourself."

His gloomy face, and particularly his jowls, were on a fast descent toward the carpet. "But why should I wish to heal when I have lost my beloved Eleanor?"

He showed her a small oval-framed portrait that fit in the palm of his hand. "It was delivered to me this evening by Captain Sherringham. Now you can see her beauty."

"Captain Sherringham delivered it?"

"Mrs. Ashby was beside herself and could not manage the task. She asked the fellow to undertake it for her, and he did so in such a kind, understanding manner that I think he must know what it is to suffer a broken heart."

Nathaniel and his good deeds again. So that was why he had come tonight.

"I see." Sensing Nathaniel's eyes fixed on her from across the room, Diana was suddenly very glad she'd gone to more trouble with her dress that evening. It was vanity, but it couldn't be helped.

Her ankle itched where his toe had touched it under the table. She was quite sure he'd left her stocking marked with boot polish, but she didn't dare look. Clumsy fool.

"My beloved Eleanor," George said, snuffling. "How can I live on without her?"

"Mr. Plumtre, it is clear she was precious to you, and your devotion to her memory does you credit. But life must be lived, sir. And as fully as one is able. Otherwise what is the point of it all? Someone reminded me recently that there is a difference between selflessness and martyrdom."

"But how can I enjoy life without Eleanor? How can I think of myself and my future without her?"

Diana sighed, looking down at her hands. "We cannot sink under the weight of sadness or regret, because that does no good for anybody." Diana thought of her mother, eaten up with bitterness because of what she didn't have, never taking time to appreciate what she did have, or that she had been lucky enough to know love and passion at least once. Many people never had that. Or they missed their chance. "We must live life while we have it."

"You too have known sorrow of the heart, Miss Makepiece? I see it in your eyes and hear it in your voice."

"I have known disappointment and heartache, yes."

She wanted to tell Nathaniel she was sorry for her tone of voice all those years ago when she'd rejected his proposal. It was true that she might have let him down with gentler words. Not that her answer could have been anything different. Even if she could have set her other reservations aside—had they thrown caution to the wind and married—they would have struggled financially.

Who could have helped them? However well-meaning, his father had limited resources back then and had managed his own affairs poorly. Most importantly, an elopement would have meant abandoning her mother, betraying her. For Diana's entire life it had been only the two of them, and she owed her mother for all those years of struggle.

As for Nathaniel, the additional burden of a wife and ultimately children would have dragged him down. Once the first glow of passion wore off, and with hard times and poverty breathing down his neck, resentment would have set in. And as her mother said, a man was free to travel, to leave. The woman was always the one left behind to raise the children.

Yet he had shown himself capable of improvement since then. He had turned his life around and found a measure of success that could not have been predicted three years ago. She could almost imagine he'd done that to show her what she gave up. What she might have had, if only she was braver. If only she had more faith in him.

"I have learned to go on as best I can," she added thoughtfully.

George Plumtre seemed annoyed that anyone might lay claim to as much grief as his own. "Perhaps your heartache was not so great, Miss Makepiece, if you are able to go on."

"I do not know the extent of your suffering, but I know my own. The agony of having to give up the chance of happiness while seeing others find love… knowing I might have had the same. Once. But that chance slipped away from me, and I let it go. In that respect, sir, our grief differs, for I can blame no one but myself."

Afraid of risking her heart, she had never been a gambler. But tonight she looked at Nathaniel, and her duties as a good daughter—a girl who never did wrong—were set aside as she awoke at last to her desires as a woman. As her own woman, seeing him for the first time.

Later that night when they returned to the lodge, Elizabeth had little good to say of the evening. "That dreadful Sayles woman! To think that I, a Clarendon, should be forced into such company. We shall become the laughingstock of Bath if it is known that we harbored that woman."

"You make Mrs. Sayles sound like a flea-bitten stray," Diana murmured. "I'm sure she is as worthy of kindness and tolerance as anybody. Should a Clarendon, with her many advantages in life, not look charitably on those less fortunate?" Although she knew her words would fall on deaf ears, she had to speak. Diana was full of nervous energy after the shock of seeing Nathaniel again.

"Charity indeed!" Elizabeth muttered. "I will not stand the Sayles woman's common company for another evening like tonight. This takes charity to obscene lengths. I hope we are not dragged into further iniquitous acquaintance. Where will it end?"

Her husband assured her that Mrs. Sayles would soon leave the area. "She ain't known for staying long in one place, as far as I hear," he boomed. "Mayhap she'll meet another fellow hereabouts and ride off with him."

"I hope she does, for she will eat her way through the Wollaford pantry if she stays another month."

"'Tis plain she had her hooks out for Sherry, but he assures me he has no interest of that sort in the lady and only brought her to her aunt for a good deed. As I said to him," Jonty said with a laugh, "no good deed goes unpunished!"

On her way up to bed, hearing her own thoughts of that relationship confirmed, Diana smiled. Sherry and his valiant deeds! He simply must stop rescuing ladies.

She forgot what a long day it had been and that she ought to be yearning for her bed. Alone in her room once the maid left, she drank Dr. Penny's tonic, wrapped her hair in curling papers, and then nestled into her plumped pillow to read another chapter of Anne Elliot's story.

> *"Poor Frederick!" said he at last. "Now he must begin all over again with somebody else. I think we must get him to Bath. Sophy must write, and beg him to come to Bath. Here are pretty girls enough, I am sure… Do not you think, Miss Elliot, we had better try to get him to Bath?"*

Oh yes, Diana thought, her eyelids finally too drowsy to hold open any longer, *do get Captain Wentworth to Bath, for Anne's sake.* Bath was a good place, and strange, wonderful things happened there.

Sixteen

No, it was not regret which made Anne's heart beat in spite of herself, and brought the colour into her cheeks when she thought of Captain Wentworth unshackled and free. She had some feelings which she was ashamed to investigate.

—Persuasion

NATHANIEL RODE OUT THE NEXT DAY WITH JONTY. When he called at the lodge, it was early and the ladies were at breakfast. The captain did not come in to greet them, because it was not an hour for visitors. There was a brief ruckus in the hall and then the two men left, taking the dogs with them.

"I must say," Elizabeth said, abandoning her kedgeree to look out the casement window and straining to watch the men ride off, "the captain is extremely well favored. It is rare to see the like these days. Perhaps some of his sartorial elegance will rub off on my husband." She sighed. "One can only hope."

Diana thought Sir Jonty cut a rather smart figure, besides which his generous character more than made up for any rough edges, but her cousin was harder to please when it came to appearances and did not care as much about what lay beneath.

Oh…what lay beneath Nathaniel's fine clothes…

Diana didn't realize how large a bite of toast she'd bitten off until it caught in her throat on the way down.

While she quietly choked into her napkin, Elizabeth returned to her own breakfast. "It is a great pity he keeps company with that dreadful Sayles creature." She paused, shrugging her shoulders. "And that is a relationship I cannot comprehend. I thought she was his mistress, but he speaks so boldly before her of seeking a bride. It is all very odd."

"I do not believe it is anything more than a friendship," Diana offered timidly. "As he told Sir Jonty—"

"You know nothing about men, Cousin, and it is best if you refrain from trying to pretend that you do. Whatever he claims about the acquaintance, I would not trust his word."

Utterly set back by this comment, Diana fell silent again.

"All men suffer a lack of judgment occasionally," Elizabeth continued through an unladylike full mouth. "Until they settle down in marriage, it is common for such mistakes to be observed and the wrong company to be kept. Besides"—she swallowed hurriedly and took a gulp of coffee before getting up to peer through the window again—"the captain is not only very pleasing on the eye but on his way to becoming extremely wealthy. Jonty says that brewery is worth a pretty penny and expanding all over the countryside with its own tied public houses."

That, of course, made up for any lapses in Nathaniel's behavior and keeping the wrong company, Diana mused. The power of money. It was indeed, as her mother had said, everything in their world.

"I know what my husband is up to, sly thing," Elizabeth added. "He wants to get the captain for one of his sisters, to be sure." She laughed. "All the ale he can drink *and* a fortune. He cannot pass that up. So he is keen to believe whatever the man tells him about the Sayles woman."

Diana said nothing, but her silence did not discourage Elizabeth, who continued in this vein.

"Susanna will probably win out, being the older, but I thought he was more interested in Daisy at the dining table and she is a cunning creature with few scruples. Susanna will have to look out for herself or her younger sister will steal him away. The sooner he is separated from that Sayles woman, the better. Oh, that hair of hers! I felt for sure it was a wig when first I saw it, but apparently not."

Diana refused to disparage that poor woman just to make herself feel better. There was too much of that going on, and that sort of talk was one of Elizabeth's favorite pastimes.

Suddenly her cousin added, "If I might say, Diana, you also made rather an exhibit of yourself last night."

Diana paused, coffee cup halfway to her lips. "Me?"

"Trying to monopolize Captain Sherringham's attention in such an obvious way. I cannot imagine what you were about. He's not likely to have any interest in you, and you ought to give others a share of the conversation."

Diana set her cup down again. "I didn't think I—"

"You pushed yourself forward at every opportunity. I did not know where to look."

She couldn't even think of a response to that. Oh dear, had she made a fool of herself?

"As for the Plumtres, there is no need for you to ingratiate yourself with them, crawling into their good graces. I suppose you thought to make me look bad and a poor sport by going along with everything."

"I merely meant to be polite, Elizabeth. They are, after all, my hosts."

"And what am I? I sent for you to come here and be company for me, not to gad about like a butterfly."

Shocked, Diana assured her cousin that she had not deliberately done or said anything to slight her in the eyes of her in-laws, and Elizabeth's energies were soon redirected in shouting irritably to the butler for more coffee.

Their breakfast was interrupted a short while later by the arrival of Sir Jonty's sisters. Having dashed in like two greyhounds after a rabbit, they were anxious to dash back out again immediately, and much to Elizabeth's evident dissatisfaction, they had only come to collect Diana and take her out walking with them.

"What about me? I am to be left alone again?" Elizabeth complained.

The girls hesitated and Daisy frowned. "We didn't think you'd want to come."

"And we planned to walk a fair distance," Susanna added earnestly, as if concern for their sister-in-law was their only motive. "The ground is still damp and we are on foot."

But Elizabeth would not let them go without her. They were forced to wait while she finished her coffee, found a coat and walking boots, changed that coat for another, went back for gloves, and then stopped to apply lip balm and rose oil.

⤝

Chattering without pause, the Plumtre girls walked as quickly as their brother had the evening before, but they took Diana and Elizabeth in another direction, toward the lake. A sister on either side of her, they gripped Diana's arms and marched her along.

"It was very good of you to talk to George yesterday, Miss Makepiece. His mood was much lifted."

"Really?" Diana was doubtful of that because he had looked just as sad when she left.

"Oh yes, indeed. He talked of you for the rest of the evening until he finally trundled off to bed."

They walked on rapidly, neither girl looking where she stepped and occasionally forcing the group into a puddle. Chattering almost constantly, the sisters paused only to shriek with excessive alarm and excitement whenever a rabbit appeared or a bird took flight from a nearby tree.

Elizabeth followed a fair distance behind, complaining about the mud and stopping often to catch her breath.

Daisy whispered, "Why did *she* have to come?"

Diana was rather hoping the exertion would wear her cousin out enough to silence her complaints, make her retire earlier tonight, and leave Diana in peace.

"Look"—Susanna pointed at Jonty and Nathaniel—"there they are. How handsome he is!"

"His shoulders are wider than Mr. Rowland's," said Daisy.

"Who is Mr. Rowland?"

"He's a gentleman who was sweet on Susy last winter, but Lizzie didn't think him good enough."

"He was not sweet on me. What a thing to say!"

"Indeed he was and you liked him."

"Well, I'm sure I did not."

"Although he was a dreadful prig, he had very good thighs and reasonably fine buttocks."

"Daisy!"

"What? He did…for riding purposes, I meant! Come on, let's catch up with them!"

Diana was dragged along again by the two young ladies, her boots slipping in the mud. She strained to look over her shoulder. "Perhaps we can sit a while on that stone bench and wait for Elizabeth."

"Good Lord, no."

"But—"

"She would not want us to wait."

"Oh, I think she would."

"No, no. Let her go at her own pace!"

They whisked Diana along, laughing and shouting for their brother, oblivious to the muddy state of their petticoats.

Finally hearing this stampede, the two riders stopped and looked back.

Diana felt her face heat up, fearing Nathaniel would think she'd voluntarily run after him like this, utterly abandoning all dignity.

"Here we are," yelled Daisy. "What a coincidence that we should run into you!"

Sir Jonty chortled. "Coincidence, indeed! You are after the captain, as I warned him."

Neither girl seemed the least ashamed to admit it. Ladylike modesty was clearly unknown to them.

Both men dismounted to greet the ladies and make civil inquiries about their walk.

"It has certainly put color in Miss Makepiece's cheeks," Nathaniel observed with a wry smile.

Breathing hard, she did her best to smile back. *Not too much, you fool. Just a little. You wouldn't want him to think you're flirting.*

She must have caught something from the Plumtre sisters, she thought helplessly, because suddenly his height and the breadth of his shoulders were too much for a well-behaved woman.

"Perhaps you're tired. I would gladly lend you my horse."

At that moment her legs did feel rather soft and likely to buckle, but she was determined to prove herself just as strong as anybody, so she declined the offer.

"Jonty was showing me the plans for his folly, Miss Makepiece." Instantly a large scroll of paper was thrust into her hands and the two men began to talk of columns and steps and Italian marble, as if she understood every word. She could go nowhere, of course, while she was holding the plans and they both were looking over her shoulders.

"What do you think, Miss Makepiece?" Sir Jonty bellowed. "Will it not look very fine reflected in the water here? When the mists rise on an autumn morning?" He pointed across the lake to where the folly was currently abandoned a quarter of the way to completion. "And in the evening, on warm summer nights with stars shining above it?"

She could not answer because, standing so close to Nathaniel's body, his heat was almost too much to bear. The best she could manage was a low hum of deep consideration, as if pondering the questions tossed back and forth over her head.

"But it won't be complete for ages," exclaimed Daisy. "Don't say we have to wait for the folly before you hold that ball you promised, Jonty! Last year it was put off because of George's fiancée. If you keep putting it off, Susy and I will be in our dotage before we get to enjoy a ball here at Wollaford."

Her brother beamed. "Don't fret, Daisy. You will get your ball." He turned to Diana. "What do you think of a summer ball at Wollaford, Miss Makepiece?"

The girls also stared at her, their faces shining with hope.

"I…think that would…be a very good idea."

"Excellent! Since Miss Makepiece agrees, we shall indeed have a ball."

Flattered as she was to be the person upon whom that decision appeared to have rested, Diana was also somewhat startled by it.

By then Elizabeth had caught up with the group. Fortunately she was out of breath, or she would surely have had a few very angry things to say about being left to struggle through the mud alone. Instead, flushed and bedraggled, she saved her darkest scowl for Diana when she found her there between the two men, holding the building plans and seemingly in the center of all decisions.

Diana did not want to be accused again of monopolizing anyone's attention or thinking she knew anything about men. Heaven forbid. She tried ducking out of the way and leaving the gentlemen to hold the plans, but Nathaniel would not take his side of the paper. Instead he reached across to point at something drawn on the plans, and she inhaled a deep breath of his manly scent—warm leather, boot polish, and sandalwood.

Newly awakened to some dangerous fancies—only now acknowledging them for what they were—and still feeling the angry pinch of her cousin's spiteful regard, Diana backed away so desperately that she almost tripped into the reeds by the edge of the lake.

Nathaniel reached out, catching her coat sleeve in the nick of time.

She looked down at his firm hand, alarm skipping and darting around inside her body.

"Do take care, Miss Makepiece," he muttered, frowning.

Suddenly there was a shout of greeting from the water, and they all spun around to see George Plumtre in a small rowboat.

"Good morning, Miss Makepiece!" He paused with his oars out of the water, letting his boat drift into the reeds. "Perhaps you will do the honor of joining me on a boat ride. The lake is peaceful this time of the morning, and I can show you where the swans nest."

Nathaniel's hand left her sleeve as if it had stung him somehow.

Diana didn't know what to do. The idea of a boat ride with mournful George was not inspiring, but he looked so hopeful. Suddenly his sisters were pushing her forward.

"Do go with Georgy. You will cheer his mood again, Miss Makepiece."

"He is in need of your gentle company," Susanna whispered. "You are so very good for him."

Horrified, Diana realized now why they had dragged her half a mile over muddy grass. She looked up at Nathaniel and saw his expression closed off in an odd way. He stared at George and then at her again, but he said nothing as the young ladies steered her toward the boat. His lips formed a straight, firm line, all merriment gone.

It was too late to refuse now; to do so would be rude. What excuse could she possibly come up with, anyway? Two moments later she was seated in the other end of the dangerously rocking rowboat and moving away from the group at the bank. She could hear the Miss Plumtres laughing and chattering, but she didn't look back.

She blew out a deep breath and tried to smile at George.

"How fortuitous that you should be out walking with my sisters," he said, apparently not at all aware of the machinations of womanhood.

"Yes," she replied with a sigh.

Diana Makepiece, you might as well resign yourself to the fact that you had your chance. No need to sulk! Sherry might have announced his intention to find a bride, but as he had said at the dining table last night, he would not ask the same woman twice, especially after the harsh way she refused him the first time.

In any case, she didn't want a man. And he would be better off with one of the Plumtre sisters. They had youth on their side and—as Elizabeth had said—considerable quickness of mind, as well as beauty.

No, no, Captain Sherringham could have no interest in Diana anymore. He had offered his horse merely to be kind, considerate of her advanced years no doubt. He had grabbed her sleeve only to save her from an embarrassing trip into the water. It was his way with any woman.

Oh Lord, Gloomy George was already reciting more poetry as he heaved on the oars and the little boat rocked with passion. This time, he assured her, the rhymes were his own creation.

Diana peered over the edge into the dark water and wondered how shocked they would all be if she dove in and swam for the reeds.

She had absolutely no doubt that only one of the men on the bank would actually leap in to save her if they thought she was drowning. Captain Sherringham wouldn't be able to keep himself from rescuing her.

That would certainly give Elizabeth something else to complain about, Diana mused.

Fancy trying to drown yourself just to get attention.

Perhaps she'd save that idea for warmer weather.

When she closed her eyes she saw his image again, framed by the sun as he removed that naughty child from her back, lifted it high overhead with his strapping arms, and laughed, spinning around. And around. His strong, capable arms.

∽

Nathaniel watched the little boat drifting away. Again she had slipped out of his grasp. As he listened to the young ladies, he realized quickly that they had settled on Diana as a perfect match for the bereaved man. Someone to bring him out of his grief.

He was forced to admit that Diana's soft, pleasing voice and sensible manner would be very good for George. But that didn't mean he had to condone the idea.

Was that why her mother had sent her to Bath? Diana seemed to be of the opinion that she didn't need a husband, but of course her mother would want to see her well settled, regardless of Diana's intentions. The Plumtres were landed and wealthy, and they had now formed a connection with the Clarendons, which must make them a suitable family—at least in Mrs. Rosalind Makepiece's view.

"We think Diana is perfectly delicious, don't you, Captain?" one of the young ladies exclaimed. "We are quite enchanted with her."

"Yes," he agreed. "Perfectly delicious." So sweet she made his teeth ache. Not to mention the other parts at her mercy. Even if she had tried to get away from his side so adamantly that she almost ended up in the lake. Was his closeness that abhorrent to her?

Good then. If she stayed out of his way, he wouldn't have to suffer so many confused thoughts and be seized by that utterly humiliating desire. Or smell her dratted perfume.

"I must see the plans for the folly," Lady Plumtre exclaimed. "Why am *I* not asked my opinion? I'm sure I know more about these things than my country cousin."

Nathaniel readily gave up holding his side of the

plans and walked a short way off, pretending to admire the scenery, but he was soon joined by the excitable Plumtre girls who wanted to point out every item of interest on their brother's estate.

"Do you like to fish, Captain?" Susanna asked. He replied that he did, but that he invariably felt too sorry for the captured fish and threw it back.

"I prefer to swim," said Daisy proudly. "I was once dared to swim all the way across the lake."

"And you sank like a stone when you were not halfway across," her sister replied. "It was lucky there were people boating that day and within reach to provide rescue."

"I did not sink! I was caught on some weeds."

"Daisy can never let a dare pass her by, Captain. Much to the detriment of my nerves."

He laughed. "A young lady of gumption, eh?"

"I am not afraid of anything," the girl assured him, chin up, arms swinging. "Why should I be?"

"Quite. I do admire a determined spirit. There are too few of them about these days. Too many women cowed by the constraints of propriety."

When they returned to the lodge for the promised luncheon, Jonty soon had Nathaniel's ear, away from the women, and made it clear that his thoughts were aligned with those of his young sisters.

"That charming Miss Makepiece would be excellent for George. Shake him out of his grief. I am so glad she came. Such a delightful girl. Something so very soothing and reassuring about her presence."

Nathaniel watched the couple together. Diana *was*

livelier than he had seen her in a long time. She was smiling and chatty, not hiding away as she used to. George trailed after her like a lost pup, and she appeared to have great patience for it. Not once did he hear her snap out a curt comment—ask the fellow whether his jacket buttons were caught on her gown or something similar, which was what she would say if Nathaniel scampered after her in the same manner. Nor did she shrink away in abject horror when that man stood near. Too near.

His irritation mounted, quite spoiling the sunny afternoon.

Damn her then, he thought crossly, if she could be impressed by a milksop who did nothing but droop over books all day. But if that was what she preferred, so be it.

When Lady Plumtre asked Nathaniel whether he would like more tea, he snapped out that he'd had enough, and everyone looked at him in astonishment. He coughed, laughed uneasily, and quickly turned to Jonty, raising the subject of hounds and their training.

Later, when the opportunity arose, he moved closer to where Diana and George were seated together and in quiet conversation. He hadn't meant to contribute to it, merely to stand near and listen, but Diana turned to him suddenly and said, "We were talking of poetry, Captain Sherringham. I do not suppose you know much of it."

Of course she would suppose that, he thought angrily. "I know poetry," he grumbled.

She looked smug. "What is your favorite? That charming nursery poem 'The Butterfly's Ball,' I suppose?"

"No. 'To the Virgins, to Make Much of Time.'"

Diana's smile was slight, oozing condescension, so Nathaniel cleared his throat and began to recite from memory.

> *"Gather ye rosebuds while ye may,*
> *Old Time is still a-flying;*
> *And this same flower that smiles today*
> *Tomorrow will be dying."*

The smile drained from her lips. Surprise lifted her brows.

He continued,

> *"The glorious lamp of heaven, the sun,*
> *The higher he's a-getting,*
> *The sooner will his race be run,*
> *And nearer he's to setting.*
>
> *That age is best which is the first,*
> *When youth and blood are warmer;*
> *But being spent, the worse, and worst*
> *Times still succeed the former."*

Until he began to recite the poem aloud, Nathaniel wasn't certain he would remember it all, but the gratification he felt when he saw how he'd shocked her helped his memory retrieve the words read long ago. Her eyes kept growing larger. He looked down into those lush green pools and swam in them.

> *"Then be not coy, but use your time,*
> *And while ye may, go marry;*

For having lost but once your prime,
You may forever tarry."

Susanna and Daisy Plumtre applauded with enthusiasm, and Jonty squeezed glum George's shoulder and bellowed that it was a timely reminder.

"I am impressed," Diana admitted quietly. "Not a word missed, Captain."

"May you never again doubt a gentleman's capacity for poetry."

"Indeed, I shan't."

"Or judge him by appearances."

"Quite." She lowered her lashes, hiding the glitter of emeralds.

"Or think he does not hold a great many things in his memory."

"They say that elephants have good memories," she pointed out.

He nodded. "Wonderful, majestic creatures, elephants."

"They also mate indiscriminately and their courtship, once the urge is upon the bull elephant, lasts less than half an hour."

Eyes narrowed, he studied her impertinent countenance. She rolled her lips together, clearly withholding a chuckle. Jonty, however, laughed loudly at her comment and eventually so did the others. Except for Lady Plumtre who apparently didn't get the joke.

"Elephants? Who cares anything about elephants?"

Nathaniel suggested, "Other elephants, I'm sure. And apparently Miss Makepiece, who has made some study of the animals, it seems."

"I find the study of all beasts interesting," Diana explained.

"I shall have to take care then, or you might start to study me."

Her lashes flickered, her brows twitched. "Perhaps I already have."

"Alas!" Grinning, he held a hand to his heart. "And what have you discovered?"

Before she could speak, Lady Plumtre exclaimed, "She's always reading books in a corner somewhere. It gives her a terrible stoop, as you see."

Everyone looked at Diana, who had no such stoop.

"I always warned her it would have such an effect," Lady Plumtre added, her tone superior and self-satisfied.

Diana picked up her teacup and soon had her ear requisitioned by George again.

Seventeen

OVER THE NEXT FEW DAYS, DIANA WAS HAULED around the streets of Bath to sample every delight in the company of the Plumtres. Remembering that Elizabeth had accused her of deliberately trying to win the family's affections away from her, she often tried to refuse the events they planned, but there was no stopping the daughters of the house. Diana began to think that if she locked herself in her chamber, they might drop down the chimney or climb through her window.

So she shopped and tasted and admired until her head spun. She was paraded about the Pump Room, and up and down the Crescent to spot new fashions. Susanna and Daisy were tireless—their mama hardly less so. Elizabeth frequently protested, trying to find reasons for Diana to stay behind with her whenever she did not want to go out.

"Diana prefers to stay quiet and at home," she would say. "She has not the urge to be out and about all the time."

But her in-laws did not settle for that. It was

shocking, but they insisted on treating Diana as a
person with her own opinions and wishes, and an
ability to speak for herself.

One afternoon about two o'clock, as they all
walked around the Pump Room, Diana overheard
a group of ladies by the fountain mention Captain
Sherringham. She discreetly followed the path of their
sly, darting gazes and saw him with Mrs. Sayles and her
aunt, Mrs. Ashby. How strange it was, she mused, that
she had run into him once again.

Bath must not be such a large place after all.

The ladies at the fountain were in a giddy state,
gossiping about his companion's brassy hair. Diana
thought them all a little too mature to be acting like
silly girls, but as much as she might wish not to hear
their conversation, it was impossible to avoid. She
certainly could not distract herself with the water. It
was hot and possessed an awful taste, worse than any
medicinal concoction she'd ever tasted.

Looking around, Diana suddenly realized she'd
become separated from the rest of her party. And the
crowd had grown, a large wave pushing her closer to
the gossiping bunch at the fountain.

"He has been avoiding Madame De La Barque
since he returned to Bath," one of the women was
saying. "He used to frequent her house, but goes there
no more. They say it's been years."

"The same of Lady Fincher, so I was told by a very
good source. He will not answer her invitations, yet
he was once quite a favorite at her afternoon salon
where, as you know"—here the gossiper lowered her
voice, although Diana could still hear clearly above

the music being played in the gallery—"all manner of wickedness went on into the small hours."

"Although he had lost favor with Lady Fincher when he told her she had bad breath. He was drunk, no doubt."

"But honest in his assessment of Lady Fincher's breath. *In vino veritas.* In wine there is truth."

They all broke into unpleasant titters.

"I heard he spent his last visit to Bath shouting rude epigrams from a theater box, losing at faro, and chasing after the wayward wife of a cabbage vendor. There was something about a rejected marriage proposal—to some little country girl. It put him in a terrible mood that winter, and then he just up and left."

"If he wasn't extremely pleasing to the eye, I'm quite sure he never would have been welcomed in any grand lady's salon. He ought to be grateful, but he bit the hand that fed him too many times."

Another woman snorted. "They'd still take him back again the moment he flashed those blue eyes. He's never sorry, because he knows how to get around the worst tempers. There is no one else like Sherry. No one can compare in the boudoir. He knows how to…"

Much to her irritation, she could not hear the next few words, because the band playing in the gallery had reached a stirring crescendo. Only intermittent gasps reached her ears.

"And then he…"

"But he never…"

"With her feet over her head, for pity's sake…"

"Under the table…"

"In her husband's barouche…"

"Dancing naked…"

"With a rose between his teeth…"

"No, no, it was an apple…"

Having heard quite enough and yet, at the same time, nothing complete, Diana set down her half-empty glass and turned away. Only to find the notorious Casanova himself directly in her path.

"Miss Makepiece, how do you find the waters?"

She snapped out a breathless, "Wet."

His lips quirked. "I meant the taste."

"Hot." Diana had no idea what her face was doing. She stared at his waistcoat, heat rising under her stays. "Bitter."

"That would be the sulfur."

"Would it? I suppose you would know, being so familiar with Bath."

"Are you quite well? You seem a little…upset. Agitated. Has someone upset you?" He looked around as if ready to confront the person, whoever it might be.

"Not deliberately," she muttered. "They cannot help themselves."

It was the first time they'd had a chance to speak alone since they'd both arrived in Bath. Diana looked around in something of a panic, but neither her cousin nor the Plumtre girls were anywhere in sight. The noisy crowd was making her dizzy as another new surge of people filed in from outside, eager to take the waters before three o'clock.

"Please don't trouble yourself, Captain. I am perfectly well," Diana managed, clasping her reticule tightly in both hands.

Suddenly he advanced. She backed away. He silently

advanced again, she moved back again, and in this way they had soon found a small space by a window.

"How is Mrs. Sayles?" she asked, trying to be civil. Ah, it was better here. A little more free air. What did he think he was doing, cornering her in this manner?

"She has a headache"—he paused—"as usual."

"Yes, a lot of things go on as usual, don't they?" Oops. She had not meant to sound so sharp. What did it matter to her what he did when he was in Bath? With his blue eyes. Under tables. Under skirts. With a rose—or an apple—between his teeth?

"Are you enjoying Wollaford?" he asked.

"Very much. The Plumtres are excellent company and wonderful hosts."

"And Mr. George Plumtre. How do you find him?"

Bemused by his gruff tone, she looked up and replied, "How do I find him?" *The same as the water*, she mused, *wet*. "I turn around quite often and there he is."

Nathaniel frowned, heaved his shoulders as if his clothes were too tight, and grumbled, "Jonty tells me his brother is quite smitten."

"Is he?" What the devil was he playing at now? Trying to discover the tenor of her friendship with another man. For what purpose? He had made it plain that he would never resume his attentions to *her*. And she did not want him to, did she?

He had no chance to say anything more about that or his motives in asking, because suddenly George, Elizabeth, and the younger Plumtres found her again, descending through the mob to reclaim their guest.

"There you are! I wish you would not wander off from where I left you," her cousin snapped. "I distinctly told you to stay there. You're so quiet I hardly know where you are from one moment to the next. It is not convenient to be dashing about Bath trying to find where you've gone off to."

Diana was confused. She did not know what to be, because nothing seemed to please Elizabeth. If she spoke up, she was putting herself forward in an ill-mannered fashion. If she stayed quiet, she was an inconvenience.

Nathaniel spoke up. "I moved Miss Makepiece out of the crowd, Lady Plumtre. She did not look very comfortable, and I thought she was in need of some air."

"Air?" Elizabeth frowned. "*Air?* What on earth for?"

Diana bit back a chuckle and Nathaniel said solemnly, "Why, to breathe, madam. Or does she require your permission to do that too?"

Her cousin's countenance wavered between fury and confusion. As usual she took her discomfort out on Diana. "If you were not feeling well, you should have said so. How was I supposed to know? I'm sure I take no pleasure in traipsing up and down the place like a tourist, but you will insist on coming out."

"I am not ill, Elizabeth. I was merely—"

"Always thinking of yourself. Not a thought for me or what I would do when I returned to find you slunk off somewhere."

Sir Jonty emerged from the mad throng at that moment and greeted Nathaniel with the usual excessive volume, while his wife continued to mutter and fume under her breath.

Once again, thought Diana, her moment alone

with Nathaniel was over so quickly. Was that why
his presence, when she had it, seemed such a luxury
now? She wished she had not overheard those women
talking. She didn't want to know all of that. When he
looked into her eyes she wanted—

Oh, she no longer knew *what* she wanted.

In any case, she needn't think he was kind to her for
any reason other than his habitual need to rescue every
maiden in distress. Even *old* maidens.

Nathaniel stayed only for a few brief words with
his new friend and to accept an invitation for dinner
at Wollaford Park, and then he made a quick retreat.

George sidled up to Diana. "My mother and Jonty
think him a splendid fellow, but in my opinion the
captain is a little *too*…jolly, don't you know?"

"I know precisely," she replied with a tense sigh.
He was too…everything.

⤜⤚

That evening after dinner, Daisy Plumtre insisted on
Nathaniel sitting for her while she sketched his profile
for a silhouette.

Mrs. Ashby and Mrs. Plumtre were together by
the fire, talking of old times, Caroline yawning loudly
beside them. Jonty, his wife, Susanna, and George
played cards, but Diana sat alone with her book,
apparently absorbed in it. Even when George asked
her to advise him at cards she politely declined and said
she wanted to finish her chapter. But oddly enough,
Nathaniel had noticed not a single page turned while
he watched her. It was a rainy evening and occasionally she looked up to watch the raindrops on the

window. Then she bent her head again over the open book, pretending to be engrossed in the story.

"Miss Makepiece is very fond of her book," he whispered to Daisy. "Do you suppose she reads sermons? From her grim face it seems likely."

"I believe it is a novel—a romantic story."

He shook his head. "I suppose she thinks she's safer reading about romance than enjoying any herself."

Daisy was busy tracing the shape of his nose on her grid-covered paper. "Don't sigh so heavily," she exclaimed, "or you'll blow out the candle!" After a pause she added, "What do you mean, she's safer reading it?"

"That must be how she gets her thrills," he whispered, trying not to move his lips too much. "She strikes me as the sort who doesn't like to get a hair out of place or a stocking wrinkled for a gentleman."

Daisy giggled. Across the room, Diana looked up but almost immediately down again. Still her page didn't turn.

Nathaniel added in a louder whisper, "Romantic novels cause young ladies to expect too much. Make them think a man ought to be everything at once and never have any faults. A poor fellow like me doesn't stand a chance when a lady's head is filled with that nonsense."

Daisy huffed, forgetting her own warning about the candle. "I very much doubt you have any problems once you decide to woo a lady."

"On the contrary. My charms have been known to fail on one particular lady at least."

"The one who refused you?"

"Yes," he growled, reminded of that pain anew.

"And did she read a lot of romantic novels?"

He nodded. "She seldom had her nose out of them."

"You must not have made it worth her while to put her book down, then."

Nathaniel turned to look at Daisy, but she immediately shouted at him for spoiling his profile.

"Now I've made your nose too bloody big again!" she exclaimed, tossing another crumpled sheet of paper to the carpet.

"*Daisy!*" her brother George shouted wearily from the card table. "*Language!*"

She screwed up her face. "I don't see why other people can use that word and I can't. I'll just start making up my own curses. Such as...as...fergalumph!"

Nobody answered her so she set to her task again, frowning determinedly. "Do sit still, Captain. I've never known such a fidget!"

All those paper roses littering the floor were the subject's fault, apparently, not the artist's. He asked the girl how much longer this would take. "I shall have to stretch my legs in a moment before they seize up with old age," he told her. "Unless I have something to amuse me and take my mind off the cramp." He glanced over at Diana again.

"It won't take long if you stop talking and moving your great big head about."

That made Diana look over the top of her book, her eyes shining with amusement.

"Miss Makepiece thinks I have an excessively large head too. See? She smiles. Although she tries to hide it."

Across the room Lady Plumtre grew annoyed that a

conversation was going on without her. It was not to be borne. Looking about for a scapegoat, she quickly found one.

"You should put that book away and join us over here, Diana," she exclaimed. "What can possibly keep you so engrossed?"

Diana looked up. "I would like to finish—"

"You're no company at all with your nose in a book. There is time enough for that when you are alone." Lady Plumtre addressed the other players at the table in a lazy drawl. "My cousin has not had much benefit of good society, so you must excuse her. She is either too withdrawn or too excitable, as I pointed out to her the other day."

Again Diana attempted to be heard. "I did not mean to be rude, but you are all occupied and I am almost—"

"Books are all she cares about," her cousin exclaimed. "It is all the entertainment she is used to, I suppose."

Diana read on, not letting Lady Plumtre's snide words force her away from her book again. She was evidently accustomed to being berated by her family.

"Poor Miss Makepiece," Daisy whispered. "She ought to throw that bloody book at Elizabeth. I would if I were her."

But Diana would never be so demonstrative.

He longed for her to speak up again, as she had the first night he was there at Wollaford. What had changed her back into the solemn woman afraid to smile?

He'd played the fool before in an effort to make her laugh. He'd teased her to try and raise a reaction. The only thing he had not done, Nathaniel realized now, was pay proper court to her.

After so many years of deliberate misbehavior, he wasn't sure he knew how.

And why should he want to?

Her opinion of him was clearly not much altered, but while she was there without her mother whispering in her ear, perhaps he had a chance to change her view of him. There was hope. That first dinner, when her face had shone and she'd conversed freely, had granted them both a fresh beginning.

There would be a certain amount of satisfaction in proving her mother wrong and showing Diana Makepiece that he wasn't the unmitigated scoundrel she still thought him. He could be a gentleman. He could make her look at him with something other than scorn.

Perhaps he could get Diana to put her book aside without sighing as if it was a great annoyance to face life itself.

"Miss Makepiece," he called out to her, "Miss Daisy Plumtre continues to draw me with a monstrous great nose. I think she makes me look like Punch the puppet. Do come and help us."

Diana hesitated, slowly looking up again over the edge of her book. "How might I help?"

"He won't sit still!" Daisy protested.

"I shall sit still if Miss Makepiece comes here and reads her book aloud to me. I know she doesn't want to give over reading, but she might at least share the pleasure with us."

Diana looked around the room. Her cousin was

preoccupied with arguing over the cards, accusing her husband of cheating. Since no one else was paying attention, Diana got up and took a chair closer to where he sat. "I can read to you, Captain, but do not ask me to explain the story up until now, because it is too long and involved and I'm sure you have not the patience for it."

"No matter." He smiled a little. "The sound of your voice will be satisfying enough."

She looked askance.

"I find it has...soothing qualities," he added. "It is the sort of voice a man cannot tire of." Just having her seated nearby was pleasing. He reached forward, turned her book over, and read the title. "Ah, yes, I remember the gist of it. A lady named Anne has broken the heart of a sailor by rejecting his proposal. Is that not so?"

"You are familiar with *Persuasion*, Captain?" Diana asked.

Nathaniel stared at her pursed lips and suffered the uncomfortable urge to claim them. "Someone I knew once before was reading it."

"Oh, do read aloud, Miss Makepiece," Daisy cried. "Anything to make him sit still. He is the world's worst model. If I was sculpting in clay he would have a dozen limbs by now."

So Diana began to read aloud.

"I can listen no longer in silence. I must speak to you by such means as are within my reach. You pierce my soul. I am half agony, half hope. Tell me not that I am too late, that such precious feelings are

gone forever. I offer myself to you again with a heart even more your own than when you almost broke it, eight years and a half ago."

He watched her mouth, following the gentle bow of her top lip and then the lower. Those lips he had kissed.

"Dare not say that man forgets sooner than woman, that his love has an earlier death. I have loved none but you. Unjust I may have been, weak and resentful I have been, but never inconstant."

Nathaniel felt her words fall over him like invisible kisses. Incredible that her voice should still have such an effect on him, after once being so unkind to him. But the speech she read might have come from his own lips.

"For you alone I think and plan. Have you not seen this? Can you fail to have understood my wishes?"

Because of her, he had changed his life. Yet Diana was unaware of the part she'd played in his success. He studied her face while she read on, and he imagined kissing the tip of her nose. Licking those naughty eyebrows. Making his way back down to her soft mouth, the color of strawberry flesh and just as sweet.

"You sink your voice, but I can distinguish the tones of that voice when they would be lost on others."

She was interrupted, her reading drowned out by a loud mazurka suddenly played on the pianoforte by Lady Plumtre, who had given up on cards and evidently did not share her cousin's love of novels.

Diana was about to close her book. Nathaniel reached over again and placed his hand on the page to prevent it.

"Read on," he insisted. "*I* hear you."

She looked down at his hand spread upon her page.

"I am listening," he told her earnestly. "To you."

He thought Daisy Plumtre might have dropped her charcoal, but he didn't know for sure. He knew of nothing but Diana's fingertips hesitantly brushing across his knuckles, easing his hand aside so she might continue reading.

However loud her cousin played, the two of them were in their own world in that moment, and nothing could interrupt it.

Few people ever listened to Diana, he realized. Even when they thought they listened, they did not hear her. But he would listen because he understood the value of what she said. He knew how her words had changed his life once before.

He didn't want to miss another sigh from her lips.

Eighteen

FORTUNATELY FOR ALL THE LADIES, CAPTAIN Sherringham had decided to stay a while in Bath, in some lodgings he had apparently rented before, near Sydney Gardens. He and Jonty were soon fast friends, being of similar social nature and affable character, and thus he was invited frequently on the Plumtres' outings. Even when he was not expected or had said he was not certain if he could join them, he invariably turned up. And usually he brought Mrs. Sayles too, much to Elizabeth's disgust.

Diana learned that Mrs. Ashby was a good friend of Jonty's mother, and as such she was a fixture at manor house dinners.

"My dear old friend has fallen on difficult times," Mrs. Plumtre explained, "and I must look after her. She has no one else, you know"—she lowered her voice—"just that curious niece, Caroline. Well…the less said about her, the better. Oh dear." A rumble of laughter shook her well-padded frame. "She is a handful, isn't she? But she might at least be company for my friend, might bring her out of herself."

Seated beside Mrs. Ashby one evening, Diana listened patiently to her tales of the angelic Eleanor, apparently a woman of more goodness and accomplishments than anybody else who ever lived. Indeed she was so perfect, her mother explained, that it was no wonder God took her up to heaven at a young age.

"The bond between a mother and her only daughter is great indeed. Nothing can break it. Even death," the lady explained drearily. "I have naught else to live for now and wait only for the day when I can join my sweet angel."

Diana thought of her own mother in similar circumstances to Mrs. Ashby—an impoverished, genteel lady with a scattering of relatives who apparently did not care about her and had left her to struggle alone since the death of her only daughter. If Diana were gone, her mother would be all alone too, she thought sadly. But her mother did not have friends like the Plumtres on her side.

"I know it must be very hard to miss your daughter," she replied gently to the lady, "but I must say, I would never want my own mother to give up on life without me. Like Eleanor, I am an only daughter. I would want my mother to make the most of life, if I could not. Indeed, if I could look down from heaven and advise her, I'd urge her to be happy, to live *for* me."

Mrs. Ashby considered this quietly and seemed to take some comfort from it. After that she often sought Diana's side in the evenings, and over time her conversation became a little more cheerful. "Captain Sherringham said I should listen to your advice, my dear," Mrs. Ashby said one evening. "He said you have a steady, serene way about you, and he was quite right."

Diana felt her cheeks warm. She happened, at that moment, to glance over and catch Nathaniel watching her while pretending to peruse a shelf of books. He looked away at once, pursing his lips in an idle whistle, hands behind his back. *Very nice thighs*, she thought suddenly. And immediately cursed herself, remembering that she was not Daisy Plumtre and ought to have more on her mind than a man's thighs, however splendid.

Caroline Sayles took advantage of her aunt's welcome at Wollaford and the Plumtres' generous hospitality, trailing along to dinner at the manor and eating and drinking as much as she could—even in her advanced state of infirmity, for she continued to be a lady of many ailments. The suffering and tending of these varied maladies made up most of her conversation.

Diana tried to sympathize with the lady and listen to her problems, but they were numerous. The only other person who took any interest in Caroline's illnesses was George Plumtre who, having lost his fiancée to a sudden and virulent fever, considered no discomfort too small to be taken seriously, no pain or symptom too slight to be ignored.

"One must take precautions," he said, hovering on the edge of his seat. "One should never overlook these things. They can soon become much worse." A moment of faintness, he assured the wide-eyed Mrs. Sayles, could strike a person down within hours.

Elizabeth despised the woman, considering her "common," an uninvited intruder. "Caroline Sayles ought to be on the stage," she muttered. "I have never known a creature so desperate for attention."

Diana was amazed, as always, by her cousin's utter lack of self-awareness.

She felt sorry for Elizabeth. Her cousin would never realize how she left herself open for mockery, but there was no way to help her. Unfortunately, Elizabeth would never acquire the ability to laugh at herself. That, it seemed, was a Clarendon failing. And surrounded by the rowdy Plumtre family—her opposites in many ways—she was quite out of her depth. It made her more bitter than usual, her nerves stretched thin.

On the other hand, Diana enjoyed her merry hosts and found herself fitting in more than she had expected. She was still able, however, to stand apart and observe their quirks, to study them from a little distance without becoming too attached, too quickly. It was not in Diana's character to throw herself into a friendship without caution, but once her trust was fully earned, her loyalty formed, the connection could never be broken.

She liked Susanna and Daisy and found them very entertaining, but they were indeed wild and somewhat unpredictable. She proceeded warily with that friendship, yielding a little more each day to their rambunctious spirits. Their mother was easier to endure from the beginning. Nothing seemed to trouble the lady unduly, and her soft voice was never raised except in happy exclamation.

As much as the Plumtre girls and their mother clearly celebrated having an appreciative guest to show around Bath, the uncomplicated pleasure they found in each other's company when home together doing nothing much was touching. The Plumtres were not afraid to show their affection and to laugh with—and sometimes *at*—one another, but never viciously. It saddened Diana when she compared their relationship to the difficult one she had with her tightly bound mother.

The sisters were enthusiastic about everything, except for lessons that required them to sit still, and their mother appeared to have no wish to discipline. Her laughter could often be heard encouraging the girls in their misbehavior, even when she later chided them in a halfhearted, ineffectual way.

When the cook at Wollaford Park had her day off, Mrs. Fanny Plumtre and her daughters spent time in the kitchen together, and Diana was invited to join them. Surprised as she was to see a lady of Mrs. Plumtre's consequence donning a pinafore and putting herself to work in her own kitchen, Diana learned it was an event to which the lady looked forward.

"I know I shall not have my girls with me forever," she whispered in Diana's ear, her eyes glittering with bright, unshed tears, "and I must make the most of the time we have together. Perhaps I can teach them something at least, the way my mama taught me. I may not know how to play a harp and I can't dance with elegance, alas, but I can cook! My girls will never go hungry, wherever they are in the world."

Diana then observed an extravagant use of flour,

sugar, and all manner of exotic spices. Some of which, when she found it later in her hair, caused her to panic that she had suddenly sprouted gray.

For the first time in her life, she enjoyed cooking and learned that it did not have to be a chore. A recipe did not have to be followed exactly, she realized. It could meander off a little. Like a tune when one hummed it to oneself.

Mrs. Plumtre showed Diana around the kitchen, larder, and distillery with great pride. Nothing in that place, she noted, went unused. Nothing was saved for a "special occasion," possibly because the lady approached every day as if it was an event. Diana thought of her own mother pushing precious ingredients to the back of the shelf, never allowing them to be opened. Almost as if she punished herself by keeping them there, yet denying her tongue the joy of tasting those luxurious or exotic spices.

Did her mother not think herself worthy of pleasure?

Well, Diana would not be that way. From now on she refused to live in a world without tasting it. All of it.

Especially proud of her gooseberry wine, Mrs. Plumtre insisted upon Diana sampling a large cupful. The brew had the curious effect of making her tongue and her feet feel soft at the same time, and although the first sip made her wince, she had soon grown accustomed to the sting. The kind lady was so delighted by Diana's response that she insisted on pouring them both a second cup, and then a third. About that time, Sir Jonty, his brother, and Nathaniel arrived on the scene.

Out for a ride that day, the three gentlemen had

come across a large elm in which a favorite old bonnet belonging to Mrs. Plumtre had sat weathering storms for several years. Apparently it had blown off her head in a gale, landed in the tree, and never been retrieved. Nathaniel was instantly taken with the desire to rescue it. George had assured him that the tree was too high and treacherous, that no one could climb it. Naturally this only made the captain more eager to perform the deed, and when Sir Jonty added the inducement of a wager, it could not be resisted another moment.

The gentlemen had returned to the house, ostensibly to find a stick of some sort, but Diana suspected Nathaniel wanted to gather an audience of gasping young ladies who might applaud his daring deed.

Entirely at the mercy of Mrs. Plumtre's gooseberry wine, she decided to join the others, despite the fact that this was what he wanted and she was, in effect, letting him think she cared. Diana trekked across the grass with them to watch the foolishness as it played out. The show-off would not be content until he cracked his head open, she thought crossly, shielding her eyes from the sun with one hand.

"Oh, do be cautious," Mrs. Plumtre cried. "It was a good hat, indeed. A very good sort of hat. But I confess I had quite given up on it and managed these past two years without it. I would not want the captain to suffer injury just for a hat I had forgotten and not bothered about for such a time! It is quite pulled about by the weather by now and that tree is a great height to climb. Should we not persuade him to give up the mission, Miss Makepiece? Perhaps you, in your gentle way, could put him off the idea. He listens to you."

"I wouldn't dare try to persuade *him* to do anything." Diana swallowed a hiccup.

The sun was very warm that day and the fresh air, combined with the effects of the gooseberry wine, made her extremely dizzy. As she stood swaying under the tree and watching Nathaniel strip down to his shirtsleeves, she felt the heat more than ever and wished she had a fan.

All for a wager, she mused scornfully. He had not given up all his old habits, it seemed.

He glanced over at her as he rolled up his sleeves to expose two broad forearms. "Miss Makepiece, do you too doubt my ability to climb this tree?"

She shrugged, struggled to curb another hiccup, and exclaimed, "It seems an extreme measure to rescue a hat."

"Extreme measures are sometimes necessary."

Even if you fall, she thought, *I'm sure you'll look wonderful doing it.*

Alas.

With a broken broom handle held in his mouth, Nathaniel swung himself up the wide trunk and began his agile climb. The ladies held their breath and Jonty looked on in admiration. George was unimpressed and made certain everybody knew it.

"I would have climbed that tree if not for the anxiety it might cause my mother," he assured Diana. "And you too, of course, Miss Makepiece."

Nathaniel continued his ascent into the branches and Daisy ran to the foot of the tree. "I can climb too. It doesn't look very difficult. I am not afraid."

Her sister told her to come away and not to be

so foolish. "Ladies do not climb trees. Do they, Miss Makepiece?"

"Certainly not," Diana managed, trying not to care that Nathaniel's riding boot had just slipped off a branch and caused her heart to plummet the same distance as she had, in that second, envisioned his body falling. "I cannot imagine a lady would ever have cause to do so."

The branch that held the lost bonnet ransom was finally reached. Nathaniel now stretched across it, using the stick to dislodge his prey from its knotted perch. It tumbled down and Daisy caught it with a shout of triumph.

Accompanied by cheers and applause, the rescuer descended slowly until he was a few feet from the ground and then he leaped, causing Diana's pulse to race recklessly yet again. The Plumtre sisters circled him in excitement, Susanna holding his discarded riding jacket. "There. I have won my wager," he said, glancing over at Diana, breathing hard, and looking for praise.

Oh, he had surely caught her looking at him with admiration for there was a sunny sparkle of surprise in those azure eyes, and then he blinked and drew his hand back through the gilded hair that had fallen onto his brow as he jumped. The gesture made her think suddenly of his muscular form naked. What it might look like.

She swallowed hard and tasted the wine on her tongue.

"What a pity I didn't make the ladies wager too," he said, half laughing and not looking at her.

"Oh, I knew you'd manage it," Daisy replied confidently. "I had no fear."

But Diana had. When she thought he might fall she was besieged with apprehension, and in that moment, she knew she would have flown to wherever he lay wounded. And all her secrets would have exploded into the warm spring air. All her passions would have been exposed. All her embarrassing fancies.

She'd better blame it on the gooseberry wine.

"*I could climb that tree*," shouted Daisy. "Who dares me?"

"Girls can't climb," Nathaniel assured her, laughing and tweaking her nose. "Girls really can't do much of anything."

"Ha! You'll see, Captain. I'll show you."

"Don't pay heed to him, Daisy," said Diana cockily. "He only means to goad you. Everybody knows women are the superior gender."

He spun around to survey her carefully, eyes narrowed against the bright sun. "And how do you reach that conclusion, Miss Makepiece?"

"Because we do not really need men. What good are they? Whenever there is anything difficult to be done, anything requiring great internal strength, it is left to the women. Men get out of it whenever they can."

"Such as?"

Diana chose the first thing she could think of. "Childbirth!"

"Oh Lord!" He stretched out his arms in a gesture of supplication. "Whenever a woman raises the subject of childbirth, I know I have lost the argument."

Mrs. Plumtre chuckled. "Aye, Captain, best give up. We ladies have the stronger case."

"But Miss Makepiece forgets one important factor."

"I do? What?"

He didn't put his coat back on, but strode over to where Diana and Mrs. Plumtre stood. "A lady cannot bear my child," he whispered, "until I first plant the seed within her."

Diana swallowed as his hushed words trickled through her, wicked and sensuous.

"She needs me for that, does she not?" he added. "Without my *strength* to provide her with a babe, her own capacity to bear one has no purpose. It is a moot point."

Oh, now her face felt hot. "That has nothing to do with anything," she exclaimed. "Such a subject!"

"On the contrary. It has something to do with everything. The mating ritual between man and woman is the very essence of life. And woman, magnificent as she might be, cannot procreate without a man." He leaned closer. "A strong, vital, potent man."

He was trying to shock her, she realized. The man was enjoying her blushes, making the most of her mother's absence. But was she not doing the same?

New Diana was bolder than the old one, and she would not let him render her speechless with his audacious conversation. So she answered smartly, chin up. "I don't want a husband. They're far more trouble than they're worth."

"Perhaps the right man will one day change your mind."

"I doubt it."

"You were badly treated by a man who broke your heart."

Before she could reply to that, he passed Mrs. Plumtre her bonnet, gave a little bow, and smiled broadly. "I am pleased to return this to its mistress."

"You are too good, Captain! And you render my daughters more in love with you than ever after that fine display of athleticism."

George grumbled under his breath, but Jonty laughed with his mother.

As they all moved toward the house, Nathaniel hung back to walk with Diana. "It is lucky I have some practice climbing trees, wouldn't you agree?"

"Is it a skill you need often, Captain? At your age?"

"Only when *extreme measures* are necessary. When I have exhausted all other methods to get a lady's attention."

She had noticed a stray leaf on his sleeve, caught in the roll of linen at his elbow. Had it not been for that wine, she probably could have ignored the leaf. But just then it seemed extremely important that she reach over and pluck it free. Her fingertips felt the heat of his strength through the sleeve. Sunlight tickled the hairs on his arms and made them glow.

His steps slowed, almost to a halt.

Diana stumbled over a clump of grass and knocked into his arm as it swung at his side. She could feel the contact in every part of her, every inch. Her thigh brushed against his and then, with both hands on her waist, he steadied her. Of course he should not put his hands on her. It was an impulsive move with no thought for what was proper, but he did not instantly let go and she did not protest. The others had walked on, Daisy still loudly assuring them all that she could climb a tree, or anything else, with as much ease as a man.

Nathaniel's gaze stroked Diana's body and meandered upward to her lips.

"The sun has put a bright glow on your cheeks, Miss Makepiece. And you're breathing very hard. Or perhaps it was the anticipation of seeing me fall. Dare I hope you worried for me, my excessively large head, and other parts of my potent, male person?"

Diana struggled to remember that he was a flirt by nature and that this was how he teased all women. She smiled haltingly. "I fear, Captain, it is not the sun or any thoughts of you making a dent in the ground that has me in an unusually unsettled state, but rather gooseberry wine."

His brows lifted. "Indeed?"

"A little *too much* gooseberry wine."

"Tsk-tsk. What will become of you so far from home?"

A bold reply flew out of her. "I cannot wait to find out."

He tipped his head to one side and squinted down at her, as if trying to read something written on her face.

"I mean to try everything I never did before," she added. "No more jars left unopened." She waggled a finger before his face. "Nothing saved for a day that may never come."

"I do not like the sound of this, Miss Makepiece." His nose twitched. "You have an air of rebellion about you."

She laughed. "Do I? Good. About time, don't you think?"

Apparently he was unsure about that. "I see I must be the somber one for a change and keep *you* out of trouble."

"Hmm. Perhaps I shall take to climbing trees," she warned saucily.

"At least I know you don't want a man. I won't have to worry about that."

"That's not what I said," she replied. "I said I didn't want a husband."

The Plumtres had just turned to see where the captain and Diana were. He still had his hands on her waist, and she belatedly pulled free to rejoin the others before her mildly dizzy state caused her to do or say something even naughtier.

Nineteen

A FEW DAYS LATER, WHILE THE LADIES WERE SHOPPING on Milsom Street, rain came down and threatened to cut their outing short. They took hasty shelter in a tea shop and as they clustered by the window, who should happen by with a handy umbrella but Captain Sherringham and Mrs. Sayles. Diana had been watching for the carriage that George Plumtre had hurried off to fetch for them, when she saw two people passing. At that same moment Nathaniel saw her and immediately turned his steps, heading inside the shop.

Her heart picked up into a canter. Since that gloriously sunny day when she, under the influence of gooseberry wine, had plucked a leaf from his shirt and confessed her desire for rebellion out loud, she had dreaded seeing him again. Would he make sport of her for being tipsy that day?

Upon sighting his tall form working its way through the huddled crowd of damp shoppers, the Misses Plumtre yelled his name in near hysteria and lavish gratitude. Anyone might think they'd been abandoned there to starvation and certain death, Diana mused.

"We've been waiting so long for George and the carriage," Susanna cried, bouncing into the captain's path and almost knocking his companion off her wooden pattens. "I begin to wonder if he is drowned and floating out there somewhere. Or he has forgotten us and gone home. He can be terribly absentminded."

"It's such a bl—wretched crush in here," her sister added. "It was fun at first to be squashed together, but now we're all very miserable and I fear we shall not get to the dressmaker's before it closes."

Nathaniel asked which dressmaker they had intended to visit, and Susanna explained, "Miss Makepiece has an appointment there at three o'clock with Madam Le Clair. She is in Edgar Buildings. We are quite desperate."

Diana hastily assured them, as she had countless times already, that it didn't matter.

"But it does," Daisy replied firmly. "You are to have that new dress finished for the Wollaford ball." Ever since Diana had made the error of showing them her "best" frock, the two young ladies had insisted she must have a new gown and then, much to her mortification, had persuaded Jonty that he ought to pay for it.

Elizabeth was so furious about the "needless expense of a ball gown for a woman who will never have another chance to wear it" that she would have nothing to do with this new dress and wouldn't even come into town that day. She had been in a sulk about the ball ever since she heard that it was now bound to happen. Her husband and mother-in-law were hastily throwing plans together in a haphazard fashion, which seemed to be their usual method. And they were not consulting Elizabeth, which only threw salt in the wound.

"But you said you wanted nothing to do with the ball," Diana had heard Jonty exclaim to his wife that morning as he was on his way out of the house.

"That does not mean I shouldn't be consulted," Elizabeth replied. "I am supposed to be the mistress of Wollaford, even if I am consigned to the lodge while my in-laws take possession of my rightful home."

"Lizzie, my dear, you know this house is much cozier for the two of us and it would be cramped for the others. Until we have offspring of our own there is no sense in uprooting—"

"Do as you will then! Why not ask my cousin her opinion, since you seem keen to take hers above mine!"

"Really, Lizzie, I wonder at the way you treat your cousin. I thought you wanted her to come."

Elizabeth had moaned under her breath. "Of course I did. One likes to have a less attractive, somewhat dowdy companion about the place. But she is being very sly and going behind my back. Even now I shouldn't be surprised to find her eavesdropping behind a door, looking to outdo me in some matter."

After accidentally hearing this, Diana had been eager to get out of the house, despite the threat of rain and even if it was to be fitted for a ball gown she would only wear once in her life. As Elizabeth had assured her.

Nathaniel was now examining the clock on the tea shop wall, as directed by Susanna, to see that it was already a quarter before the hour. "Might I escort you to the dressmaker with the aid of my umbrella?"

he asked Diana. "Unless you prefer to wait for Mr. George Plumtre."

The young ladies looked at her expectantly. They had been pushing her at their brother for days now, but the necessity of a perfect new ball gown undid all that. Temporarily, at least.

"Mrs. Sayles can wait here for the carriage with the others," he continued, looking quite innocent. "I should not like you to miss your appointment, and here I am with an umbrella to put to good use."

One likes to have a less attractive, somewhat dowdy companion about the place.

Diana considered, glancing at the clock and then the blurred view through the rain-spattered shop window again. Finally she said, "Very well. Thank you. It is most kind."

He offered his arm and she took it.

❧

Nathaniel extended the umbrella over them both as they stepped out to the street.

"We'll never get there in a quarter of an hour," she murmured.

"Have faith, Miss Makepiece. Look at it this way. With everyone else taking shelter, we have the path almost entirely to ourselves." He grinned down at her. "And at least you have the handsomest bull elephant in Bath to escort you."

She shook her head, hiding her smile. Or trying to.

"And I have the most beautiful lady on my arm."

"Don't talk nonsense." She flushed, just like the first time he had told her she was beautiful.

·"You know me, Miss Makepiece. I am all nonsense."

Glancing upward, she said softly, "Ah, but I don't know you, Captain. We have only recently met."

"So we have! I must admit, sometimes it feels as if we have known each other ten years or more," he replied with a wink. "I am so comfortable in your presence."

He loved having her hand tucked under his arm, holding his sleeve. It was not at all annoying. Nothing like having Caroline Sayles pawing at him.

A few other folk were braving the rain, but as he had said to Diana, the path was mostly their own. He held her closer to his side and she didn't comment about that being improper. In fact, it almost felt as if her fingers had just stroked his arm again, with no fallen leaf to use as an excuse this time.

"Here is a shortcut," he said, steering her around a puddle and a lamppost to walk down a narrow alley between buildings. Now they *were* alone.

His thumping heartbeat seemed to match the sound of the rain hitting his umbrella.

"I would like to explain to you about Mrs. Sayles," he said.

"Why? It is no business of mine."

Nathaniel looked down at her. She was staring ahead to the end of the alley, her face shaded by the umbrella. "I have been taking her about the town because she has no one else who will, you know."

"There is no need to explain yourself to me."

But he wanted to. "And her aunt prefers Caroline to be out as much as possible." He sighed. "They live in a very small house and I can quite see her point."

"Yes."

He cleared his throat. "I wouldn't want you to assume that Caroline and I—"

"As I did before, you mean?" She stopped walking and turned to face him. "I listened to gossip when I shouldn't have."

Nathaniel had not expected so much understanding. Usually women ranted and railed. They seldom apologized for leaping to a conclusion. Again he was struck by how different she was from other women he'd known.

"I should have waited to see for myself before I judged," she said in her calm voice.

He nodded. In the shadow of the umbrella her eyes were bright and luminous. "We must walk on," he murmured. "Your dressmaker—"

"Captain, I think you should kiss me."

He stared. Was his mind playing tricks on him?

"My lips," she said, "are cold."

Nathaniel looked at her warily. "This is very sudden, Miss Makepiece. A kiss between two strangers? It can hardly be proper. Have you been at the gooseberry wine again?"

"Not yet, but I might be reduced to that if you do not obey me."

Obey her, indeed! "More of your rebellion?"

She nodded. "Let this be my apology."

"For?"

"Heeding gossip."

Slowly he bent his head. She hitched a little higher on her toes. Their lips met. It was a soft brush, no more than that. But it warmed him from head to foot. "Now it is your turn, Miss Makepiece. You must tell me about George Plumtre."

"What about him?"

"He's always hovering around," he replied grump-ily. "I don't like it."

She laughed at that. "Oh, don't you? It must be hard for the shoe to be on the other foot then."

"Meaning, madam?"

"You, Captain, are surrounded by women wher-ever you go."

He frowned. "I cannot help that."

She pressed her lips together, that little dimple appearing in her cheek, and her left eyebrow quirked.

"I cannot," he insisted. "It's not as if I beg for their attention."

"Of course not." She sighed. "Then how can I help it if George Plumtre likes my company? I am cheering him up. I am providing a dutiful service to the poor fellow. Just as you provide your services to so many ladies."

Nathaniel stared at her, not knowing what to say or how to manage this rare jealousy. He had continually assured himself that George was not important, but his confidence was severely tested by this uniquely difficult, challenging woman. And she was in a rebellious mood, as she'd already confessed to him. Gooseberry wine was the first step to the potential abandonment of petticoats, in his experience.

"You may as well kiss me again," she whispered. "We're going to be too late for the dressmaker anyway."

As if he needed her permission! He was about to kiss her again anyway, whether she suggested it or not. But he had to smile. Only Diana would frame her request for a kiss in such a way, as if she really didn't want one of his at all.

So he tipped her chin up with his fingers and kissed her again, harder this time, hungry and heated. The umbrella shifted and rainwater spilled down the collar of his coat, but he did not care. Her small hands came up to his face and touched it tentatively, tracing the curve of his cheek and running gloved fingertips over the light stubble.

"What are you doing to me, Diana?" he muttered, bemused, lost.

"Becoming acquainted with you again, Captain." She ran the tip of her tongue along his lower lip. "From the beginning."

"I sincerely hope you don't plan to introduce yourself to other gentlemen this way."

She put her hands around the back of his neck now, under his wet collar, linking her fingers together and easing his head down for another kiss. He groaned deeply, wrapped his free arm around her waist, and tugged her up against his body.

Her tongue shyly explored his. Nathaniel held back, not wanting to scare her away, letting her advance at her own pace. Nor was he ready to risk his heart on her again. Not yet. He had gambled all before and lost.

But his pulse raced. Her perfume filled his senses, lifting him out of that rainy alley and into a fragrant summer meadow somewhere.

Then she lowered her heels again, slipping down his body. Her gaze met his and held it. As the rain ended and the sun came out again, everything around them seemed to be sprinkled with diamonds. But nothing compared to the breathtaking beauty of her eyes glittering up at him.

"I give you permission, Captain, to seduce me."

～

Diana Makepiece, what has come over you?

Oh, she didn't care. She didn't want to think sensibly. This powerful, driving need had taken possession of her. The feel of his arm around her, the heat and strength of his body against hers was more than any flesh-and-blood woman could withstand.

And that was all she was. A flesh-and-blood human. A woman with faults like any other.

Needs and desires like any other.

What was he waiting for?

While she had stood in that shop staring out at the rain, a little voice inside her head had told her that she would see Nathaniel.

He will pass by at any minute. Any minute he will come.

Was it premonition or simply her wishful thinking? Or was it because she had grown accustomed to the sight of him popping up wherever she went?

Then he was there, a tall streak of sunlight appearing in the midst of the gray rain. The wings of excitement, as feverish and wildly unnecessary as those of a fifteen-year-old girl, lifted her up until she felt as if she floated several feet above the ground.

"Well?" she demanded. "Have you nothing to say?"

"About what?"

"Seducing me."

Nathaniel kept his arm around her, the umbrella

still held in his other hand, while he examined her face carefully, thoughtfully.

Impatient, she warned, "If you don't bloody well hurry up and say something, I shall take back my permission."

His eyes narrowed. "That Daisy Plumtre is a bad influence on you, I see."

"But you like merry, lively girls who speak up for themselves, take risks, and don't trouble over too much deep thought."

Slowly he smiled. "I like *you*, Diana Makepiece. I think I might like you better than any other."

She stepped back. Or perhaps it was more of a sway.

"When you're not scowling at me and putting up prickles, of course. Or decrying the purpose of my manly parts." He drew her close again, and when he sighed, she felt it travel through his body and into hers.

"I want this to be part of my adventure in Bath," she told him. "I am quite decided. Since I shan't marry, why not take a lover?" Diana discovered she rather liked saying that. It rolled very pleasingly off the tongue. Again she thought of her cousin's words, *One likes to have a less attractive, somewhat dowdy companion about the place.*

That would not be her. "I am determined," she added.

He stared. "You are determined, are you indeed?"

"I am. And since you have experience…and, I hear, considerable skill in the bedroom, why not you?"

He inhaled sharply. "Miss Makepiece, you are quite possibly mad."

"Yes. Quite possibly, while I am in Bath I shall be mad. So?"

A breathless laugh shot out of him.

She reminded him slyly, "*Gather ye rosebuds while ye may.*"

Nathaniel rubbed his chin slowly with his long fingers, a devious spark in his eyes.

"Oh dear," she murmured, "what now?"

His eyebrow wavered.

"I would prefer, madam, to thaw that icy heart of yours with a very respectable courtship. And despite my occasional clumsiness, I am not an elephant, so I would like a courtship with you that lasts longer than half an hour."

"*You* want a respectable courtship?" She didn't believe he knew how.

He raised her hand and kissed the leather-clad knuckles. "Let Miss Makepiece be duly warned that she is about to be severely, thoroughly, and painstakingly wooed. As she never has been. As the lady deserves."

"I see," she managed, more than a little breathless. "That's all very nice, I'm sure. But I just told you my intention. Surely the wooing is unnecessary."

"Not at all. Nothing *I* do, madam, is unnecessary! I hope you are ready, Miss Makepiece. Seduction is not merely a one-act play. It comes in three parts. With intermissions."

"Oh?" She laughed. "I look forward to your efforts, Captain. I'm sure they will be vastly…entertaining."

He pursed his lips, offered his arm again, and they walked on. "Entertaining, eh?" he chided.

"I do hope you won't be climbing any more trees to impress me. It is so easy to break a limb at your age."

He chuckled softly. "I can assure you, no further trees or limbs will be harmed in the process of this wooing."

She had no idea what he planned to do to her, but the anticipation was even greater than watching him scale that elm tree in foolish pursuit of a bonnet.

⌘

"I have a great deal of time for Sherry," Sir Jonty told Diana the following afternoon at Wollaford Park as they all sat in the conservatory and listened to the girls play harp and pianoforte. "He is a splendid fellow, and I should not mind him asking for one of my sisters. Not at all."

The subject of this discourse stood nearby, hands behind his back, focused on the ladies playing. Sun shone through the glass panels and lit him up from head to toe.

"He does seem very pleasant and amiable," she replied in a whisper so as not to disturb the music.

"If only the girls weren't quite so rough about the edges, what ho?"

Diana pretended she didn't know what he meant.

Jonty sighed gustily. "I know Lizzie don't think much of 'em. They ain't refined enough."

"They are delightful girls!"

"But they ain't without fault. I love my sisters, but I know what they lack."

She had to admit that the girls ate with their elbows on the table from time to time, and she had once seen Daisy fixing her garters midway through the pudding course.

"I wish they were more demure, Miss Makepiece,

more like you. I see how George admires your gentleness and your manners."

She stared ahead. "Oh?"

"Fellow lights up when you enter the room. I suppose you had lessons in deportment and the like, eh? Those lessons Lizzie is always pushing at me for the girls."

"No, indeed, we could not afford them. But my mama is very keen on proper behavior and it has been drummed into me since childhood."

"You were fortunate to have her, then."

"Yes," she said slowly, "I was."

"At least you can mix with society and never be out of place."

Diana was amused that he thought so. If only he knew. However calm and at ease she might look on the surface, she was very different inside. But perhaps he was right and her mother's training had helped her hide those anxieties and emotions so that no one ever guessed the turmoil beneath.

While it would indeed be nice to have a genial, demonstrably loving mother like Mrs. Plumtre once in a while, it was also useful to have a mother capable of giving direction. Fanny Plumtre was an amusing, benign lady, but she was quite without any authority over her daughters. She gave both girls suggestions, none of which were ever taken, and yet she bestowed her kisses upon her daughters anyway.

Jonty lowered his voice and suddenly became very solemn, as she'd never yet seen him. "I fear for my little sisters. Wouldn't like the girls to be looked down upon in the future. I know my wife considers me boorish, but that is just the way I am, Miss Makepiece. She knew that when she took me on. 'Tis too late for me to change and I see no reason for it. 'Tis different for a man, of course. I have a thick skin and not much troubles me. But Susy and Daisy—I should like them to belong, to fit in a little better."

Diana was moved by his great fondness for those two sparkling creatures and envious of the easy way he expressed it. He loved his sisters and didn't hide it, didn't see anything amiss with letting them know. Of course, that did give the girls rather too much rein, because they knew they wouldn't be punished. They knew how to get around their adoring great lummox of a brother.

"I should send the girls to your mama, what ho? Let them come under her strict thumb." He laughed, back to his usual jovial self. "I think they would soon upset the peaceful quiet of your little village, Miss Makepiece."

"Oh, it's not so very quiet there. I believe as much goes on there as in Bath, but not as many people get to witness it."

A short while later, while there was a pause in the music and they all applauded, Sir Jonty left her side to speak to his sisters. Diana saw George Plumtre getting up and moving toward her, as if intent on taking his brother's vacated seat, but suddenly Sherry was there instead, claiming the spot. George was obliged to divert his course midstep, and had only two choices—to return, looking foolish, to his own chair, or to take the empty one beside Mrs. Sayles. He chose the latter.

Diana's heart skipped giddily as she felt the tapestry

cushion beside her sink and, in her peripheral vision, saw Nathaniel's legs stretched out and crossed at the ankles, the leisurely pose of a man who was comfortable and self-assured. Here he came to do his "wooing."

"You look very well today, Miss Makepiece."

"Thank you, Captain."

"The flowers in your hair have distracted me all afternoon."

She had rather impulsively taken some white baby's breath from a little posy on her dressing table and tucked it into her hair. "Yes," she replied, feeling foolish. Hopefully she would not now break into Plumtre giggles.

"Looks like pearls from a distance, or little stars caught up in all that luscious midnight hair."

Diana threw him a hasty, bemused glance. "Very poetic, Captain. I'm sure if you look closely you may see some gray among the midnight."

He laughed, leaning back into the corner of the sofa. "No, not a strand. I think you must have found the secret of eternal youth here in Bath."

Susanna Plumtre now gestured for Diana to take her seat at the pianoforte, but Sherry abruptly shifted a few inches closer and trapped her skirt under his thigh. "Stay a moment," he murmured from the corner of his mouth.

"As it happens I am not in the mood to play, so I will pretend I haven't seen her."

"How lucky for me that you are not in the mood to play. With them." His hand found hers on the cushion between them, and he stroked the back of it gently with one fingertip. She shivered.

Jonty's sisters were excited about a concert they longed to attend. This discussion soon swept everyone up in a whirlwind of noise, and the two people on the sofa were temporarily forgotten.

"Certain expectations have been raised by your behavior, Captain," Diana warned him steadily. "You spend so much time at Wollaford that Sir Jonty thinks you will make an offer for one of his sisters very soon. He is beside himself with joy at the prospect."

He chuckled. "You know why I come here, Diana."

"To ride out with Sir Jonty and rescue stray hats?"

"Of course." He suddenly stretched his arm along the back of the sofa and tickled the nape of her neck, twisting a small curl around his finger. "Hats and other lost items that no one else dare retrieve."

If anyone looked over at the sofa, they would see his impropriety. Diana made an effort to slip her skirt out from under his thigh, but then his hand left the curl and came down to cover her fingers. Her breath squeezed out in short, hard gasps.

"I come here to see you," he whispered. "To admire your beauty, which strikes my heart anew each time I see it. No flowers in your hair can compete with that. They wilt in comparison to such delicate features. They bow their heads in deference."

"Oh, do stop. You're making my spleen ache."

"That's not your spleen." He leaned closer. "Don't pretend you can't see your own beauty, Diana. False modesty is not becoming. Be bold and know what you are. Know your own worth and stand up for it." His breath warmed her skin, skimming over her cheek with a partial kiss that was also a sigh, unheard and unseen by anybody but her. Then he stood and left her, strolling over to join the others around the pianoforte.

She saw him whisper something to Jonty, who then looked over his shoulder at Diana and exclaimed, "Miss Makepiece, you must attend the concert with us too, of course. Sherry says you have a fine ear for music."

"We'll all go," Nathaniel said firmly.

Jonty clapped his hands together, making his wife jump in her chair. "It will be a jolly company," he roared.

"Diana will not want to go," Elizabeth grumbled. "She has no reason to attend a concert, and she has been out too much as it is. Why would anyone want to sit and listen to music for hours on end with no respite? There will be no one there of any account, I'm sure. Diana can stay with me."

Every eye was suddenly upon Diana. There she was on the other side of the room, seated alone on the sofa and minding her own business, but now startled to be the center of all focus. She drew her feet further under the sofa and clasped her hands tightly together, taking up as little room as possible while she was being observed with pity and irritation.

"But the Viscountess Blakeney and her companion, Lady Dodsworth, will attend," Nathaniel cunningly intervened. "I was almost certain you would want to be there, Lady Plumtre. I'm surprised to hear you criticize a concert patronized by those ladies."

That naturally changed Elizabeth's mind for her, but she found another reason for Diana not to be included. "There will not be enough room in the barouche for all of us. I refuse to be packed in too tightly yet again."

"But that's part of the fun," Daisy exclaimed.

"Indeed it is not! It is undignified to arrive at the assemblies all squashed together, and I must wear my new taffeta silk which crumples if it is not well spread out."

Daisy fell back into a chair without the slightest attempt at grace and exhaled a hearty "*Fergalumph!*"

There was a pause and then Sherry said, "It is a concert of Bach, and Miss Makepiece was just telling me that he is a favorite of hers. You would not leave your house guest behind, surely? Even if it costs you a few more wrinkles."

Diana had never told him that Bach was a favorite, yet it was true. Somehow he must have found out.

Elizabeth's scowl might have shriveled the toes of a lesser man. "I merely point out the practicalities. My husband never thinks of them while he is inviting all and sundry on these jaunts."

The others blanched at hearing Diana described as "all and sundry," but she was not surprised. She understood now that she'd only been sent for because Elizabeth had anticipated a "frail" cousin's support in everything she said against the Plumtres. Expecting a Clarendon ally, a pale shadow, Elizabeth had instead found herself even more disgruntled and outnumbered.

"I'm sure we can arrange something," said Sherry, "if Miss Makepiece *does* desire to attend." He looked over at her, the blue of his eyes so intense and touching her in a shockingly intimate way. Encouraging and supporting all at once. "Does the lady desire?"

"Yes," she managed, slightly hoarse and ignoring her cousin's hard stare. "I should like to attend the concert."

"Good." He grinned broadly. "That's settled then!"

"What about me?" Caroline Sayles demanded. "I like to hear a good tune."

This, of course, had been one of Elizabeth's greatest fears when the invitation first began to expand. "We definitely have no room for you in the barouche," she replied speedily.

"Surely we can make room," said Daisy. "Having everybody crammed in makes it more fun!"

Clearly disgruntled, but with no one else taking her side, Elizabeth was obliged to say, "Captain Sherringham must find space for Mrs. Sayles then, if she means to come too."

There was a pause, and then Nathaniel said, "Mr. George Plumtre, I believe I heard you mention a splendid new curricle recently purchased. One that is free of drafts and has a cushioned seat of the highest quality."

Awoken suddenly to his chance of being and doing something important at last, George somberly assured the group that he would take a passenger in the new curricle about which he'd boasted earlier. And then he added, "Miss Makepiece will be quite safe with me."

Nathaniel's face fell, his plans obviously trumped, but Diana saw the keen smiles of his sisters and mother, so she could do nothing but accept George's offer, not wanting to disappoint them. She caught the tail end of Nathaniel's scowl before he turned away again.

She raised a hand to her cheek, where she still felt the brief and secret graze of his lips.

Those flowers in her hair were definitely causing mischief.

But she had not set out to cause any jealousy. At least, she did not think she had. It was a wickedly pleasant sensation, no denying it. Was it possible that she enjoyed it a little too much?

She had better come to her senses and put a stop to it. Tomorrow at the concert, she would make certain George Plumtre knew she regarded him as a friend only and nothing more.

As for Nathaniel…he told her it wasn't her spleen that he endangered. She suspected he was right.

Unfortunately she felt her cousin's eyes regarding her with chilly resentment, worse than before, and Diana wondered if she was not the only one who had begun to suspect.

Twenty

NATHANIEL BORROWED A CURRICLE FROM A BUSINESS acquaintance, but he did not ride to Westgate Buildings to fetch Mrs. Sayles. He rode to the lodge early, knowing that Diana was always punctual and would probably be waiting with her coat on. Didn't want her having too much time to think and come up with excuses when he turned up at her door instead of George, did he?

To his surprise, she was not waiting but still above stairs. Nathaniel was shown into the drawing room where he found Jonty and Lady Plumtre in evening dress, ready for the concert.

He hurriedly explained there had been a change of plan with the travel arrangements. "Mrs. Sayles was feeling under the weather and decided to stay at home with her aunt. Since I have the room, I thought I had better fill it with Miss Makepiece."

"But what about George?" Sir Jonty exclaimed.

"I understand there was some trouble with the new curricle. He said he would be delayed and asked me to make his apologies." Nathaniel didn't like to lie to his new friend, but Diana was worth it. He would do anything for her, he realized, and to have her company for himself alone.

"Well, that's a dashed sorry business! I warned him not to buy off that fellow Wilson. I've never had any luck with the vehicles he sells, have I, Lizzie?"

His wife ignored him and focused her spiteful eyes on Nathaniel. "Diana has been in such a tizzy all day. I cannot think why. It is only a concert."

Jonty replied, "She must not get so much excitement at home. 'Tis no wonder she is all at sixes and sevens. These young ladies do like to make a bit of a fuss over their pretty frocks." He strode to the brandy decanter on the sideboard. "Anybody want a stiffener before we go?"

His wife pulled on her long, white gloves. "Well, I doubt anyone cares what dress she wears. No one is going to be looking at *her* amid such exalted company, are they?"

"I shall," Nathaniel replied quietly.

Sir Jonty didn't hear. Discovering the crystal decanter lighter than he expected, he now marched to the door, shouting at the dogs that got under his feet and hollering for the butler to bring another bottle.

His wife, however, had heard Nathaniel's comment.

"I hope you know, Captain," said Lady Plumtre, "that my cousin is not in the market for a husband. Although you stated your own desire for a wife, Diana did not come to Bath for *that*."

"Is that so?"

"She is to be my companion in the future. Her

mother needs somewhere to put her, naturally, and I can give Diana a home."

"I doubt that is her mother's plan." He stopped hastily, remembering they were not supposed to have met before. "Most mothers want their daughters to marry well. They don't generally resign them to the life of a spinster lady's companion, especially when they are still so young."

Lady Plumtre laughed scathingly. "Young? You have been misled, perhaps by the eccentric way my sisters-in-law have encouraged her to dress. Diana Makepiece is soon to be eight-and-twenty. As for marriage, she gave that idea up some years ago when she broke off a long engagement. Her mother surely knows that Diana thwarted her own prospects then. She cannot expect another such chance to come her way. She has no dowry, nothing to recommend her really beyond a neat embroidery stitch and some little bit of skill at the pianoforte. She would have taken that other man while she could, if she had any desire to marry."

Her husband was on his way back across the room, tripping over his dogs a second time. "But, Lizzie, our George is quite besotted with her. Has his heart set on the lady."

She spun around to face him. "For pity's sake, stop calling me by that dreadful name. I am Elizabeth. If you cannot remember it, don't call me anything. And how can George be set on anybody when he was, not two weeks ago, grieving for another woman and swore he would never recover?"

Jonty's face reddened and he got on with pouring the brandy from a new bottle.

"As for Diana," Lady Plumtre continued snidely, "she is the worst woman for a man like George. She is cold and callous. Strung her fiancé along for two years and then, without the slightest warning, sent him away into the arms of another woman. Completely out of the blue she decided she could not marry him. So you see, Captain Sherringham, Diana is not looking for suitors. She is resolved to a future as my companion."

At first Nathaniel felt anger bubbling up inside. Of course the bloody woman wouldn't tell him that *she* was the one who ended the engagement to Shaw. What was she afraid of? That Nathaniel might think she did it because of him? That she had ever regretted her choice?

But the anger turned to something else when Diana entered the drawing room a few moments later. He began to wish he had accepted a glass of brandy from Jonty after all, for suddenly he needed the courage. He, who had never lacked it before around a beautiful woman.

She had sent Shaw away. She had defied her mother after all. Could this be the truth?

As for Diana being resigned to spinsterhood and spending the rest of her life at Lady Plumtre's beck and call?

Not likely. Not if he had any say in the matter.

She claimed to want only a lover, a temporary amusement while she spread her wings in Bath. But he was not prepared to let her go again.

He suffered a jolt of guilt as he thought of George whose heart was supposedly set on Diana. It was not entirely believable, considering the fellow's mournful demeanor only so recently put aside, but she was an exceptional woman. Perhaps George Plumtre truly did have intentions toward her and it wasn't merely a case of Jonty's optimism taking that leap.

Was it wrong for him to want her still? To sweep her away from George?

She wore a dark burgundy gown, simple and elegant, but she needed no embellishments. He realized it was the same dress she'd worn at the Manderson assemblies. Tonight, however, it looked different. Or was it simply the woman inside it who had changed? Her hair was softly curled about her face and tied up with a few bands of ribbon in a Grecian style. Small pearls hung from her ears—the only jewelry.

"Well, I must say!" Jonty exclaimed, almost dropping his glass. "You look quite lovely, my dear."

A light pink suffused Diana's cheeks and she looked at the carpet, her thick, dark lashes lowered. "I am sorry it took so long, but I had to wait for the maid."

"Well, if she hadn't made an undue fuss over dressing me, you might have had her sooner," her cousin remarked. "She was all thumbs dressing my hair and could not get it the way I wanted it. Useless girl. I really don't know why I bother taking such young girls in to train them."

"Because she's cheap, ain't she?" Jonty laughed. "And it gives you someone else to shout at other than me, Lizzie."

Before Lady Plumtre could start berating her husband again, Nathaniel stepped up and bowed. "Miss Makepiece, I would gladly wait thrice the time for the pleasure of escorting such a beautiful lady to the Bath Assembly Rooms on a Wednesday evening."

Her lashes lifted and he saw the gleam of shock. "You're here for me? But where is George… Mr. Plumtre?"

Probably about to read a forged note from Mrs. Sayles begging him to fetch her from Westgate Buildings, he mused. "He had some trouble with his curricle and sent me in his place so you would not miss the beginning of the concert. Such a gentleman he is."

Diana gazed at Nathaniel as if she didn't believe a word of it.

"Shall we go?" he said.

She hesitated, but finally took his arm. "Something about this is very odd. If not for Bach," she muttered from the corner of her lips, "I would stay here and not mind if I was late."

"Cheers to Johann Sebastian then." Nathaniel steered her quickly out to his borrowed curricle before anyone could discover his ruse, or before he changed his mind and gave in to the unusual occurrence of a guilty conscience.

❧

Beside him in the small, well-sprung vehicle, Diana watched the glittering lights of Bath flash by. The satin sky above them was not yet as dark as it would be, but already dotted with stars. The warm air drifted around her like a soft, silk cape with only a gentle breeze stroking her face as they dashed along.

"Lady Plumtre tells me you mean to become her companion," said Nathaniel suddenly. "That you are resigned to being an old maid, to living at her side and serving at her beck and call for the rest of your life."

What a horrible thought! She chuckled.

"She can give you a home, she said. When your mother no longer can."

"How charitable of her."

"And *you* ended the engagement with Shaw," he said.

Diana sighed heavily, watching stars and puddles of lamplight reflected in the river as they approached the bridge. Her mother must have told Elizabeth, she thought. "Yes."

"Why?"

"That is an intimate question and I cannot answer it." Diana's heart struggled to keep a steady beat. She still had not learned how to discuss what she felt, or even to believe it herself. Although so much was different here—*she* was different—sooner or later she would have to go home to face her mother again. It was all very well to be a new woman away from her mother's view, but then what? Could this change be lasting for her?

He was still the naughty captain at heart, the accomplished, artful lover, the bold rogue. She was quite sure he'd fabricated the entire story about George's curricle. Naturally, he wouldn't worry about what would happen when his deceit was exposed and he'd have to face the consequences. He thought only of the here and now, of what he wanted in that moment.

"What happened to Mrs. Sayles this evening?" she asked coyly.

"She is unwell."

"But she is always unwell. In the two weeks of our acquaintance I've never known that to stop her from going out into society or missing an invitation, however begrudgingly it was granted."

"I am sure Mr. George Plumtre will find room to bring her. If she should recover suddenly."

"When he fixes that broken curricle?"

"Yes." He smirked.

Diana shook her head. "It was rather cruel of you to leave Mrs. Sayles behind."

"But she wouldn't know whether she'd missed the beginning of the concert or not. You would. Like your cousin, she is only coming tonight because it's a social event, not for the music."

There was no arguing with that. Whatever wickedness he'd employed to arrange their trip together, she was grateful for it. Did that make her as bad as him?

They didn't wait in the Octagon Room for the rest of their party. Sherry took her directly into the Tea Room where the concert was being held. He was quiet now, thoughtful perhaps.

Diana became aware of people turning to watch them pass. There were appreciative smiles and respectful nods, evident curiosity and keen interest. She could not imagine that any of it was for her in that old gown. It had to be for Sherry who, as usual, stole more light than any other man in the room. How lovely it was to be on his arm. She had imagined herself shrinking, squinting, and shriveling in such a bright, hot glow, but when he smiled at her with genuine pleasure she forgot her fears and stretched into the warm light. His smile was just as effective as a spoonful of Dr. Penny's tonic.

On the way to their seats, he stopped and introduced her to several folk. They knew him through his business it seemed. He had asked her first if she would mind meeting them and she had replied in mild surprise, "Why would I mind? Of course I would like to meet your friends."

They were pleasant, well-spoken, witty people who greeted her with polite cordiality and seemed not in the least startled that Sherry would be in the company of such a shy, plain girl. Well, not so plain, she thought, remembering that he had accused her of false modesty. She was getting accustomed to looking in the mirror and not immediately finding all her bad features, looking instead for the good, the passable, and the slightly improved.

Nor was she so shy anymore. Diana had proven to herself that she could be entertaining and hold her own in a conversation. She'd had plenty of practice at the Plumtres' table where it was necessary to be loud. One might starve otherwise.

They took their seats. The lights were lowered and the chatter of the crowd muted. He had made sure to arrive separately from the others in their party because he wanted to sit with her away from all of them. He didn't want her to suffer the distractions and demands of that noisy bunch, because he knew what music meant to her. Over the years of their acquaintance he had witnessed her yearning to simply enjoy the music while everyone around her prevented it.

Tonight he wanted her to know that he understood,

that he was not the empty-headed buffoon she thought him to be. Well, not always.

He might not be as clever as she was about music, but he knew what it was to be frustrated, to want something badly and never quite be able to capture it.

And he was wooing her, as he'd warned. He gave her all his attention.

Several women at the concert recognized him, but he carefully avoided their searching gazes and waving fingers. If Diana noticed, she gave no sign.

As the music began, he reached for her gloved hand and held it lightly on his thigh.

She did not struggle to take it back, and her fingers eventually relaxed as the slightly plaintive notes of a slowly soaring melody took hold of her senses.

Nathaniel wanted to say much to her, but tonight he would be quiet and let her enjoy the music.

According to the printed program at which she'd glanced as they sat down, this was Bach's Concerto in D minor for two violins and orchestra. She would never forget. That rather uninspired name had given no clue as to the heart-wrenching beauty of the music they were about to hear. Although familiar with the composer's work, she had never heard this piece and it was instantly carved into her soul.

With her hand in Sherry's, she let the music claim her. Felt the poignant notes steal inside her veins and fill her with exquisite joy. Never had she been able to hear an entire piece from beginning to end without interruption.

He could have brought her jewelry or some other fancy gift, which perhaps she might have expected from the old Nathaniel trying to impress her. Instead he gave her this moment, knowing her better than anyone. It would cost him—perhaps end his new friendship with Sir Jonty once he knew that Nathaniel had lied to steal her away from George that evening. So many people would be annoyed and upset.

Yet he had done all that to sit beside her and make sure she enjoyed the concert.

Reckless, risk-taking Sherry.

Diana closed her eyes, not just to hide the tears that filled them, but to let the music take over completely. Into her very bones it came. And she tightened her fingers around Sherry's hand, squeezing.

There was no other sound but the music and her heartbeat in her ears.

❧

"*Sherry! I thought it was you from behind*," the woman shouted to him as they passed through the Octagon Room after the concert. "I've never seen you so still. I thought you must be passed out drunk! But I couldn't hear you snoring."

He winced. Couldn't remember the woman's name. Julia perhaps? Jenny? Damn it.

Diana had not said a word to him since the music began, but she seemed in haste to get out of the place now that the last note had been played. He tried to keep up with her as the crowd surged around them.

Another woman to the left of their path also waved

a program at him. "Sherry! Sherry! What are you doing here? You never were one for music, as I recall!"

"I didn't know you were in Bath, old chap!" another fellow bellowed behind him.

Nathaniel struggled onward, keeping Diana's head in his sights as it bobbed in and out. Where the devil was she going in this much haste?

At the doors their progress was hampered by a cluster of folk all trying to get out at once. He caught Diana's sleeve to hold her back, and instantly wished he had not because they came face to face with another woman with a high-hoisted bosom and a very low-cut gown. Her thick perfume hung in a cloud around them.

"Sherry, darling!" she cried in a gushing breath of gin and aniseed. "I wondered when you would come back to Bath. I thought you had deserted us. No one fun ever calls in to see me anymore!" She noticed then that he was with Diana. Her heavy, languid gaze swept down and up, and then she smiled. "Do call upon me soon. When you are free."

He moved to pass her and she stuck out her closed fan, poking it into his chest.

"I have missed you, Sherry. All the girls have."

"Excuse me." He pushed the woman's fan away and hurried after Diana again.

When at last he was outside in the fresh air he found her standing by the horses, tears in her eyes.

"Diana, none of those women meant anything to me," he began. "I went there to play cards, not—"

She silenced him with a gloved finger to his lips. "Don't say anything. Take me away from here. Now. While there is still time for us."

"Time for us?"

"The Plumtres will find us at any minute. I saw them in the crowd. And then you will have to explain your actions to them."

"What do I care?" he muttered.

"*I* care," she said. "I don't want a scene to spoil the evening. It's been so wonderful. Please, don't let it be over yet."

Without another word he helped her up into the curricle.

&

He'd expected her to insist that he take her back to Wollaford, but instead she wanted to see his lodgings.

"Show me where you stay when you are in Bath," she said.

He hesitated. "It's not the sort of place one takes a lady."

"Then pretend I am not one."

"Don't be ridiculous, Diana."

"I am being daring, determined. You accused me before of not being so."

But he had said those things to her in frustration when he was trying to find a way into her heart and wanted to make her show emotion. "I cannot take you to my lodgings."

"Where is it then?" she demanded. "A house of ill repute, such as those you apparently frequent while here?"

So much for not wanting the evening spoiled. "No! It's a perfectly respectable boarding house for single gentlemen, but the landlady doesn't allow female guests in the rooms." One hand guiding the reins, he reached for his handkerchief and passed it to her.

She snatched it from his hand. "I'm not crying about all your women, so don't think I am," she said. "The music was too beautiful, that's all. It left a deep impression upon me."

He wasn't sure he believed her.

Perhaps reading his doubt in the fluttering amber of passing lamplight, she added, "The music was sad, hopeful, sweet, and bitter all at once."

"Does that mean you liked it, or not?" One could never be sure with women. Not one like her, anyway.

"Yes," she replied sulkily, blowing her nose hard.

"Well, that's alright then." They rode on a while and then he said, "At least now I know you have some feelings. Finally, tears! For music, of all things."

She sniffed, blinking her wet lashes.

Nathaniel took a deep breath. "There have been women in my past, Diana. Doesn't mean anything."

She was quiet.

"A man cannot change his past," he said, "only his future." He cleared his throat and the horses cantered along, the wheels of the curricle rumbling over cobbles. "I hope that the woman I marry can accept me despite my faults and will not hold past mistakes over my head each time she thinks of them."

"You want her to ignore so much, never to know about those women, never to ask. Is that treating her fairly? You would want—expect—to know all about her past."

He frowned. "What past could she have had?"

Diana snorted. "See? You want her to ask you nothing, yet she must hide nothing from you."

"She should have nothing to hide!" He turned his head to look at her and then he repeated, "What past could she have had?"

"She must know nothing of yours. Why should you know about hers?" Her eyes shone, even with her face in shadow.

"I didn't say she should know nothing," he muttered, suddenly peevish. "I said she shouldn't think of it or bring it up every time she wants to start a quarrel with her husband." The thought of Diana having experience of that kind had never occurred to him. According to Sarah Wainwright's gossip, Diana hadn't even wanted to kiss William Shaw. But was that the truth? Two years of an engagement was a long time for a man to go without trying something.

He would have.

Who the devil was engaged for two years and didn't even share a kiss, for pity's sake? Oh, no indeed, she must have… He couldn't bear to think of it.

Jealousy struck as it never had before, like a serpent's tongue.

"I think she should at least know what you did with your paramours," Diana said. "She should know that much."

"Very well," he exclaimed hotly, "I'll show her." He turned the horses toward Sydney Gardens.

Twenty-one

WITH THE WONDERFUL MUSIC STILL SINGING THROUGH
her blood, Diana was flying that night. She didn't want
to go home to her book and her bed. Not yet.

This moment with Nathaniel was magical, the sort
of moment that might never come again.

Of course she knew there were many women in his
past. Nathaniel had never made any secret of it. Seeing
their eager faces as they tried to catch his eye had
merely reminded her of the fact. He had experienced
much that she had not, and tonight she was forced
again to consider the disadvantages of being a woman
in this world.

Diana had always accepted the fact that if she
did marry one day, her husband would have more
knowledge in certain matters. Unlike her friends, the
Book Club Belles, she had never been particularly
keen to know about relations between husband and
wife. William Shaw had certainly never inspired those
yearnings within her. But Nathaniel...oh, Nathaniel
had always upset the rhythm of her pulse.

She'd assumed it was because he was forbidden. He

was a man she knew she could not have, the naughty book she could never open. Her mother had warned her about him from the first time they met.

Now that she finally allowed herself to admit her feelings for him, they flourished inside her. They had grown too quickly for her to manage, and tonight they took over completely.

But Nathaniel treated her gingerly, barely daring to touch her. That was not how he had been with other women, she was quite sure. Diana did not want to be treated as if she were made of dainty china and might break.

"I'm stronger than I look," she whispered.

He had halted the curricle under some trees off a deserted path in the park. It was quiet, the air warm and still.

"Touch me the way you touched them. I want to know what it's like. With you."

"Diana—"

"Now," she commanded. "I want you to touch me. Everywhere."

She guided his hand to her breast as they sat beneath the whispering trees, and he felt the hard, thrusting beat of her heart.

"I am supposed to be wooing you properly," he groaned. The silk taffeta of her gown was soft and warm under his palm as he explored her shape.

"Yes, well… I don't have patience for that." She kissed his cheek, licked his ear, nibbled his lower lip.

"The music did something to you tonight."

She stroked his thigh with a bold hand, then reached for the fall of his breeches.

"Diana," he moaned, sliding down into the grass with her.

"Hush." He felt her fingers inside his breeches, venturing eagerly forth. And then she made a small sound when she found what she sought, her hand closing around it. "You gave me a lovely gift tonight," she whispered. "Let me give you something in return."

Nathaniel knew that he would need all his willpower tonight to keep from finishing what she began, but at that moment his protesting mind was blank. His body and his white-hot desires took over.

He felt for the hooks on the back of her gown and loosened as many as he could to tug it down over her shoulders. Her skin shone like a polished pearl in a slender shaft of moonlight that filtered through the leaves above. A sweet but very faint scent of lavender reached his nostrils and he inhaled deeply, taking in as much of her as he could while kissing her throat and the curve of her exposed shoulder. The yearning he'd tried so hard to stifle in her presence now pushed at the bindings of his will, desperate to break free.

His lips traveled down over the swelling flesh of her bosom above her corset. He could just make out the darker shade of her nipple under the lace chemise. He let his tongue sweep over it, ruffling and dampening the delicate lace, allowing himself just that one taste. But her nipple instantly rose to attention, pricking through a hole in the thin, dainty border of lace and taunting him. Wanting more. He could not bear the temptation and took her nipple again between his lips. He closed his eyes.

She gasped, trembling. Her hands stroked his manhood, fingertips tracing slowly up and down the length as it grew and stretched. The heaviness and heat of his desire for her mounted.

The pounding in his temple became faster, harder. His breathing was shallow and quick, but he couldn't hear hers. Was she holding her breath?

He sucked gently and felt her arch under him, writhing.

Her perspiration was sweet, intoxicating, and as he licked it from her skin, Diana's body responded keenly, stretching and arching. Was she humming? Some sound touched his ears, not much louder than a flutter of butterfly wings.

It was, he realized, just like his lusty dreams in which she came to his bed. As his wife.

His wife. Not a hussy.

She was a lady. Thinking of her mother's disapproving face was enough to shrink a man's plums to prunes. "Diana." Her hasty wriggling had succeeded in slipping the chemise down and freeing her breast. The wet nipple jutted upward enticingly. "We must not."

It didn't even sound convincing in his ears and yet it was his voice, his protest.

"I told you, I want a lover, Sherry."

Nathaniel reached down, meaning to pull her hand out of his breeches, but his fingers brushed her garter instead and then her thigh. He immediately forgot what he'd been aiming for.

With a grunt he lowered his mouth again to her breast, wild with hunger.

She made an odd purring sound, her free hand grabbing his hair, her fingers scratching his scalp.

Lost to reason, he touched her between the thighs, felt her dewy softness rubbing against his palm and then his fingers. He could feel her pulse thudding away, rocking her entire body as he fondled her, exploring, teasing, and tending with slow strokes and quick ones.

She murmured his name, his hair twisted around her fingers, her other hand tugging on his erection until he thought he would explode.

When he felt her peak and heard the groans, Nathaniel had to calm his own desires. His heart was racing, his body seized in the grip of raw lust. He wanted to claim her then and there, but that would undo everything he'd been working for these past few days in her company. Even what he had done now was more than he should have.

But the ice queen had turned into a demanding vixen.

He kissed her while she still trembled, her mouth open on a small, sharp cry of delight, her eyes closed. He tasted her tongue, sucked on it, licked her lips, lingering over her.

She was like no one else. He wanted all of her, including her heart, not just possession of her body.

"The sky will soon be lightening," he whispered. "I must return you to your hosts, before they send out a search party and have me clapped in irons."

"But surely we have ages yet."

Nathaniel sighed and gently kissed her brow. "I fear not, my love. I've kept you so late it's early."

Yes, it would soon be a new day. New for him in so many wonderful ways.

❧

He delivered her to the lodge and would have come in with her to explain to the others why they were late, but she made him go. A weary-faced footman answered the door and let her in.

"Lady Plumtre is in the drawing room, madam," he told her gravely, his eyes coldly disapproving of her tumbled hair. She'd tried, with Nathaniel's assistance, to put the arrangement of curls back together again and failed miserably. Captain Sherringham wasn't nearly as skilled at repairing a lady's disordered wardrobe as she'd imagined he would be. And she was rather pleased about that discovery.

"Thank you, but I think I'll go directly to bed. I am dreadfully tired." Thus, Diana slipped upstairs to her room. It might be rude, but she could not face Elizabeth's censorious scowl or any prying questions. Not tonight. Nothing should be allowed to spoil the beautiful evening she'd just enjoyed.

Of course, she might have known that Elizabeth would not let her rest in peace. Knuckles were soon heard on the bedchamber door, and Diana—in the process of changing for bed—was forced to answer the angry tapping.

"Elizabeth, I am tired. Please, can this wait until morning?"

"Oh, I'm quite sure you are tired. And it *is* morning."

"Goodness gracious. Is it really?" Diana tried to sound concerned, but unfortunately the music was still playing in her head and Sherry's kisses were imprinted on her flesh. She was drunk with the joys of discovery.

"What could you be thinking to ride off alone with

him, to willfully separate yourself from us and come back at this hour?"

"In truth, Elizabeth, I had no notion of the time. I was enjoying myself too much."

Her cousin stared, eyes popping. "Your mother will hear of this."

Diana sighed. "I expect she will." But it was too late for her mother to do anything about it. She was far, far away.

"You knew that he lied, I suppose—about George's curricle."

She felt her cousin's frosty gaze scraping over her face and looking at the hanging, droopy curls that had been flattened by the exertions of her evening and now dangled untidily against the side of her neck and down to her shoulders. "Not for certain. Not at first."

Elizabeth marched around the room, fists clenched at her sides. "What do you suppose Lady Dodsworth and the Viscountess thought of you, gallivanting about with that man? He has a terrible reputation, so I hear. It all came to light this evening, but I cannot say I was surprised. I suspected as much from the beginning. I told Jonty it serves him right for jumping into an association with a man about whom he knew so little, but he would not heed me."

"You should not believe gossip, Elizabeth. It is not ladylike."

Her cousin whirled around. "How dare you say that to me? How dare you think to tell me anything? The way you behaved tonight has caused me nothing but shame. Oh yes, Lady Dodsworth saw you at the concert. *Holding his hand in public and with no engagement between you*. Nothing more than an acquaintance of a few weeks. Someone told her you were a Clarendon, and when she approached me, I did not know how to explain and apologize for such behavior."

Diana folded her arms. "I am only half a Clarendon," she pointed out. "I daresay you might blame any wickedness on my father's blood." What would Elizabeth do, she wondered, if she knew what else of Nathaniel's Diana had held that night. More than his hand. Much more.

"The less said about your father, the better!"

Walking to the window, Diana opened it wide to let in fresh air. "I should tell you, Elizabeth, that I have known Captain Sherringham a great deal longer than a few weeks." The confession came out of her mouth before she could think to prevent it. In that instant she wanted to shout her happiness out loud through the window. She wanted people to know. Especially Elizabeth, who thought Diana could not know anyone or anything of interest.

Her cousin gripped the brass bedpost with straining, clawed fingers. "I knew there was something amiss with that man! He was too full of smiles, too quick to befriend everybody."

Diana laughed. "You liked him well enough when you learned of his fortune."

"No matter how much money one has, breeding cannot be bought. That was confirmed tonight by his careless, scandalous behavior."

"You sound like my mama." Diana shook her head. "I may as well tell you that I am the woman who once rejected his marriage proposal, a decision I have come to regret since I know now what I gave up and how I allowed myself to be persuaded by the will of others." She felt the breeze on her face, gentle as his kiss. "But I blame only myself. From now on, choices will be my own, whatever they are and wherever they take me. I'm sorry if that does not comply with your plans for me, but you see, I do have a life of my own and I was born to live it, not to live for anybody else."

Elizabeth stood in shocked silence for several moments, and then she walked out and shut the door hard behind her. Diana had no doubt that a letter would immediately be penned to her mother. And before many more days had passed, she would be summoned home.

Tomorrow would be time enough to worry about that.

She climbed into bed and stretched with a lusty sigh. Just one more chapter to read before she closed her eyes.

> *"I have been thinking over the past, and trying impartially to judge of the right and wrong, I mean with regard to myself; and I must believe that I was right, much as I suffered from it, that I was perfectly right in being guided by the friend whom you will love better than you do now…*
>
> *"Do not mistake me, however. I am not saying that she did not err in her advice. It was, perhaps, one of those cases in which advice is good or bad only as the event decides; and for myself, I certainly never should, in any circumstance of tolerable similarity, give such advice. But I mean, that I was right in submitting to her…"*

Diana knew that her mother had persuaded her against Nathaniel for sound reasons. She had always known it. She had made a coolheaded decision to reject his proposal, being perfectly sensible for both of them since he could not be.

But she and Nathaniel were the same people they had been back then. She could no longer keep her heart out of the equation. This rebellion had not begun when she drank too much gooseberry wine, or he came back to Hawcombe Prior, or even when she told William Shaw that she couldn't marry him.

It had begun when Nathaniel kissed her under the arches of the Bolt, catching her unawares when she'd thought she had all the facts before her. His kiss had made her realize there was something she'd forgotten. Something she'd left behind that only a reckless, brazen, tree-climbing man would come back to find for her.

Twenty-two

RISING EARLY THE NEXT DAY, NATHANIEL RODE immediately to Wollaford, where his first order of business was to apologize for the deception with the curricle. But he found George Plumtre out and his sisters apparently at a dress fitting in town. His mother greeted Nathaniel as she always did, apparently not bearing any grudge toward him for keeping Diana apart from them at the concert.

"As long as Miss Makepiece enjoyed herself, Captain," said Mrs. Plumtre earnestly, "all is well with us. We have grown very fond of the lady. We *all* have grown fond of her."

He knew she meant George, of course.

"I had hoped, madam, to have a word with your younger son this morning. Is he expected to return soon?"

She assured him that George would be gone some time, but she did not seem able to say where he went. Or if she knew, the lady had been commanded not to inform Nathaniel. There was something strange about it, but he did not want to make her uneasy, so having stayed a polite quarter hour, he took his leave and rode to the lodge.

His reception there was less forgiving. Jonty was not at home either, and after a hasty inquiry, he learned from the footman who opened the front door that Diana was also gone, off to the dress fitting with the Plumtre sisters. This left Lady Elizabeth Plumtre in the drawing room when he entered. She made no attempt to hide her disdain and accused him at once of being out to cause scandal and besmirch the Plumtre name. Not to mention the Clarendon reputation.

"I wish you would take that awful Caroline Sayles and leave Bath before you cause any more trouble. Surely you have imposed upon my husband's hospitality long enough. Even he is not so dim as to continue opening his doors to a man who embarrasses his family, flirts shamelessly with his little sisters, lies blatantly to his face, runs off with his wife's companion, and leaves a notorious concubine to distract his brother."

"Yes, I am aware that my actions last night were not those of a gentleman. I came here today to apologize to George and to Jonty."

"And yet neither of them are at home to you. Can you be at a loss to realize why? You are not welcome here, Captain. You have, as they say, outstayed your welcome at Wollaford. I suggest you stay away for your own good. And for Diana's."

He had nothing more to say that could be civil and decided he had better leave before he lost his temper. There was a time when he would have uttered a parting rude remark to make the lady fall down in a dead faint.

But she was not worth the breath.

Fortunately, he knew where that dressmaker was located, did he not?

❧

"I am not certain. It seems a little…low at the bodice." Diana looked in the long mirror. She had rarely seen her full reflection except in a clean window, and even then it was usually distorted. Today she could take in the entire shape and it was worrisome, to say the least. Had she grown plumper in just a few weeks, or did her new ball gown and undergarments provide her with several inches of more obvious curves? The food at Wollaford Park was always very good, and she had eaten plenty of it. Perhaps she ought to slow down, she mused.

No need to try everything put before her.

She flushed, thinking suddenly of Nathaniel and all the things she meant to try with him.

The dressmaker smiled and showed her that a pretty lace tuck could be used if she felt herself too exposed. But Susanna and Daisy exclaimed that they really didn't think she needed it.

"Why should you hide your bosom?" cried Daisy. "There is nothing amiss with it and everyone knows it's there. If men had a bosom, they'd show it off at every opportunity."

Diana corrected her. "One does not say *bosom*, Daisy."

"Then what does one say?"

"One should not generally refer to it at all."

The girls laughed at her blushes, and the dressmaker took her down the corridor to a changing room where

Diana could slip out of her new gown in privacy. She was relieved to escape inside that small room, close the door, and no longer have to look at herself in the mirror. It was most disconcerting to see oneself from the toes up.

Hands began to unhook her from behind and she thought nothing of it, assuming one of the dressmaker's assistants had waited for her to return from the viewing room.

Until she realized the fingers were very slow and not at all dexterous. And rather more keen on tickling than in removing her gown. She turned in surprise.

"Sherry!"

He placed a finger to her lips and she hastily swallowed the sound.

Drawing her closer, he kissed Diana and she felt the joy take hold of her again. Would every time he kissed her be like this? She hoped so.

She whispered, "How did you get in?"

"I have connections in Bath." He grinned.

Of course he did, she thought. How many other women had he waited for in these little rooms? She didn't want to know.

For now he was her audacious, wicked Sherry. And she was complicit in his crimes.

"I knew this was yours," he added, pointing to the familiar muff hanging from a hook on the wall. "I had to see you, Diana. Make certain last night was not just a dream."

Oh, she knew how he felt.

She nodded, catching her breath.

Slowly he kissed her again, gently, and then made

his way down her throat. "Hmmm." He pressed his wet lips to her breasts where they rose and fell above that fine lace. "I like this gown. I approve."

"I am glad. I've never had a gentleman pay for my dress before."

He dropped to a stool in the corner and she sat astride his lap, exploring his hair and his face with eager, nibbling kisses. "A gentleman?" he growled. "Who? Tell me the blackguard's name."

"Sir Jonty, of course."

"You lie. It's not Jonty who pays for this." He hooked one finger around the silk and lowered it to plant another kiss against her breast.

"It is!" She wriggled, reaching for the fall of his breeches.

"It is some man with designs upon you." Nathaniel stopped her hands and pinned them behind her back. "Some rake who plans to get under this pretty frock."

"Nonsense!"

"Oh, yes, it is. A man who wants this"—he gathered up the skirt and tickled his way up her thighs and over her stocking tops—"and this." He spread his fingers, tightened his grip around her thighs, and slid her closer. "And this."

She gasped as he touched her in that intimate spot.

"This sweet treasure," he whispered.

Diana tried to keep silent, but he did not make it easy. He knew exactly how to touch, caress, withdraw, and tease.

With his other hand he reached up to run his fingers over her trembling, lowered eyelids. "But he also wants these." His caress traveled to her ear, looping a stray curl behind it. "And these." Down across her

cheek his fingertips swept, to her lips. "And these."
Then finally down to her breast where he placed his
hand over her heart. "And this."

"This rake wants a great deal too much," she
managed.

"That's why he pays for your gown," he assured
her huskily, the other set of fingertips pressing and
circling, quickening their strokes.

"I assure you he—uh. Oh."

"Hmm? What's that, Miss Makepiece? I didn't
quite hear that." He grinned slowly.

Her body quivered, her nerve endings tingled, and
every muscle in her body tightened as the blissful
waves rolled over her.

With his entire hand he cupped her sex and
squeezed, intensifying the tremors until she bit her
tongue and tasted blood.

"He wants all of you, madam," he whispered.
"That's why he has already paid the dressmaker for her
services. And her discretion."

Diana opened her eyes. "You? But Sir Jonty—"

"Will find the bill already paid. Anonymously,
of course."

She wasn't sure how to feel about that. "I don't
want you buying things for me."

"You wanted a lover," he reminded her softly,
sliding a finger over her damp, sensitive flesh. "This is
the sort of thing lovers do."

She had to take his word for it. His eyes were very
light and very blue that day, and she imagined floating on her back in a warm bath. Naked. An indecent
thought of the type he was more and more often

planting inside her mind. Apparently without meaning to do so.

Suddenly, her mind made up, she slid off his lap and went to her knees between his strong, broad thighs. Before he could stop her, she had freed his roused organ from his breeches.

"Diana," he groaned. "Take care. Don't go too far. I can't hold—"

"But darling," she purred, "this is the sort of thing lovers do." And she lowered her mouth over his staff, suddenly extremely glad for one of those shocking conversations she'd once overheard between Rebecca and Jussy.

Nathaniel's thighs tensed, but his hands fell to his sides, then to her hair. He grunted, shifting on the stool. "I can't hold back," he muttered under his breath.

Well, as Jussy would say, when a person was in trouble anyway, they might as well make it worth their while.

∾

He helped her up when she was done and set her on his knee again.

"Make love to me," she whispered. "All the way."

"Here?" He chuckled softly. "Demanding, aren't you? And altogether too reckless today."

"I'm tired of waiting."

"It would ruin your lovely new white frock," he murmured in her ear, his breath skittering over her skin.

"Then take it off me."

He laughed huskily, softly. "Oh no, no, no. That would be more temptation than a rake like me can withstand." Even one that had just spent, he mused. It wouldn't take him long to be roused again in her presence.

"Then don't withstand," she urged.

"Diana, behave yourself." He grabbed her wrists and kissed her palms.

She pouted. "It is just my fortune, sir, that the moment I am ready to misbehave, you are determined not to."

"I think we misbehaved quite enough," he muttered. "This rebellion of yours…"

"What about it?"

He trapped her chin in the vee between his thumb and fingers. "Is it only for me?"

Nathaniel Sherringham had never been so uncertain in his life.

✎

About to give some pert, evasive answer, Diana stopped and reconsidered. A certain vulnerability was apparent in his expression. She had never seen it before, and it made her want to put her arms around him, to lay her soul bare before him.

But for how many years had she watched this merry rogue flirt and seduce while she stood in the shade, desperately trying to keep her heart locked safely away? Not knowing whether to take him seriously at all. She recognized now how much she had yearned for him. But that old Diana had punished herself, forbidden herself the pleasure—just as her mother stored those precious spices on a dark shelf and never dared use any.

She smiled at him, her heart aching with so many emotions. None would be denied any longer. Diana took his fingers and pulled his hand away, saying gently, "No. This rebellion, Captain Sherringham, is for me. And only me." It was about time, she thought, that she did something purely for herself.

He nodded, his narrowed gaze on her lips. After a breath, he said, "Stop writhing in my lap. You're being an unbearable tease."

The solemn moment had passed.

"Does it hurt, then?" she said, brows curved.

"Immeasurably," he assured her.

"I thought I just cured it."

"That, I fear, was temporary."

Fingers tapped against the dressing room door and a polite voice asked if she needed assistance.

"No, thank you," she called back. "I'll be out shortly."

Nathaniel slid the shoulders of her dress down and kissed her skin, nuzzling the valley between her breasts where they rose above her new chemise. She felt his lap growing under her again and shifted her weight to his left thigh.

"You will come to the Wollaford ball on Friday?" she asked, running her hand carefully over the ridge in his breeches.

"After last night, I ought to keep my distance from Wollaford. I don't want to cause trouble. Christ, Diana, I should never have driven off with you like that. What must they all think of me?"

"That has never bothered you before!" Keeping his distance? He was not doing that now, she thought, amused. "You had better come to the Wollaford ball, or folk might think we have something to be guilty about when I have assured them all on the contrary."

He finally gave her a lopsided smile, like a boy caught misbehaving. "Very well. I will see you there, Diana. Save a dance for me. If you are not scooped up by all the other gentlemen who will fall under your spell in this wretchedly exquisite gown I so foolishly purchased for you."

Diana wanted to laugh out loud, but of course she could not. For once she believed it when he told her how she looked. Her heart thumped madly, joyfully. Yes, she felt beautiful at last.

She kissed his lips hungrily, devouring his soft groan of desire. Was he waiting for more assurance that he was the only one? He did not push for it and she was relieved, for she might have given in. This carelessness was harder than it looked.

He slid a hand between her thighs, under her fine new gown again, drawing his fingertips slowly and tenderly over her roused flesh until she wanted to purr. As her neck arched and her head went back, he kissed the base of her throat. "I should make you promise to dance with me all evening," he murmured, his breath warm, tickling her moist skin. "I have never felt so possessive in my life. So envious of any man that looks at you."

"Poor Sherry. I'm sure you'll manage." *I had to*, she thought. *For years I had to.* She gasped, shivering, caught in the grip of passion as he caressed her skillfully to yet another slow, blissful peak.

"Even when you are out of my sight, Diana," he groaned hotly into her breast, "you are never out of my mind, damn you. I swore I would not make a fool of myself again with you. It's an obsession. It must be."

And then he took her over the edge and she plummeted, biting her tongue to keep from crying out. Her eyes closed tight, she melted—parts of her quite literally.

Well, he had always said he would thaw her out.

She tipped forward to lay her head on his shoulder as he leaned back against the wall of the tiny dressing room.

"If it's an obsession," she whispered, "it cannot last. It will burn itself out."

For a moment he said nothing. She felt his heart thumping hard against her own. Oh, what were they doing together?

"Stand up," he growled suddenly, his hand still caressing her intimately.

Should one ever disobey a command from a man when he seemed annoyed under these circumstances?

She swiftly decided to comply. A naughty imp whispered in her ear: *You know very well what you're doing, Diana. Pricking his temper. Tantalizing and teasing. Being wicked and revolutionary and flirtatious. Being everything you were always warned against. And didn't think you could ever be. Enjoying every bit of it.*

This gown was not the only new thing she was trying on.

Nathaniel leaned forward, and holding her hips in a firm grip, he placed his mouth in a very unexpected place and repaid the favor she had done for him.

The next time an assistant came knocking on the

door to see if she needed help, she was utterly beyond speech and Nathaniel was obliged to answer for her in a high-pitched squeak.

∾

He wanted to hear her say she loved him. He needed it. Otherwise he might just be a part of her rebellion, a passing fancy. Nathaniel had never been as uncertain as he was now with her. None of his other relationships had ever been like this. He had never faltered. Never smoldered as he did this time. With her. For her.

It took every ounce of willpower to keep her waiting, but he wanted this to be right, to be done properly.

Diana was blossoming, but he didn't want to rush her. He would make this the way he'd imagined in his dreams.

He would wait for those precious words from her lips.

Twenty-three

OVER THE NEXT FEW DAYS HE KEPT HIS DISTANCE. He did not come to dine at Wollaford and Sir Jonty was busy organizing the grounds for the ball, as well as overseeing the building stages of his folly by the lake. The weather was fine but not remarkable. There was a sense of unease, of something changed in the air.

Diana could not settle or feel any contentment until she saw Nathaniel again.

She knew her cousin had written to her mother. No doubt a letter would soon arrive summoning her home to Hawcombe Prior. In the meantime she was mostly confined to the lodge, Elizabeth making a great deal of unpleasant fuss anytime she expressed a desire to go out.

"Poor George," she snapped at Diana, a few days after the Bach concert, as they sat sewing in the drawing room. "You have caused him terrible pain by being so attentive one moment and then running off with that scoundrel Sherringham the next. I do not know if George will ever recover. Just as he had begun to let his heart heal again. I hope you are satisfied with the havoc you've caused."

Diana sought Sir Jonty in his library that afternoon after hearing sounds of his return and the usual ruckus from his spaniels. She would never bother a gentleman in his library, but Sir Jonty was not the sort to stand on ceremony and had been so generous that she felt it necessary to speak with him directly, rather than rely on Elizabeth to convey her apology.

He seemed surprised to see her there, but he put aside his copy of the *Bath Chronicle* and listened without interruption as Diana assured him that she had meant no harm to his brother, and she was sorry if her friendship had been misconstrued as anything more.

"Well, no, dear Miss Makepiece… I'm sure… George… I'm sure it is nothing to be anxious about. Do not distress yourself on that score. I only hope you have not been inconvenienced. We did think there was an attachment between you and George. But…that is how things go, I suppose." He smiled. "You have helped open his eyes and his heart again. We are all grateful to you for that, my dear Miss Makepiece. And…as long as you have not been injured…then all is well."

Glad to get that off her chest—but a little puzzled about why he thought she might have been injured— she left him to his newspaper, his pint pot of black porter, his tobacco pipe, and his peaceful library. After all, the poor man had few places in that small house where he could escape his wife's nagging.

❧

Nathaniel received a visit from Jonty the day before the Wollaford ball. His first thought was that the man had come to inform him that his invitation to the ball was rescinded.

This, however, was not the case.

Despite Lady Plumtre's insistence that he was no longer welcome at Wollaford, Nathaniel found Jonty in much the same good humor as usual. There was only a little awkwardness as he greeted Nathaniel and looked around his small room at the boarding house.

"I remember a time when I enjoyed my freedom in such lodgings as these," he said, smiling. "But then my papa died and left me Wollaford. Thus I was obliged to find a wife and settle down."

Nathaniel waited, sensing his friend had something preying on his mind. Jonty paced back and forth, hands clasped behind his back. Finally he stopped, looked at Nathaniel, and said, "I came today on my brother George's behalf."

"Oh?" It had to be about Diana.

"You know—I'm sure you have seen by now—his attachment, his growing fondness for a certain lady."

Dropping to a chair by the window, Nathaniel nodded. His mind had been filled with nothing and no one but her since their last encounter.

"George has been...cautious when it comes to giving his heart again. After his sad loss."

"Of course. That is understandable."

"But now he finds a woman in whose company he takes great pleasure. A woman he fears you may have some prior claim upon."

Nathaniel said nothing. He leaned forward, resting his forearms on his thighs, hands clasped. He did not want to lose Jonty's friendship, but neither was he going to give Diana up and clear the field for that wet cabbage leaf George.

"So my brother asked me to inquire about your intentions related to that lady. He does not wish to encroach upon another man's…property."

"I very much doubt she would appreciate being referred to as my property," Nathaniel said, darkly amused.

Jonty proceeded to walk up and down again, clearly uncomfortable with his task as messenger in this affair but anxious for his brother's sake. "My wife thought you had given the lady up, but George wished to be sure. The lady herself seemed…uncertain as to where she stood in your life."

Naturally, Lady Plumtre was eager to get him away from her cousin and would want to think he had given up. He stared out of the window and saw Diana's face, her green eyes watching him steadily, thoughtfully. This rebellion of hers… He sighed and shook his head. She had enchanted poor George too.

"Well, old chap?" said Jonty.

Nathaniel stood. "The lady is capable of making her own choices," he said carefully. "I think we should let her choose the suitor she wants." Then he laughed curtly. "It might, after all, be neither of us. She has been a trifle unpredictable of late."

His friend blew out a great breath. "I daresay you are right, Sherry. Let the lady choose. George will have to take his chance like everyone else. Perhaps it will do him some good. I have rather tried to protect him from the world, you see. Sheltered him as best I could. Alas, he was then unprepared for the weight of grief when he lost Eleanor. He had not learned to stand on his own feet, to face misfortune. That, I fear, was my fault, having never let him know any." Jonty paused. "I believe Miss Makepiece has helped him climb out of that pit of despair in which he wallowed. She has been so patient and kind. Has even offered to help my sisters. I am indebted to the lady."

It was plain to see why Jonty wanted Diana for his brother. He saw her as serving a purpose for his entire family. "Yes," Nathaniel muttered stiffly, "she is remarkable, isn't she?"

What did *he* have to offer her? He had begun to build a future, but he didn't have a house to put her in. He had lodgings here and there. Didn't even keep a carriage of his own.

Nathaniel Sherringham—thirty years old and of no fixed abode.

Perhaps that was why she only thought of him as a potential lover. Nothing serious.

The conversation turned to other matters, but Jonty left soon after that, with a firm handshake and having secured a promise from Nathaniel that "this business" had not and would not change the friendship between the two of them.

Twenty-four

THE DAY OF THE WOLLAFORD BALL WAS GRIM, COOLER, and spoiled by rain, confining everyone indoors. But by the evening the air was warm again and dry. Only the ground remained damp.

"Naturally," Elizabeth complained. "That will allow every foot to bring mud into the ballroom."

"At least you won't be the one required to get on your hands and knees and scrub the floor tomorrow," Diana pointed out.

Her cousin glared at her. "I pray you will remember your place this evening and bear in mind the trouble you've already caused by being thoughtless and flighty. Putting yourself forward."

"But Sir Jonty assures me his brother is not at all unhappy. I do not think George was as attached to me as you thought."

"Diana, it's time you learned that men know almost nothing when it comes to matters of the heart."

She couldn't help but laugh at that. "Quite true."

The Plumtre girls were so excited that they flew down the steps of the manor house to greet Diana that

evening. Sir Jonty had brought the ladies over from
the lodge in the carriage—at his wife's insistence—to
save their dancing slippers from the wet ground, and
before her foot had touched the gravel, Diana was
whisked into the manor house to admire the flowers,
the buffet table, and, of course, their gowns.

Mrs. Plumtre had not yet seen Diana's new ball
gown and she exclaimed in delight, "How pretty, Miss
Makepiece! My goodness, it quite brings a tear to my
eye, seeing you look so well. The air here at Wollaford
has been of much benefit to you, I think." She reached
up and patted Diana's cheek in a motherly way. "Your
cousin tells us you will soon be going home. We shall
miss you, my dear."

Her heart faltered. Going home. Yes, she knew
Elizabeth wanted to be rid of her. She had not fulfilled
her expected role at Wollaford and was now considered more liability and competition than anything.

"I shall miss all of you too," she said sadly.
"Very much."

"Then you must return to visit us every summer."

But Diana doubted her mother would let her leave
Hawcombe Prior again, once she learned about her
riding out unchaperoned with Nathaniel, spending
hours alone with him in Sydney Gardens, and coming
home as the birds began to sing. That would take
some explaining.

The ballroom at Wollaford Park was a long, Tudor-
paneled hall with a black-and-white tiled floor, two
large hanging chandeliers, and a massive fireplace that
tonight was filled with flowers and a large paper fan
painted with exotic birds and butterflies. Some chairs

were set around the walls for those who did not dance,
and at the far end of the room there was a raised
wooden dais upon which a group of musicians played.
It was the grandest ball Diana had ever attended and
she might have been overwhelmed by the grandeur, if
not for Mrs. Plumtre's unfussy manners.

Only now did she fully appreciate her new white
gown, for it helped her courage a great deal. She was
exceedingly grateful to Susy and Daisy for insisting
upon having it made for her. She would have felt
terribly out of place in her old "best" frock, despite
her mother's efforts to improve it. And that thought
made her sad, because it forced Diana to consider all
that her mother had left behind for love and a moment
of passion. All the pleasures that her mother had never
known—the balls and fine gowns and carriages that
kept a girl from mud upon her slippers. All those
things Diana now had the opportunity to know.

The ballroom quickly began to fill with guests and
music. Diana had no time to hide in a corner and
observe, because the Plumtre sisters took her up and
down the chessboard tiles to meet those few friends she
had not yet encountered in Bath and to be reacquainted
with those she had. She looked around for Nathaniel,
but there was no sign of him for the first hour.

Diana was dancing with Jonty when she saw Mrs.
Ashby and her colorful niece arriving. That was not
going to please Elizabeth, she mused, wondering
what would happen when her cousin saw they'd been
invited. Currently holding court beside the buffet
table, Lady Plumtre was in her element among those
grander folks she considered worthy, a queen bee

showing off her husband's ancestral home, tonight able to ignore the fact that her living quarters were in the lodge by the gates.

As the evening wore on, Diana danced continually. There was no shortage of partners and no time to rest, but she looked eagerly for Nathaniel, and at last, there he was.

❧

Nathaniel spied her almost at once because, despite the crowd, her elegance and grace stood out just as they always had before. In her virginal white gown she looked seventeen again. Suddenly all those years since did not exist.

He crossed the floor to where she stood. When she turned and found him there beside her, Nathaniel took her hand without a word. Again, he would not spoil the music, knowing what it meant to her, how she enjoyed every note. When she began to speak, to admonish him for being late, he silenced her with a finger to the lips and a softly muttered, "Say nothing, Miss Makepiece. Not yet."

"But I—"

"Do not spoil the beauty of the music. I requested the piece especially for you."

And as soon as she heard the first strains of the violin, he knew she recognized it as the tune that had entranced her at the concert. She smiled, her eyes glistening with gold and emerald. "This is not fitting music for a ball, surely," she whispered.

"Have you ever known me to follow the rules, Miss Makepiece?"

"No," she admitted with a wry smile.

"Then even if nobody else takes to the floor, you and I shall dance. We can't let the music be wasted, can we? This is special, for you and me. It is our music, whether it's for a ball or not."

He led her out onto the floor and every face turned toward them. Many folk had taken seats when they heard the first soft notes, assuming this to be a piece of interval music and expecting refreshments of some kind.

But Nathaniel would dance with the woman he loved and to hell with what was usual. Jigs, minuets, and cotillions were for ordinary people. He and his beautiful Diana—who was anything but ordinary—would dance to their own music.

Tonight Miss Makepiece was seen and admired as she should be, brought out of her corner and into the light of those fine chandeliers. He was proud to dance with her and felt every envious eye upon him.

Her gloved fingers were laid gently over his, but he stroked them discreetly with his thumb. It was the most contact he could expect for now.

As they danced, there was no more speaking. The other guests were hushed, startled perhaps by the odd choice of music and not knowing what to do. Only the Bach could be heard, soaring around them.

And since they were dancing without conversation, Nathaniel let her know with his eyes how stunning she was tonight, how glad he was to dance with her.

Later he would ask her whether George Plumtre had proposed yet. Although he was quite sure she'd turn the fellow down, he didn't want the Plumtres—or her mother—holding him to blame. It must be entirely her choice and seen to be.

As their music came to an end, so did their tranquil moment of solitary togetherness. Susanna hurried up to Diana and asked if she had seen Daisy at any point in the last half hour. Nathaniel said that he thought he had seen her with a group of young people going out through the glass doors and onto the terrace for some air.

Susanna groaned. "She's going to ruin her dress outside in the mud and Jonty will be furious. I promised to keep an eye on her but she slipped away."

"We'll find her," Diana assured the anxious girl. "I would like some air myself. Go back to your partner and enjoy the dance."

༺ஓ༻

They went out onto the pretty terrace, ostensibly to admire the starlit sky and the blooming roses on the trellis. But Diana was in need of a kiss.

Fortunately, Nathaniel was of the same mind. He drew her behind a particularly lush climbing rose and kissed her.

"Thank you for the music," she whispered. "How clever of you to remember."

"How could I forget? That music will forever be etched in my mind as I heard it the night Diana Makepiece first held my hand in public and caused a scandal."

"You're late. I began to think you would not come. That my cousin had chased you away."

He grinned. "Trust me, she tried."

Diana reached up and drew her fingers down his cheek, then across his lips. While they were dancing and he'd forbidden her to speak, she'd had so many things she wanted to say, but now they stood in silence. Somehow that was more meaningful than if she had exploded in chatter. She'd never known him this quiet, this calm. It was as if he'd finally worked all that restlessness out of his soul.

But perhaps she just hoped that was the case.

"Has George spoken to you?" he asked.

"George? Why? About what?"

"I believe he is going to propose."

She frowned. "To me? What for?"

Nathaniel laughed softly. "Then I know what your answer will be. Let him down gentler than you once did me."

"I told you I don't want a husband."

Those blue eyes grew misty. "You are decided. Yes, I remember."

"I can be free to do as I please. Like men. Why not?"

"Because you're not a man. You're a woman." He began to sound annoyed, his voice tight.

"But I will no longer be bound by the constraints of propriety, Sherry. And in the eyes of most people, since I have not married and produced babies, I'm not even a woman. Therefore, I shall act like a man and enjoy a satisfying love life."

His brow creased. "Diana, you take this rebellion of yours too far."

"What's the matter, Sherry? This recklessness is what you find admirable. Or is it different when a woman takes control?"

Suddenly she heard voices shouting, a shriek of alarm. They both turned toward the sound.

"Was that Daisy? What on earth is she up to?"

Their quarrel cut short before it had properly found its pace, they hurried down the terrace steps and across the lawn, following the noise and a darting, leaping flame that led them toward the lake in the distance.

Daisy was halfway up the unfinished marble steps of her brother's partially built folly. With her were several young people from the ball, two of them holding lit torches.

As Nathaniel neared the scene, he shouted sternly at Daisy to stop at once and climb no further. Diana added her plea to his, and the young girl paused to look over her shoulder. She was laughing, her face pink in the flickering torchlight.

"I am not afraid," she exclaimed. "They dared me to climb up. It's more difficult than that silly tree." Apparently she didn't care that she was showing her ankles, or that her brother had expressly forbidden her from entering the folly until it was completed.

Nathaniel glared at the young men and women present. They now looked rather sheepish, as if they wished to slink away and hide in shame for encouraging this display. Once again he ordered the wayward Daisy to stop and come down. He could see the marble was slippery from that day's rain, and in a panic he envisioned her tumbling to the hard ground below.

But she laughed madly. And then she leaped, taking flight and shouting for him to catch her.

A split second later and he would have dropped her, but somehow he caught the reckless bundle and set her on her feet.

Diana began to admonish the girl, but she was laughing again, exclaiming at how much fun it was to fly through the air. "Don't be such a fusspot! It was nothing." The girl turned boldly to her audience. "And now you owe me a guinea!"

"I suggest you go back to the house," Nathaniel said. "Your sister is looking for you, and you shouldn't be out here in the dark so far from the ball."

"I don't know why you're being a fearsome grump," the girl exclaimed. "You're usually much more fun, Sherry!"

He frowned. "There is a time and a place, young lady."

Diana said gently, "Do come back to the house, Daisy. You'll get your lovely gown ruined out here."

The girl seemed to relent. She heaved her shoulders, pouted, and started walking out of the folly, but suddenly she ran back to climb the unfinished stairs again. This time her feet slipped worse than before as she climbed with more speed and less caution.

Nathaniel shouted at her. She laughed down at them.

"You didn't think girls could climb. I told you I wasn't afraid of anything, didn't I?"

"Daisy!"

Her next step was interrupted when she caught her toe in the hem of her gown.

Nathaniel lunged forward to catch her, but he was too slow this time.

The small figure tripped, lost her footing, and fell

through the air to land—so it seemed to him—directly on her head.

With everyone screaming around her and chaos breaking out, the limp girl opened her eyes and groaned, "*Oh, fergalumph!*"

Then she fainted.

❦

Nathaniel carried her back to the house, and Diana organized the girl's friends into an orderly procession behind him. There was no point in everybody panicking, as she told them. No point in calling out who was to blame.

"Take her through the kitchen," she whispered to Nathaniel. "We don't want the guests to see her like this. I'll take the others back into the ballroom and get her brother."

He said nothing but merely nodded, his face white, his eyes staring. As he carried the unconscious bundle, blood leaked from Daisy's brow onto his coat.

Diana laid a hand on his arm. "You could not have prevented it, Nathaniel."

Again he nodded. She left him at the kitchen door and quickly steered the other young people around to the terrace, advising them to say nothing to anyone about the incident. She would not want Mrs. Plumtre to hear of this until there was time to prepare her gently. And time to clean the alarming blood from Daisy's brow.

On reentering the ballroom through the French doors, she spied Susanna and quickly told her what had happened. "Do you know if there is a doctor here? Anyone with some medical knowledge?"

Wide-eyed, Susanna nodded. "Doctor Smith and his wife."

"Good. Find them and take them to the kitchen as discreetly as you can."

Having given Susanna this task to keep her busy, Diana searched for Jonty. Unfortunately, as she was informing him of the tragedy, his wife came up behind them and demanded to know what they were whispering about.

From then on, there was no chance of keeping the accident from being known by all the guests. Within moments, Elizabeth's overwrought and utterly unnecessary shrieks could have been heard from every room in the manor house.

∽

The injured girl was laid on a settee by the fire and examined by the family doctor. She still had not regained consciousness. Her mother wept; her elder brother was near frantic. Lady Plumtre raced around the kitchen creating more havoc and providing no assistance.

But Diana remained calm and capable, making tea and listening attentively to the doctor, then relaying everything to the girl's mother in uncomplicated terms. Comforting everyone.

Nathaniel watched it all unfold, feeling useless and accusing himself of having inspired the girl to attempt her daredevil antics. No one else had pointed a finger of blame in his direction, but they did not have to. He had felt it keenly himself from the moment her foot slipped on the wet steps.

Reckless Sherry. Had he not been so eager to

impress Diana by climbing a tree, the thought of such activity would probably never have formed in the girl's head. But young Daisy had followed him around, looked up to him, and constantly tried to assure him that she was fearless.

He had laughed and teased. Encouraged her mischief, when he should have known better.

Lady Plumtre was the first to turn and look for him as these same thoughts apparently occurred to her. "I suppose 'tis no wonder you were there when she fell, Captain," she said. "She was showing off for you, no doubt."

Before he could respond, Diana said firmly, "The captain was trying to stop her. She wouldn't listen. It is not his fault that she fell."

Nathaniel stood. "I should have caught her. I was too damn slow."

"Don't blame yourself," Diana exclaimed. "She would have leaped whether you were there or not."

He shook his head.

"You have been nothing but trouble for this family," said Lady Plumtre, her eyes now fully dry and gleaming with their customary hot spite. "Now this. A young girl's life snatched away from her because of you. I hope you are content, Captain."

George dashed in, having belatedly heard the news. "What happened?" He drew himself to a fast halt when he saw Nathaniel. "*You*, sir?" He had seen his sister-in-law pointing her accusing finger and, without knowing anything about the circumstances, seemed ready to believe the worst. And to act upon it.

"I ought to call you out," he blustered. "I should

indeed. Where are my dueling pistols?" Turning in circles and nervously clutching the front of his waist-coat, George looked for some invisible valet with that nonexistent box of pistols.

Diana began to explain to him that the captain had not caused this accident or done anything untoward, but George was overexcited and seemed anxious to impress somebody.

When she looked for Nathaniel again, he was gone.

"There he goes. Sneaking off like a criminal," said Elizabeth smugly.

Her nerves frayed, Diana could not bear another moment of her cousin's meanness or her selfish disregard for others.

"Elizabeth," she murmured quietly, "have a thought for someone other than yourself. Think of Daisy, of her mother. This is no time for accusations."

Her cousin's voice rose another pitch. "How dare you presume to tell me what I should think? Daisy is *my* sister-in-law. Not yours."

Jonty abruptly turned to his wife and snapped, "Be silent, Lizzie, for pity's sake. Diana is right. This is not about you. For once something is not about you."

Elizabeth's face drained of all color. She swayed, her mouth falling open, but she was rendered speechless.

While George continued to rant and rave about "calling the villain out," he made no move to go anywhere but instead sat on the nearest chair and poured himself a glass of wine.

Diana ran out to find Nathaniel passing through the hall, going out into the night.

"Nathaniel! Don't listen Elizabeth. No one blames you for this. Of course they don't!"

He stopped, his head bowed, looking unusually dejected. "I blame *myself*, Diana."

"No! That is quite ridiculous."

"There is a certain amount of truth in what your cousin said. I've caused you trouble, Diana. I should have stayed away from you when I found you here, but I couldn't." He shook his head, his lips tight. "I couldn't! Now your mama has more reason to despise me. Not that she required any."

"I don't care." She had thought this was about Daisy, but he seemed to have more on his mind.

"I do," he replied firmly. "I've been care*less* too often." He stared at her, his eyes full of sadness and disappointment in himself. "Please let me know how she fares. If there is anything I can do…"

Diana whispered, "Yes."

"I've got to go… I… Good-bye."

In the next breath he was gone.

She stood in the hall, a breeze through the open door playing with her skirt. She had gotten a little blood on her lovely new gown, she realized.

There was no time to go after him because she ought to be with Daisy, keeping the others calm.

But why had he said "good-bye" that way? As if this was the end.

Twenty-five

JONTY AND HIS MOTHER APPOINTED DIANA TO SIT WITH Daisy. They thought her the best person for the role, the most capable, the kindest. Although overwhelmed by the extent of their trust in her, Diana did not mind the task. It gave her time to get her thoughts straight and kept her out of Elizabeth's way. The invalid had regained consciousness, but she was not yet herself and did not want many visitors. She enjoyed nothing as much as Diana sitting by her bed and reading to her. The days and nights passed quietly in this fashion.

Nathaniel had called on Mrs. Plumtre the day after the tragedy and brought with him the best physician in Bath—a specialist in head injuries—to examine Daisy. The man dutifully looked his patient over, conferred with Dr. Smith, and pronounced her "a very lucky young lady." He had no doubt she would recover fully, given time.

Mrs. Plumtre had assured Nathaniel that no one laid any blame at his feet. "But I do not think the fellow believed me," she told Diana. "He looked so distraught, poor man."

He visited every day for a week, bringing flowers and gifts for the patient, but he kept his distance from Diana. The patient, meanwhile, being a young lady of generally stout health and even stouter defiance against lying in bed, soon rallied.

One day, just as Daisy was improved enough to complain about her egg not being boiled the way she liked it, there was interesting news.

Susanna ran into the room to announce that George was engaged to Mrs. Caroline Sayles.

This was, of course, horrifying for Elizabeth—worse even than the accident that had rendered her sister-in-law unconscious. What made it even more unbearable was that her husband had known about the imminent engagement for some days and had kept it from her. Even her mother-in-law had known about George's growing affection for the brassy-haired lady and been sworn to secrecy. Jonty explained that anxiety regarding Captain Sherringham's possible claim upon the lady had necessitated this discretion.

"George didn't want to step on the good captain's toes, of course," Jonty told Diana. "I thought there might still be some…attachment, and Mrs. Sayles herself seemed to think there might be. But Sherry said he would let the lady make her own choice. He did not stand in George's way."

She was puzzled by this, because Nathaniel had told her unequivocally that there was nothing between him and Caroline Sayles. Someone somewhere must have formed a misunderstanding.

They learned that this romance had begun on the night of the concert. While Nathaniel had been concerned about how his "kidnapping" of Diana might cause trouble, George and Caroline had found their own scandal.

"Elizabeth is furious," Susanna whispered. "She thought that when the captain left Bath he'd take Mrs. Sayles with him." She giggled. "Now she will never be rid of her."

Diana's heart leaped two beats. "The captain left Bath?"

"Oh yes, he's gone. Quite gone. We shall all be quite bored without him, shan't we?"

Once again he'd left, she thought angrily. One curt good-bye while he was walking away from her and that was all the care he gave, even after she'd opened up so much for him, tried to prove herself daring and bold, instead of being the meek girl he once thought her. Even when he visited Daisy in her sick bed, he made no attempt to see Diana alone. He barely looked at her. Wretched man.

What else could she have expected from that scoundrel?

Her little rebellion was over and in a few weeks she would return to Hawcombe Prior, her own departure from Wollaford delayed now only by her nursing duties at Daisy's bedside.

She kept a stoic face while the two girls lamented the captain's departure, but inside she ached. During her stay at Bath, Diana had learned so much about herself, had even learned to like the woman inside, to forgive her for the sinful thoughts that sometimes crept in. Had learned to loosen her stays and worry less. Had learned to speak up for herself and what she wanted.

Now, as her time there drew to a close, she

discovered something else. That pain she felt was not indigestion or colic or anything amiss with her spleen.

It was love.

❦

"Nate, you might have told us you were buying the Pig in a Poke!" his sister exclaimed when he arrived back in Hawcombe Prior on a sunny morning in early July.

"I bought it for the brewery," he explained. "But I've decided to take up residence there too."

His father was delighted, Rebecca no less so. Not everyone, of course, was quite so pleased to see him back again. And back to stay.

While he supervised the raising of a new sign above his tavern, Sam Hardacre rode by with his cart and gave a reluctant greeting. Nathaniel waved for him to stop.

"Have you asked Lucy to marry you yet?" he demanded of the ruddy-faced carpenter, coming directly to the point.

The man's face gathered like a fist. "She ain't interested in me. Not now she's moving on to bigger and better places."

Nathaniel shook his head. "There is no better place." He should know, he mused, having traveled so much and having seen so many other towns and villages.

"She won't stay for a humble fellow like me."

"Then don't be so humble! If I were you, I'd take the bull by the horns and snap that young lady up. Don't let the chance pass you by." He had seen Lucy watching Sam, waiting for him to notice her so she could pretend to look elsewhere. She was a girl who had yet to reconcile her mind to what her heart wanted. He had some familiarity with that.

"You sound like a man with regrets, Cap'n."

"Yes," he agreed, "but I mean to change all that before it's too late." He leaned against the side of the cart and looked up at Sam. "If you want some advice on how to win that girl of yours, you might want to read one of those novels. It seems that's where the ladies get their ideas these days."

Sam thought for a breath and then said, "I'd rather learn from a man of experience, Cap'n." He grinned. "If you'll teach me."

Nathaniel rather liked that idea. No one had ever asked him to teach them anything. He straightened up, knuckles resting on his hips, and said with all due solemnity, "Very well, young Master Hardacre. You come by my father's house for dinner this evening, and we'll see what we have to work with."

Something caught his eye across the common. Sarah Wainwright was fluttering about, looking as if she'd lost something.

"Seems Sir Morty is off wandering again," Sam observed. "That damnable pig gets around. If you ask me, he needs a lusty sow to help him stop that restlessness."

Nathaniel trotted over to help, as usual unable to ignore a lady's distress. He followed the indignant screams and a trail of damage into Mrs. Makepiece's walled vegetable garden. Somehow Sir Mortimer Grubbins—the prizewinning Oxford Sandy and Black pig who was the unofficial mayor of Hawcombe Prior and Sarah's pet—had found his way through Mrs.

Makepiece's passage while she cleaned her floor with the front door open. Now, having trotted directly through her kitchen and out her back door, the pig romped happily among her neat lines of cabbages, onions, and carrots in the garden behind her house. The lady chased him in circles, swiping at the beast with her straw bonnet, but he seemed to think it all a jolly game, his trotters cantering back and forth, gleefully making more and more mess.

There was no time for the lady to react against Nathaniel when she saw who had come to her aid with Sarah. Desperate to be rid of the rampaging beast, and with her own energy and dignity depleted, she could only let him help.

Fortunately for Nathaniel, he was not wearing his best suit of clothes. Within a few minutes the pig was safely corralled and on his way back to Willow Tree Farm. Sarah apologized profusely to the lady, and as they came back out through the front of the house, Mrs. Makepiece managed to reply that there was not *too* much damage.

"You will make recompense, Sarah, of course," Nathaniel said to his step-niece.

"Yes, of course!"

The grim lady muttered, "I'm sure I'll survive." She was breathless, disheveled, and not quite able to look Nathaniel in the eye. She had avoided him since his return. He wondered how much she knew about Diana's time in Bath, how much Lady Plumtre would have told her out of spite.

On his way out, he noticed a water stain on the wooden floor and looked up to where a damp patch was visible on the ceiling between the low beams. It was turning yellow with age, the plaster cracked.

When he pointed it out to the lady, she explained dourly, "That spot leaks whenever it rains. Has done so for some time."

"Why did you not ask my father or brother-in-law to have it fixed?" She was, after all, one of his father's tenants.

"I... We can manage, Captain."

"Madam, if that patch spreads, it could bring down the plaster. The water could be rotting into the wood now."

She stared up at the ceiling and wrung her hands in a tight knot.

"It will only get worse," he added. "Must be coming in somewhere through the wall and soaking the beams between floors." Nathaniel made up his mind. "I'll bring a ladder this afternoon and see if I can mend it. And I'll help you tidy that garden too."

He gave the lady no time to argue. Brisk, efficient, and determined, he took the bull by the horns, just as he'd advised Sam Hardacre.

In the past he had fought against the woman, always pulling in the other direction like in a tug of war. What could she do, he wondered, if he stopped pulling and helped her? Beat him with a shoe? Or her straw bonnet, as if he were Sir Mortimer Grubbins, that other beastly pest?

Apparently she chose to do neither. He had cunningly outplayed the woman. With kindness.

⚜

When Diana received a letter from Justina she took it quickly to her bedchamber, thrilled to have news from home. She missed her friends in Hawcombe Prior and was surprised her mother had not yet commanded her to come home.

My Dear Diana,

What has become of you, I wonder, in the world of Bath? I know I told you not to write and to save it all for when you returned, but I grow anxious to hear of your terrible adventures. Which had better be many and wicked to make up for these weeks we have suffered without you.

Things here are much the same. Well, almost. The tavern has a new landlord. A most interesting fellow and a bachelor. I do not know that you will think much of him though.

You will never guess what has become of Lucy Brydges! She has decided not to go to Basingstoke and juggle a parade of suitors after all, but to marry Sam Hardacre and stay here in the village. When the moment came to leave us all behind, she was not as brave as she thought, nor so ready for life without her friends.

I write therefore to inform you of the wedding arrangements. Lucy has no time to put pen to paper because she has so many other plans to make, but she desires very much that you return to enjoy the celebrations.

I am told that there will be cake, and more importantly, the Book Club Belles are all to have new bonnets.

My Wainwright will send the carriage for you.

I can think of little else to persuade you of how much you are needed here, except to say that whatever holds you in Bath cannot be as dear to you as those of us who wait for your return.

&

One week later, Diana stepped out of the Wainwrights' carriage, walked through her mother's gate, and stopped in shock when she found Nathaniel Sherringham in his shirtsleeves, applying a new coat of paint to the open front door.

Her mother came out into the hall at the same moment, a cup of tea in her hand, offering it to him.

"Diana!" she cried. "Good Lord!"

He almost dropped his brush and spun around, flicking paint across his linen shirt. "Di...Miss Makepiece."

Her mother recovered first. Not waiting for Nathaniel to take the cup from her hand, she set it on the narrow hall table and stepped by him to take one handle of her daughter's trunk. "Well, you might have written to let me know you were on your way, for pity's sake!"

"I wanted to surprise you, Mama." She glanced sideways at Nathaniel as she followed her mother into the cool house, but he turned away and got on with his work.

"You certainly did that. I thought Elizabeth would keep you there until September at least."

As they walked into the kitchen, Diana stopped her mother with one hand on her shoulder. "Are you pleased to have me back, Mama?"

"Of course, Diana."

They set down the trunk and embraced. Diana breathed deeply of her mother's scent and all that was familiar. "I missed you, Mama."

"Well, goodness, I should hope so. Now sit down and I'll pour you some tea while you tell me all that happened."

"I think, Mama, you have a few things to tell me first."

Her mother's eyes were wide and innocent as she reached for a clean cup and saucer. "I do?"

Diana's pulse was scattered. "Why is Captain Sherringham here?" she whispered.

"Oh, it is nothing," her mother replied nonchalantly. "He's been doing a few odd jobs about the house. Making himself useful. Seems to think he can slide into my good graces."

"But what is he doing here in Hawcombe Prior?" She had thought him gone forever. Justina's letter had not warned her about his return. That sly woman!

"He has purchased the tavern, would you believe? Took it over from Bridges. I cannot think why a man like that would wish to settle here. I should have imagined that London or some other large, noisy place suited him better."

The tavern! Of course. That was why he had come back. He was the bachelor Justina thought she would not find interesting. Diana smothered a chuckle.

Suddenly her mother took her hands and stepped back to inspect her properly. "You look different, Diana. Confident. Your eyes are shining as I have not seen them since you were a little girl."

She smiled. "I *am* different, Mama."

"And better, I hope?"

"Oh yes, Mama. I feel like a new woman."

"Then it was worth it to lose you for a while." Her mother kissed her gently on the cheek. "But I felt the loss of your company, my dear, very much."

"I thought you would have sent for me to come home by now." She licked her lips and added cautiously, "Did Elizabeth not write to you?"

"Yes, a very odd, disjointed rambling letter, of which I could make neither head nor tails since many lines were scribbled over. Her spelling has not improved, I see. Nor has her use of punctuation." She sighed, reaching for the teapot to pour a cup for her daughter. "But then I had a letter from Mrs. Fanny Plumtre in the same day, and she was most eager for you to stay as long as you could. She said what a good friend you have been to her daughters. They sound rather wild, I must say."

So apparently her mother still did not know Nathaniel had been in Bath. Had Elizabeth thought better about telling her?

Oh, it was good to be home, she thought, standing in the old kitchen. How quiet it was there, compared to Wollaford. Her life at home might be more predictable and less elegant, but she had missed it.

She glanced back over her shoulder and down the narrow passage because she could hear Nathaniel whistling. It was...

Their music.

She hid her smile in the teacup and watched her mother puttering about the kitchen, only half listening to her stories of what had happened since Diana left. How odd that her mother would let Nathaniel into the house at all, let alone bring him tea. Perhaps she too had learned to change.

❧

He was sitting with his father after dinner that evening when the bell rang. It woke them both from a drowsy game of backgammon.

"Who could that be at this hour?" the major exclaimed. "Don't show them in here, Nate, my boy, or I shall have to put my shoes back on." His father liked to remove as many garments as he could while at ease in his own parlor, and he was always loath to put them back on.

So Nathaniel went out into the hall and opened the front door.

"I brought this month's rent," she said pertly, a little net purse dangling from her finger.

"Diana? At this hour?"

Not waiting to be welcomed in, she walked boldly into the house. He thought for a moment, knowing he ought to quarrel with her about the impropriety of this late visit, but then he closed the door and said in as formal a tone as he could manage, "Go through to my father's study. End of the hall."

He knew his father would probably be asleep soon by the parlor fire, if he was not already. With his father asleep, he and Diana were, in effect, alone together in the house. Her mother could not know where she'd gone. She wore neither coat nor bonnet, brazenly flouting the rules. Must have been a spontaneous idea, he concluded. The woman was having a lot more of those these days, and he wasn't sure whether he liked it.

What would she do next?

Following her into the small study, he said, "Miss Makepiece, could this not have waited until the morning?"

"No. It's overdue."

But when he reached for her purse, she put it behind her back and dodged aside with a low chuckle. Apparently the lady was in a playful mood. He propped his behind against the leather-topped desk and folded his arms. "Took you long enough to come home, Miss Makepiece," he muttered. "I began to think you'd decided to stay and marry George."

Her eyebrows arched high. "George prefers Mrs. Sayles—*your* friend. Didn't you know? They are engaged."

Nathaniel paused, surprised, then laughed as he realized he should have seen it coming. "That explains a curious discussion I had with Jonty."

Diana walked up to him and pushed her way between his thighs, sliding her arms around his neck. "You left Bath abruptly. Not a word to me."

"Once I knew Daisy would recover, there was nothing else I could do. I had outstayed my welcome at Wollaford, and you were needed there."

Her fingertips gently stroked the back of his neck, and he quickly felt the growing heaviness of want traveling the length of his spine and settling in his loins. Her soft lips were mere inches from his, and she tempted him by letting her tongue out to moisten them. "And you came here. Why?"

Nathaniel took her hands to keep them out of trouble. "I wanted to be here, waiting for *you* this time. Since you complained that women are always left to wait for men, I decided to prove to you that I was capable of waiting. *If* you came back."

"Why wouldn't I?"

His heart clamored to hear her say she loved him. It was a pathetic, desperate state to be in, but there was nothing he could do about it.

Diana leaned back and he released her hands. "I saw the letter to my mother, by the way. The one that supposedly came from cousin Elizabeth," she said.

"Did you? That's nice."

"You intercepted it somehow."

He sighed and shook his head. "Would I do a thing like that?"

"Yes."

They stood looking at each other for a long while. He was not going to confess anything until she did. Not this time.

Diana held the net purse out to him again. "I'll be going then."

"I think you had better, Miss Makepiece. Wouldn't want anyone to talk. You know how gossip spreads."

She sniffed, gave him an odd look, turned, and walked out, her head high, her proud nose in the air.

Nathaniel sagged against his desk and exhaled a low curse. That damn, stubborn woman. Would he ever get her to take that biggest risk of all?

❦

The wedding of Lucy and Sam Hardacre was a merry affair at the Hawcombe Prior church, followed by a breakfast at the Pig in a Poke.

A large amount of ham, tongue, cheese, and eggs was consumed, but much of the cake ended up on the floor when Sir Mortimer Grubbins escaped his sty again and decided to invite himself to the party.

Amid the chaos, the parson's wife sought Diana out to tell her she was looking "a little more rounded" after her trip to Bath. "And I am pleased to see the curl returned to your hair. But you came back with no husband? Such a pity. Here you stand at another friend's wedding, poor thing. What shall we do with you?"

Diana smiled. "As it happens, Mrs. Kenton—and I must ask you to keep this under your bonnet as you are the first to know"—she lowered her voice to a whisper—"I think I might soon find a husband after all."

The lady almost jumped out of her shoes. "But who is the fellow, Miss Makepiece? Gracious!"

"That I cannot tell you, for I have not yet asked him myself."

"Asked *him*?" The lady's eyes popped. "Surely you mean that he has not asked you, dear."

She laughed. "Oh no. This time it's my turn. I know this particular fellow won't ask me. I wounded him once before, you see, so now it's up to me to do the asking."

Ever since she had walked up to her mother's gate and seen him there, Diana had known what she must do, but getting up the courage was not easy. First she'd had to let Lucy's wedding go by, because she would not want to distract anyone from that joyful occasion.

When the Book Club Belles had gathered earlier to salvage what they could of the flower garlands to decorate Sam Hardacre's cart, Diana had felt her secret burning inside and longed to tell someone. Mrs. Kenton just happened to be a handy ear, and of course she—unlike Diana's friends—would have no suspicion of the gentleman's identity. Poked and prodded into silencing the gossiping woman, Diana now felt the great satisfaction of telling Mrs. Kenton something the woman didn't know and could never have guessed.

The next afternoon, Diana sat with her mother in the kitchen, quietly sewing. She thought back to that long-ago day when Nathaniel had proposed to her. She remembered almost running home and her mother commenting on her heightened color. Diana had gone to bed early but could not sleep. Her mind had churned relentlessly over Nathaniel Sherringham's proposal, and unable to rest, she had gotten up early the next morning. She was in the kitchen putting on her walking boots by the fire when her mother came down to remind her it was wash day.

"Where are you off to so early?" Mrs. Makepiece had exclaimed, glaring at her daughter above the bundle of bed linens she carried. "I need help here, young lady. I hope you don't think to go gallivanting about the village with those friends of yours, leaving me here to struggle alone."

Diana sighed heavily, remembering the anguish she'd felt, the indecision. She had thought to run and see Nathaniel before her mother came down, but she'd forgotten it was the day to tackle all the laundry.

"And you left your window open again, Diana,

letting all that frigid cold air in." Then, leaning toward the fire she had casually tossed a small, palm-sized crumple of paper into the flames. "Sometimes I think you deliberately court a cold, young lady, just to get out of your chores."

The burned paper had not signified much at the time, but now, thinking back to that chilly morning, Diana set her sewing aside and said to her mother suddenly, "What did you do with his note, Mama?"

"His note? Whose note?"

"Nathaniel's note. The one he left for me before he went away from Hawcombe Prior four years ago."

"I don't know what you're talking about. You're very flushed, Diana. Are you feverish again?"

"No, Mama. I am quite well. Better, in fact, than I have been for a long time. My eyes are open. And so is my heart."

Ashen, her mother stared. "What fancy have you got into your head now?"

"I wanted to give you a chance to confess and tell me you were wrong. Tell me you are sorry."

"Why would I do such a thing?"

"Burn his note, or tell me you are sorry?"

Her mother shook her head, apparently speechless.

"You found it, I suppose, on the floor of my bed-chamber that morning." Diana spoke slowly, softly. "I remember I had left my window open and you went in to close it, because you chided me about it. That's when you would have found his note."

Still nothing from her mother.

"When you brought the bundle of bed linens down for the wash, you had his note with you. And you burned it in the fire. That is what happened. Is it not? He told me he tied it to a crab apple to send it through my window, and now I remember the kitchen smelled a little like baked apple that morning. I did not think anything of it then."

Her mother must have pricked her finger because she grimaced, caught her breath, and bit her lip. "I have no inkling of any note. What are you talking about?"

"Mama, you knew that if I went out that morning I would go to him. You saw me lacing my boots and so you reminded me about the laundry. Because you knew…" She caught her breath and swallowed a sob. "You knew how I loved him."

Now, at last, she could say it out loud. The walls did not crumble.

"You knew it before I did. Mama?"

Her mother looked up slowly. "Yes, I knew. Do you think it gave me any pleasure, Diana? I saw you were in love, and that is the worst thing in the world for any woman to feel. Certainly the very worst reason to marry!"

"But Mama, you had love. It doesn't happen to everyone. Some people live their entire lives without it. Yet you found it. Even for the short time you had together, you and Papa had love."

"And look what good it did me. I wanted the best for you, Diana. Always!"

"But not a marriage of love?"

"Good heavens, no! I saw how you loved that man, and I couldn't bear to see you brokenhearted."

"You didn't think I was capable of winning his love in return, Mama? Capable of keeping his heart for long? Did you find so little strength in me that you imagined I couldn't help him, couldn't be good for him? As he could be good for me?"

"All men are duplicitous and fickle, Diana. I have told you that many times."

"I would have made a difference in his life and he in mine."

"Oh, that sheen would soon have dulled, believe me. Once he found something else or someone else… I could not let that happen to you as it did to me. I wanted more for you."

"Regardless of what I wanted?"

Her mother's eyes glistened with unshed tears. "Man cannot live on love alone."

"And I cannot live without it. I don't want to."

Her mother looked into the fire. "I never meant for you to be unhappy for so long. I thought it would pass."

"Did it pass for you, Mama?"

To that there was no answer.

She forgave her mother for burning the note. What else could she do? It was in the past and now everything had changed. They were all starting from the beginning. Besides, Nathaniel had gotten his revenge when he intercepted that letter from Elizabeth and kept her mother from knowing what Diana had been up to in Bath.

"You must know, Mama, that I will always look after you. I would not abandon you."

"Don't be foolish, child."

Diana took a small, wrapped parcel from her sewing basket and passed it to her mother. "I brought you this from Bath."

It was slowly and carefully unwrapped—a fragrant lavender pillow embroidered with a very pretty peacock, his tail on display. Her mother studied it for a long time but could find no fault with the stitching.

She shook her head. "All that detailed work just for a little pillow. Who would have the time to sew such a thing that is purely decoration? Such a waste of fine thread too!"

"A lady named Eleanor Ashby. Her mama gave it to me as a parting gift. Just in case we never get that real peacock you wanted."

Then her mother smiled, sniffed the sweet, dried lavender buds inside the pillow, and ran her fingertips gently over the embroidery again. "I'm sure this will do me even better. Real peacocks make an awful lot of noise and mess, so I hear, and they can be temperamental."

The pillow was given pride of place on her chair in the parlor, where it was much admired by every guest, and Diana quite often caught her mother smiling at it.

The subject of the burned note was never again mentioned, but as the sun began to set that evening, Mrs. Makepiece suddenly reminded her daughter about the fruit-picking party with the Wainwrights at the Midwitch Manor orchards. "You had best go and fill a basket with as much as you can," she said. "Then I can get started on this year's jam, can't I?"

As Diana walked through the door, her mother called her back to tuck some violets behind her ear. It was the closest she would ever get to an apology.

Twenty-six

THE AIR WAS MELLOW, THE BEES DROWSY. IT WAS ONE of those amber summer evenings when the world felt a little drunk on rich scents and bright colors, when the day had been long and hot. A light breeze ruffled the long grasses and scattered little clouds of dandelion seeds. A rabbit sat on its haunches, pondering the scene, whiskers twitching, ears alert. And then, hearing her approach, it ducked away, bouncing into the hedgerows.

As Diana strolled down the lane, she watched two sparrows taking turns bringing food to their fledglings. How hard they worked. It was no easy thing to raise children, as her mother would say. Again she imagined that one of those sparrows might be the bird she had rescued from the Manderson assembly room several months ago in the spring. Not only had it followed her home and built a nest there, but it had found true love in Hawcombe Prior and raised a chirping brood.

She came to the gates of Midwitch Manor and found them wide open, welcoming anyone who wanted to share the labor that evening and take home a basket of fruit. The orchards flourished, producing more fruit than the Wainwrights claimed they could manage, so they always generously shared their bounty with the other villagers. Diana greeted the Book Club Belles as they appeared, moving slowly in and out of the trees with their baskets.

Somewhere nearby, one of the villagers played a viola—a surprisingly elegant accompaniment to the curses and squeals of Sarah Wainwright, who once again pursued Sir Mortimer Grubbins on another trail of merry destruction. The orchards were a favorite playground for that stubbornly independent pig, and if an event was taking place there, he was sure to be in the thick of it.

Humming along with the tune of the viola, Diana made her way through the trees and bushes, looking for one face in particular.

She found him picking blackberries, the ends of his fingers stained with juice.

Pausing for a deep breath, she looked at the tall figure with the sunlit hair.

Now or never, then.

"Captain Sherringham," she called out, striding toward him and swinging her empty basket.

He turned and smiled when he saw her. His admiring gaze went directly to the violets tucked above her ear. "Miss Makepiece, I hoped you would join the party this evening."

"I wouldn't miss it for the world."

Glancing at her empty basket, he tut-tutted. "Best make haste or the others will take all the fruit."

She licked her lips. "Well, I rather thought you might share yours with me."

His eyes narrowed. "Now why would I do that?"

Diana glanced down at his full basket. "That's more than one bachelor can use. It'll be wasted."

For a long moment he looked at her, hands on his hips.

"Especially a wandering bachelor who never stays long."

No reply. Impatient, she set her empty basket in the grass, stepped closer, and tipped her head back to look up at him. The sun was just drifting below the trees, sending a soft golden light over his brow and kissing the tips of his lashes.

"Are you staying here, Nathaniel? Or will you get restless feet again in the winter?"

He considered her thoughtfully, head tilted to one side. "Apart from trips necessitated by my business, I plan to spend a large portion of my year in Hawcombe Prior. To make this my home."

"I see. And you will need someone, I suppose, to manage the tavern when you are not here."

"I shall begin my search for applicants forthwith." He plucked a blackberry and tossed it skyward, catching it in his mouth. He chewed. "So I'm not going anywhere, Miss Makepiece. You won't be rid of me again. Hard luck."

She rolled her eyes. "I feared as much."

"Say what you want to insult me, this is where I want to be. Your sulky face won't put me off. Pinch me, poke me, curse me. You, madam, are stuck with me."

"Then will you marry me, Nathaniel Sherringham?" she demanded in a loud, clear voice that caused several folk nearby to stop and look at them. "I know you won't ask me again, so I must ask you and risk my heart, the way you once risked yours."

His eyes widened. He set down his basket.

"I am in love with you," she added, "and that's all there is to it."

Slowly, he stepped toward her and put his arms around her waist, drawing her against his body. As if they were quite alone in that orchard, no one watching and listening in amazement. "What about all my faults? They are many, as you like to point out."

She sighed. "Nobody is perfect. Not even me."

He smiled down at her, his eyes shining. "True. We might not be perfect, but—"

"We are perfect for each other."

Nathaniel had taught her to speak up, and she had shown him that sometimes it wasn't necessary to speak. Sometimes all one had to do was listen.

He kissed her in full view of the other fruit pickers and the Book Club Belles. It was by no means a sweet kiss or anything that might be misinterpreted as harmless or innocent.

Somewhere in the raspberries, Mrs. Kenton quietly fainted. It was the only quiet thing she'd ever done.

※

"What made you change your mind, Diana?" he asked.

She looked surprised. "You climbed a tree for me. What else could I do? I wouldn't want you injured by trying even more desperate measures."

Nathaniel laughed, his arm around her as they walked along. She was his at last. The woman who had been out of his range for so long had finally reached down and offered her hand. He would never let it go again.

❧

Who can be in doubt of what followed? When any two young people take it into their heads to marry, they are pretty sure by perseverance to carry their point, be they ever so poor, or ever so imprudent, or ever so little likely to be necessary to each other's ultimate comfort. This may be bad morality to conclude with, but I believe it to be truth; and if such parties succeed, how should a Captain Wentworth and an Anne Elliot, with the advantage of maturity of mind, consciousness of right, and one independent fortune between them, fail of bearing down every opposition?

—Persuasion

They left the wedding feast early, not caring if anyone noticed.

Alone at last, they slowly removed the petals from each other's hair and then all the layers of clothing until they lay together, naked finally, no barriers in their way.

"I love you, Mrs. Sherringham."

Below them in the tavern, the villagers continued celebrating loudly with their tuneless singing and noisy stamping. Perhaps they hadn't even noticed the groom sweeping his bride away. Diana had last seen her mother reluctantly forced into dancing by Major Sherringham, who had drunk just enough not to care about his gout. While the major danced clumsily, making up most of his steps, her mother insisted on trying to correct him. But that was what made her happy—keeping control, getting things right. Everyone was used to it, even the major, who merrily disregarded her instructions.

The newlyweds had slipped away to their cozy haven above. There, with the windows open and the harvest moon shining in, they finally made love.

Nathaniel entered her carefully, the last act in his "wooing," the moment for which they had both waited. One more patiently than the other, for Sherry had finally learned how to manage his impetuous nature. He had won what he had yearned for every day for ten years.

Diana wrapped her legs around his hips and kissed him fiercely, lovingly, having learned to give herself up to passion, to let her heart live.

It was, for both of them, well worth the wait.

Epilogue

SHE WASHED THE TAVERN WINDOWS WHILE NATHANIEL trimmed the ivy. Singing away on his ladder, he had apparently forgotten she was directly below, because cuttings and various leaf-munching insects kept falling on her head, making her jump. Of course, when it came to her husband's motives, she could never be sure if he did it on purpose to try and make her scream. Now that he had finally raised "emotion" out of her, he enjoyed doing it often. Especially the kind that made her shriek and chase him.

Diana bided her time until he came down the ladder, and then she made certain to accidentally spill water from her bucket down his breeches and over his foot.

He glared at her, his jaw tight. "You'll pay for that, Mrs. Sherringham."

"Do you know how many caterpillars have fallen onto my shoulder this past half hour?" she replied primly.

"Oh, so you admit you deliberately tipped that bucket."

"I admit nothing of the kind. I merely point out

that you should pay attention to your surroundings and take more care." She shook her head, lips pursed. "Really, you're not fit to be up a ladder and holding something sharp. That is simply asking for trouble." As he advanced menacingly toward her with the pruning shears, she aimed her wet rag and tossed it.

With a splat it hit him full in the face and then dropped to the ground. He blinked and started forward again. "*You're* asking for trouble alright, woman."

"Put those shears down!"

He did, but he still chased her around the building, soon catching her in his arms and holding her to the ivy-coated wall.

They were still there ten minutes later, kissing and lost in their own intimate world, when they heard someone clearing a throat.

Both looked over at the street in front of the tavern.

A coach and four had pulled up some moments earlier, unnoticed by either of them.

Sir Jonty Plumtre peered out, grinning. "There you are, Sherry! Sakes, this little village is not at all easy to find. I began to think you'd made it up. Almost got run off the road up there by an enormous pig. Guess who I've brought along to see you."

And then his sisters shoved him aside to look through the carriage window and shout excitedly. "Here we are at last! Aren't you pleased to see us? Jonty said you'd agreed to let your mama teach us how to be ladylike."

Oh dear. Had she done that? Diana could vaguely recall a conversation with their brother along those lines, but she didn't believe she'd committed her mother to such a task. This would require some explaining indeed.

Daisy shouted as she leaned out of the window, "We're going to have so much fun in the country, and we can't wait to meet the Book Club Belles."

Diana had a feeling that Hawcombe Prior and the Book Club Belles would never be the same again.

Acknowledgments

Thanks to my friends and supporters, and to my dad, who is always in my thoughts.

About the Author

Jayne Fresina sprouted up in England, the youngest in a family of four daughters. Entertained by her father's colorful tales of growing up in the countryside and surrounded by opinionated sisters—all with far more exciting lives than hers—she's always had inspiration for her beleaguered heroes and unstoppable heroines. Visit jaynefresinaromanceauthor.blogspot.com.

Once Upon a Kiss

The Book Club Belles Society
by Jayne Fresina

The Perfect Hero

When handsome, mysterious Darius Wainwright strolls into town, the Book Club Belles are instantly smitten with his brooding good looks and prideful demeanor. It's as if he walked out of the pages of their favorite new novel, a scandalous romance called *Pride and Prejudice*. But Justina Penny can't understand why her fellow Belles are starry-eyed in the newcomer's arrogant presence—surely a wicked Wickham would be infinitely more fun...

An Unlikely Leading Lady

Justina is the opposite of Darius's ideal woman—not that he's looking for romance. But when he discovers her stealing apples from his uncle's orchard, he can't resist his own thieving impulse. A stolen kiss from the mischievous Miss Penny leaves Darius wanting much, much more. If it's a dashing villain she desires, Darius is more than willing to play the part...

Praise for *The Most Improper Miss Sophie Valentine:*

"Eminently witty." —*Publishers Weekly*

"Decidedly humorous, as well as sensual...a true charmer of a read." —*RT Book Reviews*

For more Jayne Fresina, visit:
www.sourcebooks.com

Sinfully Ever After

The Book Club Belles Society
by Jayne Fresina

— ❧ —

To Rebecca Sherringham, all men are open books—read quickly and forgotten. Perhaps she's just too practical for love. The last thing she needs is another bore around—especially one that's supposed to be dead.

Captain Lucius "Luke" Wainwright turns up a decade after disappearing without a trace. He's on a mission to claim his birthright and he's not going away again until he gets it. But Becky and the ladies of the village Book Club Belles Society won't let this rogue get away with his sins. He'll soon find that certain young ladies are accustomed to dealing with villains.

— ❧ —

Praise for *The Most Improper Miss Sophie Valentine*:

"A unique historical romance…pleasingly edgy." —*Booklist*

"A true charmer of a read." —*RT Book Reviews*, 4 Stars and KISS nominee (favorite historical heroes of the month)

For more Jayne Fresina, visit:
www.sourcebooks.com

A Gentleman's Game

Romance of the Turf
by Theresa Romain

How far will a man go

Talented but troubled, the Chandler family seems cursed by bad luck—and so Nathaniel Chandler has learned to trade on his charm. He can broker a deal with anyone from a turf-mad English noble to an Irish horse breeder. But Nathaniel's skills are tested when his trained Thoroughbreds become suspiciously ill just before the Epsom Derby, and he begins to suspect his father's new secretary is not as innocent as she seems.

To win a woman's secretive heart?

Nathaniel would be very surprised if he knew why Rosalind Agate was really helping his family in their quest for a Derby victory. But for the sake of both their livelihoods, Rosalind and Nathaniel must set aside their suspicions. As Derby Day draws near, her wit and his charm make for a successful investigative team…and light the fires of growing desire. But Rosalind's life is built on secrets and Nathaniel's on charisma, and neither defense will serve them once they lose their hearts…

Praise for *Secrets of a Scandalous Heiress*:

"Romain's novel is a bright light. Well written, filled with likable characters and topped off with a mystery." —*RT Book Reviews*, 4 Stars

For more Theresa Romain, visit:
www.sourcebooks.com

The Infamous Heir

The Spare Heirs
by Elizabeth Michels

——————— ❧ ———————

The Spare Heirs Society Cordially Invites
You to Meet Ethan Moore: The Scoundrel

Lady Roselyn Grey's debut has finally arrived, and of course, she has every flounce and flutter planned. She'll wear the perfect gowns and marry the perfect gentleman…that is, if the formerly disinherited brother of the man she intends to marry doesn't ruin everything first.

Ethan Moore is a prizefighting second son and proud founding member of the Spare Heirs Society—and that's all he ever should have been. But in an instant, his brother's noble title is his, the eyes of the *ton* are upon him, and the lady he's loved for years would rather meet him in the boxing ring than the ballroom.

He's faced worse. With the help of his Spare Heirs brotherhood, Ethan's certain he can get to the bottom of his brother's unexpected demise and win the impossible lady who has haunted his dreams for as long as he can remember…

——————— ❧ ———————

Praise for *How to Lose a Lord in 10 Days or Less*:

"Rich with wit and charm." —*Publishers Weekly*

"[A] richly emotional, wonderfully engaging romance." —*Booklist Online*

For more Elizabeth Michels, visit:
www.sourcebooks.com

QUANTITY SALES

Most Dell books are available at special quantity discounts when purchased in bulk by corporations, organizations, or groups. Special imprints, messages, and excerpts can be produced to meet your needs. For more information, write to: Dell Publishing, 666 Fifth Avenue, New York, NY 10103. Attention: Director, Diversified Sales.

Please specify how you intend to use the books (e.g., promotion, resale, etc.).

INDIVIDUAL SALES

Are there any Dell books you want but cannot find in your local stores? If so, you can order them directly from us. You can get any Dell book currently in print. For a complete up-to-date listing of our books and information on how to order, write to: Dell Readers Service, Box DR, 666 Fifth Avenue, New York, NY 10103.

Also by Diana Blayne

DENIM AND LACE